(av) Nov 19

GRISTLE'S REVENGE

Book 2

GRISTLE'S REVENGE

Carol Salter

Wayside Publications

Published by **Wayside Publications** Manston,
Kent CT12 5AW

First published in Great Britain
In 2018 by Wayside Publications

Paperback ISBN 978-0-9933174-6-0
Kindle ISBN 978-0-9933174-7-7

pegu design

Cover Design by Lucie at Pegu Designs
www.pegudesigns.co.uk

Printed and Bound by Book Printing UK
www.bookprintinguk.com

List of Illustrations

1

Kidnapped

PURITY Springfield lagged behind her mother Shine, who was on another of her 'shiny' gathering sprees. She was bored, bored, bored. So bored, she'd started listening to those annoying parrots overhead prattling on about their leader, the Green Goddess. Anything was better than remembering how bored she was.

Her back was aching between her shoulder blades again too, where the segments of her adult wings were due to sprout. The fact she couldn't reach the spot to rub it better, made it all the more intolerable. *If one more person comes up to me and asks how I am, or when my wings are due to sprout, I swear I'll tell them where to shove their wings!* she resolved.

Purity hated looking like a pathetic ladybug. *Why can't my primary feathers have grown already? I want to do more than hover above the ground like some flying beetle. Is it too much to ask?* She glared over her shoulder at her infantile winglets, sighing for the hundredth time that day, ignoring her beautiful sky-blue hair which hung in long tresses down to her waist, a perfect match for her wide blue eyes.

They're taking so long to open. Her father had told her over and over, that this was the result of her dual heritage and they would be even more spectacular and exciting because of it. *That's my dad, always the optimist,* she thought grudgingly.

Her father's wise words didn't help today. She squinted at the two titchy pink wings she'd had since her walnut-shell birth. They looked so out of proportion to her growing teenage body, though her mother said they were still beautiful. "Mothers always say that!" she muttered.

"Did you say something dear?" mumbled Shine, head deep inside a council litter bin reaching for an empty custard tart case in the bottom.

"No Mum," fibbed Purity, crossing her fingers behind her back and praying to Mother Gaia that her nose wouldn't grow as long as Pinocchio's.

The boating pool café was in better shape these days. It was unrecognisable from the time before when Gristle, the evil Heath witch, had left it a mass of seething lava. The S.P.R.A.T. (Serious Property Requiring Action Team) had toiled twenty-four seven to restore and regenerate the place to its former glory. They'd worked from descriptions taken of the place in the sixties. The pool had been renewed till the water sparkled. The buildings re-built and re-painted to their previous specifications. The whole site had been improved and invigorated receiving more custom as a result. Already humans were thinking they'd imagined the volcano-thingy in the pool despite photographic evidence to the contrary. A number of folk - responsibly bewitched to forget - were disregarding any mention of it, saying, 'Hasn't that nice man from Scotland done a sterling job?'

Local mortals watched in their thousands as the multi-millionaire entrepreneur came to Ramsgate supposedly to revamp and re-brand the place. The episode wasn't unlike Margate Pier which a migrating Sea Serpent demolished in nineteen eighty-six and everyone blamed on a hurricane. True, the hurricane had interfered with its sonar causing it to veer off course into the pier, but it was the sea beast which levelled it. The number of times S.P.R.A.T. re-built it in the dead of night, only to have humans damage it again a few days later. In the end, they let the mortals have their way after one of the Team was nearly blown up whilst lugging the last of the timbers back.

Shine was face down in the litter bin when Purity experienced a strange, repellent sensation. It felt like something thick and greasy was sliding down both her arms, pinning them to her sides. She shivered. Someone couldn't be walking over her grave because fortunately, fairies don't have graves, returning instead to the ether from whence they came, but Purity had overheard mortals saying the phrase and it fitted her feeling exactly.

Unsettled by the feeling she called out to Shine.

"Mum, come on, I'm getting cold," she sighed, another fib. *I'll go straight to the Neath Realm if I'm not careful.* She looked at her mother's petite feet dangling upside down in the air like some strange blue shoe plant.

"Just a moment dear," answered Shine, her soft, sultry voice echoing from the depths of the waste container.

"There's a lovely Chinese take-away tin in here and ours is starting to wear at the edges."

The feeling of greasiness increased. Purity wrapped her arms around her body to reduce her shivers.

Shine jumped, banging her head on the inside of the bin when she heard her daughter's terrified scream. She emerged covered in litter, appalled at the horrific sight which greeted her.

Her captivating daughter was screaming and there, wrapped like a vice around Purity's beautiful slim waist, were the most disgusting pair of skinny red hands she'd

3

ever seen. They came complete with warty knobbly fingers and the filthiest, grey curly fingernails. Shine stared in terror as the revolting hands began dragging her precious child towards the gaping black hole from whence they came.

Shine flew to her daughter's side. Grabbing Purity's arms, she wrapped her own hands around them and pulled. Purity, in turn, grabbed her mother.

"Mummy," she wailed, her eyes wide with terror. "Help me, save me!"

Her terror was infectious. Shine pulled for all she was worth, but while Purity was strong for a fairy, Shine had never been strong. She was no match for the dreadful thing beyond in the blackness, which was hauling Purity into its dark chasm. The creature was unrecognisable, but she knew it was far too powerful for her pitiful efforts. Her child was disappearing in front of her eyes and she was unable to hang on much longer.

Unwilling to accept what was happening, for misery lay in that direction, Shine tried, in those few vital seconds, to reassure her daughter, regardless of the helplessness she felt inside.

"Don't worry darling," Shine answered, attempting to sound calm, though in truth she was petrified because she felt her grip falter. "We'll find you, wherever you are."

Purity started to cry. She realised her mother's strength was failing. The hold on her from the unknown attacker increased. Purity was wrenched away from the only life she'd ever known, disappearing from her mother's grasp with a loud undignified 'pop.'

The dimensions settled back to their usual positions and Shine collapsed on the ground weeping.

"My baby. My life and love. Gone forever," she sobbed, tears cascading down her soft pale cheeks soaking into the dry ground beneath.

2

Gone!

Harty found his wife lying curled up next to the litter bin. When she and Purity failed to return home at their agreed time in the afternoon, he guessed they might be on Royal Esplanade and Shine had forgotten the time as usual. It was her favourite haunt for shiny things. He figured, she'd either got carried away, or had fallen into a bin and couldn't get out - he'd had an experience like that.

He never forgot the time he'd been captured inside a tree, many years ago, by a dreadful hunting spider. He still had nightmares of those six beady eyes staring down at him in the darkness. He shuddered, quickening his flight to find Shine, as a terrible image flashed through his mind of Purity in danger.

Shine was an almost lifeless ball, worn out by her torrent of tears. Lifting her into his arms, he held her close crooning to her.

"Shine, my sweetheart. Talk to me." She didn't reply. "Where's Purity? Shine?" A distraught sob left her chest and the tears fell anew. This simple action caused Harty to gasp. He knew then, that something awful had happened.

Harty's heart raced in his chest like a tiny bird. He didn't know what was wrong but judging by how frozen the ends of Shine's wings were, it was bad. Very bad, if she was showing signs of the dreaded IBS - Iced Blood Syndrome.

"Gone." Shine managed to whisper.

"Gone?" Harty echoed, puzzled. She nodded and began sobbing again. He hugged her to him and carried her back over the road to their nearby home in the West Cliff area of Ramsgate. *Purity. I need to find Purity. Where is that girl? She'll be able to comfort her mother and find out what is wrong.*

★★★★

Things had happened quickly for Gristle the Heath witch, twelve years earlier. Harty had been correct thinking he spied a Neath Demon during the final showdown with Gristle in the West Wood. He had dismissed the idea initially, but he was not wrong. Crogg had watched the exciting duel, through a small tear he'd made in the fabric that held the dimensions apart.

There was no way the skinny demon had the inclination, or strength to pull the heath witch through into his dark dimension. Or, make the tear big enough for her to pass through, but an angry troll? Onk's rage, combined with Gristle's spell casting, in such close proximity to the tear, magnified the magical field, till it was large enough for the body of Gristle the witch to sail - wailing and cursing - through it. Her withered body slipped through the tear smoother than a piglet covered in goose fat. The fabric popped back into its original shape, sealing shut once she'd passed through. Gristle hardly felt a thing.

One moment, the huge shape that was Onk was howling, and shaking her in his arms till her teeth rattled - what she had left of them. The next nothing - literally nothing. Gristle couldn't see, hear or feel a thing. Before she entered the nothingness, she thought she imagined someone wailing in pain, but didn't know where that had come from, certainly not from her.

After a few seconds, she corrected that assumption; she could definitely smell something. It wasn't very nice even to her insensitive nose. She'd made a lot of very smelly potions and this was worse, far worse than any of those. On a scale of one to ten, this was about fifty-three.

As her eyes adjusted to the dim gloom, she noticed she wasn't alone. A small, red skinny creature sat next to her in the darkness. *If he's waiting to be thanked for saving my life, he'll be waiting a very long time*, she cackled to herself.

****

The early years had been hard work. The final movement spell, supposed to have sent Onk elsewhere, had back-fired onto Gristle instead. Moving her, not only several yards away, but because spells notoriously played up around trolls, shifting her in space too, sending her straight into the Dark Neath Realm.

The realms were never the same after the Rift Wars. Warring warlocks had split them asunder, shifting time in the process and moving all magic out of sync with humans. After many centuries apart, the vast population of humans no longer believed in magic. Fairies and their like were relegated to myths and legends, though many still lived on Earth. The planet would have been destroyed completely, were it not for the surviving warlocks and witches coming to their senses. They created a place of safety surrounding Earth called the In-between. The In-between cushioned and protected Earth and those who knew the way through it to the six magical realms beyond were highly prized. There were other ways to move directly from Earth into a realm, but individuals did so at their peril.

Gristle began planning her revenge on Onk immediately after her failed duel with him. She captured Crogg easily with a gullibility spell, just like she'd used on Lenny. With no choice, he became her servant and willing accomplice. With Crogg at her beck and call, Gristle soon uncovered his skill at creating openings between the Neath Realm and Earth. He'd stolen the secret of creating holes, or tears, from the mighty Neath lord he'd been indentured to, but he didn't have the magical ability to move them or make them bigger.

The tears were just big enough for a skinny three-foot Neath demon to squeeze through, but not large enough for anything the size of Gristle's body, however wizened. Armed with the knowledge that escape was possible, Gristle spent all her time crafting a spell which would enable her to move any tear to where she needed it, and, more importantly, to enlarge it. Obsessed with her plan, she never once considered climbing back through the tear into the mortal dimension once she'd mastered its creation.

Over the years she'd experimented, adapting and refining Crogg's original spell, until one day, she managed to create a tear into Earth's dimension which she could manipulate. Using creatures residing in that hellish place, which Crogg brought to her as test subjects, Gristle learnt the restrictions of her casting with many unfortunate and ghastly results.

With Crogg doing all the manual labour, Gristle designed first a small hovel for them to live in. Over the intervening years he expanded and extended their home until it resembled a large house with many levels, both above and below ground. Most of the internal walls were made from the bones of Gristle's failed experiments or local stone.

Just like on Earth, Gristle survived by performing small

castings for the larger Neath Realm inhabitants, of which there were many. To supplement her income, she used her preferred method of changing creatures into food, preferably rabbits, her favourite meal.

Obsessed with her failure to destroy the city troll in the West Wood all that time ago, Gristle doggedly continued with her original plan to capture the fairy babe who had eluded her. Finding out that the unborn fairy, now almost full grown, was the daughter of the mulberry elf Harty Springfield, and, more importantly, was special to the city troll, made Gristle more determined to succeed with her plan. She kept the results of her experiments and ultimate goal a secret, paranoid that someone would force her to share her tear-making abilities. She lacked the insight to see this is exactly what she had done to poor Crogg.

"If any of those foul creatures here in the Neath knew of my ability, they'd be trying to escape themselves," she whispered to no one, as she dribbled down her hairy chin. This statement demonstrated just how mad Gristle had become, for creatures of the Neath hated the Light Realms. They trembled at the mere mention of the name and dreaded any time they were tasked with going into the light by their masters. It appeared Gristle had no intention of leaving the Dark realms - ever.

The very first tear Gristle managed to perfect came out, naturally, in the West Wood in Thanet. It was where Crogg had created his tear to observe the showdown between Gristle and Onk, and it was the last place Gristle had been on Earth. Gristle's tears didn't exist very long each time she created them, lasting only seconds initially, but with much practice, she learnt how to sustain and move them about. Making tears between dimensions expended huge amounts of magical energy and tired Gristle greatly. She required some time to recover before she could attempt the process again.

When she spied Purity Springfield and her mother on the Esplanade - with her goal literally in sight - she was overwhelmed with greed. The twelve long years of waiting were over. Together with Crogg, she began enlarging her tear, making it ready, drooling down her raggedy clothes in excitement, till the tear was big enough for the demon to pull the young fairy through.

****

The years had been kind to the City Troll Onk and his warrior troll wife, Gem. Over the past twelve years, they had birthed five strong children. Unlike fairies, trolls gave birth as humans do. Onar was their eldest child, a son, now aged eleven. Ustar, their eldest daughter, aged nine - the 'ar' ending on the first name denoting eldest son or daughter. Twins aged four. Tera, a daughter, and Tepp, a son. And, youngest of all, a third son, Reex, aged two. Reex was a total surprise and spoilt by all the family members.

Female trolls' fertility years were brief, in comparison to their longevity, covering a decade at most, enough time in which to conceive and birth a child. Any offspring, like Reex, birthed after ten years was a rarity, held in great esteem by the clans. Great things were said to befall such individuals according to troll law. Onk was such a troll, born fifteen years after his parents' union, and their only son.

Following the showdown with Gristle, Onk had taken his troll maiden off in the manner of trolls everywhere. They were duly united, becoming an officially-mated pair. As such, Onk was off-limits to all other females. Onar, their son, the result of their first union arrived fourteen months later. A troll pregnancy takes five months longer than a mortal human one and has a far noisier birth.

Onk's emerging clan - there were no other clans in East

Kent – didn't live far from the Springfield home, as a troll judge's distance, just outside Thanet, at a place called Upstreet. Their rambling home, nestled on the rise where Upstreet looked down over the flat, fenlander fields, faced the tiny hamlet of Sarre.

Onk had become a troll of some substance since marrying his wife, for she had brought with her a small treasure trove. This, along with Onk's own endeavours, ensured their family had enough to live on comfortably.

Onk's fame had spread once the local rooks broadcast his banishment of the witch in the West Woods. In his wife's opinion, Onk was much more faint-worthy to females of their species now. He'd kept his hair long and wavy, a throwback to past times which Gem loved. Modern city trolls wore their hair very short, either pulled out in clumps resembling the human bed-head look or, shaved down one side often with zig-zag lines. Onk also retained his love of hats, wearing a wide variety of headgear. From structured berets and fedoras to free-style objects and strong, bag-for-life hats with a variety of mottos, pictures and logos.

Gem, the warrior troll maid, incarcerated for centuries within the walls of an enchanted castle in the West Wood, loved the twenty-first century. She loved their home and its modern conveniences like taps and toilets which hadn't existed in her time. She enjoyed the views looking back across the fens towards Thanet, her previous prison, but had no inclination to ever live there, despite Shine's urgings for Gem's family to move closer. *Too many unpleasant memories,* guessed Shine and she'd be right.

The Springfields visited often, their own home much too small to accommodate Onk and Gem's noisy and growing brood. Despite the distance between their homes, the children of both families grew up together and Purity was treated like a troll child feeling very much at home in either place.

"Purity, Purity are you home?" called Harty, entering their home underneath the oak trees on West Cliff heights. His wife, still enclosed in his arms, shuddered. There was no response to his call. The bottle-tops strung on horse-hair threads covering the doorway tinkled, but otherwise, everything was still and quiet.

"Where is that girl?" Settling Shine on their bed, he covered her trembling body with their swans-down throw, a wedding present from their neighbours. Kissing her on her forehead he sat next to her, staying till she fell into a troubled sleep.

Harty didn't want to leave Shine alone. Who knew what state she'd be in finding him missing as well when she woke up. However, so far, he hadn't been able to get any sense out of her mumblings and he needed information. Hoping she'd be okay for a few moments, he flew up into the nearest oak tree and asked Shirley, their neighbour, if she could stay with Shine while he searched for Purity.

"Of course, happy to help out," the squirrel replied, her tail whisking this way and that as she spoke. "While you're looking, could you watch out for my Leon too? That squirrel is one continual worry. My mother told me he'd be trouble and she was right."

Harty smiled. Squirrels were the same the world over. The males always making mischief and the females always grumbling and going on about the warnings their mothers gave them, which they never seemed to take any notice of. He remembered the previous pair who lived above them, both long gone now, though their numerous offspring lived hereabouts.

Harty returned to the Esplanade scouring the bins searching for some sign, some clue that might tell him what had befallen his wife and their beautiful daughter.

The parrots above were no help either. They always exaggerated. So, you couldn't believe a word that came out of their pointy mouths. Several of them had inferred that they might, or might not, have seen Shine and Purity over by the bin next to the boating pool cafe. He floated over to the spot and searched the ground, and then, in the fading light, he saw them. Two parallel lines in the nearby grass, like something, or someone, had been dragged roughly ten feet along it. There were also several places where clear outlines of tiny shoes like his wife wore, appeared deeper in the dirt as if she was exerting energy against something. Harty's invisible worry antenna already squirming, raised its head higher as he visualised the battle played out on the ground in front of him. He realised the thing being pulled, against her will, was probably his daughter Purity. He dropped to the grass in disbelief.

"No wonder Shine is in shock. She is such a gentle soul and if something terrible has happened to Purity..." Harty stopped mid-thought as he realised there could only be one possible conclusion for Shine's state and the drag marks ending so abruptly.

He tried his best to consider other outcomes, but his heart knew the one thing that would have resulted in Shine's wings freezing with IBS, was contact from the Neath Realms.

****

Onk flew into a rage when he heard about Purity's abduction. He stamped up and down outside his home causing the earth to shake and his chickens to start laying eggs at an alarming rate.

After checking in on Shine again - she was still uncommunicative - Harty had flown as fast as his wings could flutter to Onk's place in the growing dark. He thought about catching a lift from a friendly blackbird who lived in the privet hedge three properties down, but he was still out foraging and Harty was desperate to do something, anything.

Gem came running outside to see who was bothering her hens. She saw Onk's face ablaze with fury, terrifying to behold if you didn't know him well, but Gem did. She'd seen her husband like this once before, when Onar, their firstborn, had fallen over the cliff at West Cliff whilst picking a bloom for his sister. That time, Onk threw himself over the edge after his son without any thought for his own safety. That selfless act increased Gem's love of her troll husband ten-fold. Both had sustained numerous injuries, but Onar would have drowned without Onk's quick thinking. It was something Gem noticed other trolls didn't have these days. Onk appeared to be unique in almost every way, from his clothing and vocabulary to his values and principles. Others, she'd observed, fell into one of two camps; dim-witted and lazy, or sneaky and nasty. She was lucky her rescuer turned out to be so brave and so good-looking. Gem sighed lovingly just thinking about her amazing husband.

Harty jumped into his favourite mulberry tree, planted and festooned with fairy lights just for him by Onk. Whilst Gem - finding Onk's rage very alluring - approached him, her eyelids fluttering.

Gem's spoken vocabulary wasn't as wide as Onk's, and though she managed to make herself understood by others, she didn't need words with Onk for they truly loved each other. Unaware of the reason for Onk's anger, and uncaring for the moment, Gem placed her ample hands on her wide child-bearing hips and growled deep and loud.

"Onk. Onk angry?" she asked, her tone laced with anticipation.

Recognising his beloved's playful sound, Onk grunted in return and strode towards her.

Up close, the sight which met Gem resembled the

14

'Incredible Hulk' having a major meltdown. It only made Gem's heart flutter more. She glanced up and spied the slender mulberry elf with the grey curly ringlets and short trimmed beard, hugging his favourite branch. Far from looking relaxed, Harty's eyes were wide and his wings were trembling. Gem wasn't sure whether her wonderful husband had frightened the elf, or whether something else had upset him. Realising now was perhaps not the best time to get playful, she changed her tactics.

"Onk go chill," she ordered, pointing off to one side. For one moment, Onk did nothing except growl back in a decidedly threatening way. Then he shook his head, looked where her finger was pointing and answered his reason-for-living.

"OK," he replied, in a bizarrely normal voice before stamping away into the darkness. Harty let out the breath he didn't realise he'd been holding. It was only the second time he'd witnessed Onk this angry, the first time had been when he'd grasped Gristle in his arms and struggled with his conscience not to squeeze the life out of her. Harty wasn't present when Onar went over the cliff, though he'd heard about it. All of Thanet heard Onk's roar of anguish.

"Harty come, safe now," called Gem, beckoning Harty out of his precious tree. Harty kissed the branch in gratitude smiling as a new bud appeared, then floated down and told Gem what he had told Onk.

He relayed the details about Purity's disappearance and Shine's failing health. Gem nodded in all the right places, then called their children to her. Despite hearing their father's bellowing earlier, the children had paid little attention to the sound. Onar, guessing their parents were 'at-it' again and that was too-much-information, had schooled his siblings on how to react when this happened.

Their mother's tone, however meant business, and the five of them appeared from various locations around their vast estate. Gem set each of the children various tasks. Onar, being the eldest, was told to assemble Onk's hunting gear. To Harty, this appeared to include every lethal weapon ever made.

Harty wondered where Gem had sent Onk, but he felt it unwise to ask at this time. Instead, he settled on the windowsill inside their front room watching the children, and Gem, coming and going as the equipment began to pile up on the rug in front of the fireplace.

As the children worked, Harty fretted. Shine was safe in Shirley's care, but he really wanted to be with her, caring for her. *And Purity? Where is my beloved daughter now? In the Neath Realms, anything can and does happen. The sooner we find Purity, the better. Time is not on our side.* Harty sniffed loudly as his emotions threatened to overwhelm him.

At some point, the required amount of equipment must have been reached, because Gem halted in her tasks and, hands back on her hips, surveyed their efforts.

"Good," she announced, staring at her brood, lined up on the far side of the humongous heap.

"Ustar, watch Tera, Tepp, Reex." Ustar grumbled at her allotted task to look after the home and babysit the youngest children, but she didn't argue. "Onar come."

Harty was surprised at Gem's orders for Onar was far younger than Purity in years. He'd presumed Onar would be put in charge of the household with Ustar a useful second.

Gem didn't wait for any reply or complaint, she marched out of the house leaving Onar to collect and carry all the amassed gear. Harty fluttered outside and rounded on Gem.

"What about Onk?"

Gem smiled sweetly at Harty, if a troll's smile could be considered sweet with rows of tombstone teeth. "Onk come," she murmured mystically. And with that, Gem and Onar took the straightest route across the fields in the dark, heading towards Thanet. Harty cached a lift on Onar's willing shoulder just like he did on Onk's.

The trio were almost on the outskirts of Ramsgate when Harty noticed a small cloud of dust rising some distance behind them.

"Onk?" Gem glanced back and grinned. "Onk," she confirmed, her smile widening. Onk caught them up several minutes later.

"Onk chilled," he mumbled, staring at his beloved with his version of puppy-dog eyes, the sight scary enough to make yoghurt turn to cheese. Gem patted Onk's wet hand and recommenced her step. It was then Harty noticed Onk was wet through. Water ran from every piece of clothing. His hair hung in long wet tails dripping more water on to his skin.

"Onk, you're very wet!" Harty exclaimed, stating the obvious. Onk grinned at his friend. "Onk chilled," was Onk's enigmatic reply.

"I'll bet you are. How did you get so wet?" he asked, taking a sideways glance at Gem, who nodded knowingly. With no small amount of pride, Onk advised Harty.

"Onk needed chilling." As if that explained everything. Harty shrugged, some things were best left alone, he decided.

Shine was a little better when Harty returned with reinforcements. Shirley had her sitting up drinking sweet acorn tea, nature's cure-all for IBS. Gem and Onk were too large to fit inside their tiny home, it was a push for Shirley too, with her wide hips and bushy tail.

Once Harty had reassured himself that Shine wasn't any worse and he had helped shove Shirley back outside, the five of them sat on the lawns with several tea lights dotted about. Harty held his wife's tiny hand. He didn't want to upset her, but they needed to know exactly what had happened in order to mount a rescue.

"Shine my dear," Harty murmured, patting her fingers. "Can you tell us where Purity is sweetheart?" Shine's eyes were red and her eyelids puffy from crying so much, even now tears threatened to spill over the edges. Harty was proud of his wife as she held her tears in check and taking a deep breath, relayed what had befallen them.

"...although it was a filthy, disgusting Neath demon who grabbed Purity and yanked her away from me," Shine relayed in faltering words, while Harty gave her strength by holding her close. "I'm sure I heard him muttering something about Gristle, that foul old witch who Onk fought in the West Wood." Onk and Gem looked at each other, remembering the time when Gem was released from her prison inside the enchanted castle.

"Surely that old witch is long dead? She was evil beyond her years and everyone knows evil witches don't live long." He looked around at his friends for confirmation of his bold statement. Nobody spoke, they appeared to be thinking the same thing. "...even if she isn't dead," he muttered, admitting what they were thinking. "She can't have held a grudge against us all these years, ...can she?" They weren't to know Gristle had done exactly that.

Harty patted Shine's hand again, more to reassure himself than her. "We'll find her Shine, I promise." Harty looked over to Onk who nodded his unspoken promise too. Despite this reassuring statement to his wife, Harty hadn't a clue where, or how, to begin searching for his lost daughter.

"She must be in the Neath Realm somewhere," he said, thinking out loud. This statement brought a shudder from his wife, for no fairy had ever returned from the dark dimensions, and here was Harty, a tiny tree elf, planning to journey there. "...and if she is we'll find her," he insisted, hugging Shine to reinforce his intention. *Am I mad? Maybe, but I'll go into the Devil's inferno to rescue my daughter,* he resolved.

Considering the conversation finished, Gem rose to her feet.

"Shine come, Harty and Onk go." Through their long years of association Harty and Shine understood their friends' brief speech patterns. Shine was to go to Upstreet and stay there with Gem and the children, while Harty and Onk set about finding Purity.

Shine nodded and went inside to fetch her things. She re-emerged a few moments later hoisting a shiny bag bulging with shiny items. She ran over to Harty.

"You be careful you hear? Don't go getting into trouble. I want you and Purity, home safe." Harty tried to chuckle and think of a flippant, reassuring answer, but it didn't come off. Instead, he settled for hugging his love tightly again, not wanting the moment to end. He watched as Shine, riding on Gem's shoulder, waved goodbye to them both, the tears falling again down her pale cheeks.

Onk stared down expectantly at Harty eager to be off. Onar had gone home with his mother and Shine. There was no way his parents would let him go anywhere near the Dark dimensions till he was older – much, much older.

"It's too late to start our journey tonight," he advised a disappointed Onk. "…and I need to pack a few things too. We'll begin at first light," he added, to Onk's unspoken question, then he disappeared inside the tunnel that led to their shiny home.

Onk often slept at Harty's and he settled down to rest in his usual spot on the grass, falling asleep within minutes. Harty, on the other hand, found sleep wouldn't come as easily for him. The last time he had travelled any great distance was to Thanet twelve years earlier.

"This time I'm not going to fall foul of any rogues or villains," he muttered, remembering the horrific episode where he was almost dragged into the Neath Realm, by a wingless fairy using a spider's nest as a lure, and an Orc as an accomplice. Harty shivered, recalling how helpless he felt after the spider's venom paralysed him. Onk had been his saviour that time. He desperately hoped Purity had been spared anything like his ordeal.

"I don't have a clue how to find Purity," he lamented, as he trotted around his home collecting this and that in the pre-dawn, the next morning. He wasn't paying attention to what he stuffed into his journey bag, much like his wife had done the night before. "She could be anywhere. I don't even know how to access the Neath Realm, or know anyone who does."

Then a stray memory flitted across his mind – *Maybe I do know someone*. The thought spurred Harty on, and he began racing about the rooms collecting items he thought would be useful.

When he'd finished gathering things, Harty had a neat travel bundle containing clothes and food. The final item was his needle dagger which he secured in his belt. It was a bit long for a knife and too short for a sword, but it was Harty's and he felt a lot safer strapping it in place. His other friend, Tiny the holly elf, always wore one and he was extremely brave.

Harty halted as he went out the door, catching his reflection in a shiny plate on the wall. He wasn't brave like Tiny, and he wasn't a hero like Onk, but this was his child and he vowed to the image in the mirror, that he'd bring her home safe and well.

3

Station

THE train station at Ramsgate was much as Harty remembered it. He'd had no need to return during the intervening years, though he understood his wife had visited a few times. The station had its queue of unremarkable people waiting at the ticket window. There was evidence that the dreaded IT infection had spread its insidious format here. An automated ticket machine stood like a silent soldier, and signs above the station steps announced departures with digital words.

The I.T. world of humans, filled the folk of the Magic Dimensions with utter revulsion. Harty was a writer, and even he couldn't understand what attracted mortals to their computers and phones. What the magic folk saw was the race of mortals moving further and further away from their beginnings and their affinity with the Earth. Some individuals appeared to spend hours, if not days, indoors, not speaking or interacting with another living being face-to-face. *Don't they know that a human soul needs living things around it to thrive, to live? Apparently not, judging by the way things are going.* Harty had watched them walk the streets blissfully unaware of life passing by. *One day, Mother Earth, or Gaia as the fairy folk knew her. One day, Gaia will call out to the mortals of Earth for help, and no one will hear her calls. They'll be indoors tapping away on their silly machines thinking they've found Nirvana, too blind to see it all around them.* Harty sighed, as he flew in through the swing doors behind a smartphone-focused traveller.

Onk wasn't impressed at having to return to Ramsgate train station either. Like Harty, he'd never felt the urge to revisit the place. Unlike Harty, his memories were of a dark, musty room, filled with spiders, mice and beetles. Though the beetles had tasted nice and crunchy they weren't enough of a lure to bring Onk back before now.

Harty, on the other hand, had much to remember. Last time, he'd squeezed through a gap in the far wall and followed a beautiful sound calling to him from the tunnel beyond. He'd discovered the amazing white mice choir with its feline conductor, a large grey cat called Tenamunday.

"If anyone has an idea how to reach the Neath Realm," Harty told Onk, as they entered the station hall, "it has to be that scary grey cat." Onk nodded. The tree elf recalled how intimidating the cat's behaviour had been, until he found out that Harty was a friend of Shine's. Tenamunday and his vicious trio of rats, were all smiles after that, to the terrorised, near-fainting mulberry elf. More so, once one of them spied Onk sitting in the darkened safe-portal room crunching beetles. They'd abandoned Harty as fast as their whisking limbs could move.

The two friends passed quickly through the large high-ceiling anteroom, taking the stairs on their right which led to the platforms. Descending the stairs, they walked the underpass. Well, Onk walked and Harty rode shoulder-saddle. Fortunately, the magic safety portal remained active in the wall underneath platforms one and two.

Safety portals, designed by elemental wizards at the Fairy King's request, existed to keep magic folk safe, providing them with a place to hide if danger threatened, like a mortal being able to perceive them. Whilst this ability was rare, it wasn't impossible, for magic folk sometimes took mortal partners. The resulting union could produce individuals able to see things they shouldn't - these mortals excelled as Magicians and Mediums in the human world.

Harty whispered the first words of opening, 'Hocus Pocus,' followed by the second phrase uttered in his head. This feature was added after one such human, David Devant, had overheard the initial phrase and discovered a door. The railway door revealed itself and they stepped inside.

New cobwebs festooned the room. Several brown house mice squeaked in alarm and froze in place, petrified at the appearance of the massive city troll. As Onk moved into the room their instincts took over and they scattered to the four corners, disappearing into cracks between the crumbling brick pointing.

Beyond this room, through another small gap, was a tunnel which in the past had led to Tenamunday, the elusive feline they needed. Harty was feeling apprehensive. *I wonder whether Tenamunday's vile hench rats still live in the tunnels?* He was also re-considering his decision to bring Onk inside the portal. *It might have been better to leave Onk outside in the fresh air, as he can't go any further on this bit of our quest.*

"Are you okay staying in here Onk?" he asked, feeling slightly guilty at making his friend wait in the dank chamber. "Only you could go outside, if you want to." Onk looked around at his friend who had alighted from his shoulder to hover level with his eyeline.

"Onk wait," he replied. He smiled widely at his friend and plonked himself down on the brown dirt floor, making shooing gestures with his hands. "Harty go."

"If you're sure," persisted Harty. "I don't like to think of you stuck in the dark alone." Onk chuckled at Harty's concern for a big lumbering troll when he was the size of a flea by comparison. Onk spoke to reassure his friend.

"Onk eat," he answered. To prove his point, he grabbed the nearest beetle scrambling across the ground and raised it purposely to his mouth.

"Okay, okay," said Harty, holding his palms up and edging backwards. "At least wait till I'm gone before you eat it please," he begged. Onk smiled and nodded. Despite his limited vocabulary, he knew exactly what to say or do, to distract his friend - he was an intuitive troll.

"I shouldn't be too long," Harty reassured Onk, more for his own sake than the troll's. "I don't remember it being far from here. I'll call you if I need help," he promised, severely hoping he wouldn't need to call on Onk. He was pretty sure his friend could demolish the wall if he wanted to.

Floating down towards the back of the room, Harty located the gap he'd squeezed through all those years ago. Taking one last look at Onk, who waved at him with a beetle held between two sausage fingers, Harty sidled sideways through the crevice. He kept his wings in tight, it wouldn't do to damage the sensitive membranes. Action completed, he edged out cautiously poking his face into the dark tunnel. It looked the same, pitch black on the right side and a faint lifting of the blackness on the left. Taking a deep, steadying breath, Harty set off down the left-hand conduit.

The journey seemed longer than last time. He knew that wasn't possible, but it felt like more time had passed, before he came to the place where the tunnel bent around a corner to the right.

Peering around the bend, he scanned the area beyond. It was the same - a huge space - considering the confines of the tunnel network. A place where numerous cables and tubes came and went leaping off into other tunnels. Glancing up, he saw the impressive glass man-hole cover which gave the auditorium its eerie light and mystery, but it was empty. Devoid of all life, feline or rodent, an apparent dead-end.

Harty rested against the dusty wall wondering what to do next. He didn't have any other leads to the dark dimensions. At a pinch, he could ask Cecil, the giant slug. He had a good working knowledge of tunnels, maybe he'd know whether the choir had moved to a new practice area. Depressingly, he realised they might have disbanded, it was thirteen years ago. Without any other ideas presenting themselves, Harty slumped back against the wall in dejection.

Should I go back to Onk? he wondered, glancing behind him in the direction of the portal. *No, I'll be fine,* he decided, shaking his head. *I need information to find Purity and Tenamunday is the only source we know.* He hadn't been there many minutes considering his options when he heard a sound. A scuffling noise reached his sensitive ears from the entrance on the far side of the chamber. Moving out from the wall, Harty crossed the space and entered the opposite entrance following the elusive sound.

The second tunnel wound round and round, it rose and fell till Harty was soon disorientated, yet still, he followed the sound. The sound didn't increase in volume to show Harty was gaining on it, it stayed the same level. Harty realised he must be pacing someone, or something, moving furtively about the same distance in front of him. Whether the creature knew Harty was trailing it, he didn't know.

They could be leading me deliberately away from Onk and safety, he realised. Harty remembered Tenamunday's menacing behaviour the first time they met. *Could this person be leading me astray, trying to get me lost so they can attack?* Harty swallowed and glanced over his shoulder, briefly considering returning to Onk. *No! I've come too far to turn back.* He had no choice, but to continue in pursuit of the imaginary foe.

"It's gone!" exclaimed Harty, not meaning to speak out loud, but the sudden lack of sound surprised and frightened him. He swivelled around in the gloom searching for invisible assailants about to leap out at him. Nothing and no one appeared, no motley gang of rats to intimidate him. He stopped his racing thoughts, listening as hard as his ears would work.

"It's still there!" he whispered in relief. The sound was quieter and becoming more so the longer Harty didn't move. "What's happening?" He started moving again at a slower rate as his ears scanned back and forth. Then he figured it out. *It's higher. It's above me.* Lifting his head, Harty tried to scan the area above, but in the gloom, it was hopeless. *I need to find the way up and fast, before the sound disappears completely and I become lost inside Goddess knows where!*

Hands on the walls, Harty paced around the tunnel for several moments, then he found it. A wooden ladder, of sorts, was leaning up against one wall. It felt well-used and fragile under his hands, but desperation was setting in his heart. It was only the beginning of their mission to save his daughter and already he felt he was failing in his duty as her father. Grabbing hold of the first rung, Harty climbed.

The ladder ended in total darkness. The outline of a mouse-sized hole greeted his hands and he scrambled through. This new tunnel was curvy, but short, for which Harty was extremely grateful. Trying to manoeuvre his delicate wings in such a confined space was precarious, he was terrified of shredding the edges against the rough walls.

He jumped out the end with a loud sigh of relief, ignoring any potentially dangerous situation that might be waiting for him. Anything was better than staying in the rodent-sized tunnel. He wasn't sure he had the courage to go back that way again anytime soon.

Checking his wing tips for damage first, he then surveyed the area. There was light coming from another tunnel entrance over to his left. He was about to move towards the source of light when movement on the opposite side caught his eye. Two red lights blinked, on and off. *Is it some kind of beacon, or warning system?* he wondered. Then they blinked again. Eyes, a pair of eyes, red eyes staring straight at him.

4

Tenamunday

HARTY guessed the eyes belonged to the creature he'd been following.

"Don't come any closer," warbled a terrified voice. "What do you want?" continued the high-pitched squeak across the distance. "Why are you following me?" Harty detected the creature's fear rising as it asked its second question. It was about ready to bolt.

"I'm looking for someone," he replied, hoping his own voice sounded friendly enough to calm and soothe the distressed animal.

"There's no one down here, but us house mice," the voice answered, confirming to Harty what he suspected.

"I know," he replied, without thinking first. His answer didn't help allay the mouse's fear. To the mouse, it meant this stranger knew about them. He wasn't some harmless individual who'd got lost as he'd imagined.

The timid creature poised to flee, his eyes darting to another tunnel in the dark, one Harty hadn't detected. Sensing the mouse's intention Harty blurted out.

"I'm a friend of Tenamunday." It wasn't strictly true, Shine was a friend of Tenamunday's, but as they were married he considered it amounted to the same thing. The mouse's decision to flee halted momentarily. If what the elf said was true, it would be rude not to stop and assist him.

"Tenamunday is not here," the mouse admitted. Harty's loud sigh of disappointment was obvious, even to the mouse.

"Do you know where I might find him?" requested Harty. The mouse thought about it for a few moments. Did he really trust this individual, this person who said he was friends with Tenamunday? The cat had taught every generation for years to trust no one, unless they wanted to return to their previous existence in cages. They'd followed his commands to the letter, even rolling twice weekly in coal dust so their white fur wouldn't show. The mouse wasn't sure.

Harty could sense the mouse was undecided. He needed something else, some proof, to show he meant no harm, that he was who he said he was.

"I heard Tena's mouse choir sing once. The singing was superb. I thought I'd gone to heaven." Harty hoped the fact he'd heard them perform might sway the frightened mouse's indecision.

"Yes, we love to sing. These tunnels have superb acoustics," replied the mouse, reacting without thinking to Harty's comment about the singing. The pride in the mouse's voice was clear and Harty's words helped the mouse come to a decision. "Tenamunday moved house. He's not here anymore." Harty's heart sank as he realised his only lead had gone. *How will I ever find Purity now?* His feelings of disappointment must have shown on his face because the mouse stepped out from the shadows into the space.

"Tenamunday now lives under the restaurant at the end of Ramsgate pier." Harty lifted his eyes and saw an unusual slate-grey mouse.

"Really? Oh, thank you, thank you so much. I can't believe it. You're a wonderful grey mouse, thank you again." The mouse shrugged his shoulders in embarrassment and smiled, then chuckled quietly as if laughing at a private joke.

"You might want to take an easier way out than the one you came in by," he advised. "Take the white tunnel," he suggested, and with a shake of his tail - which Harty could swear released a sprinkle of coal dust into the air – the mouse fled.

****

It looked like they were out for an afternoon stroll along the promenade, as Harty and Onk headed down the long stone pier hugging the bay, which held the marina in its arms. The harbour area of Ramsgate was picture-postcard pretty, with its Victorian facade and buildings, its flocks of boats resting on the water like drowsy dappled ducks. Humans congregated around the many cafes and bars edging the seafront roads, whilst braver folk not concerned about the low sea wall, chanced the pier to sample the French fare served at the Brasserie.

The pier was lively with walkers, both magical and human, out for a constitutional. At various intervals, fisher-folk scowled at passers-by, for interrupting their ritual commune with marine life. Refusing to be cowed by these interlopers, they left lines, tackle, bait, and the grisly remains of butchered kills, lying inconveniently across the walker's route.

Harty shuddered. He hated seeing fish sprawled on the concrete gasping for life. It reminded him of the time all those years ago, before Purity was born, when fish fell from the sky in their thousands. Onk, however, had no qualms.

"Mmmm, fish," he mumbled, clearly recognising a good food source when he saw it. Harty realised why Tenamunday had moved to the end of the pier, there were fish leftovers aplenty. Wrinkling his nose, he adjusted his position on Onk's wide shoulder as they continued towards the concrete building at the end. It was no surprise there was no sign of Tenamunday when they got there.

"I guess we start searching." Onk grunted his reply. Neither of them had a clue where the elusive moggie might be hiding. "I don't think Tenamunday will be inside the restaurant. Let's start at the end of the pier and work backwards." Onk nodded his agreement as usual. Harty lifted himself up into the strong air currents and scanned the area from above, hoping a bird's eye view would help - it didn't.

"See anything?" he called down, circling above Onk's head like a large mosquito. Onk grunted again, he couldn't understand why they didn't just shout, so he did.

"Tena," he bellowed, cupping his mouth in his hands to cast his voice back and forth. "Tena, Tena, Tena," he repeated. At first – silence. Onk was just about to repeat his catchy refrain when a sound reached his ears.

"No, no, no. No more. I am going to go deaf!" came the exaggerated reply, as a grey cat came slinking out of a gap in the wood shuttering beneath the restaurant. As it appeared the cat's body seemed to shimmer and melt like it wasn't quite in the same dimension as Earth.

"I think they heard you all the way to Canterbury from here," he continued to grumble. Onk smiled. He was pleased. If that was true, Gem would have heard him and that thought made his smile wider. Plus, he'd located the strange moggie they were searching for.

Tenamunday looked almost exactly as Harty remembered him. He was grey and intimidating and gave Harty the collywobbles. He seriously hoped the cat could assist in their mission to enter the Neath Realm and find his daughter. There was no alternative.

"So, Mr Harty Springfield, what brings you out to see old Tenamunday after these many years?" Harty swallowed anxiously, as the cat jumped up on one of the wooden groynes and began washing a tattered left ear. It was the least damaged of the two, the right one was worse, resembling an overworked doily. The cat had obviously fought its share of battles during the intervening years. Closer inspection revealed several scarred areas across his face and a deep one running down his right flank. Tenamunday was ageing.

Disliking Harty's scrutiny of him, the cat turned its head in mid-lick and regarded the elf, one paw raised. Lightning fast, a set of claws shot out from inside the innocent looking paw. Harty ducked. Tenamunday smiled, enjoying the effect the appearance of his claws had on the little tree elf. Onk wasn't so intimidated and was fed up waiting for the conversation to get going.

"Purity stolen," he announced, in typical brief Onk fashion. "In Neath Realm." The cat stared at the troll in amazement his jaw dropping open, his pink tongue resting on his lower teeth. *So, it's true, the troll can speak,* Tena mused.

"Shine's beautiful daughter, stolen!" exclaimed the cat, recovering himself. "Why didn't you say so before! I'll help in any way I can, my dear troll." Harty noticed the cat didn't include him in that sentence. It seemed Shine held more sway than the mulberry elf no matter how closely-related. He sighed. It was becoming a habit, but it didn't matter as long as they rescued Purity.

"Yes," added Harty, joining the conversation. "We think she is being held inside the Neath Realm. Can you help us get there?" He crossed his fingers behind his back. The cat turned its head towards Harty as if astonished he was still there, then he shimmered fleetingly and disappeared, his body fading out like a rainbow in the sun.

"Well, that was a great help!" Harty groaned, sinking down onto the wooden decking. "Now we don't even have a lead." Onk ambled over, his face just as despondent and sat down next to Harty, the wooden planking protesting at his weight.

"Gone," Onk said, stating the obvious.

"Yes Onk," replied Harty, dropping his head in his hands, "Gone." They both sighed simultaneously.

With nothing else to do, the dejected pair sat on the end of the stone pier dangling their legs over the edge. Neither of them had a clue what to do next. The row upon row of tiny white yachts bobbed up and down, while the tidal waters ebbed and flowed. Harty couldn't help but admire the way the sunlight glistened off the crest of the waves and the chrome fittings of the boats. Onk admired the way the fish swam around the docks and imagined them with a handful of chips. Eventually, Harty voiced his thoughts.

"It doesn't look like the cat is coming back anytime soon." Onk nodded. "Seems we're on our own again Onk." Onk nodded again. Onk had a good grasp of spoken words, but he still preferred to use non-verbal responses in conversation where possible. No point wasting valuable verbal effort, he felt. "How on Earth are we going to get into the Neath Realm Onk?" Onk thought about it, it was a difficult question.

He remembered the previous times he'd seen the Neath Realm. The first was when Harty got kidnapped in Crystal Palace Park. That time, a demon called Crogg, sealed the rip he'd created in the dimensions. The second time was in the West Wood when he lobbed the ugly, evil witch Gristle across the clearing. The demon Crogg had appeared there too, but afterwards, Harty advised him, Gristle's spell had closed the tear. Two tears both closed. The only other times Onk thought, was when Fimm the boy-ghost crossed over and when Dog the dragonlet returned to his mother. Onk was about to tell Harty this, when the air beside them glimmered and Tenamunday re-appeared.

"We thought you'd gone for good!" exclaimed a somewhat peeved Harty. Noticing Harty's annoyance the cat deliberately paused to wash his right ear. The couple waited. When Tenamunday decided they'd suffered long enough, he lowered his paw to the ground and spoke.

"Whilst it is true I am able to cross into other realms. The Neath Realm appears to be beyond my capabilities."

"What do you mean?" replied a disbelieving Harty. "I watched you vanish. Where else do you go?" he demanded, his curiosity outweighing his displeasure at the cat's power-playing tactics.

"If you must know, I've never really thought about it," Tena answered dismissively. Harty's eyebrows shot up his forehead. Even Onk looked sceptical, not an easy expression to pull off on such a large, craggy face.

"You don't believe me!" remarked Tena, holding one paw above his eyes. "That hurts," he added in mock indignation. Realising his theatrics weren't working and that Onk was staring at him like he wanted to eat him, Tena explained further.

"Look, I know I leave this dimension, but I've never actually considered where it is I go till now. I can tell you it's not the Neath Realm, or anything like the Neath."

"How can you tell?" interrogated Harty.

"For one thing, where I go is light and airy and it's pleasant to go there. When I popped back this afternoon, I managed to find someone, and they told me it's called the In-Between. That's why I was gone so long. Time in the

In-between is different. I was only there a matter of minutes for me, but for you hours have passed.

"Why would you go somewhere when you don't know where it is?" persisted the mulberry elf. The cat shrugged, this line of questioning was going nowhere. He decided to offer another proposal.

"I can tell you that I can't reach the Neath Realm. That's where I tried to go while you waited."

"Well, that's that then," mumbled a forlorn Harty, his eyebrows assuming their earlier position. "I might as well go home and tell Shine, our daughter is lost forever," he mumbled, his voice heavy with the sadness inside his heart. The cat stopped him by holding out a paw.

"I didn't say I couldn't help, just that I couldn't reach the Neath." Tena paused considering his next words. "But, I might know someone else who can." Seeing Harty about to ask who, Tenamunday added. "This creature lives on Earth but goes to the place I go. He may be able to travel further than me. However, contacting him and getting him to listen, is going to be hard work."

"Why."

"Because he's a wren."

Harty could see the difficulty a cat might have trying to approach a wren. Getting him to listen and believe he didn't want a tasty snack would be a challenge.

"Where does this wren live?" he enquired, his hopes re-igniting.

"This wren lives part of his time here in Thanet, and the other part in the In-between," answered Tenamunday. The cat was speaking about the trans-dimension - the place where dragons and yetis hung out. Harty knew of it.

Meanwhile, a wonderful aroma had hit Onk's nostrils. It was coming from the bins below the restaurant. They smelt amazingly good, so he began rifling his way through the refuse. Aware Harty might think his behaviour rude -

he'd learnt a lot about manners since marrying Gem - he called out, his head inside the metal bin.

"Onk listening," he shouted, in case Harty thought he wasn't. Harty was used to his wife having her head halfway inside a bin most of the time, so Onk's behaviour didn't faze him in the slightest.

The news from Tenamunday, that a flighty wren might be their only way of gaining information leading to the Neath Realm didn't help Harty's mood. Already feeling stressed and worried, they now had to find not just any bird, but a wren - a species which was recalcitrant at the best of times - there was no alternative.

"Did you manage to find out the bird's name?" Harty enquired, fluttering like an enticing toy in front of the cat's face. Wrens were terribly stubborn birds, refusing to speak to non-wren folk, unless they were properly addressed by their full name.

Tenamunday stared at Harty unblinking for a moment, as if mesmerized. He was trapped in feline-mode, as Harty provided him with the opportunity for a tantalizing morsel. He shook his head, covering his almost fatal move to swipe Harty from the air, by pretending to inspect a front paw. Fortunately, Harty mistook Tena's reactions for embarrassment at his comment about the wren's name. He was about to apologise for even considering Tenamunday would forget such an important point, when the cat vanished for the second time.

5

Wren

"I DO wish he'd stop doing that! He could at least warn us first," grumbled Harty. He looked over at Onk for his support. Onk just smiled. He liked the cat's fade-to-black, it was impressive, but he didn't want to antagonise his worried BFF. Harty settled down, deep in thought, on the top of a concrete bollard to await the cat's second return. Doing so, he narrowly missed the iron railing running through it - iron could be deadly to fairy folk. Onk put his hand over the offending item, providing protection for his preoccupied pal. Harty smiled gratefully, when he realised what Onk had done.

Tena returned after only a few minutes this time, shimmering into existence as he stepped across the divide between Earth and the In-between. Tena wasn't completely sure why, or how, he could do such a thing, but he knew it didn't do to tempt Fate the Aspen fairy, by asking.

"Malachi Maximus Mallory," Tena intoned solemnly, as if he were giving a sermon.

"You've got to be kidding, r-r-right?" stuttered Harty in amazement, lifting off from the bollard.

"Nope," smiled Tena. "Malachi Maximus Mallory the Sixteenth to be exact."

"And, I don't suppose you have any idea where we can find this Malachi Maximus Mallory the Sixteenth?" asked Harty, still amazed a bird so tiny, could possibly possess a name which was clearly longer than its own body. The cat's smile widened.

"Yes, I do," smirked the cat wickedly. "I believe he lives in the park at the end of the West Cliff." Harty wasn't sure why the cat was grinning so inanely, but he was reluctant to inquire in case he didn't like the answer.

Onk, had finished his foraging in the nearby restaurant bins, before Tenamunday vanished for the second time. He had decided that he would return here once their mission to save Purity was complete. Although the leavings were few, they were excellent quality, high cuisine at its best, as proved by the small amount of leftovers on offer.

They left Tena at the end of the pier, feigning the excuse that he had a new batch of mice to train. Harty suspected there was something the cat wasn't telling them. He hoped it wasn't bad, because they could really do with something good happening right about now.

The destination wasn't far from the pier and both knew the route well. They crossed the tiny car park and started back along the harbour wall, Harty riding on Onk's shoulder, because it was quicker.

Over the years this practice had become second nature to them. Harty didn't need to ask for a lift, and Onk didn't need to agree. They were friends, close friends, the type of friendship where each knew what the other thought or felt. They were good together, helping each other out of several scrapes and incidents. One time, rescuing an errant Onar from a sink-hole when he was playing on Pegwell beach.

Another time, helping evacuate local tree elves when a fire broke out in the children's play area of George VI Park. They made a good team and loved each other like brothers, regardless of their species and size. They had more things in common than they had differences.

Onk made good progress walking up Royal Esplanade hill. *He still has that way about him*, Harty mused. He observed all manner of creatures stopping to stare in wonderment at Onk, while he strode past oblivious, head held high, his long locks undulating with his swaying gait. *His taste in fashion has improved considerably, probably something to do with having a wife,* Harty surmised, acknowledging Shine's effect on his own wardrobe. Gone was the potato-sack clothing and garden twine embellishment. These days, Onk wore 'proper trews, along with various tunic tops. His first ever T-shirt, his favourite, found when they arrived in Thanet and depicting a rock band, had been relegated to a drawer. Onk had refused to let Gem throw it away.

Around Onk's neck hung his perennial assortment of trophies. One in particular, always attracted Harty's attention - a small walnut shell. It held a special place in his heart. Empty now, no longer the refuge of the unborn fairy who became his daughter. Shine had added her own touch to it, covering the precious item in foil so it stood out amongst Onk's treasures; a couple of cat collars, a crow's foot and some starfish skeletons.

They walked the length of the Esplanade, or rather Onk did, each lost in their own thoughts. Uncannily, both were reminiscing about a moment years ago, when the storm-to-end-all storms hit Thanet, and it rained fish! It had been a prelude to a momentous occasion. Neither of them had known then, that each would discover their beloved, and Harty would gain a daughter. Onk glanced down at the little man riding on his shoulder and smiled.

"Harty special," he murmured. Harty grinned.

"Onk special too," he answered. It was their unique phrase to each other, to show just how much each cared. Feeling strong in heart they entered the park.

As parks go, the park at the end of Royal Esplanade wasn't humongous. It had one entrance that led to a large square patch of grass which held the children's play area. Around the circumference inside the six-foot-high Victorian wall, was a gravel path with various rocks and trees planted along its length. It was a nice place to go on a sunny day with young children. It was safe, if a little too secluded when alone.

The West Cliff Park was not however exciting. Gone were the amazingly scary playground rides like the witch's hat; instead risk-assessed RoSPA equipment stood empty and just plain boring.

Harty scanned the nearby trees and bushes looking for any signs of life, be it animal or magical. No birds twittered in the trees, no animals scampered across the grass. There was more life in Ramsgate cemetery.

"Why is nobody here?" questioned Harty, turning to Onk for an answer. Onk spread his arms wide and shrugged his shoulders. He didn't know either. He ambled over to the playground equipment and started pushing the tiny toddler swing back and forth. Rusty from lack of use it made a high pitched, irritating squeaky sound. Harty was just about to ask Onk to stop, because it was getting on his nerves, when somebody else beat him to it.

Flying in from an unknown spot within the park came a tiny brown wren. It landed on the top metal bar of the swings and began berating Onk, telling him to desist from making such a terrible racket. It warbled at him in tones of major indignation, the noise quite loud considering the size of the bird. It appeared that Malachi Maximillian Mallory the sixteenth had arrived.

It became pretty clear why nobody else lived in the Park, Malachi wouldn't allow it. If anyone tried to take up residence, he would hassle them to such an extent that they threw in the proverbial towel and left. Harty could see why. He'd only witnessed the bird's outraged behaviour for a few moments and already the wren's incessant tone was getting on his nerves. It was more annoying than the swing. Still, they needed to be on good terms with the bombastic wren to get him to assist with their mission. Harty didn't have a clue how they were going to coerce this domineering individual into helping them.

"Get out! Get out, this isn't your Park. Go away! Go back where you came from, you're not welcome here!" Shouted the infuriating tiny brown bird, flitting from the swings to the slide and back again.

"That's not very nice," replied Harty hotly. He could feel his ears turning red and his wingtips curling. He was finding it difficult to stay polite considering the bird's demeanour.

"I don't have to be nice. This is my home, not yours. I can be as nice or as horrible as I choose, and no one can do anything about it," snarled the wren. Harty had never seen a bird snarl before, he hadn't thought it possible, till now.

The wren somehow forgot all about Onk. He had that effect sometimes, when he didn't want attention. It was amazing, considering how large he was. It was almost magical. The wren made the same mistake, turning to face

Harty whom he assumed was the leader of the duo. Onk had his own brand of common sense and he'd saved people's lives on several occasions using it. Nobody's life was being threatened at present, but Onk didn't like people or animals, or wrens - who were not polite.

As swift as a swift, Onk swooped. In one seamless movement, Onk's arm flowed through the air and encapsulated the wren as it flitted back to the swings for the forty-second time. The wren didn't stand a chance. Onk's large, smelly hand plucked it from the air like an avian grape. He hadn't harmed the bird, but his fingers closed around it, imprisoning it within a fleshy cage. If the sound the bird made when it was moaning about Onk's squeaky swing and their presence in the park was annoying, that was nothing compared to the hullabaloo it made within Onk's hand. And then it was gone.

Onk wasn't to know that trapping a creature, who could move between dimensions was doomed to fail. Feeling the pressure release as the bird vanished, Onk opened his hand to find the bird had flown, leaving a token of his disapproval on Onk's palm.

"That didn't work very well," muttered Harty, not wanting to blame Onk, but unable to put the blame elsewhere.

"Onk sorry," mumbled Onk, and he was. He didn't realise what would happen, and neither did Harty until it did.

"What do we do now?" asked Harty, looking up at his big friend. "The wren was our only source of information. How on earth are we going to get to the Neath Realm to save my daughter now?"

Unknown to Onk and Harty, Malachi Maximillian Mallory the sixteenth hadn't gone very far. At this moment, he was perched in a tree about ten feet above their heads, well above Onk's head anyway.

"Why didn't you say that?" twittered the wren from his safer perch. "Instead of grabbing me like a toy. It's not okay to go around grabbing people." Onk shook his head and Harty stared at the ground, it was his attempt to appear apologetic.

"We're sorry, aren't we Onk?" Onk nodded and added.

"Onk sorry Malley."

"What did he just call me?" exclaimed the disbelieving wren. Harty, worried about offending the wren further, rushed to reply.

"H-h-he didn't mean it," he stuttered, a sure sign Harty was feeling stressed. "He's a troll, a city troll, they struggle with long words."

"Long words! What long words?"

Harty didn't want to say anything more about the wren's name. They'd already upset it by Onk snaring it and now they were about to have issues with his name.

"Your name, while impressive, is very complicated for a troll to say," Harty suggested diplomatically. The wren didn't notice the comment about the troll, all he heard was the word 'impressive'. It brought him down out of the tree and back on top of the slide where he sat surveying the two individuals with careful scrutiny.

"This is my place," he stated. "Nobody comes here. Nobody visits. Unless they need something important. Something only I have the ability to give. I heard you talking about the Neath Realm."

Harty, seeing a glimmer of hope, grabbed it.

"Yes, my daughter Purity has been dragged into the Neath Realm through a tear. I don't know where she is. I don't know why they took her, but I must get her back. Her mother will die of a broken heart if I don't."

"Broken heart," echoed Onk. And as he said this his hand reached up to his face and he wiped away a tear which had fallen from his eye. If the wren was surprised at the troll's

43

ability to speak, he was absolutely stunned by his show of emotion. In Malachi's experience, trolls didn't have emotions. They ate, fought and generally had a good time at other people's expense. He was intrigued.

"If you get into the Neath Realm what are you going to do when you get there?" queried the pretentious little bird. Harty hadn't given that a great deal of thought. He'd been trying to figure out how to get into the realm. Exactly what they'd do when they got there, was anyone's guess. *I have a troll, after all. Surely that counts for something?*

"You don't know, do you?" interrupted Malachi, with a hint of superiority in his voice. Harty was worried, maybe the bird wouldn't help if he thought they were a risk to him. Maybe, Malachi Maximillian Mallory the sixteenth was well-known in the Neath Realm. Perhaps, judging by his initial behaviour, he'd hand Harty over to the Neath Demons too. Harty shuddered.

He remembered Crogg. Those horrible spindly red arms yanking him towards the greasy black nothingness. And yet, here they were trying to gain entrance into the very place he still had nightmares about. *My daughter's in there. She's a child, alone and probably terrified. If she's still alive. No! I mustn't think like that. She is alive. She has to be alive, there is no other possibility I will consider.* With that belief firmly placed in his head, he shook himself and spoke again to the wren.

"Please, can you help us? We need to find my daughter. We know she is in the Neath Realm, and no I don't have a plan, but I have Onk and I trust him with my life."

Malachi was touched by the mulberry elf's short speech. Of course, he knew a way into the Neath Realm, but he never made things easy for anyone. These two would have to earn their tickets to the Neath like everyone else.

"I might know of a way in," advised the wren, "but I'll need something in return."

Harty figured something like this was coming. It seemed nobody did a good deed anymore, without expecting payment of some kind.

"Okay, it seems we have no choice. We don't have another way in. What's your price?"

"I'll need to think on that," replied Malachi. "Come back in a couple of hours and be ready to leave Earth."

The wren wouldn't be moved from his decision. He refused to let them go immediately no matter how much Harty pleaded and Onk gave another eye brimming performance. Harty and Onk trooped out of the park, frustrated at having to wait. They headed along the Esplanade towards the boating pool and cafe. On one side of the establishment was a small piece of grass where they sat watching the seagulls take advantage of the shallow safe water.

There weren't many people about, it was a weekday. Children over five were still being collected from school, and adults - in the majority - were working. A few mums pushed their all-weather-terrain strollers with toddlers or babies wrapped inside plastic cocoons. Elderly couples sat drinking tea under parasols which were secured to the wooden benches in front of the cafe. Some had dogs, which took advantage of the bowl of water put out for them by the thoughtful café owner. It was calm and quiet and somehow bizarre.

****

Gristle had become quite proficient at creating small tears directly from the Neath Realm. Creating larger tears, tears big enough to allow a person to fit through, required a great deal of concentration, energy and downright hard work. Gristle had created peep holes at many sites across Thanet, and at this moment, unknown to Harty and Onk, she was staring at them from the other side of the pool. She saw the worried expressions on their faces and revelled in it.

"If they think they're worried now, just wait till they come here," she cackled, for although grabbing Purity had been her objective, her aim was to make Harty and Onk suffer. If she could kill them in the process, so much the better. Harty's precious daughter would remain her slave, until Gristle became bored and sold her to a Demon, in exchange for something she wanted.

The near future wasn't looking very good for either Harty or Onk. All they knew was that Purity had been kidnapped, probably by the evil witch, but they didn't know she was still keeping her captive. They were playing right into Gristle's hands. After a short while, Gristle stepped away from her peep-hole, rubbed her palms together in anticipation and grinned, displaying a large amount of blackened rotting teeth.

****

Malachi didn't wait for the troll and elf to return as pre-arranged. Instead, he sought them out and found them lolling on the grass.

"I wondered if I'd find you here. I've decided what it is I want."

"We need to be clear," persisted Harty, worried they might be agreeing to something that could be a trick. "We won't do anything which jeopardises my daughter's life. That is our condition. Take it or leave it."

"I don't see that you're in any position to make conditions," pouted the wren. Till that moment, Onk didn't realise a wren could pout. It looked decidedly odd on an animal with a beak, he concluded. "We'll see," continued the wren unperturbed. "There's something in the other realms I want. Something I can't bring back on my own

46

because I'm too small." *Malachi must go into the Neath Realm often,* realised Harty, completely missing the fact that Malachi had made no mention of the Neath. *What would a trans-dimensional wren want?* he wondered.

Since the wren had appeared at the boating pool, Harty noticed he'd been edgy. He hadn't settled once, moving from one patch of grass, to the wall and back again. Always checking over his right shoulder, as if worried that somebody invisible was watching them, or more correctly watching him.

"Is something wrong?" Harty asked. Onk stood up and began pacing. Onk had noticed the change in the bird's demeanour too. Gone was its dominant posturing. Instead, it was positively anxious and ill at ease.

Malachi didn't know specifically that Gristle had been watching them, but he felt something wasn't right and he knew to trust his instincts. They had saved his life on more than one occasion. He wasn't going to tell his newest 'friends' of his growing apprehension, but he was beginning to regret leaving the safety of his Park to come down the Esplanade - there he was safe. Unknown to the other two, the park had been ward-protected for him by high-level warlocks, so no one else was safe there - except Malachi.

"Come on, we better get going," he urged, apparently eager to be moving. We have a way to go and I'm not quite sure how we're going to get someone the size of a small mountain through the gap."

With Malachi leading, Harty and Onk left the peaceful scene behind and followed him into the residential area behind the green. The houses up the road behind Royal Esplanade weren't as grand, or as large as those facing the coastline, but many were elegant and spacious - it was a much sought-after area of Thanet. Harty, flying instead of riding, surveyed each property they passed. He'd become quite knowledgeable about local properties, their histories and valuations. He estimated these homes, though not commanding a sea view, would still obtain a respectable price.

They turned first left at the junction and followed the wren as he fluttered down towards Pegwell Bay hotel. Halfway down on the left, the new houses changed, and old flint walls re-appeared, along with the remains of the once grand Courtstairs Manor.

Harty had researched the Manor when Onk and Gem were looking for a family home. It was important to fairy folk to know the history of a building. They didn't want to find any bad spirits occupying places they were considering as homes. The property had been built in the late 1800's by Tomson and Wottan, who were believed to own the oldest brewery in Britain dating back to 1554.

Thomas Tomson brought the original Ramsgate brewery in about the 1680s. Later Thomas Wotton was made managing partner and together, they purchased a second brewery in Cannon Road, Ramsgate. A private underground telephone line was installed between the two breweries – also the first in England. The brewery ceased to exist when it entered into an association with the national chain of Whitbread's in 1957.

The Courtstairs property was taken over briefly by the

Royal Air Force during World War Two. After that, Thanet Council purchased the site and used it as a hotel until they sold it in 1972. Since then it had been bought and sold several times, running as a hotel and then as a venue for conferences, weddings and other occasions until its permanent closure in August 2012.

The wren took them past the locked gates of the forlorn Courtstairs estate. Harty paused, staring in through the iron rails at the sad, empty building. Onk following his gaze, noticed a woman, dressed in pink, standing in one of the upstairs windows looking out at them. He thought to wave at the pretty lady for she looked sad and lonely, just like the house. *A wave might be just the thing to cheer her up*, he decided. He glanced at Harty for confirmation and when he looked back to the window - she'd gone. She reminded Onk a lot of Fimm, the young boy he'd met, also in an abandoned home, all those years ago. That was the day before he met Harty Springfield the Mulberry tree elf – his true friend. Onk continued to reminisce as he trudged along, remembering his first ever "Pretty," and how amazing it was that it became Harty's daughter, Purity.

The wren flew slowly down the sweep of the road past the public house and hotel, until it came to a road where the traffic had been barred. Animals and magic folk didn't pay heed to human traffic signals. They flew or climbed over the barrier and continued on the unused road which meandered between the empty fields towards Pegwell Bay.

Harty took in the vast seascape view, the fields running down to the bay, the houses standing like soldiers at attention staring blankly out at the mud flats and retreating tide. Sandwich huddled in the distance and Deal pier stretched like an extended arm on the horizon. Inland, the lone experimental metal windmill, which hadn't turned to the wind in decades, stood forlorn and abandoned, waiting to go the same way as Richborough power-station cooling towers had on a cold March day in 2012.

They'd walked, or flown, quite a way from Ramsgate town, when the wren changed direction, heading towards the picnic area on the green above the derelict Hoverspeed base. The buildings and craft were long gone, the large concrete apron the only remaining testimony to mortals' inventiveness. Above this, overlooking the bay like a Norse sentinel, stood the resplendent replica of the fabled Hugin Viking ship, a long-time tourist attraction.

Harty didn't have a clue where the wren was taking them. He was even more surprised when the wren flew up, disappearing over the side of the Viking boat. Harty followed him, while Onk clambered, first over the railings avoiding the spikes, and then over the boat's side to join them.

"Why on earth have we come all the way out here?" asked a puzzled Harty. "You can't mean to tell me, that the opening to the most terrifying realm in all the twelve dimensions is inside this Viking ship!"

"I knew you wouldn't believe me. It's much easier to show you than tell you," grumbled Malachi sullenly, and with that, the tiny bird vanished.

"He's done it again! Why does everyone keep doing that?" muttered Harty to Onk, who was preoccupied rearranging his neck ornaments. Onk shrugged his shoulders but said nothing. "I do wish they'd say something first, it's so unnerving." As Harty finished complaining the wren reappeared.

"I'm not sure how your troll is going to fit in there," the wren stated, hopping up and down on the boat gunnels like they were too hot to touch. "But, we'll give it a go." Unbelievably the wren vanished for the second time in as many minutes.

"And there he goes again! I'm getting quite sick and dizzy

with all this," mumbled Harty, settling himself down on the edge of the boat. Onk was amused. He found it fascinating the way the tiny bird, like the cat earlier, was there one minute and gone the next, but judging by the thunderous look on his friend's face, he didn't think Harty would be impressed with his observations, so sensibly, he stayed silent.

"I'm more worried about what his request is going to be," confided Harty to Onk. Finished with his jewellery arrangement, Onk had changed to reviewing the bottom of his trousers. Naturally, they weren't his best pair, these were mostly for travelling, but he was beginning to dislike the loose thread hanging from the left leg hem. He had an urge to break it off, like he'd seen Gem do with her teeth if the children's clothes frayed, but his teeth were a long way from the bottom of his trousers.

City trolls were not very bendy creatures, not lovers of yoga or other flexible pursuits. They enjoyed stamping and shouting mostly. With this in mind, Onk had recently started karate training. It suited his mood well, and whilst he didn't require self-defence strategies - being a huge scary troll - he liked the friendship of his fellow students, a couple of Tarmac Orcs - formerly of the M25 pack - and several species of ogre.

The shouting and stamping was the best reason for going. Unfortunately, during an extra enthusiastic lesson, the class in unison had literally brought the roof down, almost killing their Sensei Tomohiro in the process. Tomohiro was a white crane, originally from Tokyo, who now resided in Sandwich Bay. After the roof's collapse, their instruction moved outdoors into the bay, to prevent further destruction. Thinking of his karate moves and his loose thread, Onk missed most of his friend's rant about the tiny wren.

"He hasn't actually mentioned what it is. I have a sneaky

suspicion it involves him having something he shouldn't from the Neath Realm." Onk, who'd lost the thread of Harty's conversation and his own regarding his trousers, nodded wisely in his best 'I totally agree' manner.

"Are you coming, or aren't you?" called the exasperated wren, appearing for the third time.

"Well, we would, if it weren't for two things," replied Harty snidely. "First, you didn't keep popping off every five seconds." Onk sniggered at the words 'popping off,' causing Harty to frown at him. "And second, we could actually follow you." The wren seemed genuinely surprised.

"You mean you can't see where I'm going?"

"Haven't got a clue," answered Harty, lifting his arms wide to emphasise his point. Onk nodded furiously beside him. Malachi looked from one creature to the other. He couldn't figure out how to solve the problem of them not being able to see and follow him.

"Onk knows," said Onk, and with that he leapt out of the boat, over the railings, disappearing onto the beach below.

Harty and Malachi sat side-by-side on one of the oars at the edge of the boat, waiting for Onk's return. They didn't know what idea Onk had, or whether it would work, but neither could think of another one, so they waited. Harty trusted Onk implicitly. He knew, regardless of his friend's brief vocabulary, that Onk was very bright and perfectly capable of producing a cohesive plan.

Onk returned about fifteen minutes later, smiling so widely that the wren shivered at the sight of all those teeth. Within his hands he held a long length of blue nylon rope, the type fishermen used to make nets. He vaulted over the railings and then effortlessly over the high side of the boat for the third time, landing with a thump that rocked the concrete moorings.

The nylon rope was thick, as thick as Onk's fingers. It

didn't need an Einstein to figure out that neither Harty or Malachi could hold it. Without a word, Onk began unwinding the twisted skeins of fibre, until the rope was a third as wide and three times as long. He took one skein and began to part it to produce an even thinner rope. Harty caught on first. Onk was trying to make a very thin rope that could be used by all three of them.

Once Onk was happy with the width of the rope, he secured one end to his right wrist and handed a thin segment in the middle for Harty to hold. He gave the other end to Malachi. Thus, they were bound together like mountaineers, and Malachi, taking the end in his beak, led them through into the Neath Realm.

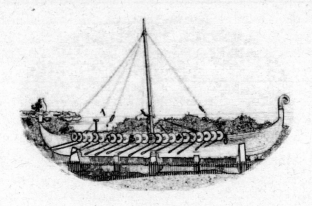

6

The In-Between

HARTY wasn't sure what he expected the journey to the Neath to be like. He knew Earth was surrounded by the protective layer of the In-between - whatever that was - and they would have to pass through it to get to the other realms. The wren advised Harty and Onk to keep their eyes, "either shut, or fixed on the ground, and think about something nice." On no account should they attract the attention of the residents. Malachi guessed neither of them would be able to do this, but he felt he'd covered his obligations by saying it. He found the occupants of the In-between very irritating, they often tried to waylay him. *Goddess knows what they'll make of this unlikely duo.*

Harty initially closed his eyes as he followed the wren and the thin piece of rope. He didn't want to see any of the expected nasty sights, but his curiosity overcame his caution. Besides, there was a strange itchy feeling affecting his skin as they traversed from Earth to Neath. It was the same sort of uncomfortable sensation he got when standing too close to iron.

He opened his eyes, attempting to locate the source of the strange feeling, and was amazed to discover a vast sea of sparkly, diamond-bright water. *Shine would love this.* The water wasn't empty either, it was brimming with life. Fish, seals and whales were plentiful and in the far distance, he was sure he spotted a mermaid jumping and twisting into the air before plunging back into the shimmering liquid.

So that's where they went! I haven't seen a mermaid in centuries. Shine is always moaning about the lack of mermaids and how she misses their singing, and here they are – they've moved into the In-between. Harty could see why, it was very tempting. A calm and quiet place where nobody hunted you, a neutral zone and off-limits to even Neath Demons. Yet it was also boring. Yes, it had a sparkly shimmer and yes, it had lots of interesting creatures, but that appeared to be the extent of it. *What do they do all day?* he wondered gazing around at the creatures floating gently on the waves.

The In-between seemed to stretch to infinity, though on the far horizon Harty thought he could make out a subtle change in colour to one side, which might indicate land. Looking forward, he saw the wren flying gallantly in front with the rope strand firmly held in his beak. Looking back, he was reassured to see Onk trogging along bringing up the rear, his head cast downwards exactly as the wren had instructed, and his mind fixed firmly on his stomach, his favourite thing.

All at once, Harty started feeling weary, his arms felt heavy and he struggled to stay aloft. It felt like they'd been travelling for hours, not mere minutes. *This can't be right. It must be an effect of the In-between,* he rationalised. *That's scary, and if I'm scared now, what am I going to be like when we reach the Neath proper?* Harty shivered trying to control his fear.

Onk looked up briefly, and glimpsed Harty's pale face. He wondered whether his friend was alright. Harty had been through a lot in the last couple of days since losing Purity. Then he noticed Harty looking out to the side, instead of staring down at his feet, or having his eyes closed as the wren had advised them to do. Following his friend's gaze, Onk turned his head. He stared in amazement at the huge expanse of water which stretched for miles on their left-hand side. He smiled widely at all the 'pretty' things moving around them.

"Pretty," he murmured, gazing out longingly across the sea. Spying the frolicking mermaid Harty had seen moments ago, he mumbled a second, "Pretty," and sighed again, his huge shoulders rising and falling dramatically. Staring up into the deep azure sky, he noticed light glinting off a fabulous metallic dragon flying high above them.

He was tempted to step off the path and wade into the shiny water, anything to get rid of this bizarre itchy feeling which had started the moment they stepped out of Earth's dimension. What he wouldn't give for a holly tree branch right now, he thought. His skin felt as if two million ants were wriggling up inside his clothes. He shook his body like a wet dog in an attempt to stop the irritation. It didn't help. He wondered whether Harty and the wren were suffering as much as him. He was moments away from undoing the rope around his wrist and jumping into the inviting looking water, when the wren disappeared - which got his attention.

When they had left Earth's realm, Onk could still see a faint outline of the wren and Harty in front of him. Here, the rope continued floating in mid-air, seemingly by itself. It was still being pulled along by Malachi, but Onk couldn't see anything in front of it. The glittering water and the itchy skin continued and within moments, Harty disappeared too. Onk was certain Harty had fallen into the water. He turned sideways, away from the magic flying rope, looking along the water's edge. In doing so he raised his right hand out to the side. His hand disappeared.

Panicked, Onk pulled his hand back from nowhere and it became visible again. Then the rope began tugging lightly at his right wrist like it was alive, so Onk tugged it back hard. Suddenly, at the speed of a bullet, there was Harty, and there was the tiny wren, both struggling to stay in flight as they were propelled backwards past Onk and into the water beyond. That got the locals attention.

Onk, realising what he had done, hauled in two very unhappy, wet and bedraggled individuals. They ended up suspended on the rope much like a child's bedroom mobile. Onk tried hard not to laugh, clasping his free hand over his mouth, while Malachi and Harty stared miserably at him.

"Onk sorry," he wheezed, succumbing to the troll equivalent of a fit of the giggles. The bizarre noise issuing from Onk's mouth, drew even more attention. Several nearby mermaids, concerned about their very wet visitors, moved closer offering to fan them dry with their tails. *Shine is never going to believe this,* thought Harty, as he hung fluttering in the breeze while a beautiful blonde female with only flowing hair to hide her attributes, smiled wistfully at him until his wingtips curled.

The mermaids, deciding that Onk needed feeding up too, supplied him with a barrel-load of sushi. This met with Onk's full approval, he was starving. He wolfed it down while the ladies watched and giggled. Once everyone was sorted to their satisfaction, either fed or dry, the three travellers resumed their exit from the In-Between, waving goodbye to the disappointed mermaids.

Onk still couldn't get his head around the subject of the various dimensions. He wasn't at all happy about stepping into the Neath, but with much urging from Harty, and the reminder that they'd done this once before leaving Earth, Onk consented to allow first his hands, then his arms, and finally the rest of him to disappear into the nothingness.

He couldn't see a thing. It was complete blackness and it smelt funny, like rotting fish and Brussel sprouts. He lifted his hands in front of his face. He knew they were there, he could feel his breath on them. He could feel the pulse at his wrist. When he rubbed them together, he could feel the touch and coarseness of his palms.

"Onk blind," came the inevitable conclusion. Harty, realising Onk didn't understand the situation tried to reassure him. He couldn't fly over to him, because he couldn't see anything either and he was worried about flying the wrong way, or worse flying into something.

"It's okay Onk. You're not blind, it's just really, really dark in here."

The wren was twittering somewhere nearby. It sounded remarkedly like a nasty snigger. Malachi was enjoying their discomfort, and Harty became annoyed.

"Why didn't you warn us?" he asked irritably. "You knew what it was like. It would have helped if you'd told us it would be completely pitch black."

"Nobody ever believes me. So, I don't tell them any-more," responded the hard-hearted wren. Harty realised from Malachi's statement that this wasn't the first time the bird had brought somebody through. *Who else would brave such a horrifying journey?* he wondered. Already the smell was threatening to make him gag, that, and the total darkness were absolutely debilitating.

Then, just when Harty believed it couldn't get any worse, a sinister grating noise came to them in the dark.

"What's that?" shrieked Harty in alarm. The noise sounded like someone being dragged over sandpaper.

"It's ok," replied Malachi calmly. "It's nothing to worry about. Sounds travel a long way here. That person is probably miles away," he added placatingly.

"Nothing to worry about?" disputed Harty, his voice trembling with anxiety. "We're standing somewhere in the dark, with who knows what waiting to pounce, and you say not to worry? Do you think we're stupid?"

"Onk here Harty," Onk interrupted, trying to reassure his frightened friend.

"Honestly, there's nothing here. If you stayed in the Shadowline you'd eventually be able to see. It's just a matter of time, a matter of letting your eyes become accustomed to the dim light. It took me over an hour the first time I came through, but now I can see within a few minutes. We're at the right place, but before I go, I need to tell you my request."

"Wait! You can't go!" exclaimed Harty, his wings fluttering in agitation. "You can't leave us adrift and blind in this dreadful place," he pleaded, hoping to appeal to the wren's compassion, if he had any.

"I'm not leaving you anywhere - yet. This isn't the true Neath Realm. This is a point where the In-between and the Fire Realm meet. Here, a thin sliver of Neath called the...."

"The Fire Realm!" exploded Harty, interrupting Malachi's explanation. "What are we doing in the Fire Realm?"

"You agreed to do something for me, if I showed you the way to the Neath. Well, I need you to collect something of mine. It is being held in the Fire Realm and I cannot enter. I can only exist in the buffers, Earth, or the Neath. So, you must collect it for me. Once you have recovered it, I will show you into the Neath Realm." Harty didn't have a clue what a buffer was, but he thought he'd identified a way forward without having to grant the wren's request.

"If we are in the Neath, then we could proceed without you."

"You could, and it is true we are technically in the Neath, but this is not the true Neath. As I was trying to say before you interrupted me, this is merely a narrow ribbon of land called the Shadowline which connects the two realms. Do you know what the Shadowline is?" Malachi asked sarcastically. Onk shook his head, but only Malachi could see it.

"I think I've heard of it," mumbled Harty, not wanting to appear ignorant.

"I'll tell you, for Onk's sake," said Malachi diplomatically. "Ever since the Rift War centuries ago, each realm has been separated in time and space. This is because gigantic rifts were created by the warring demons and warlocks between each dimension. To prevent the realms decaying, and to stop them from falling into the rifts, the remaining warlocks created an area of land, or sea, to act as a bridge, called a buffer. Each realm has a buffer. For Earth, the In-between is its buffer, protecting it from all other realms. It is also the only buffer that touches all the remaining buffers at some point along its circumference. The buffer between the Neath and Fire Realm is the Shadowline. How will you get to the Neath Realm if I don't lead you there?" questioned Malachi.

Harty still couldn't see anything in front of his face, and Onk wasn't offering any opinions in the dark. They had no option. Harty doubted they could find their way back to the In-between, let alone return to Earth.

He'd heard a lot about the Fire Realm; how hot it was for one thing. How extremely dangerous it was too, and how a nasty species of fairy, called the Incendiary Sprite, lived there. If he was worried about them entering the Neath Realm, Harty was petrified about visiting Fire. He had always been frightened of fire.

"What choice do we have?" he mumbled. He'd committed them to finding his daughter and if that involved finding this wren's possession first, then so be it. He had nothing to lose and there was no way they could find their way home from here without the wren.

"I can't see you, so how can we follow you into the Fire Realm?" Harty enquired, adding his own sarcasm into the conversation, once he'd made the decision to continue. Malachi ignored Harty's obvious scorn.

"I can't enter the Fire Realm," replied Malachi. "But, I can create an entrance for another person to enter. It's one of the things I do. Individuals come to me for access to the Neath Realm, much more than they ever do the Fire Realm."

"Why?"

"I don't ask them, and they don't tell me. They just pay me and go. That is until one of them stole what belonged to me and left it there."

"What is it, that is so precious to you, a wren who can travel almost anywhere in the dimensions, that you need us to get it for you?" Harty probed.

Malachi was silent for several moments following Harty's question. Harty was worried that the wren may have left them stranded in the blackness, until a quiet voice nearby said, "My egg. The last egg my mate laid before she - died."

Harty didn't know what to say. He thought the bird to be a heartless individual, but this showed a gentle side to the creature that Harty didn't expect.

"Surely, such a thing would have perished by now?" he said bluntly, his curiosity, as usual, getting the better of him.

"It's enchanted," responded the subdued wren.

That was all Harty needed to hear. An enchantment. His mind travelled back in time at the mention of that one word, to the events surrounding his daughter Purity's birth. How could he not help this bird? In the dark, he felt the pressure wave of something large moving about. Onk brushed passed him.

"Onk help find egg," he murmured. Harty exhaled. It seemed Onk had made his own decision. "Come with me," whispered the wren, and without another word, Harty felt the familiar tug of the string on his arm.

He didn't know how the wren managed to create openings in the dimensions. It was something to do with him poking his beak against the fabric that separated each one, he guessed, since the bird didn't seem to have any magical ability or pockets in which to keep a wand or runestone.

One minute, all three of them were in total darkness, the next, a pinprick of bright fire glowed like a ruby, lighting up their surroundings, making all their appearances devilish red.

The pinpoint of light grew as the bird niggled and jiggled the fabric of the Fire Realm. Soon, it was large enough for someone the size of a Mulberry elf, like Harty, to fly through. Before he could approach, however, Onk took the initiative and poked his little finger into the hole the bird had made. He pulled and stretched the rip in the fabric of the realm until it could accommodate a troll, and with that, he stepped through, removing the rope knot from his wrist as he went. Harty followed, leaving the bird alone in the darkness of the Shadowline to await their return.

Harty never thought in all his long life that he would ever leave Earth. Now in the space of a few short hours, he'd entered the In-between, the Neath briefly via the Shadowline and was entering the Fire Realm with not one, but two quests to fulfil. Fluttering down next to Onk, they gazed out on an alien landscape of heat and fire and steam.

Neither had a clue where to start looking for Malachi's egg. In front of them was a road heading off towards the horizon, it seemed as good a direction as any. Harty thanked Mother Gaia that it wasn't yellow and made of bricks.

He glanced behind him, but the tear had vanished, healed like it never existed. Onk had already dug a hole in the warm ground and placed two rocks on the far side to indicate the location of the Shadowline entrance. Malachi had promised to check it regularly.

They agreed rest was what they needed first. There was no night and day here, but it had been a strenuous time for both. They had travelled first to the train station, then the pier, after that the park and finally the Viking boat. Admittedly, Onk had done most of the walking, but Harty was emotionally exhausted too. They settled down not far from where the wren had deposited them and slept.

When they woke, they set out, having no idea of the time of day, though Harty guessed it was probably the following morning. Deciding he felt safer sitting with Onk, Harty landed as gently as thistledown on his friend's shoulder. Onk smiled. Sensing his friend Harty needed some reassuring he started singing.

The city troll had a pretty good voice, somewhere around the baritone range, but every now and then he would drop a complete octave then sweep back up as if he hadn't noticed. After a brief spell singing, Onk changed to humming instead. He seemed to have decided that humming was more appropriate to his current mood, though what tune he was actually humming Harty didn't have a clue. Whatever it was, it made Onk's chest, neck and throat vibrate and was a bit like sitting on a washing line in a high wind for the little elf. Despite this, Harty was content to remain a passenger for the time being.

As they hadn't planned to travel to the Fire Realm searching for Purity, neither were dressed for the increased temperature. Soon, Onk had removed his tunic top and Harty his fleecy jacket. They saw no other travellers as they traversed the flat, featureless road and nothing appeared in the distance. Harty wasn't sure whether they were travelling through an unpopulated area, or whether the folk nearby were in hiding. He suspected once they saw buildings, they'd see people. His suspicion proved correct.

Onk had covered about six miles when the barren landscape changed. At first, the scenery had been empty, moonlike, with dark crevasses around them. Now, empty stone-built houses appeared at the edges of what looked like fields, although no crops seemed to be growing in them. The spaces were marked out like fields with boulders lining the boundaries between properties.

They came across more and more of these small crofter-type houses built of stone, sitting at the edge of empty stone fields without any sign of life. That is until the dwellings started getting larger.

Onk noticed them first, strange grey-skinned people. He'd never seen them before and neither had Harty, and Harty knew a lot of people. They stared out at the couple from glassless windows set high up on the second floor of their homes. They didn't say anything. They didn't do anything. They just watched as the two friends continued down the road which ran through the centre of their community. The road expanded turning into a highway as the homes increased. Harty's instinct told him they were inside their homes, in relative safety, for a reason, and he was proved right – again.

7

Fire

"ONK, you don't think those people will harm us, do you?" whispered Harty, into his friend's left ear. Onk lifted his head from studying the grey road and gazed up at the grey people staring down from their windows. As he caught their eye, the people one-by-one moved back into the darkness. Onk smiled.

"Onk knows," was his enigmatic reply.

Harty wasn't sure whether Onk's statement implied that he knew who these people were, or that he knew they weren't dangerous. Conversations with Onk remained difficult at the best of times. His succinct vocabulary had taught Harty valuable lessons regarding the way folk communicated. His observations led him to realise that misunderstandings were commonplace, and often due to the way people spoke, rather than what they meant. He surmised, the multiple languages might be the reason behind lots of disagreements between humans.

The sky had been red and the temperature hot, ever since they had stepped through the rip in the Shadowline. Onk glanced back over his shoulder, surprised to see the sky behind them a deep purple, while the sky ahead was becoming a deeper blood-red. High up in the ether he spotted a metallic shadow moving across the sky from east to west, but it vanished as quickly as it appeared. Unable to track it further, he turned his attention back to their current situation.

The bizarre people never left their homes, but a menacing feeling remained on Harty's mind and he couldn't shake it despite Onk's reassuring presence. The elf was deep in thought, considering what to do should the people all rush out as one, and attack them, when Onk abruptly halted, almost catapulting Harty into the grey dirt ahead.

Fortunately, Onk had a habit of stopping without notice and Harty automatically grabbed his long wavy hair to save himself from falling. Squinting into the distance, he tried to see what had made his friend pause. He couldn't see anything amiss. Their surroundings looked the same as where they were standing, as far as Harty could make out.

"What's wrong Onk?" asked Harty, looking at his friend in puzzlement. "Why have you stopped?"

Onk looked over at Harty on his shoulder, then pointed to the ground. Not six inches from the edge of Onk's hairy square feet, the ground ended. Harty gasped. Using Onk's hair as rope, he leaned forward to peer down into a bottomless chasm. He swallowed hard.

"I don't want to know if you nearly stepped off the edge," he gibbered. "Looking at it is freaking me out. Would you mind stepping back a few paces please Onk?" requested Harty, forgetting that he could fly and was therefore quite safe. Onk obliged, but as he lifted his weight off one foot to step back, he felt the ground behind his heels crumble. His heels levered up and down on the edge of nothingness like a fitness fanatic doing calf raises on the stairs. Onk knew the ground behind them had vanished too - he wasn't a stupid troll.

Leaving his feet, or more precisely his toes, exactly where they were, since that seemed the most sensible thing to do, Onk turned slowly around from the waist to assess his situation. He was a physically fit troll with good core muscles, thanks to hours exercising in his home-made troll-proof gym - on top of his karate.

Harty's air swallowing continued when he realised they, or rather Onk, was standing on a narrow strip of ground with a chasm on either side. Looking back, he saw the people had finally left their houses and were standing on the far side of the rear chasm. They didn't make a sound. They didn't jeer, they didn't heckle, they stood like grey ghosts. It was very eerie, and it made Harty more than anxious. He knew they were waiting for someone or something.

The tiny piece of ground on which Onk stood was roughly three feet wide. This ribbon of safety ran away both sides into the distance. In front and behind them were chasms. They had no clue how deep the chasms were, or where they went.

Onk, deciding he'd had enough standing still regardless of the lack of terra-firma beneath him, began moving about. His stamping feet caused much of the soil to start sliding down the sides eroding their precious foothold further.

"Stand still Onk! yelled Harty. "If you keep stamping about like that, there won't be anything left for you to stand on." The elf was terrified for his friend's safety, he could fly away, but Onk was in a more difficult predicament. The chasms were wide, much too wide for even someone the size and strength of a troll to leap. "Stay here," Harty commanded. "I'll fly along this ridge and see if the land widens, or the chasms narrow." Onk nodded. Taking Harty's advice literally, he stood absolutely rock still.

The locals looked on; if they were amused they didn't show it. *They're obviously interested in us, or they wouldn't have left their houses,* thought a worried Harty. Once he was reassured that Onk wouldn't move, he flew along the ridge to the left of the troll. It wound back and forth not unlike a meandering river, then it stopped suddenly swooping down into the chasm where the two ravines met.

"That's not very promising, or helpful," muttered Harty, staring down into the black abyss. "Only the right side to check. I hope I have better luck on that side." Fortunately, he did, though not as much as he would have liked. Two-thirds of the way along the right edge, the chasm in front narrowed. It was still a massive gap to Harty, but it was the only way out. He hoped Onk was a good jumper. *I've never seen him jump,* he realised, it had never been necessary. *I hope he can.*

Harty returned to his trapped friend who, getting bored with standing, was sitting swinging his legs over the edge.

"Onk what in the Goddess's name are you doing!" exclaimed Harty in absolute horror. He watched unbelievably as more soil shifted and dropped away into the chasm below. "You could fall in!" Onk didn't seem bothered in the least, he shrugged his massive shoulders and reached around to remove the backpack he'd been carrying. "You're not going to eat at a time like this are you?" The incredulity was clear in Harty's voice. "Aren't you worried?"

"Onk hungry," was Onk's response. He began stuffing his face with the cold sausage and chips that Gem had packed for the journey. It wasn't the only food in his bag. Gem, knowing her husband's appetite, had packed a variety of meals which she hoped would last Onk a couple of days. Onk finished his six-sausage snack, and wiping his hands down his trousers, returned the bag to his shoulders. It made Harty realise he was hungry too. He wondered what Shine had packed but decided it wasn't the time or place to investigate.

"We need to get you off here Onk."

"Onk ready," he replied, lurching to his feet and scattering even more soil into the chasms below. There wasn't a lot of soil left on the space where Onk was standing and beneath it appeared some type of stone which neither of them had seen before. Harty flew down to inspect it and discovered when he touched it, it was warm.

"I suppose it's to be expected that the rocks would be warm," he commented, right up until the moment the rock moved. "Oh, my Goddess it's alive!" Almost on cue, a deep-throated groan filled the air around them. Harty knew that whatever it was, it wasn't good.

"Come on Onk, move now!" Onk got the hint and moved, following Harty along the right-side ridge to where the gap narrowed.

"You'll have to jump across here Onk." Onk stared across the space. It was doable, he decided, if only he hadn't just eaten Gem's meal. At this moment he wasn't sure he could make it. He stared down at his belly patting the fullness of it. Harty's eyes followed his movement, then widened as he saw what was happening behind them. Unknown to Onk, the ridge he was standing on started moving, the far end began lifting, sending showers of soil into the abyss.

The grey people on the edge chose this moment to get excited. They began jumping up and down and yelling. Attracted by the sound, Onk glanced over at them, catching sight of a huge snake-like beast rising regally behind him. He wasn't intimidated; he roared a challenge to his adversary.

"No Onk, you can't fight, we have to go!" urged Harty, but Onk didn't want to go. He was looking forward to fighting this beastie and Harty knew it.

"We need to save Purity. That's what we came for!" he bellowed in Onk's ear. Onk's mind was divided. He could never turn down a challenge, but he loved Purity like a daughter and he'd never give up on her. Sighing loudly, to express his displeasure he moved to the edge, bent both knees and crouching, leapt across the gap.

Landing on the other side, he did a brilliant impression of the Incredible Hulk enraged, just to show the creature he wasn't intimidated, then he swung his locks of hair around his head in imitation of a shampoo commercial and turned his back on the fight.

The stone serpent, only its head and upper body fully awake and mobile, stopped in its tracks. It was astounded that someone had the nerve to stand up to it by hollering a challenge to fight, especially when it wasn't ready to do battle. Then it spied the tiny grey people yelling and jumping about, all excitable and unnecessary, on the edge of the chasm. It decided it would be much nicer, if it was a little bit quieter. All the noise was making its head ache; not a good thing for an animal coming out of hibernation.

The snapping and biting it inflicted, didn't make the place any quieter, because quite a lot of screams ensued as a result. The stone snake rapidly became disillusioned with the grey folk's over-animated performance. Stomach filled, he stretched and stretched some more, until his long serpentine body rested back down in a long line between the edges of his gigantic nest.

Inside the nest, hundreds of tiny serpents wriggled and writhed around their parents. Luckily, only the smaller of the two parents had woken. The larger female, three times the size of the male, was resting on the far side. She was harder to irritate and wake up. She stayed deep in slumber as Onk wove his way across her spines like a tiny ant.

Harty and Onk left the grey people and their serpent gods behind as Onk walked into a new landscape full of stalagmites. They were a bit tricky to negotiate and several had lost their pointy tops, by the time Onk found his way through the forest of needle rocks. At the far side, they found the reason for the rosy glow in the sky. A wide river, not of water, but of lava, flowed in front of them, blocking their progress.

In the distance, beyond the river, they could make out what looked like a large town or small city. It was difficult to say which because of the high wall built around it. Their next puzzle to solve was how they were going to reach the settlement. Onk sat down and concentrated on removing several stubborn stones from between his toes, subsequently missing the launch of a vessel from the opposite bank.

"It's a boat Onk!" trilled Harty, rising into the air in excitement as he noticed movement on the far bank. "A boat that floats on lava!" Onk wondered what type of boat could float on lava. The boat drew nearer and Harty finally had the opportunity to study one of the grey people up close, for one of them stood in the stern steering.

The individual in question, was a man who appeared to be in his mid-thirties using Earth's ageing system. His skin was grey and seemingly hard like stone or gravel, giving his species that greyish appearance. He didn't smile. He didn't talk. He didn't even wave them onto the boat. He stood stoically, soundlessly, as if part of the fixtures and fittings. Harty had never met anybody so flat and empty. He quickly became bored with the scrutiny of the grey man and turned his attention to more pressing matters.

"I wonder what counts for money here?" he said to Onk.

Harty didn't have long to wait to find out. He was amazed to discover the grey man accepted anything that came from outside the Fire Realm. He could see why the wren's egg had been stolen, its value here was probably enormous. Both had loads of stuff from Earth and it didn't take a lot to make a grey person very happy. Though smiling didn't seem to be in his non-verbal vocabulary.

Their transport was a very shallow draft punt boat, at

times the lava was mere inches away from their unprotected bodies. The heat was immense and Harty was sure his wings were beginning to melt. Onk, as stoic as usual, said nothing. He was as happy as a pickpocket imp at a music festival - he'd never been in a boat on a river before. The Viking ship didn't count as it was in dry dock. The boat appeared to be made of rock, but Harty couldn't understand that. *Surely a rock boat wouldn't float?*

Whatever magic or law of physics that enabled the boat to float, it managed - just. The boatman collected them and saw them safely to the far side. The only mishap, a small burn on Onk's forearm where he recklessly attempted to 'test the water.' Luckily, the boatman grabbed his arm in time to prevent any serious harm.

Onk clambered out and Harty flew over the edge, feeling much better having ground below him, even if it was hard stone. Now he thought about it, he hadn't seen a blade of grass, a leaf, a tree, nothing living except people and creatures since they arrived. Harty decided he was safer flying after their last incident, leaving Onk to continue their journey on foot while he fluttered close by.

Onk's preferred pace was to stroll, exuding an air of superiority and maleness, however Harty noticed that Onk's measured tread was increasing. Soon, instead of strolling, Onk was trotting, then running, and finally almost galloping towards their goal. Onk's speed meant Harty had to fly faster, unless he cadged a lift.

"What's up Onk?" asked Harty, flying in close to speak to his friend.

"Hot."

"Yes, it is hot here," Harty agreed, thinking Onk's reply didn't answer his question.

"Could you slow down please," asked Harty, struggling to stay level with Onk's impressive run.

"Hot, hot," Onk repeated twice more.

"I know it's hot, but I'm getting hot just trying to keep up with you."

"Hot foot," added Onk, that one extra word making all the difference. Harty understood. It wasn't just the air that was hot, apparently the ground beneath Onk's feet was becoming hot too.

Onk had never taken a shine to shoes. He detested having his toes enclosed or trapped, he enjoyed wriggling them freely and flexing his feet. He complained bitterly when forced to wear footwear by his wife, for special occasions. Getting Onk into shoes was like taking a sullen teenager to buy clothing, when all they wanted to do was play on their Xbox twenty-four-seven.

Onk ran and ran without stopping until he reached the outer wall of the settlement they'd seen in the distance. Butting up to the wall were brick structures like steps, or small bridges, set above the ground. Onk immediately hopped up onto one of these artificial structures, and sighing with relief, sat down. He lifted his feet to inspect his damaged soles. Harty saw both were red and blistered in places. The ground had truly been that hot. *How are we going to continue in our quest to find my daughter, if Onk can't place his feet on the ground,* Harty wondered.

"Obviously these artificial steps have been built for folk who cannot tolerate the heat, so there must be some type of service to prevent, or ease people's pain," suggested Harty to Onk. "Wait here Onk, I'll go inside to find help."

It was a brave decision, and it wasn't until the words were out of his mouth, that Harty realised it was a fool-hardy one too. He'd just offered to go alone into an unknown city without any support, or weapons – discounting his needle sword. Onk seemed okay with Harty's offer though, for he nodded in his usual way.

"Off I go," he announced dramatically, half-hoping Onk would stop him. He didn't. Taking one last look around to get his bearings, Harty flew up and over the city wall, feeling incredibly brave and stupid at the same time. He stayed high in the air trying not to attract attention, but that plan became perilous when he found out he wasn't the only airborne creature, and most of the others could breathe fire.

A fire-breathing griffin passed within inches of him, nearly frazzling his gossamer wings. He gulped and recalculated a flight trajectory which would remove him from its path. Circling down he recognised the classic layout of a High Street with shops and market traders. *I might find assistance for Onk amongst the retailers,* he decided. Descending to eye level he approached another grey citizen.

"Excuse me. Could you assist me and my friend please?" Clearly this trader had never seen a tree elf before. It was the first open expression of surprise Harty had seen since arriving, unless you counted the grey folk shouting and screaming. A look of utter amazement crossed the trader's face before he managed to reset his expression to blank indifference.

"What assistance do you require?" he asked in formal, flat monotones.

"My friend is stuck outside the city wall. The ground here is too hot for him to walk any further."

"Ah!" replied the trader catching on. "He's on the resting steps is he not?"

"Yes, he is," answered Harty, thankful this bland man understood the problem and hopefully knew how to fix it.

"You need Phrack Blaster."

"Excuse me?"

"The dwarf, Phrack Blaster. He'll have him sorted out in no time. You'll find him down by the clock tower this time of day."

The trader waved his hand in the general direction of a large Plaza ahead of them. Harty thanked him and flew on to find the dwarf with the typical dwarf name.

74

Phrack Blaster was a European stone dwarf. What he was doing in the Fire Realm was anyone's guess. Harty found a short, stout fellow shaped like a barrel with salt and pepper hair and full beard, bent over a cobbler's last, making shoes. These weren't any old shoes, these were special cope-with-the-heat shoes. Harty watched mesmerised as the dwarf - wearing heavy metal earrings and hair beads reminiscent of Onk - fashioned and stitched a shoe made from fire lizard skin. Fire lizards lived near volcanoes, and their skin, impervious to heat, made excellent footwear. The only drawback being that the skin was extremely tough and couldn't be worn without being treated first.

Harty didn't know all the mechanics behind the tanning of lizard skins, but it involved immersing the hides in a secret solution, then working on the inside to ensure it was soft enough to wear comfortably. This process took several months before the skins were sufficiently supple to work on. Phrack Blaster appeared to be a Guild Master of some prowess, judging by his skill with the current shoe on his last.

Harty didn't know how much it would cost to purchase a pair of shoes large enough for a city troll. He guessed a considerable amount of lizard skin would be needed, not to mention the length of time to fashion and stich them. *I wonder whether the dwarf takes Earth items as currency like the ferryman? The only dwarves I know take gold, silver and precious stones and we don't have any of those.*

"You gonna float there all day gawping, or do ye have business for me?" the dwarf bellowed over his last, making Harty jump because of his sensitive hearing. His wing tips jittered. *He's scary,* thought Harty. *A bit abrupt too, but straight to the point.* Harty, like Onk, liked people who didn't mess around with unnecessary words. The dwarf reminded Harty a lot of Onk.

"I need to purchase a pair of shoes," he said, recovering

his poise and acutely aware his voice sounded reed thin next to the dwarf's deep baritone.

"Well, I didnae think ye came here for a wheelbarrow," the dwarf replied, chuckling at his own joke. "What type of shoes ye after?"

Harty swallowed, he seemed to be doing a lot of that lately. There were a lot of situations where he felt out on a limb.

"I need a pair of shoes for a city troll."

"Didnae see many city trolls in the Fire Realm, let alone in Incandesonia," stated the dwarf, taking the shoe he'd just made and placing it on a growing pile of identical footwear. "I ken see how shoes might be an issue. Where's your troll noo?" asked the dwarf, pretending to cast about for signs of someone behind Harty.

"Oh, he's not here," supplied Harty, realising the dwarf was searching for Onk. Phrack's bushy monobrow rose in implied astonishment. "No, I left him outside, on the steps, resting his feet." The dwarf smiled, deciding the elf was none too bright.

Mistaking the dwarf's expression as a request for more information and assurance, Harty explained they were doing a friend a favour by searching for something he'd lost, before returning to Earth. He didn't elaborate further, because he wasn't sure what the true story was surrounding the wren's egg.

"Well?" said Phrack. Harty didn't catch on as the dwarf continued to stare at him. "I'm going to need him here to take his measurements."

"Oh, yes," Harty turned to go, then he realised Onk might struggle walking this far into the city. "His feet are really sore, and I think they might be a bit burnt. He ran all the way from the lava river."

At that comment, the dwarf raised his eyebrow again.

"Surely not?" he replied, a tinge of disbelief evident in his voice.

"Yes," assured Harty, "he really did."

"Wait here." The dwarf jumped up from his last and left his workshop. Within minutes, Harty heard the sound of a wagon approaching. It was pulled by two of the thinnest animals Harty had ever seen. He didn't have time to question the dwarf about them, only gaze in amazement at their long necks and thin spindly legs. How an animal that thin could pull a big heavy wagon was beyond his comprehension.

"Which way?"

"This way," pointed Harty, flying ahead of Phrack Blaster and his team of strange beautiful creatures. *So, this city is called Incandesonia,* Harty mused, as he led the way. *It makes sense, a fire-related name for a Fire Realm city.*

****

"Now that's something I didnae see every day," declared Phrack Blaster, pulling up to the steps where Harty had left Onk.

Fed up with sore feet, and not having access to a stream to cool them off, Onk was sitting licking the sensitive skin in the hope his saliva would have the same effect. It didn't seem to be working, in fact, they were stinging more. Onk wasn't a medical troll, if there ever was such a thing in the troll nation, so he wasn't aware troll saliva had extremely high acidic properties. It was useful at killing off errant bugs, if any managed to beat a troll's amazing immune system, but because of its high acidity it burnt almost as much as the hot ground Onk crossed earlier.

"Onk, I've got help," called Harty, fluttering over. Onk smiled at the wagon which was obviously his ride.

"Nice," he mumbled, his tongue still engaged in podiatry repairs. He appreciated a street-cool vehicle when he saw it. He admired the high metal arches set over wide fat

77

wheels, the sleek team pulling – obviously racing trained. But, what got most of his attention was the awesome paint job done on the wooden components. Both sides had received a customized fire effect in red, outlined with gold. While the front and rear ends sported realistic flames streaming out in blazing orange. The wheels hadn't been left out either, with small flames picking out the spokes.

"Sweet," added Onk, envious of this newcomer, if he owned such a thing of beauty.

"Glad you like it," replied Phrack, jumping down from the buckboard. He lay the reins across the brake mechanism, content that his matched pair of thoroughbreds wouldn't budge without his orders.

"Took me a while to decide on the design and source paint, that wouldnae bubble and run in this heat. Got what I needed sent in from Earth." At the mention of Earth, Onk's mind flitted back to thoughts of his beloved Gem and his children.

"Onk from Earth," he announced, thumping his chest with pride. Onk was proud of his heritage.

"I can tell from the accent," replied Phrack. "North London, if I'm not mistaken. I was there a few decades back." Harty's eyes widened hearing this piece of information. Magical folk weren't supposed to be able to cross the dimensions willy-nilly when they pleased. There had to be more to this dwarf than he was letting on.

"Shall we get ye out of here, old man?" Onk, ever the minimalist nodded and clambered happily into the flatbed, though he wasn't sure he liked the term old man, he was young in troll years.

"Harty come," Onk called, lying back in the bottom of the cart like he owned it.

"I'm coming don't you worry. I was just waiting for you to get your big bones up there first, so you don't squash me."

"Onk never do," replied Onk, unsettled by Harty's comment.

"I know Onk, I was only joking," smiled Harty, settling down next to his friend and patting his arm in reassurance.

As they travelled back into Incandesonia, Harty used the luxury of sitting down to survey the town and its inhabitants. Once through the wide town gate, guarded by the local law enforcement guards, the main cobbled street ran towards the town centre. Phrack explained that this was where the municipal buildings and museum were located. Behind those, and well away from trouble, were the richer, more affluent residences, while cheaper accommodation housed the city's poorer residents near the gate.

Harty noticed that generally folk looked well-shod and fed. There were the inevitable street children and beggars, who probably made a good living judging by their full cheeks and snug-fitting clothing. *Incandesonia is doing well as populations go*, he reflected, as the wagon and team pulled up next to the cobbler's home.

8

Lou

Purity had been locked in the darkened room, without a timepiece, or change of light from night to day to mark the time. Consequently, she had no idea how much time, or how many days had passed. At intervals, she heard the sounds of creatures moving along the corridor outside her room. Judging by the growling, slurping and dragging noises, she didn't want to make their acquaintance any time soon.

Her parents had raised her to be polite, to respect her elders and other species and most of all, to be kind to them. These creatures sounded ancient and feral. Her instincts told her they wouldn't be impressed with her good manners. They wouldn't show her kindness should she try to break the lock of her door - it was the only thing keeping her safe.

No one had physically hurt her, or manhandled her, since that initial point where she'd been dragged through the tear. She'd watched broken-hearted as her mother fell backwards onto the grass, sobbing, and the tear had zipped shut faster than a weasel's sneeze. Following that, there was nothing she could do, nowhere she could go. She wanted to beat the disgustingly smelly demon, but in the pitch black she couldn't see where he went. She heard him though, heard him sniggering in the dark.

He told her she could stay exactly where she was, in the dark alone, or follow his voice to light and safety. She didn't think it was much of a choice, for Purity was a creature of light and needed its sustenance to survive. So, she followed the voice which sang an off-tune ditty about a witch who became a toad. To be honest she didn't need the voice. The Neath demon's odour was terrible - it smelt like Orc cheese - and it was far easier to follow her nose than her ears.

The two of them paced along in the dark, him apparently able to see as clear as day and Purity, lost and blind. The tears began then, rolling down her cheeks in silent protest at the unfairness of her situation. The singing stopped, and the stench became stronger.

"Yous crying little girl? No need to crys with Crogg beside you." The young Neath demon reassured her. Purity sniffed, his voice was oily and repugnant, but these were his first kind words.

"Why did you steal me?" she sobbed. "I've never harmed anyone. I wouldn't harm you."

"I knows," sighed the demon, moving closer in the darkness, his voice lowering to a whisper. "She wants you, and Crogg always follows mistress's orders. No beatings and lots of food. All Crogg wants these days. No more, no less."

Tears were new to Crogg. He'd never seen them before. Raising one gnarly fingertip he captured a teardrop as it fell from Purity's jaw. She didn't notice, not possessing the demon's night-sight. Lifting the tear, Crogg brought it to his lips and touched it to the tip of his tongue.

"It burns! It burns!" he yelped, cantering away in the

dark, leaving Purity alone, while he soothed his scalded tongue. "Strong magic," he whispered to himself, "stronger than she...."

Purity didn't have a clue what the Neath demon was gabbling on about. She'd heard him scamper away but didn't know the reason. She listened for his return heralded by stones and gravel shifting underfoot. During this time, she stood waiting, hoping, on the one hand that he wouldn't leave her to her fate while on the other, wishing he would stay away long enough so she could find a place to hide.

Crogg wasn't gone long enough for Purity to make good on her intentions, so now here she was locked in a bedroom inside a witch's home, still in the dark. Someone had been feeding her. She didn't know who. Maybe Crogg? Whoever they were, they waited until Purity slept. When she awoke the food was on the small box next to the bed. She'd tried staying awake the first couple of times. Whoever brought the food must have been watching her, making sure she was asleep before they entered the room. Now she was tired from boredom and weak from lack of light.

The witch, Gristle had visited her once, on her first day in captivity, lighting the room for a brief couple of minutes to survey her captured prize. She didn't look at all like Purity imagined a witch should look. She looked like someone's wizened old grandmother with grey curly hair, bright blue sunken eyes and thin lips. She'd cackled evilly and rubbed her dry leathery hands together, not saying much, just staring at the young fairy like she'd found a pot of rainbow gold. Then the light went out and Purity guessed the witch was gambolling about the room, at least that's what it sounded like, as her cackles came first from one direction and then another before the door opened and she left, never to return.

Now after several sleep periods, Purity's vision had

adjusted so she could make out the objects scattered around her room. Their outlines were depicted by the insipid light coming in via the gap under the door. She could also determine some shapes that passed the door though the majority were meaningless. She discerned several low slung, horse-like creatures and on occasion, a cat, but the rest? She preferred not to know.

The food was welcoming and edible and the room functional. *What I wouldn't give for a change of clothes. I don't even have paper to leave a note for the provider of the meals*, she bemoaned.

There's something else here in the Neath too. I felt it the moment the tear in the dimensions closed. It's like I'm expected, or more, that someone is waiting for me.

Purity was pretty sure the strange feeling didn't have anything to do with her confinement and the horrible witch's designs on her. It was indefinable, but she had plenty of time to consider the sensation, and the ensuing emotions it caused within her.

Purity wasn't a psychic, medium, or even a sensitive, but she was sure there was someone in the Neath, who knew her, or more importantly, knew she was here. The sensation felt like being touched or stroked lightly on the inside of her head. Though it was a bit creepy, strangely enough it didn't frighten her. Gristle was all the fright she needed. It was weird; she sensed the other entity seemed curious and interested. *It has to be another person like me, a rescuer? Please, let it be a rescuer.*

After the fifth sleep period, of Purity's confinement - she didn't count naps - there was a change in the routine. She heard the patter of small feet which stopped outside her door. A key turned in the lock and the door opened. While the light didn't exactly flood in, it was a dramatic improvement on the dismal gloom.

"Mistress says, if you's agree to wear these, you's may

have freedom of the house." The tiny person outlined in the doorway bowed low, and struggling with their size, came forward bearing two silver rings. As she moved further inside the room Purity could see it was a thin waif-like, female hedgerow imp. "They's spelled," the imp explained.

Purity looked down at the bangles hanging from the imp's arms, the confusion on her face obvious. "They go's around your ankles," continued the imp, pointing to her own ankles enclosed in smaller versions. Purity shivered, but nodded her acquiescence, lifting first one leg and then the other, as the female imp bent down to place the anklets around her graceful limbs. The silver irritated her skin, but not as much as iron would have done. She said nothing, knowing the other fairy must feel the same as her.

The individual was a Hedgerow imp whose species originated from Earth. *How did this imp survive? Why didn't she die of shock entering the Neath?* Purity didn't know. Hedgerow imps were roughly the size of a stag beetle and often, quite literally, dropped down dead if frightened or startled, even by mistake. *To survive in the Neath this imp must have a strong constitution,* which was rare for her species. Her task done, the imp rose, and, without a word took Purity's hand, leading her out of the darkness and into whatever passed for daylight in the Neath Realm.

Purity had guessed she was in the Neath, from the instant the noxious demon closed the tear. The overwhelming darkness, the demon and the smell, not to mention his constant moaning about the disgusting painful light. Later, Crogg made sure to tell her repeatedly, she must be a she-devil for burning his tongue so badly. When Purity asked how, he admitted he'd tasted her tears. His admission gave her the final confirmation she needed. In school she'd learnt that Neath demons could not tolerate tears, and now she knew why.

Her father, Harty, had regaled her with the story of his kidnapping about fifty thousand times, from the time she was able to clamber onto his knee and listen. Finally, when she could bear it no more, she made him stop his retellings by sitting him down and regaling him with his own story, word for word. He'd never repeated it again, sure in the knowledge that his daughter had learnt enough to be careful. And she had been careful - right up to the point where she'd been pulled through the tear.

Holding the Hedgerow imp's hand, she followed her through the house. They ended up in the kitchen, and despite the noises she'd heard during her incarceration in the room, she didn't see a single creature, which amazed her. In the kitchen, a plate of food sat on the table, the same type of food that had been placed in her room while she slept. *This imp must be the unknown person who has been supplying my meals.*

"Sit, eat, tomorrow we works." Purity didn't like the sound of that. Work? She'd never worked. Sure, her parents made her do chores, empty the bins, put the laundry out, and wash up, but work?

"What type of work?" she asked the imp, curious despite her dislike of the word 'work'.

"You's see tomorrows," was the imp's mysterious reply, though she did tell Purity her name - Lou.

That night Purity didn't sleep in the dark bedroom alone, she joined Lou in the kitchen settling into a space made up beside the fire. It was warm, if a little smelly, but snuggling down next to Lou felt better than sleeping alone and listening to things go bump in the night.

A few hours later Purity woke. Something had woken her, but she couldn't figure out what it was immediately. In the ebbing firelight, she caught sight of something dark slinking into the room. It was an animal of some kind. It was lean and low, and covered in black fur. In alarm, she elbowed Lou in the side. Lou raised her head, smiled and settled back to rest.

"Is just Gussie," she murmured, through half-closed eyelids.

Purity watched entranced as Gussie slid around the edges of the room, checking the corners and sniffing them loudly, then sidling over to the two fairies and, with Purity holding her breath, it settled down to sleep covering their feet.

The animal's breathing slowed, becoming steady and deep. Purity was tempted to reach out her hand and touch the soft silky fur which tickled the ends of her toes, but she resisted. *Can this get any more bizarre?* she wondered, as she re-joined her companions in sleep.

She woke again several hours later as morning began. There was little change in the light outside the grubby kitchen window, just enough to see the animal still asleep across her legs.

"I named him Gussie, 'cause he looks like a Gussie," whispered Lou, waking up next to her. Purity couldn't begin to understand what Lou was speaking about, so she stayed silent as Lou continued. "We's can't move till he's gone. I don't think's he'd hurt us, but I's not taking any chances."

"Does he belong to the witch?" asked Purity intrigued.

"Oh no!" exclaimed Lou seemingly horrified at such a suggestion. "If the mistress knew she'd kill Gussie. Or worse, eats him. I never knows with her. No, we's don't tell her." Then realising Purity might, she added, "You's not tells either?" Seeing the fear in the imp's eyes Purity shook her head. "Of course not," she promised.

Lou sighed, and both watched as the silky creature called Gussie, about the size of a small sausage dog, woke. Purity studied the creature. She couldn't see any ears or mouth, though two jet -black eyes glanced her way as if feeling her scrutiny upon him. Gussie slinked back across the floor before disappearing out through the back door.

Purity would never have guessed in a million years, make that one million trillion years, what work, she and Lou would be doing over the next few days. Each morning they rose from their place by the fire, warm from the stove and Gussie's furry pelt. Purity would watch him slink silently out of the room like a graceful furry snake on legs. She marvelled at how beautiful and luxurious he seemed. *Fancy something that lovely existing in the Neath Realm,* she reflected each morning.

Lou led her out the back door. If she'd had any thoughts about running away, the view that met her eyes outside put an end to that. The landscape was as black as ink. She couldn't tell where the land finished, and the sky began. Right in front of her, things grew out of the ground in various shades of grey, on grey soil, with grey walls surrounding, what she presumed was a garden of some sort. It wasn't any type of garden she wished to visit or tend. She sincerely hoped that none of the meals she'd eaten had been made from the plants growing there. In addition to their lack of colour, the plants were weedy and spiky and not very appealing as food.

Lou took Purity around the garden following a gravelly path. On the far side of the house was an outbuilding, the type people keep their animals in, and animals is what Purity found. These weren't fluffy, slinky adorable animals like Gussie, these were fire lizards and snakes, and all manner of spiders. From tiny spindle-legged ones, to exotic coloured varieties with thick-jointed knees. Purity shuddered in loathing. These were animals out of other people's nightmares.

"What on earth are we supposed to do with these?" she asked, staring transfixed at row upon row of cages filled to bursting with these animals.

"Well firsts we's has to weed them out by separating the older ones."

"And how do we do that without being bitten, maimed or killed?" replied Purity, a tinge of sarcasm in her questioning tone.

"We's say a spells which makes them as light as bubbles. Then we's grabs them using these," answered Lou, apparently missing Purity's sarcastic tone. She held out a pair of long wooden tongs with sharp-tooth metal grippers at the end. They looked very painful for anyone caught on the biting end of them.

"They look like something out of a horror film," stated Purity in alarm. She grabbed another pair of tongs and stood there working them open and closed.

"We's are in the Neath Realm," answered Lou tersely, Purity's sarcasm not completely lost on her, though the film reference went right over her head.

"Why are there so many?" Purity asked, waving her pair of tongs about as she practiced grabbing thin air with them. Lou looked at her like she was stupid, but she replied anyway.

"They's mating."

"Oh," said Purity. Then, catching on, repeated, "Oh!... ...How long before … you know?" Lou grinned.

"Every three nights."

"No!"

"Yes."

"No!" exclaimed Purity in utter disbelief.

"Is we's going to talk all day, or is we's going to work? Cos' mistress gets angry if we don't works." Purity didn't want to meet the witch again, once was enough.

"What do I do?"

Relieved that the simpleton girl was settling to work Lou showed her the ropes.

That evening a weary fairy pulled her body under the coverlet by the fireside. She was asleep before Lou joined her, or Gussie arrived for the night, and didn't wake till after he'd left come morning. Each day continued the same, and Purity, not used to manual labour was exhausted to numbness within a few short days. The strange sensation that had plagued her when she arrived in the Neath, seemed to have vanished with her concentration on the appalling work.

Lou and Purity repeated the same tasks every day. The first day she'd been horrified by what was expected of her. She refused to do some of the jobs, saying she'd rather die.

Lou seemed to know, that Purity couldn't bring herself to kill anything. She didn't blame her. When Lou first arrived in the Neath, she couldn't do the nasty deeds either, but it was surprising what starvation made you do, how you gave up your conscience for a small crust of bread and a bowl of slop.

Lou took over from Purity, amid much exaggerated grumbling and sighing, though in reality she wasn't that concerned. Purity watched, tears running down her face at the brief, painful life these critters had. She decided snakes, spiders and lizards weren't so bad after all – witches were far worse if they inflicted such torment and death.

Lou envied Purity, but she pitied her too. She'd overheard Gristle planning her revenge on the folk who she blamed for imprisoning her in the Neath. Crogg and Lou were trapped too, unknowingly ensnared by gullibility spells which Gristle used to great effect. It was only a matter of time before Purity received the same spell too, then she would remain in the Neath forever. That would be good for Lou because she'd have a friend. Lou couldn't remember ever having a friend. She'd forgotten more about her life before Gristle than she remembered. There was Gristle and Crogg, then Gussie and now Purity. Lou was determined not to lose her newest, best friend to any of Gristle's plans.

★★★★

The shoes Phrack made for Onk were humongous. Harty watched Onk stomping up and down Phrack's workshop like a troll in a toyshop. They were Onk's first ever handmade pair of shoes and he was very proud of them. The very opposite of teenagers forced to go shoe shopping with their parents. They hate every pair their mother suggests, while she hates every pair the teen likes. Onk loved his new shoes. They fit nicely, were warm and cosy, but most importantly the soles of his feet didn't burn. Phrack also supplied Onk with a wonderful jar of dwarf burn cream. "As used by lava mining dwarves every-where," he said. The cream soothed his second degree burns a treat.

Harty was getting jittery in his spot by the window. He didn't think they could afford such wonderful shoes, or more correctly, boots, since they came up to Onk's ankles.

"There must be at least eight lizards for each shoe," he mumbled. "It'll cost a fortune. What are we going to do about payment?" The dwarf hadn't mentioned payment. He'd watched Onk happy in his new footwear and felt rightly proud. There was no finer feeling than a customer happy with his shoes. *Another satisfied customer, payment next, but will they be agreeable to my idea?* he wondered. Phrack decided to approach the delicate subject and see how they responded.

"So, ye like the boots?" he asked Onk.

"There, I knew they were boots," Harty groaned under his breath. "That'll cost heaps more."

"Onk love boots," he grinned back at Phrack like a child at Christmas. "Strong, soft," he continued, really getting carried away.

"About payment," continued Phrack.

"Oh no here it comes, get ready to give those boots back Onk," moaned Harty to himself as he sat on the window ledge.

"I was wondering whether ye'd do me a favour in return, instead of currency."

"Really!" shouted a surprised Mulberry elf. Onk grinned wider.

"Yes, I've had enough of the Fire Realm. I'd like to look further, travel, see something of the other dimensions."

"You want to come with us?" asked a disbelieving Harty.

"No, I want ye to collect me when ye leave Incandesonia. I need time to sell my workshop space and gather my equipment." No self-respecting dwarf would ever leave his goods behind.

"We're not really going back to Earth," confessed Harty, his wingtips curling with emotion. "We're heading for the Neath Realm." And so, Harty told the dwarf the whole story, beginning with the showdown years ago and ending with Purity being kidnapped.

"So, you see, we have to go on. We came into the Fire Realm to locate this wren's egg, so he will take us to the Neath Realm and I can rescue my daughter." What Phrack said next surprised both Onk and Harty.

"I have a daughter," he murmured, casting his eyes down to the floor. Dwarves found speaking about their emotions embarrassing. He glanced up briefly, catching their astonished gazes, and, before he lost his nerve, he continued. "Aye, I haenae seen her in decades. She lives in the Neath Realm. Married a Stone warlock and moved there." Phrack stood for a moment, communing with himself, then he made a decision.

"If it's the Goddess's will, then I must follow. I'll come with ye to the Neath Realm. It's travelling and in the precise direction I should go."

"Are you sure?" asked Harty. "It's likely to be very dangerous." Harty looked to Onk for confirmation and Onk nodded.

"A bit o' danger nae frightened me, laddie," replied Phrack. "Besides I ken where the egg might be.

"Really?"

"Aye. Where ye planning to stay?"

"We haven't decided yet."

"Ye ken rest here until we leave if ye like. It isnae much but its dry and warm."

"Thank you, that would be great," answered Harty, for both of them. Phrack showed them to a space beyond his workshop where they could sleep. Scanning the area, Harty found several soft leather off-cuts on a shelf and curled up there, while Phrack hastily prepared Onk a temporary bed on the floor.

****

"Tell me again, what are we doing here?" whispered Harty, as they waited in the shadows of a nearby building.

"Shhhh, they'll hear ye," mumbled Phrack Blaster, edging back into the concealment of the doorway. Onk hadn't come with them because Phrack had said the mission needed stealth and finesse. Onk wasn't exactly built with those qualities in mind. When Phrack was happy the guards had gone, he looked up at Harty floating above his head.

"If I haed known ye were noisier than your companion, I might hae brought him instead." Harty huffed at such a suggestion.

"I can be quiet. I just don't know why we are being quiet that's all." Phrack sighed.

"We're." He corrected himself. "I'm being quiet to observe the guards' routine, but ye very nearly gave us away."

"Oh, sorry," apologised Harty, dropping down so their eyes were level.

"It's okay, don't do it on the actual night, is all."

"I'm still not sure why we're here, in stealth mode,"

Harty persisted. The dwarf was learning the hard way that Harty, though more vocal than Onk, wasn't necessarily the sharpest pencil in the box.

"Here is the Incandesonia Museum, where all the wonders of the six realms are supposed to reside, and your wren's egg is probably inside if it's in the Fire Realm," answered Phrack.

"Really?" Harty was interested. He tried, but he couldn't see the building in the dark.

"Why does it have guards if it's just a museum?"

"Exactly my question. There never used to be guards watching the outside of the museum, something's changed. Something valuable must be inside, maybe it's your egg? That's' going to make it harder to steal."

Harty became indignant at the word 'steal'.

"We're not stealing, we're returning the egg to its rightful owner."

"So, ye say."

"I do say, I do say indeed," responded Harty, pulling himself up to all four and a half inches. Recognising he'd gone a bit far pulling the tree elf's wing, Phrack relented.

"Okay, rightful owner, I understand."

"I hope you do. I wouldn't do anything so low as steal…" It was the dwarf's turn to look incredulous.

"Really! And what pray tell did ye plan to use for currency for Onk's boots?" No amount of verbal blustering could cover Harty's curling wingtips shouting out his guilt.

"In all honesty, we hadn't thought that far," replied Harty, "when you offered your solution."

"I did, didn't I?"

Just then the noisy guards returned for another brief inspection of the area. Phrack and Harty shrank into the shadows once more.

"Breaking in at night doesnae look good," muttered Phrack, once they'd arrived back at his workshop. "We need to check out what they're guarding and whether it's going to be moved soon."

"I can do that with Onk, we can go in tomorrow as tourists."

"Okay let's do it. We don't get many visitors to Incandesonia. It might look suspicious if I suddenly decided to visit the museum after living here years. You two fit the bill perfectly as tourists who'd be interested in the city's exhibits and curios."

Next morning saw Harty and Onk, complete in his wondrous new boots and a jaunty felt hat, queueing up to go inside the museum. Onk had always loved hats. When Phrack gave him the opportunity to choose clothing to look more like a tourist, he chose the hat.

The curators appeared to be charging an entry fee for the first time today. Luckily, Phrack had had the foresight to supply them with a few coins in case of need. Onk glanced upwards, observing the guards stationed on the roof. As he turned his head back down to Harty to advise him of his observation, his eye – always lured by shiny objects – caught sight of a metallic gleam, glistening in the fiery daylight on the far edge of the city. It was too far away for Onk to distinguish its outline, and he lost sight of it as the queue shuffled forward into the shadow of the building.

If they thought gaining entry to the building during the night with only four guards on duty was going to be difficult, during the day the number of guards seemed to have trebled. Harty was glad they decided to pay as tourists, so they could assess their chances first.

He watched the steady stream of folk passing through the museum. *Museums seem to have the same visitors regardless of the dimension*, he mused. There were the slightly zany, hip-dude, secondary school teachers with their bored groups of teenagers. The slightly wacky primary teachers with their wide-eyed infants. There were individuals wandering about with nowhere else to go, and couples not gazing at any exhibits, just gazing doe-eyed at each other.

Harty swallowed, the sight reminding him that he'd left his poor wife Shine alone with only Gem for company. *How she must be suffering with both me and Purity gone from her side,* he reflected guiltily. *It would be so good to have access to an Earth smart phone right now. On the other hand, it's not likely to work outside of Earth's dimension, so maybe not so smart.*

Inside, they wandered from exhibit to exhibit pretending to be interested in the stuffed heads and exotic displays. They halted at the entrance to another dusty room where, 'Rare Animals from the Six Dimensions,' was grandly announced on a large banner hanging over their heads.

Harty was puzzled. There were no valuable items on display, nothing to explain the presence of the increased number of guards. There were no queues to see amazing new, or priceless artefacts, despite what the banner at the room's entrance announced. The usual shards of pottery nestled in glass display cases with tags identifying their age and location of origin. Row upon row of dead insects, pinned flat onto paper trays, sat alongside unremarkable fossilised remains. It was a relatively normal museum as museums go. That was till Harty tried to enter one specific door, then Hell's Pixies broke loose.

They came at him from every direction. He'd never seen so many Hell's pixies in one place, apparently employed as extra security in addition to the regular guards. They converged on Harty's position, making him feel like a felon before he'd attempted to commit any crime.

"What are you doing?" questioned the head Hell Pixie, catching Harty off-guard. His status was obvious by his red beret, whereas his two dozen troops all wore green ones.

"Ahh! I was looking for the little boys' room," Harty blurted out, trying to think of a plausible excuse.

"Well, you're not going to find it in there," scowled the pixie.

Trying to stay in character Harty asked.

"Do you know where I might find it?"

"Up the toe of my boot, if you don't move along!" replied the irritated guard.

Hell's pixies were never a happy bunch, probably because their lives comprised of two parts. They lived the first part in the light realms and when they died there, instead of returning to the ether, they passed over, not to heaven but to a second hellish life in the Neath Realm. Most wore a permanent scowl, especially when they met other creatures of the light realms and remembered their past lives.

Harty feigned indignation and fluttered off. Onk, stomping along in his new boots followed on behind.

"You see that?" The head pixie turned to his closest subordinate, watching Onk traipse past. "Those boots must have cost a small fortune." The guard in question nodded his agreement, it was more than his wings were worth to disagree with his disgruntled boss.

Realising the Hell's Pixies might continue to follow him if he looked too suspicious, Harty went on to examine the dead animal displays in the next room, there was a slim chance the egg might be amongst them. When both were sure the guards had lost interest in them, they sat together to discuss their progress, Harty gliding down smoothly to land on the stone bench next to Onk.

"I can't find it Onk. Have you seen it?" Onk shook his head. He was getting fed up looking at rows of dead things. All he saw were dead objects that he wasn't allowed to eat.

"I once heard someone say, if you've considered all the logical options and not found the answer, then the answer, however illogical, must be the answer." Harty had lost Onk after the first part of his convoluted sentence. Onk displayed his confusion by waggling his eyebrows up and down like he'd seen Gem do.

"That means, if the egg isn't here, it must be in another part of the museum they're guarding. How on Earth are we going to find it, let alone get it?"

Onk had had enough of walking around boring rooms. He decided it was time to take matters into his own hands - literally. He grinned at Harty in reply, then walked to the wall on the opposite side of the room that was covered in paintings. He appeared to spend a few moments scrutinising one depicting a large swan-like creature then, without warning, lifted the painting down like he worked there, said, "Punch." And did.

The hole was sized exactly right for Harty, who flew through it quicker than a greased pickpocket imp through runny treacle. In a flash, Onk replaced the painting, and whistling an odd tune, stomped away like nothing had happened.

Harty was away from prying eyes. No one walked or flew on this side of the building. He glanced left and right confirming he was in a long empty corridor. Getting his bearings, so he could find his way back, he flew up near the ceiling and travelled towards what he guessed, was the suspect door he'd tried to open earlier.

Hearing voices he slowed his flight, edging around the corner cornice to peer down at the owners of the conversation - two fat, greasy goblins.

"I told you, I told you no one would look for it here and I was right," announced the first goblin.

"I know, but I still have that feeling. You know, that feeling I get a bit before things go wrong."

"What can go wrong? You've paid for more Hell's Pixies than I've got teeth and that's a lot," reassured the first goblin, grinning widely to show his companion the large number of teeth he possessed. His colleague didn't seem impressed, judging by his head shaking from side to side. Harty realised he was listening to a couple of individuals involved in very shady dealings.

"We can't afford to have it stolen before she gets here tomorrow. She's paying a lot for this haul and the egg is the icing on the cake."

Harty almost squealed in excitement. *The egg! They've got the egg!* It was all he could do not to shout it out loud and had to resort to holding his belly to stop his excitement from leaking out. It was a well-known manoeuvre to stop silliness exploding. *Get a grip Harty,* he told himself. *Besides, the egg is being moved elsewhere tomorrow, that means we only have tonight or now.*

The two characters moved away from the mountain of objects resting against one wall. Harty guessed this was the haul leaving tomorrow that the two goblins were discussing. He had to locate the egg in the pile before it was moved, or the goblins returned, and there was no time like the proverbial present.

Flying around the ceiling he positioned himself above the pile of items. He saw stuffed animals, jewellery, herbs and spices, live creatures in cages, but no egg. He dropped lower. A couple of engraved boxes caught his eye. They were the right size for a wren's egg to fit snuggly inside. *Can I open the boxes before I'm discovered?* He wondered.

He reached the first box without a problem, lifting the lid gently he peered inside. A large blue stone rested on a pink cloth. The second contained a ring, and the third, a coiled dead snake. He almost dropped that box on the floor as he recoiled, thinking the snake alive. The fifth and sixth were empty, obviously waiting for their treasures. *Where's that pesky egg?*

The voices returned, becoming louder, the owners of the haul were coming back. Harty lifted to the ceiling and disappeared around the corner of the room, just in time to listen to their on-going conversation.

"Should we put the pixies in here?"

"Might be a good idea. There's a brute of a troll hanging around out there. I don't trust trolls ever since my sister ran off with one."

"No!"

"She did. Don't know what she saw in him."

"What are you doing?" The first goblin asked, as the other leant over to check one of the boxes.

"Just checking. I told you I can feel it in my noggin. Something's going to happen. You should trust my noggin."

"You always say that."

"And I'm always right, am I not?"

"Mmmm, I'll go arrange that extra Hell's Pixie guard in here."

"Ok," replied his partner. "I'll check on the other stuff outside."

Harty was terrified. Once the Hell's Pixies arrived there'd be no chance to grab the egg. *What shall I do? Go check the other stuff, or re-check that first box again which the goblin couldn't leave alone?* He opted for the box. It was nearer.

He spiralled down towards it and lifted the lid. It was just a pretty blue stone, not the wren's egg. Harty sighed unable to hide his disappointment. Then the stone shimmered. Only slightly, a thin sliver of change, but enough for Harty to recognise the object had a glamour set upon it, disguising it as a stone. He reached his arms out and lifted the stone. At his touch, the stone turned into an egg. Harty gasped in delight. It was light too not like a stone, like an egg, a wren's egg. Grasping it to his body, he rose into the air, and struggling, hurried back along the passageway to where Onk had punched the hole.

He found the hole in the wall as a Goddess awful cry went up behind him. All Hell's Pixies broke loose.

That was Onk's signal to move the painting. He found Harty sitting in the gap behind it. Staggering with the weight, Harty settled into Onk's outstretched hand. Onk closed his fingers gently over him. Palming Harty and the egg, Onk raised his hat and pushed both underneath. He replaced the painting, then stomped towards the doors and freedom.

How Harty managed to fly with an object almost as big around as he was, Onk could only guess. Without a backward glance, Onk stormed towards the exit, as the two goblins and their retinue came out of the protected door at the rear of the building.

"Slow down!" cautioned Harty, from the relative safety of the dark hat. "Make it look like you're bored." Harty was unable to see the result of his instructions.

Onk stopped in his tracks. Giving a preening shrug, he flung his long greasy locks about him almost accidentally dislodging his headwear. Harty grabbed a handful of hair with one hand, pulling the egg towards him with the other and hung on.

There were various species visiting the museum that day, including some young and very impressionable female teenage orcs accompanied by their warden, who insisted on being called teacher. The girls' reaction to Onk's behaviour was classic. They drooled down their hairy chins at the vision of loveliness he represented, and a couple swooned.

"Oh Miss, looks at him," Brianna cooed, her strong Neath dialect identifying that she hadn't been born in the Fire Realm, but sent to school there. She pointed in Onk's direction. "He's ever so luverly." The teacher wasn't as impressed, but she did appreciate a good pair of legs when she saw them. Forgetting her role as warden/teacher for a moment, she replied.

"Mmmm yes, quite nice, I suppose. Though a bit tall for

me." Secretly, she thought he was 'luverly' too, though it would never do to say as much to her charges.

"He's dreamy," cooed a second orc soaking the front of her bib with saliva.

Onk didn't notice any of it. He didn't know the effect he had on females, and in any case, he was immune to their charms since marrying Gem. She was his fated, *One True Love*.

"Look that troll's getting away," yelled the larger of the two goblins.

"Don't be stupid! How would a troll get through that titchy hole in the wall? No, what we want is that iddy-biddy elf. The one the pixies stopped earlier. It's him that's stolen our stuff. Not some blooming great lump of a troll, no matter how good he looks." The other goblin gave his colleague a side-ways look.

Onk slowed his walk following Harty's advice. He sauntered through the main door like he was the Goddess's gift to the dimensions. And maybe he was.

9

Kaduru

"YOU should have seen Onk," enthused Harty, once they'd returned to the safety of the dwarf's workshop. Phrack had thoughtfully provided them with a midday meal of fruit, which they devoured while Harty fedback on their adventure. They were both famished. Onk decided, a life of crime made a person very hungry indeed.

"It was amazing and terrifying, and Onk was awesome!" Harty tore into the fruit he'd chosen. "They totally ignored Onk. I heard one of them say, he couldn't possibly have climbed in through such a tiny hole. They're obviously not very bright," Harty sniggered, the sticky fruit juice running down his arms as he waved them about in his excitement. "They forgot it would take someone with the strength of a troll to smash a hole in the first place." He flexed his biceps to reinforce his statement. "I'm guessing one of the goblins liked Onk, judging by the look he gave him." Harty smirked at his friend. "Probably couldn't think straight with all that hair-waving. I was under his hat, and I felt it." It was

Onk's turn to give a side-ways look. He shook his long hair in negation.

"Onk taken. Onk belong to Gem."

"Of course you do, Onk. I was only jesting." Harty wolfed down more fruit in his happiness at their successful mission, oblivious for once, to his friend's discomfort. Onk frowned, clearly unhappy with Harty's comment.

"Well, ye have your egg. What next?" asked Phrack Blaster, swiftly changing the subject.

"Now, we go back to the wren. Give him the egg, and he leads us to my daughter." Harty glanced at Onk for confirmation, but Onk's face was downcast. He appeared to be concentrating on eating his fruit.

"Ye make it sound simple."

"It is simple. Simple plans work best, don't they Onk?" There was no reply to Harty's question. Harty turned to face his friend, but Onk had left the room. *How did I not notice that Onk had gone?* He sat for a moment thinking about the comment he'd made earlier to Onk. He tried to appear confident to Phrack, but he didn't really feel that way. Especially, when he realised Onk hadn't agreed with him. Hadn't agreed with anything, now he thought about it.

"I need to go and find Onk." Rinsing his arms in a bowl of water, Harty left in search of his friend.

Onk hadn't gone far. He was sitting outside the workshop on a low boundary wall, swinging his feet and staring at the ground. Harty approached.

"I'm sorry Onk." Onk looked up. "I shouldn't have said those things. I shouldn't have teased my best friend. Will you forgive me?" Harty settled on the wall.

Onk looked down at the little man who was so tiny he could squash him with one hand and smiled.

"Onk forgive Harty. Harty friend."

"And you're my friend, my best friend." Onk nodded and let out a deep sigh.

"Onk misses Gem."

That single short sentence made Harty feel bad. He'd forgotten that his friend Onk, had joined him searching for Purity, while his wife and family were waiting, without word, at home. This wasn't Onk's mission, it was his. He'd not only upset his friend but made him sad thinking of his loved ones so far away. It was inexcusable.

"I know. I really am sorry. I didn't mean to remind you."

"First time away," Onk continued, his voice becoming quieter. Harty moved closer and patted the back of Onk's hand with his own tiny one. Onk looked down again and smiled for a second time. He knew his friend was trying to make him feel better.

"You're not alone Onk, not alone." Onk nodded.

They sat on the wall in silence for most of the afternoon, their friendship bond re-established once more, getting up when Phrack called them inside for a much-needed drink.

The dwarf wasn't sure about Harty's so-called simple plan. He decided to ask Harty for more details as they sipped their beverages by the fire. Harty remembered the route they took to get to Incandesonia didn't exist anymore. They'd need to find a new way out.

"One thing's for sure, we can't go back the way we came," he admitted. Onk nodded his agreement, reverting to his usual form of dialogue. "Sure, we can cross the lava river, but the land between that and the grey people might be a problem since we woke the creature up."

"Creature? What creature?" asked a confused Phrack, not liking the sound of what Harty was saying one bit.

"Onk and I had a bit of trouble getting here," Harty hedged. "The journey wasn't easy or straight forward." He looked towards Onk for affirmation and encouragement. Onk nodded again, his long locks doing a vertical Mexican wave behind him. "Purely by mistake of course," Harty

104

stressed trying to placate Phrack's worried tone. "We woke up some kind of serpent. When the serpent realised he couldn't eat Onk, because by the time it woke up fully Onk was too far away, it turned around and ate a lot of grey people standing nearby instead.

"Oh goodness," gasped Phrack.

"Onk wanting to fight," interrupted Onk, demonstrating to them that he was capable of constructing a proper sentence as well as fighting.

"Anyway, I don't think they'll be happy if we go back that way," Harty concluded, and Phrack was forced to agree.

Harty suddenly found his throat constricting as his brain processed the word's he'd just spoken. *Onk and I sentenced those people to a cruel and gruesome death, so we could survive. There hadn't been any other way*, but that didn't make him feel any better. His words dried up as his heart filled with shame. Phrack, astonished at Harty's revelation, didn't notice his abrupt silence.

"You woke up Kadru and lived? I've never heard of such a thing!"

"I think," Harty responded in a small voice, "I think he was more interested in eating loads of grey people than us." He took a deep breath. "Either way, the land is unsafe, and the remaining people are likely to be too angry to let us pass. I know I would be if strangers caused my relatives to be eaten."

"It's a good thing the female serpent is tougher to wake up, stated Phrack solemnly. Otherwise, you'd not have lived." Harty's mouth dropped open and Onk blinked at Phrack's words.

"There's another one?"

"Oh yes, she is much much larger and cannier than the male. Ye dinae take advantage of her so easily. She's aggressive and very protective of her bairns." Phrack was becoming more amazed at the luck of this strange duo.

"I'm thinking if you've upset the Stone folk and Kadru, you're right, I'd best find us a safer route."

"Really? That would be wonderful Phrack," Harty enthused, his panic receding. "I was dreading returning that way. Onk tried to challenge the serpent last time too." Onk grinned at Phrack's raised eyebrows which had reached his hairline in amazement. He couldn't believe the troll's audacity threatening a stone serpent and surviving.

"We have to cross the river first. Ye dinae upset the boatman too, did ye?"

"Not unless his family live on the far side of the river, no," assured Harty.

"Good. The boatman has no family. He is bonded to the river." Harty didn't know what that meant but wasn't about to ask questions.

"We'll leave in the morning once I have sold my final pair of shoes."

"Do you have to sell everything here? Can't you take some of your wares with you?" asked Harty. Harty was a little bit envious of Onk's new boots, he'd been hoping the dwarf might make him a pair. If they left all his materials behind there'd be no wonderful lizard skin. As if reading Harty's thoughts, Phrack moved over to his cabinet. Opening the door, he reached inside and pulled out the tiniest pair of booties, fit for an elf. Harty squealed in delight and Onk, thinking they were under threat, looked around for someone to smash.

"I got a bit bored waiting, and these took no time at all to cobble. I thought you might have had enough of flying."

"They're wonderful," squeaked Harty, his wing tips curling back and forth to announce his pleasure. "I was going to ask, but…"

"I'm glad you like them. Put them on," interrupted Phrack, not wanting to become embarrassed by his small act of kindness. Harty wheeled around the room in them.

"Look Onk look, a tiny pair like yours!" Onk clapped his hands together in glee.

Onk nominated himself custodian of the wren's egg before they left Incandesonia, placing it in a small bag he kept secured around his waist under his tunic. Harty had never seen the bag before and wondered what Onk kept in there, but when he tried to peek Onk became secretive, turning away before he could spy its contents. Once satisfied the egg was secure, Onk zipped up the bag and whispered, "Pretty."

Harty sighed hearing the word pretty. He was taken right back to London. Sitting in his Mulberry tree by the Thames. Onk was smiling down at a pink cocoon containing an unborn fairy which would shortly become Harty's daughter. A tear rolled down his cheek as he saw the scene again inside his mind.

"Pretty," he echoed, squeezing his eyes tight shut and wishing his daughter well wherever she was.

They left mid-morning the following day, after Phrack had sold his wagon and beautiful pair of racing Gerenuks. He'd miss them, but they wouldn't fit on the boat or be useful on the rest of the journey. He wanted to ensure they went to caring owners, so he'd taken much less than they were worth.

They travelled on foot towards the lava river and the ferry crossing. The journey to the river was much slower than when they arrived because Onk could afford to stroll, wearing his fire-resistant boots. Plus, the dwarf had joined their company reducing their pace further. The mooring pier was empty when they reached it. Harty still found it difficult to tell the time with no sun or moon, but Phrack assured him it was late afternoon.

The river wasn't wide. The far side could be seen with ease, however, there was no sign of the boat or the boatman. Phrack looked both ways up and down the fiery river – nothing. It was impossible to cross a flowing lava river, the heat coming off it alone was enough to boil water.

"We'll wait a wee while," he announced, and sat down on the gravelly bank after laying out a dark piece of cloth big enough for all of them to sit on. He advised them that it was heat-proof and comfortable. Harty flew down off Onk's shoulder to enjoy walking some more in his new boots, the novelty not yet worn off, as he stepped over to the blanket.

"These boots are fabulous," he informed the dwarf, as he continued pacing about in them.

"I'm glad ye like them. The stitching was a mite fiddly, not as neat as I'd like."

"But even so," insisted Harty. "They are lovely."

"Good, I'm glad. Nothing thrills a craftsman more than appreciation of his work."

"I do, I love them Phrack. You must let me repay you some way."

"Journeying with you, that's payment enough."

"That's not payment," Harty stated. "That's companionship."

"Whatever ye say, it is enough."

A short while later, Phrack seemed to notice a change in the air, or something Harty missed, because he rose to his feet.

"He's not coming," he informed a rested Harty and Onk.

"The ferryman? Why not? Where would he go?" questioned Harty rising into the air.

"He's either sick, or he's been told to stay at home, or he's… ." Phrack left the last word unsaid. It didn't do to tempt Fate. Harty choose to ignore the unsaid word.

"Who would tell him to go?" he pressed, opting to follow up the second suggestion as Phrack began rolling up their blanket.

"Who do you think?" responded Phrack, turning to face them. "Goblins."

"Goblins!" exclaimed Harty. "Not the ones from the museum? What do we do?"

"We don't sit around here waiting to be caught, that's what," replied Phrack, pushing the blanket into the travel bag he had brought. "Come on, we need to find another place to cross."

Harty fluttered onto Onk's shoulder.

"Is there another place to cross?"

"I hope so, I really do," replied the sombre dwarf, "or we're in trouble."

Phrack took Onk and Harty west along the river bank. He seemed to know roughly where they were going and Harty had no better ideas, so they followed. As they walked, Harty riding in his usual place, the sky changed colour from a rosy hue to a deeper ruby with streaks of russet. Phrack stared up at the sky and sighed.

"We need to find shelter, there's a fire storm brewing." They hadn't seen a storm since their arrival in Incandesonia, but Harty took Phrack's word for it.

"Where are we going to shelter? This place is barren and empty," said Harty, turning in a circle. "There is no shelter for miles."

Phrack smiled, and reached into his voluminous travel bag pulling out, what looked like another ground blanket.

Harty and Onk had never seen a storm like it. It didn't rain water, or snow, or even hailstones, it rained fire bombs and lava. The three travellers were safe under Phrack's hastily assembled awning. It came complete with foldable poles which were positioned one at each corner and one in the middle to prevent the bombs from having prolonged contact with the fabric and burning through. Instead, due to their velocity they bounced on and off again. It was a tight squeeze for Onk and if he hadn't been wearing his boots, it could have been much worse. With his long flowing hair and size, he was a bigger target than Harty or even Phrack.

"The storms are caused by a volcano erupting some-where in the realm," said Phrack, bending to apply some of his magic cream to Onk's left wrist. It sported a burn from where a fire bomb had bounced off the canopy onto his outstretched arm. "They usually last a couple of hours and most people shelter from them, except the bairns, who like to play chicken – till they get burnt."

"That's awful. Don't their parents stop them?" asked a horrified Harty.

"It's ok, they rarely get hurt and when they do, no one dies very often." Harty shivered. His daughter was far too precious to him to ever let her do such a reckless thing.

10

Stone

"COME on, we's catch the tail end if we's hurrys," called Lou, racing off into the garden. They didn't get much free time, but a fire storm reaching this far inside the Neath was an extraordinary event.

"They're more commons in the Fire Realm than here," she explained, to a breathless Purity catching her up. "It's exciting!" the tiny imp enthused. "When the bombs comes we's duck or jumps out the way." Purity couldn't see the fun in doing that.

"Isn't it incredibly dangerous or something?" she queried.

"Yes. No, Maybe. Oh, I don't knows. Is fun is all," said Lou, wondering whether Purity was going to ruin her brief episode of enjoyment. "Look the sky's turning, gets ready to jumps."

Purity was about to ask Lou which way, when a boulder a foot wide and on fire, landed not three feet from her position. She screamed and jumped away from it. Lou laughed out loud.

"You's have to look up and watch's them coming,

111

otherwise, they's likely smack you on the heads," she giggled. Purity didn't think it was a giggling matter, but she raised her eyes to the sky as instructed. Within moments, another glowing red object appeared above her in the black sky. As it drew nearer, she saw the flames stretching out behind it like taffy – and jumped. It landed exactly where she'd been standing. She didn't have time to consider the consequences, as a second object appeared. She jumped again. This one landed several feet away. In front of her, Lou was jumping this way and that, avoiding a whole barrage of flaming rocks. Purity was thankful only a few came her way, but those that did kept her eyes and mind occupied.

She had thought the storm might be a distraction, enabling her to attempt an escape. She hadn't planned on the storm distracting her – which it did. Purity was puffing as the last rocks dropped short of them. Lou plopped down on the grey soil and pouted, disappointed that the storm was moving away.

"That was certainly a good workout," Purity commented.

"What's a workout?" asked Lou intrigued.

"Exercises you do to stay fit."

"Why in the Neath would you's need exercises to stay fit when there's works aplenty?" Lou chortled, finding the whole idea ridiculous. *She has a point, our daily workout involves plenty of physical work, lifting and moving cages and animals.* Even with the lifting spells, the two girls still needed to push and pull the equipment.

Storm over, they retreated inside, away from the empty blackness.

****

Harty Onk and Phrack, waited out the brief fire storm at the edge of the Fire Realm, sheltering under Phrack's amazing fire-resistant awning. When the storm was over, Phrack collapsed the poles, rolled up the awning, and folded the ground sheet they'd used. Both disappeared inside his mysterious bag like they never existed. Phrack had tried to explain dimensional transcendentalism, but it was beyond Harty's comprehension.

They continued along the bank, Harty puzzling over the ferry's disappearance. He was wondering where the boatman had gone. He hoped the man was poorly, though not too poorly of course. It didn't do well to dwell on other possibilities. He gazed at the lava flowing beside them, the heat radiating from it making his left side all toasty. *That stuff will destroy anything, even a boat.*

They walked several miles before Phrack called a halt. Harty was sitting in his usual shoulder-riding position, otherwise, he couldn't have kept up with Phrack's step, let alone Onk's. *Onk's been quiet for the longest time,* thought Harty. Though he wasn't a big conversationalist, Onk liked to hum and sing when he strolled, a silent Onk was a sign he was troubled.

"Is everything ok?" he asked, leaning a little closer.

"Onk thinking," came the common reply. Onk thought a lot. He thought about a great many things, some small and some huge. Like, how many elephants could fit on a football field wearing high heels, and where do weasels go to die? Onk was quite a philosopher, amazing Harty with his vast knowledge and understanding of the dimensions. *Perhaps it's true, trolls' brains do spread into other realms, because Onk's thoughts are vast.*

Harty knew Onk's thoughts weren't always connected with their current activities either, so he didn't assume the troll would be considering their problem. He'd found that out many times to his detriment during their long relationship.

One time, he'd complained about his aching back and

Onk had muttered, "Snake wee." Harty, thinking it a cure, had searched far and wide for snake wee, finally locating some at the local Howells Zoo, almost being swallowed by a provoked python in the process.

Arriving home clutching his small pot of wee he proceeded to smear it over his painful back. His wife Shine was disgusted for it smelt like three-week-old dead mice. Gem, who was visiting them at the time, roared with laughter falling backwards off her chair onto the concrete outside the Boating Pool Café. When she recovered sufficiently to speak, she advised Harty that Onk had been trying to remember the last time he'd smelt anything like the aroma of dead mice.

"Is it useful?" he asked Onk, wary of making assumptions around his friend.

"Maybe," Onk replied wisely.

Harty was always prepared to listen to Onk. He lifted himself up from Onk's shoulder and hovered in front of him. Phrack paused too, to see what Onk might say next. This troll aroused a sneaking sense of admiration in him. His previous experience with trolls had been that they were stupid, slow and uncouth. Onk was none of these, he was a troll who commanded respect and maybe a little bit of awe too.

"Onk can build boat," he stated simply. Harty and Phrack looked at each other, then back at Onk.

"Really?" they both said simultaneously. Onk nodded.

"That would be very helpful indeed my strong friend," answered Phrack. Onk liked it that Phrack called him 'his friend.' It made that warm fuzzy feeling rise up in his chest. Not as far as it did for Harty and Gem and their combined children, but enough to be pleasurable. Onk smiled.

"Tell ye what," Phrack continued. "If we have nae discovered any passage across the lava flow by sunset," *Whenever that is,* thought Harty. "We might take ye up on

114

your offer Onk." And thus, their next step of action was decided.

Their trudge along the near bank failed to throw up any kind of bridge, path, or boat. Phrack finally turned to Onk, who was staring, captivated by a beautiful bird-like creature wheeling and swooping in the sky on the far horizon. The light glinting off the bird's wings made Onk smile and reminded him of something, but he couldn't quite remember what. Regardless, he liked watching the pretty colours twist and turn.

"It's over to ye now Onk," said Phrack, interrupting Onk's revelry.

"Need those." Onk pointed to the tools hung round Phrack's belt. Phrack gasped in surprise.

There are few things in the dimensions more precious to dwarves than their tools. It was not uncommon for them to sleep with them, or wash with them – when they did wash. Phrack was no exception. He loved his tools and if tales were true, he kissed his tools each night before retiring to bed to thank them for their effort, though no dwarf would ever admit to kissing anything.

Asking to hold a dwarf's crafting tools was like asking to hold their new first-born – unthinkable. Yet here was Onk, not only asking to hold, but requesting to use his equipment. Phrack decided he hadn't heard Onk correctly. Was this troll whom he almost revered, asking to sully his perfect instruments of craft? It sounded like it.

Harty cleared his throat preparing to defend his friend. He guessed, based on Onk's request, that Onk didn't know about dwarf etiquette, but he did know Onk wouldn't have asked unless the tools were essential to do the job.

"Why do you need Phrack's equipment Onk? Harty stuttered. Like Phrack he was a bit dumbstruck.

"Onk need to make own tools," he answered, oblivious to the unspoken tension radiating off the dwarf. It was a simple request to his roving troll mind. Hearing Onk wanted to make tools, caused the dwarf to ease slightly. *If Onk wants to make tools,* he reasoned, *that means that he likes them, honours them and knows the importance of a precious set of working tools.* Harty picked his metaphorical way through the conversation, trying to seek a solution to both their needs. *Phrack needs to keep his tools safe.* Was it the light or had the dwarf's face blanched at Onk's request? *Onk needs tools to make a boat.* A light bulb lit up in his mind.

"Onk can you draw the tools you need?" asked Harty. Onk nodded.

"Phrack, could you make the tools he draws?"

"Probably," answered Phrack, the tension in him dropping another notch.

Harty led Onk over to a spot of sandy ground and asked him to draw what he needed. Onk drew a stone hammer head, then a stone chisel.

"I can make those," replied a relaxed Phrack, not realising how tense he'd been up till that point. He hunted around, finding some likely looking rocks to work on. Meanwhile, Onk searched for a boulder which might become a boat. It didn't take either of them very long. Phrack handed Onk the tools he'd created and Onk set to work. Soon, the air was filled with the sound of stone on stone and lethal shards and fragments of rock were spraying everywhere. Phrack and Harty retreated to a safe distance.

"Is there a chance that someone might hear Onk making the boat?" asked Harty, worrying about the noise levels.

"Maybe, if someone's following us, but we're a long way from any towns."

No one appeared to challenge them and Onk worked on into the late evening carving out a rough dugout. When he finished Harty didn't know, he fell asleep sometime after dark, or what passed for dark in the Fire Realm.

When they all awoke in the morning the 'boat' was

complete. It wasn't the most beautiful craft. It wouldn't win any prizes for sleekness or style, but it looked 'up to the job' as Shine would say. Onk had even fashioned two basic paddles which looked cumbersome and heavy to use. There were times, like now, when Harty was glad he was small and could fly.

Phrack pulled out the cloth they had used as a blanket to sit on the day before, from his Mary Poppins style bag. He covered the interior of the boat with the heat resistant lining. Once the troll and dwarf were reasonably happy with the 'ship-shapeness' of the boat, they manhandled the solid craft down to the river's edge. It wasn't like a real river with water in it. You couldn't wade in and push the craft off, not unless you wanted to melt your legs during the process. It was a tricky bit of manoeuvring, and one Harty was again glad he didn't need to help with as they held it at the edge of the flow and stepped onboard. Harty joined them, crossing his fingers as they cast off.

Although Harty knew rivers flowed, he hadn't expected the lava to move so rapidly. The boat seemed sea-worthy, or lava-worthy, enough. No holes or leaks were obvious, and it didn't start sinking immediately which Harty took to be a good sign. He had no idea how they'd bail the craft out, if it did start taking on lava. That thought made Harty give a small hysterical giggle, until he considered how in the Goddess's name they would 'abandon ship'. He realised they wouldn't, which was the most unsettling thought of all, not least because he'd be left alone to rescue his daughter.

The lava pulled them along at a rate of knots on a path parallel to the bank. Harty wasn't sure how far they should travel this way. He watched Phrack and Onk trying to keep the boat to the edges where the flow wasn't too strong, so they could control their tiny craft better. Harty decided to voice his biggest concern.

"When do we get off?" he enquired, his anxiety escalating despite the fact he was in no danger personally.

"I've bin trying to keep an eye oot for a likely landing on the other side," replied Phrack, his brogue becoming stronger. "I dinnae want to risk taking this fragile wee thing into the middle of the flow till we're sure. We might nae have a second chance." Harty didn't think the boat was fragile; it was made from stone. Besides, the ferryman's boat survived crossing the lava on a regular basis. He was about to say that very sentence when Phrack interrupted his thoughts.

"We might need to tae a chance soon," he continued. "I dinnae think the boat will hold up much longer despite Onk's sterling work." Phrack had been very impressed with Onk's stone masonry skills, noting that he had the makings of a quality craftsman. "It's a shame we dinnae have the luxury of a warlock to charm the hull." That comment answered Harty's unspoken questions and increased his anxiety ten-fold.

Harty looked closer at the bottom of their boat, the blanket there seemed to be turning a different colour, it was redder.

"Is the lava coming through?" he asked, his wing tips starting to curl with fear as concern for his friends rose higher.

"It's' trying," was Phrack's worrying reply. "Dae ye think ye could take a glance from high up. See if there's anywhere ahead we might land?"

Harty lifted into the air without a second thought. The thermals were fantastic to fly in, if a little hot and dry. He scanned the far bank traveling ahead of them down the river.

"There's a likely place not too far. Do you think you can make it?" he called down.

"We'll hae tae, won't we Onk?" Phrack answered for them, as Onk was concentrating on rowing hard, plus he didn't have a clue what Phrack was saying.

Onk and Phrack rowed into the centre of the lava striving

for the far side. The sweat dripped off their skin as they struggled with the jostling currents, using the makeshift oars, which Harty noticed were melting from their continual immersion in the lava.

"The place is coming up," yelled a frantic Harty, staying in mid-air to direct their course. "There, you can see it." A spur of land jutted out into the lava flow rising up to form a lip about three feet above the river's surface. They didn't need any encouragement after that, both put their backs into it, forcing the boat to the far side and safety. They were about ten feet away when a small puddle of lava appeared in the keel of the boat.

"Lava!" screamed Harty. The boat travelled five more feet. More lava poured into one end of the vessel tilting it precariously. With no time left, Phrack and Onk lunge-jumped for dry land, the dwarf grabbing his travel bag at the last moment. They made it with mere inches to spare.

Harty was panting, and he'd just watched it, not taken part in the dangerous endeavour.

"I'm glad that's over," he announced, wiping his brow. They both stared at him, then turned their gaze back at the boat as it sank, stern first, into the red river and disappeared.

Phrack lay on the ground panting, trying to catch his breath after his terrifying ordeal. None of them noticed that the ground was cooler on this side of the river, which was fortunate otherwise Phrack, laying stretched out, would have had burns to add to his breathlessness.

"It's a long time, since I had to jump, anywhere," he puffed. Onk, on the other hand was standing upright looking like a boxer waiting for his opponent, bouncing back and forth on his toes – till he realised there was no adversary. He deflated, after watching his masterpiece of stonework melt into the lava.

"Oh, Onk I'm so sorry you lost your boat," commiserated Harty.

"Never mind his boat, what about my blanket!" moaned Phrack, realising his useful and most expensive piece of fabric had succumbed to the flow. He wasn't sure whether it would melt, disintegrate, or become part of the river, washing up somewhere miles from here. If it did, he hoped someone would appreciate its worth, it cost a great deal of currency.

Sighing, Phrack turned over on his other side, facing away from the river to recover, he didn't want to be reminded of his loss by looking at the lava.

"Harty," called Onk, noticing the tree elf was suddenly out of sight. "Harty," he roared a second time, a tinge of concern edging his tone.

Harty came zooming back across the sky towards Onk.

"It's okay Onk, I'm here. I was checking the way ahead. There's a path on the other side of this field of stones." Onk nodded and waited while Phrack got himself together, which involved doing an inventory of the remaining stock inside his Gander bag. Harty thought it funny to give a bag a name, but now didn't seem an appropriate time to question it, when the dwarf was grieving the loss of his dearly departed *blanky*.

The journey rowing down the river appeared to have exhausted Phrack completely, and though it was still fairly early, they agreed to cross the innocent-looking plain in the morning, camping nearby the river that night. Phrack was shattered both physically and emotionally, though he wouldn't admit it. Both rowers sported minor burns on their arms and legs from lava splashes which needed tending.

Harty volunteered to do a bit more scouting before it got too dark. He re-checked the well-travelled path half a mile in-land. The area surrounding their position didn't look inhabited and that was good. He saw no sign of pursuit which reduced his anxiety levels.

It was just as well they decided to rest for the night, for unbeknown to the travellers, the place was a death-trap come nightfall. As the day's temperature dropped so the land moved and settled, opening cracks, crevices and sink holes in the dark landscape. The new day's heat forced these closed again, as the ground swelled to cope with the rising temperature once more. It was a land of two distinct personalities and species. Creatures which hid below by day, wandered freely at night and only the city troll's presence discouraged their attacks.

Onk removed his beloved new boots, not wanting to sleep in them. He didn't want them stolen either, so he strung them around his neck on a piece of cord, courtesy of Phrack.

Next morning, as the sky turned pale pink they broke camp, Onk sporting his boots wrapped around him like a muffler, despite the growing warmth of the day. Harty was fascinated by the changes in the sky's hue, though he didn't have any idea what this signified, or why the sky was red in the first place.

"You know it's really beautiful here," Harty remarked, admiring the sky line.

"When the environment isn't trying to kill you, you mean," countered Phrack. Onk smiled, nodding. The dwarf was still slightly rattled by the previous day's events. Yesterday, he'd been reminded of his own mortality and didn't like it one bit. He hadn't factored dying in a stone boat filled with lava onto his bucket list.

Dwarves lived long lives, not as long as fairies and elves, but at least a couple of centuries - barring accidents – providing their hearts contained goodness. It was well documented that individuals whose hearts were tainted with evil, regardless of their species, lived the shortest lives. Consequently, white witches - the kindest of all magical folk, - lived indefinitely.

Phrack realised now, that he had lived a comfortable, safe life in the town of Incandesonia. *What have I got myself into*? he wondered, knowing it was too late to turn around and go home. His home, his workshop, wasn't there anymore, he'd sold it along with his beautiful racing Gerenuks, on a whim to travel and seek out his daughter. *I hope I don't live to regret my decision.*

Onk had barely taken five steps into the stony area when his right foot sunk into the warm ground up to his knee. Anticipating more heat, he pulled it back out quickly and was amazed to discover, rows of stones,' roughly two inches in diameter, sticking to it. Harty flew close to inspect the phenomenon.

"They're not stones at all Onk," Harty enthused, "They're living things! I've never seen anything like it. Creatures that look like stones." Seeing that Harty had only ever lived on Earth, his experience in this department didn't count for much.

"We'll have tae go around," muttered Phrack, keen to get underway. "We cannae go stepping on innocent creatures like they're nothing."

"I'll go and look for another safe route through," offered Harty, flying up into the air.

Meanwhile Phrack, fascinated with the little animals, bent down to examine them in more detail. They didn't seem to be doing much, just clinging on to Onk's lower limb like they were saving themselves from drowning, like air-born limpets. Having had enough of these shenanigans, Onk leant down and attempted to pluck them off his hairy foot. As he grabbed hold of the back of one stone, a nasty row of pointy teeth appeared on the other side of it. The teeth sank into the tender skin on the instep of his foot.

At this point any normal person would have yelled like billyo, jumping around shouting 'owww' and 'ooooo' because feet are relatively sensitive, especially to mortals.

Onk however was made of stronger stuff, and while he didn't complain he did a good impression of a flamingo flapping this way and that, as more of the little blighters sank their dentally-enhanced mouths into his foot.

"Onk, hold still, let me see if I can remove them," offered Phrack.

As if understanding Phrack's words, the stones increased their grip on Onk, causing him to jump about even more, in the style of a frenzied war-dance. Finally, having had enough and not worried about the fangs, Onk leant down and ripped the offenders from his appendage, regardless of any injury he might receive.

"The little demons!" remarked Harty, returning at this point and staring at the damage they'd caused to Onk's foot.

"That's it!" Phrack exclaimed. "I remember."

"What's it?" queried Harty.

"Demons. They're demon stones," answered Phrack.

"You mean this whole area of stones are demon stones?"

"Probably," replied Phrack. "I dinnae suppose you happened to find a way around this area while ye were scouting our route last evening?"

"Eh? No, and there's not another route through them either," admitted Harty. "Do you have any idea how we get across these demon stones to the path beyond?" he asked, and then a more important question crossed Harty's mind. "Are they dangerous?"

"It depends. I remember they have lots of very sharp, pointy teeth... and they can move."

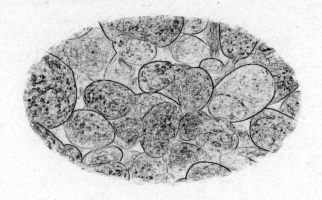

11
Colours

"I THINK Onk already found that out!" answered Harty, whilst Onk glared menacingly at Phrack for that bit of late news.

"I think it's something to do with having special protection," murmured Phrack, scratching his wide brow.

"Do you two have any ideas?" Phrack asked, looking from Onk to Harty and back again. They both shook their heads.

"There must be something we can do," grumbled Harty.

Onk sat down to sort out his burnt, and now bleeding lower limb. Harty decided to scrutinize, in greater detail, the stones Onk had managed to pull away. Most had gone into the lava river, but a few had missed the river, landing instead on the edge. These were trying to scuttle back to the mother-load whenever they thought Harty and the others weren't looking – which meant some sentience. Harty positioned himself in front of one such individual.

"We need to get across your home and we don't want to hurt any more of you. Can you tell us how to do that please?" Harty beseeched the inert stone, on the premise that being polite and nice to someone never hurt.

The stone creature was touched. No one had ever said 'please' to him before. He hesitated to reply because his species didn't speak to lower life forms.

"Please," asked Harty again, the sincerity in his voice clear. The stationary stone moved half an inch.

"It moved, it moved," Harty shouted calling the other two over. They stared dubiously, Harty was ever the optimist. "Honestly, it moved," he insisted, pointing to the small round stone sitting by itself. "It moved. So, did the others earlier." Phrack and Onk knelt down trying to get closer to Harty's level – but not too close – they didn't want a repeat of Onk's foot.

"Go on then," urged Phrack thinking; *we don't have any other plan and if the elf's going loopy I might as well join him.*

"Mmmm, what shall I say?" asked Harty, tongue-tied now he was in the limelight.

"Ask it how we can get across," suggested Phrack.

"I don't think they can speak like we do," he replied.

"Since when did you become an expert on demon stones?" said Phrack, staring eyeball to stone.

Harty edged closer to his selected stone. He was usually terrified of things with large sharp teeth. Being four and a half inches tall he worried the stone might leap up and bite him in half. Harty considered his communication skills for a moment. He was a prolific writer and on Earth had published many stories under his latest assumed name C. M. Salter. Mortals hadn't the slightest clue that several of their fantasy novels were written by the modest Mulberry tree elf.

He hadn't taken any courses in creative writing or communications skills to improve his knowledge, like he knew mortals did. They learnt about behaviour and cognition and all manner of jargonised words. He worked and wrote from his gut. He supposedly lived as a germ-obsessed recluse, in a high security penthouse in South Kensington, owning the whole building to maintain his privacy. His current literary agent, Reginald Smiliswift, - one of many over the years - was sworn to secrecy via a closed-mouth spell. Smiliswift dealt with the day-to-day running of Harty's publishing career. He was a wealthy elf and accessed any funds he and Shine needed, thanks to modern technology, via internet banking on a smartphone secure in their underground home - though it had taken the devil of a time to drag it in there. He often moaned about the overuse of the IT tech, but he had to admit it made a tree elf's financial business much easier.

"If they can't speak," he postulated, stalling for time, "it doesn't mean they can't communicate. We need to find out how they communicate." Onk was up for the challenge. Taking his life, or more accurately his skin in both hands, he selected two stones, approximately four inches in diameter. Picking them up delicately, by the very tips of his index finger and thumb, like a lady selecting a cream cake, he placed them facing each other on his outstretched palm.

At first, the stones merely sat, like stones, and then one stone changed. It started out a blackish-grey, then like a magician, before their very eyes it became greyish-black. It wasn't anything to sing and dance about and, if the three of them had not been observing intently they might have missed it.

"The one on the left changed colour," declared Phrack.

"Yes, it did," agreed Harty. They waited a while longer and the right stone turned from slate grey to midnight black.

"They communicate by changing colour."

"Yes, so that's what we need to do. Do you have anything in your Gander bag of different colours?" Harty requested.

"I might have," replied Phrack, becoming cagey and elusive. Harty was already fed up with Phrack and his precious Gander bag and the journey had only just begun.

"I don't want to pinch anything," he sighed, exasperated. "See if you have some minor things of different colours is all." Phrack retreated and sat on a large half submerged boulder on the ground, while he perused his items.

"What about this?" he queried, lifting a green wooden cat from the bag. Harty didn't have time to ponder why the Stone dwarf had felt this item important enough to bring with him.

"Good, see what else you can spare."

Onk surprised him next, by producing a bright pink clothes peg from somewhere on his person, before Phrack could identify a second object. "Where in the Light Dimensions have you been hiding that? No, don't tell me, better I don't know the answer."

Taking the green cat and the pink clothes peg from Onk, Harty walked over to where Onk had laid the stones while he extracted his peg. They hadn't moved, but both were now grey.

"Here goes nothing," Harty said, standing in front of the stones.

He placed the two objects on the ground. *How am I going to use them?* he wondered, then he had an idea.

"I'm going to see if they can understand our language, but just can't speak first."

He addressed the stones.

"This colour," he pointed to the green cat, "is 'Yes.' And this colour," he pointed to the pink clothes peg, "is 'No'."

He didn't expect them to move or bite the objects and he wasn't disappointed, nothing happened. The stones remained resolutely grey.

"This is where it gets complicated," he remarked, looking over his shoulder to Onk and Phrack who were sitting fascinated, side by side on the large rock. He turned back to the stones. "If the answer is Yes, I need you to go this colour – green."

The stones both surprised him by turning a dirty shade of green. Onk jumped off the rock in excitement, clapping his hands. The stones both turned black.

"Onk sit down you're scaring them. I think black means frightened." Onk looked down at his sore foot and back at Harty. "Well maybe not frightened, but something negative." He tried again.

"If the answer if No…" before he could finish both stones turn a puce pink. "That's the idea, now let's see if we can get somewhere." The two stones were quite enjoying themselves. They'd never been singled out for special treatment like this and now a lower life form was pathetically trying to communicate with them. They both laughed again turning black.

"Hello stones," welcomed Harty. "Will you let us cross the plain without harming us?" The stones turned pink. "Oh!" He exclaimed. He hadn't expected 'No' to be their answer.

"Ask them if there's a way around?" Phrack called out, his nose halfway in his Gander bag. Harty wondered whether he had food in there that he wasn't sharing. Without Harty needing to repeat the request the stones turned green.

"Now we're getting somewhere," smiled Phrack. "Can ye show us?" he added. One stone turned green and the other pink. "Now that's just confusing," he moaned.

"I think that means 'maybe,'" said Harty, the stones both turned green.

"Why do I feel a payment coming on?" said Phrack. The stones turned black briefly, then green again. "Ah! No change the dimensions over, currency always makes everything go around," he philosophised. The stones liked the dwarf's statement they flashed black and green again.

"I think you're confusing them," muttered Harty, feeling he was losing command of the situation. The stones turned pink.

"There ye go," said Phrack, he couldn't help feeling a wee bit triumphant. "It seems the stones and me are on the same wavelength. I wonder what thing stones could need?"

They all stood and looked about. There was nothing to see except stones. It looked like a case of twenty questions was about to start.

After fifteen questions of yes/no Harty was beginning to lose the will to exist.

"What else is there?" he demanded, staring at the stones, willing them to do more than turn green and pink with alternating questions.

"I don't think asking them if they wanted to take a short kick into the lava helped," offered Phrack. "Ye just made them angry." The stones had turned a vivid yellow after that question.

"Well, they're being obtuse deliberately," Harty remarked. "I bet we answered their question ages ago. Why do I get the feeling they're laughing at us?" The stones both turned black. "See! They both went black again."

"I thought we'd already decided black meant fear?" asked Phrack, trying to clarify the colour-coding communication system.

"I'm not so sure now," muttered Harty.

Onk had left well alone up to this point. He felt Phrack and Harty could manage this section of the trip. After all, he built the boat which got them this far, even if they couldn't leave the place now. That wasn't his fault.

However, city trolls are not known for having much patience. One sure sign it was ending, was when they started marching up and down. Onk had marched up and down so much during the birth of their first child that he created trenches several feet deep in their living room floor.

Not wanting Gem upset about the state of her home, Onk had dug the floor down further. The family home now boasted an extensive basement level beneath their property and Onk stayed outside for the deliveries of their remaining children.

Onk had already built, or rather worn, a channel in the segment of earth between the river and the stone plain. It resulted in a thin strip of earth which was weakening with each length he paced. Unbeknown to the troll, if he continued pacing the river would soon undermine the soil and flood the area they were standing on.

Onk stopped pacing not a moment too soon. He walked over to the two stones.

"Want eat?" he asked, they flashed pink. "Want fight?" Pink again. "Want go?" They flashed green. Problem solved. Onk plopped his bottom down on the large, convenient rock next to Phrack.

"Did you see that, they flashed green!" Harty exploded.

"I didn't see. Say it again, Onk," Phrack requested.

"You want go?" repeated Onk, as if for the benefit of small children. The two stones flashed green again and again, and to everyone's surprise the colour green started rippling in waves of green across the plain. Their answer prompted a new problem.

"Even if they do want to come with us, how on earth are we going to move a massive field of heavy, biting stones?" grumbled Harty, who was getting fed up with the whole enterprise. He hadn't forgotten the chunks they took out of Onk's foot.

As if in reply to Harty's comment a rumbling noise started up all around them. Onk noticed the loudest noise was coming from directly underneath their bottoms, so he and the dwarf jumped up. Just in time as it happened, the huge rock turned green, then began moving of its own accord.

It was then that the three travellers realised that demon

stones came in all sizes. They stared amazed as the large rock which they had till moments ago been perching on, extracted itself from the soil at the edge of the river and slowly stretched. It flowed like taffy until two legs and two arms sprouted, then a round head evolved.

After a lot of pulling and twisting, a tall stone giant stood in front of them. It was very clearly a female stone giant. Many of the stones across the plain migrated towards her. On reaching her, the nearest ones flowed or rolled up her body, becoming accents for her eyes, ears, lips and hair. Other stones became clothes and footwear. The whole effect was incredible. A living, moving statue of female perfection. Each stone was still a stone, but they changed shape and size and colour to become whatever they needed to be. Out on the field of stones, a path was created in the gap left behind.

Harty was admiring the finished individual when another sound made him turn. The strip of land on the far side of Onk's pacing had finally surrendered, it could hold back the lava no more. With a weak 'pop' like a boy taking his finger out of a dyke, it succumbed to the river's pressure.

Lava poured in mere yards from where the Demon Stone giantess stood. She, Onk and Phrack were about to be burnt alive, regardless of the earlier escape from the boat. The stone giantess turned red. Any stones not absorbed into her structure dashed to the breach plugging it with their bodies and their lives.

Stone upon stone flung themselves into the gap attempting to fill the space, and it worked. The stones that arrived first were fused into a stone wall holding back the red river. The late arrivals became supports and buttresses. The threat to Onk and Phrack was cancelled as millions gave up their lives to save one individual.

"Did you see that!" Harty exclaimed. "They gave up their lives to save us, to save her!" The stone giantess turned

131

green. The trio were humbled by the loss of so many lives. It didn't matter their size or species, it was the fact they laid down their lives so that others might live.

Harty was reminded of all the soldiers graves in the cemeteries of London where he and Onk had passed so many years ago. These weren't soldiers, but like them, these stone people gave up their lives for something they believed in, something which personified all the best in their species and this giantess in front of them, was their Queen. Onk, Harty and Phrack bowed to the Demon Stone queen. It felt the right thing to do.

The four of them travelled along the path created inside the stone plain, thinner now so many had given up their lives. Harty had to keep pinching himself to believe it was real, that the demon stones wouldn't roll back any minute and devour him.

As they moved along the path, the stones each side of them radiated different colours. Harty guessed this was in honour of their queen and he was partly right. These were in fact the colours of the different clans within the population. Each clan acknowledging their queen and wishing her, and their brethren, safe passage. The queen in turn, rippled with colours reflecting their clans, signifying that she recognised their status. She wished them well and advised them to continue to exist and grow, informing them that one day they would meet again.

Joining the travelling party, and feeling slightly sad, she left behind her millions of adoring subjects and stepped out on her first adventure in the real world.

12

Deceived

THE hedgerow imp arrived in Gristle's spell study, struggling with the cup of mushroom tea the witch had demanded a few minutes earlier. Lou used the lifting spell to good effect for a variety of tasks including serving her mistress, but the cup, regardless of its weightlessness, was bigger than she was.

Oblivious to the imp's presence, Gristle sat by the window pondering her wicked plan. She had been relying on Harty to come looking for his daughter, hoping that the stupid city troll might tag along too. She hadn't expected them to detour into the Fire Realm for some unknown reason. Getting irritated with Harty's daughter doing nothing in return for her keep, she'd set her to work looking after the farm. Lou gently placed the cup on the nearby table and retreated.

"That new girl is proving to be quite an asset and a fast learner, according to Crogg," Gristle muttered to herself. "Maybe I'll keep her. Teach her things, instead of that puny hedgerow imp who can't lift a saucepan without needing a rest."

Gristle had no idea that Lou was within ear-shot. "Good workers are hard to come by. Plus, I haven't eaten a tasty rabbit pie in years, not since coming to this wretched place." For some reason no matter how hard she tried, only folk from the light realms, like Earth, made flavoursome rabbits. That irritated Gristle no end.

Although Gristle called the Neath Realm, 'a wretched place' she quite liked it. True, she hadn't enjoyed the taste of rabbit in a long while, but she hadn't grown any older either. On Earth, she'd been aging at an alarming rate. Here, it appeared her rapid aging process had slowed and perhaps stopped all together. *If I could only reverse the effects, this place would be paradise,* she grumbled.

Like Earth mortals, many magic species required food to live and Gristle was no exception. There were no humans in the Neath to change into rabbits, so Gristle made do with Neath denizens. Those unfortunate enough to chance upon her abode were transmuted into animals, but she found she could only turn them into creatures which existed in the Neath already, that included snakes, spiders and fire lizards. The lizards were difficult to kill, just about impossible to skin, and though succulent, were very chewy. Gristle missed nice, soft rabbit meat which melted in her mouth. She decreed long ago that food 'should want to be eaten.'

"Food should fall apart or melt in your mouth. Not fight you every step like an aging wrestler. Seems I always have to make sacrifices to survive," she mumbled, to no one in particular.

Lou wasn't happy hearing Gristle's comments regarding Purity and herself. She had thought that Purity would be her new bestest friend. She imagined them working together and spending their free moments – as brief as they were – doing fun things.

Lou had been Gristle's number one girl for as long as she could remember. She didn't want any Light Realm usurper snatching her position. Though she'd given Purity the impression it was horrible living with Gristle, it was the only home Lou could remember. The tiny imp was happy knowing her place in the scheme of things, the unknown terrified her. *What if Gristle throws me out? Or, worse stills eats me! Purity has to go,* Lou decided, her concerns escalating as she imagined her life in the Neath all alone. *I'll 'help' her escape, then claims no knowledge of it.*

They'd got into quite a routine between them. Each morning Lou would rise first and get the breakfast going. Purity would rise and re-stock the kitchen wood pile. It wasn't real wood, but she called it that because she didn't want to admit it was old bones. The bones were all that remained of the animals Lou slaughtered each day. These were placed inside a basement door at the rear of the building to dry out. Snake and lizard skin was valuable and recycled, but the spiders' hard exoskeletons were not. Gristle utilised pieces of spiders rather than their whole bodies in her evil work. The spiders' broken-down bodies were then added to the pile of bones for burning - nothing was wasted in the Neath. Eyes and venom were vital for spells and potions. Fangs from spiders and snakes made impressive and valuable jewellery. It took a lot of bones and spiders' skeletons to make up the fires.

Gristle and Crogg ate most of the lizard meat, while Purity found out she and Lou were expected to eat the snake meat, with Gussie eating any offal and leftover parts. It was a remarkable achievement in recycling. The weird plants and mushrooms in Gristle's garden were also used in her spells, a few parts of those were edible too. Lou taught Purity which parts of the plants were safe to eat, and which were fatal.

About two days later while sweeping the stairs outside the study, Lou overheard Gristle and Crogg speaking again about Purity. Lou's ears pricked up.

"She's a good worker," he acknowledged, when Gristle asked for a report on Purity's progress. "Cleans up well and can carry more than Lou," he added.

"She is lucky to be living with someone like me, so fair and giving," Gristle replied, nodding as she considered her newest servant.

Lou knew from experience, that Gristle transmuted people into critters when she felt they had outgrown their usefulness. She had thought that being so tiny, Gristle wouldn't see any point in changing her, but now it seemed to Lou that her life might very well be in danger.

Later that afternoon, Lou announced that Gristle had given them both a special task which needed to be done in the evening before it got too dark.

"We's have to do it now and again," she lied. "It's a bit tricksy on my own trying to carry them, but with your help it should be easy."

"What are we going to do?" Purity asked, clueless to Lou's scheming.

"We's have to…" Lou stopped in mid-sentence to make sure she'd memorised the words correctly. "…infuse the stock. Yes, that's right, those are the words Gristle said, 'infuse the stock'." She sat back satisfied with her completely fictitious sentence.

Purity was puzzled. Lou hadn't mentioned such tasks before. She'd never called Gristle by her name either, not that Purity could remember, it was always mistress this, and mistress that. However, she acknowledged that her understanding regarding the ways of witches and how to raise spiders could be written on the back of a small tadpole, so she followed Lou as directed.

As evening fell, they rose from their cosy place by the fire and together, slipped out the back door. It was black as usual, but not yet night. Night in the Neath felt heavier and greasier, like someone had poured dirty motor oil into the air. Lou seemed confident enough, she'd even brought a bucket.

"Picks up the buckets then," she admonished, like gathering baby spiders was the most normal thing in the world.

"Why are we collecting them at night?" Purity enquired.

"Because they sleeps in the day silly girl," giggled Lou. It was the first time Lou had called Purity silly, and her giggle had a nasty edge to it. Something wasn't right, but Purity had no choice. "Come on slowworm," urged Lou over her shoulder, ahead of Purity in the growing dark.

"Hold on, what about the anklets?" reminded Purity. "I thought we couldn't leave the house with these on?"

"Oh those!" Lou sniggered from up ahead. "Didn't I say? They's only works in the daytime to stop you's running away."

"Why in the Goddess name, didn't you tell me that before?" asked Purity, catching Lou up. "I could have left days ago," she wheezed, not used to the sudden burst of speed. Lou looked horrified then quickly changed her expression.

"Only idiots goes out at nights," she grinned mockingly. "Come on we's needs to hurry before it gets too dark."

Purity's mind was in a daze, without thinking she followed Lou's voice as they travelled further from Gristle's home. In the beginning, she could make out the outline of the building on the skyline. The further they moved away, the harder it was to see, even squinting.

"Lou," she called. "Isn't this far enough?"

"Oh no," came Lou's voice from somewhere to her left. "We's about half way now."

"Really?" Purity didn't like it. If Lou weren't with her she'd be totally lost by now.

"Lou?" Lou didn't answer. "Lou, where are you?" Nothing. "If you're playing jokes it's not funny." Still nothing. "Please Lou, I don't know what I've done to upset you, but I'm really sorry." Purity couldn't know that just existing was too much for the jealous imp.

Lou sat not far away listening to Purity stumble about in the dark. She shoved her hands over her mouth to stop from giggling and watched with glee as Purity walked farther and farther away. *She'll never find her way back now*, grinned a happy Lou. Rising from her place of concealment, she dusted herself down and using the night-sight, that all hedgerow imps are born with, went home.

Purity walked on for hours. She had no night vision and realised pretty quickly that Lou had decided she didn't want her around anymore. *I wonder whether Gristle will get angry and turn Lou into a spider? I doubt it, who will see to the farm if Lou isn't around? On the other hand, Gristle might come after me and Goddess knows what she'll do when she finds me!*

Purity had wanted to leave, to escape Gristle's clutches but she'd rather have done it with a plan, a route and at least some food and drink. Now she had nothing. She hadn't planned to continue walking, but her mind was churning over Lou's deception and the clue's which Purity had ignored. She knew the landscape was blank for miles; Lou had told her so, but now she wondered. *Was that a lie too? I could step into a sink-hole or worse. Maybe I should stop until the light returns. Then I'll be better able to plan my route.*

Lou meanwhile, covered Purity's absence for a few days before she informed her mistress of her disappearance, because she didn't want her found and brought back. It was hard work pretending and doing the work of two people. There were a couple of tricky moments when Crogg asked where Purity was. Lou simply lied. She seemed to be getting good at it. She managed it for two days, but by then she was exhausted and couldn't keep up the pretence anymore. Plus, Gussie had disappeared too and Lou felt more alone than ever. Maybe sending Purity away wasn't such a great plan.

Purity rose early from sleep the morning after Lou's desertion and noticed something reassuringly familiar. Gussie was spread across her legs sound asleep. At her movement he roused and woke up. It was the first time Purity had ever seen Gussie fully awake close up. Usually he was slinking out of the back door as she woke. He was beautiful, and she couldn't suppress her comment.

"What a beautiful creature you are Gussie," she sighed, reaching her hand out to stroke him without thinking. Gussie shrank back, ducking his head low. When he saw there was nothing in her hand to hit him with, and her fingers were spread wide, he allowed her to touch his fur. Something Lou had advised her never to do if she valued her arm. Lou sported several scars which she said Gussie caused. Purity was beginning to wonder if these were more lies.

"Beautiful," she repeated. "… and so soft." Gussie liked Purity's touch. He liked her gentle tone too so he stayed put, letting her stroke and finally tickle him on top of his head and behind his ears. *He was in paradise.*

"As much as I love petting you," interrupted Purity after several minutes. "We can't stay here all day. I need to find people I can trust and food and water. Plus, that strange sensation from earlier has returned and I feel like I'm being watched – again. It's the first time in days that I've been on my own, excluding you Gussie."

Lou had been an almost constant shadow around Purity, without her and work as a diversion, Purity could sense the other person's presence again. She didn't get any feelings of hostility, just curiosity and awareness, and something else, something deeper.

Gussie rose and waited patiently as Purity shook off her concern about the unknown observer and prepared to move off. He began making odd chirping noises, the first sounds she'd heard from him, and he kept running off in the opposite direction to her. When she failed to follow he returned to her, chirping and trying to trip her up. Falling to the ground for the second time she remarked on his antics.

"Gussie, I don't want to go back to Gristle and Lou. Do you understand? I need to find other people, people who don't want to keep me as a hostage or slave." When she stood, Gussie continued to undermine her legs till she fell for the third time, scraping her knee.

"Ouch!" she squeaked. Gussie was by her side in an instant. Despite her protests, he licked her knee, which made her squirm in disgust, then the skin healed before her eyes. She couldn't believe it. She touched it and wiggled and jiggled her knee to experiment and assure herself it wasn't a dream – but it wasn't.

"How did you do that Gussie?" she asked, leaning down to stroke Gussie who'd settled in his usual place on her toes. A noise sounded somewhere off to the left startling Purity and making her feel vulnerable.

"Oh, my Goddess," she whispered to Gussie crouching down on the ground next to him. "I hope that's not Gristle coming after me. We need to go now," she mumbled, her voice trembling with fear.

Once more she rose, with the intention of creeping away in the direction she'd chosen, until Gussie threatened to thread between her legs and trip her again. "Okay, okay," she relented, panic edging into her voice. "You win, but this better not be the route back to the witch's house or I'll be considering how good you look as a pair of slippers!" Gussie whined at her threat, but then led the way in his direction regardless.

They walked for a long time without encountering anything. Purity realised they weren't heading back towards Gristle's home, because she was pretty sure they would have come across the garden by now. It appeared Gussie was taking her somewhere else. Gradually, the landscape altered, slopes and dips developed making a change from the grey flatness. Large boulders came into view and ahead of them on the horizon, the outline of foothills.

Purity was tiring and, recognising that she needed a rest, settled on a convenient boulder where she could spy the landscape around her. She removed her worn shoes and rubbed her sore feet. She wasn't used to walking so far, normally she'd bumble along using her infant wings. In the low light of the Neath, she'd been concerned about flying into something. Her wings, although useless for confident flying, were her safety net in case she stepped onto a concealed cavern.

"Where are you taking me little one?" she inquired, scratching Gussie's head. "I'm sure we've been walking for days. At least we haven't encountered any beasts or evil creatures, I suppose that's good." Gussie chirped his reply. Sighing at their inability to communicate, Purity replaced her footwear and rose. "Come on then, wherever you're taking me can't possibly be worse than having to kill small animals." Chirping loudly, Gussie led the way.

****

On the edge of the Fire Realm, Onk, Harty, Phrack and their new companion considered their next move. They were miles east of where they needed to be, to meet up with the wren at the entrance to the Neath. They'd crossed the demon stone plain without mishap with the stone queen as their escort and protector. They continued through stony landscapes where, more bizarrely, odd stones dropped off or joined the stone queen as she walked. It was as if they were scouting and returning with information, either that or she had some trouble keeping her form cohesive, Harty wasn't sure which.

Deciding they had travelled far enough for one day Onk stopped and called a halt.

"Food and sleep," he announced, taking on the assumed role of command. No one disagreed. Harty and Onk unrolled their sleeping bags. Phrack pulled one out of his Gander bag, along with a small portable stove. He proceeded to light the stove, which was filled with some type of oil then popped several part-baked loaves inside. Harty watched agog and Onk drooled. He had his jerky, but fresh bread was always a welcome addition.

The stone queen stood by Phrack and the stove, unmoving. Phrack felt a little uncomfortable with her standing so close. He guessed she didn't know about personal space or he would have said something about it.

"You don't need to sleep I guess." he stated, turning his head from his stove to look up at her. The queen turned her head too, regarding Phrack in turn. She appeared to be examining Phrack, rather than considering his statement and it made him feel even more uncomfortable. In reply, she flashed pink, while a thin strip of green briefly lit up one side of her torso. "I'm guessing that means not often." The queen turned her body completely towards Phrack and a brilliant green strobed her surface.

"Do you eat?" he enquired. As if on cue, several stones dropped to the floor from the queen's belly and scuttled away. "I figure that's a yes too." The greenness didn't change. Harty, who was fascinated by having a queen within their midst, flew over to sit down next to Phrack.

"I wonder if she has a name?" he said to the dwarf, who was bending down to check on his loaves.

"I should imagine so," replied Phrack standing back up. "Everyone has a name." The queen tilted her head and turned pink. Onk joined in the conversation.

"No name."

"No name," mused Harty. "How sad." It was Harty's turn to be regarded by the queen. He found it even more unnerving than Phrack, to be stared at by an unblinking stone giant, and said so.

"It's considered rude to stare," he said bluntly, without thinking. The queen stepped back clearly chastised and hurt by Harty's comment, turning an insipid orange in the process.

"What have I done? Harty was mortified.

"I think you just told a queen off," commented Phrack wryly, a smile lighting the edge of his mouth.

"I am so sorry your majesty," Harty grovelled, hitting the ground on his knees, his forehead in the dust. The queen stared down at the tiny man no taller than her index finger. She could end his life just by lifting her foot. Her subjects were discussing the method of his execution for the insult to her person. Turning from orange to bright pink, she informed them that they were in strange lands with odd customs, and they should accept that mistakes in protocol might happen. Her subordinates acquiesced but weren't convinced. In their opinion, the little winged man needed putting in his place.

"She said no, she said no. Oh, my Goddess she's going to kill me," wailed Harty, knowing she had the power of stone.

"Calm down Harty," interjected Phrack. "I don't think telling someone not to stare is punishable by death." And, normally he'd be right. "We need to find a name for our queen though. We can't keep calling her 'queen'. What if the wrong people heard?"

Harty stayed where he was on his knees in front of the queen because he felt he needed to make up for his crass behaviour.

"The wrong people?" he queried, from his position low on the ground.

"You know unsavoury, unscrupulous folk, ones who if they heard the word 'queen' might get nasty ideas about trying to rob her."

"Oh, those type of folks." Harty shuddered and Onk growled to show his displeasure.

The queen, recognising Phrack as the wisest and most courtly of the group, listened to his words. She didn't like the sound of 'the wrong people' either. Her subjects bristled with concern at this new dilemma, causing a brief multi-coloured light-show to flash across her head and neck.

"Pretty," murmured Onk smiling. The queen turned her face to Onk and smiled too.

The several dozen stones who'd left earlier chose this moment to re-appear, though these seemed fatter and darker than the ones who had originally left. The trio watched in wonder as the stones re-attached themselves to her belly. The queen sighed and sat down.

"Seems like she's been hungry a while as well," remarked Phrack. The queen grinned at him displaying several stone teeth, her previous concern about the 'wrong people' temporarily diverted by a full stomach.

Thinking to make amends for his rudeness, Harty sat back on his heels trying to think of a suitable name for a queen. He knew a fair bit about stones, from dealing in the stock exchanges with the money he'd made from writing. He considered Beryl and Jet because they were good short stone names, Alexandrite and Iolite because they changed colour like the stone queen, but they just weren't regal enough.

"Upala." Harty stated.

"Pardon," said Phrack, thinking Harty had wind.

"Upala," he repeated. "For the queen's name, its means precious stone in Sanskrit, an Indian Earth dialect, and she is a precious stone." Harty turned to the queen and wisely bowed.

"I'd like to make up for my rude comment by bestowing a name fit for a queen. I believe you are Upala, a precious stone."

The queen liked it. She turned vivid green.

"That's settled then," concluded Phrack, as they all noticed the queen's brilliant shade of emerald green.

"Welcome to our humble party Queen Upala. This is Harty Springfield." Phrack pointed to Harty. "A mulberry tree elf." Upala didn't know what in the six dimensions a tree was, but she nodded her head as protocol demanded. "This is Onk, a city troll." He waved in Onk's direction. Onk nodded and Upala nodded back. "Both are from Earth, in the light dimensions. While I, am your humble servant, Phrack Blaster, a stone dwarf." The dwarf gave a deep, courtly bow after addressing the queen formally. The queen knew all about dwarves and stone. The queen acknowledged the dwarf's bow and, with introductions complete, everyone settled down for the night – even Upala.

The following morning Upala was gone.

13

Egg

"WHERE did she go?" asked a bewildered Harty. "I've flown high over the area to search for her but there's no sign."

"I don't think she's gone far," smiled Phrack, "Look." Onk and Harty stared at the spot where they'd last seen Upala. Several of her subject stones were sitting calmly – if stones can sit calmly.

"If they're here, Upala can't be far away," he suggested. At that moment, the earth beneath Phrack and Onk's feet shifted, causing them to stumble about and land in an undignified jumble on the hard ground. Fortunately, Harty had remained airborne and wasn't affected.

Several more stones appeared to join the ones sitting on the surface, then, inch by inch the whole of Upala appeared lying horizontal on the ground where she had gone to sleep. It appeared stone queens slept underground. Upala rose, dusted herself off, re-arranged her body to her liking, and looked set to face the day.

"I wish I had that ability," lamented Phrack, slightly in

146

awe of this beautiful stone creature. Stone dwarves were by nature attracted to stone and Phrack was no exception.

****

To say Gristle was cross when she found out Purity had gone missing was an understatement. She was livid, and when she was livid she had a tendency to fall back on her nasty habit of turning things, into other things. She'd learnt the hard way, it was better to create than to destroy, and remembered not to change things she was going to need later. That included folk, or objects, which made her life easier. These days, unless she was in a fearsome blue rage, she changed only unwanted, unnecessary things.

Her last blue rage had created the Tedium Zone twelve years ago when she first arrived in the Neath. In her blue rage, she destroyed everything till there was almost nothing left for miles and there wasn't much to start with. It wasn't like Earth, full to bursting with material objects and doo-dahs that easily morphed into other items and thrived. Nowadays she compromised. She settled on changing the land just behind her house and garden instead. Where once the ground was flat and barren now tall trees and boulders appeared. For example, the trees she created wouldn't last without sunlight, food and water, just long enough for Gristle to send Lou and Crogg out to recycle every last inch of the timber, leaves and fruit. Yes, she created fruiting trees. Gristle was learning.

Meanwhile, she despatched a squad of her Demi-Golems to hunt the ungrateful wretch of a fairy down. They wouldn't stop until they found Purity and brought her back. They didn't need to eat or sleep, they didn't get ill. There was only one thing that could kill a demi-golem and that was in short supply in the Neath.

Gristle had created the Demi-Golems by accident whilst

dabbling with some necromancer spells. She'd practiced initially on dead animals, snakes, spiders etc. but the results produced some unsavoury hybrids, two of which tried to gnaw her foot off until she turned them into plants. They now adorned her garden.

Gristle finally realised that to create matter which could at least follow some basic orders she needed to utilise creatures with higher thinking skills, so she employed Crogg to haul in as many of his fellow dead demons as he could locate. He wasn't happy about the process, but a hex which identified them as fluffy bunny rabbits, worked a treat on the young Neath demon. He had no problem dragging dead rabbits home. Thus, her planned army of Demi-Golems emerged.

****

The rescuers had been travelling some time over the dark daylight landscape and Harty was beginning to worry - as usual. He was concerned that they wouldn't be able to find the right place to cross back into the Neath Shadowline. This was despite scoring the entrance with a magic marker and following an almost parallel course to their initial journey.

Onk was their navigational aid in all trips. His sense of location was uncanny, a common asset of city trolls. Place a city troll anywhere in the twelve dimensions and he'd find his way either home, or to any identified location. It may take several years and many dimensions, but he would get there – eventually. This ability did not extend to female trolls, much to every male troll's relief.

Harty needn't have worried. Onk let out a humongous roar and they all ran, even Upala, to see what horrendous beast was devouring him. It was the marker. Harty had heard trolls were renowned for their uncanny sense of direction, but until this minute he'd never really believed in it. Even when Onk found his lost son, Harty had believed it was co-incidence. Now in an entirely different continent and realm, Onk had found one specific point. Harty's belief in his friend was confirmed.

"How did you manage to find it?" Harty asked, the last tiny bit of disbelief fading from his voice. Onk shrugged; he didn't know. He'd never bothered listening to the mechanics of troll location theory in school. He just pointed his feet in the direction he wanted to go and sooner or later he found it. He was glad Harty was pleased, he liked pleasing his friend.

Onk knew he didn't have much education, that he was nowhere near as educated as his friend Harty. He did know his children were not going to be like him. He and Gem agreed their children would be brought up differently to common troll rearing practices. They made all of them attend their local school, even though they hated going and moaned constantly about it.

Luckily, Gem supported him, telling the children, 'there's nothing worse than a stupid troll.' Onk smiled as he thought of his wife and children far away. He was glad they were safe from harm. No Neath demon was going to drag any of them away. Thinking about his children his mind turned to his adopted niece. Purity was strong – for a fairy – but she wasn't in the same league as trolls. He wondered how she was fairing. He hoped she was safe somewhere and not suffering. His fists clenched, and he wanted to pulverise something when he thought of her scared and alone. He couldn't express his concerns to Harty, he was stressed out enough, without Onk adding his views, so he kept his worries to himself, and prayed each night to the Goddess that she was alive.

"What's the plan now?" asked Phrack, who'd not been party to the original scheme.

"We wait for Malachi to return," replied Harty stoically. "He said he'd check back twice each day. We may have missed his first check-in today."

Onk, being Onk, had wandered off in search of food. The Fire Realm was limited on wild food provision. However, where the realms buffeted against each other, the edge was fluid, shifting several feet on occasion. The odd animal might stray too close and enter the realm unknowingly. Once there, an animal was likely to die quickly from lack of food and water. Kindly people, who cared about animals, didn't live in the dark dimensions judging by what Onk had seen so far.

Onk found exactly what he was after, a couple of miles south of the marker. Spread out on a hot rock was a bottle-nosed dolphin baked to perfection in the heat. It had probably been there a week judging by the desiccated state, but the dried meat would replenish his packet of jerky and keep him going a while longer. Plus, the taste reminded him of his favourite meal -fish and chips. While he was dismantling the remains, he found an interesting item attached to one of its flippers.

"Pretty," he announced, immediately placing it in his 'pretty bag'. Onk started the practice of carrying his pretty items in a small bag kept around his waist some years ago. He found it incredibly useful, and after his run in with Gristle, realised broadcasting to the world you had 'pretties' was not such a good idea. Handling the small blue bell carefully he dropped it into his bag, and like always, – promptly forgot about it.

They stayed at the marker for the rest of the day. Onk returning a couple of hours later to find Phrack and Harty settled in front of a good fire. He crouched down next to it and Upala, who until his return had been standing still as stone, copied him. Harty noticed she had taken a bit of an interest in Onk. He hoped Onk would let her know he was married before she became too enamoured. If not, as his friend, he would take Onk aside and advise him.

Afternoon came and went and still no wren appeared. Onk contented himself by gazing at the strange bird-like creature flying on the horizon. It was too far away to make out clearly and he wondered whether the others had seen it. He noticed that it never strayed far from their position, but it didn't seem to pose a threat. Onk decided it was unlikely to be a problem. He was content to watch and marvel at its graceful dips and turns as it travelled across the sky.

"You don't suppose something's happened to Malachi do you?" mumbled Harty, worry never far from his thoughts. Onk turned to face his friend.

"No," interrupted a stern-faced Phrack, before Onk could utter one word of support. Phrack had already learnt that the tiny mulberry elf needed positive reassurance every now and again to reduce his anxiety levels. "If you say he'll be here, he will be." Onk winked at Phrack. Upala watched their interplay, not understanding their facial expressions but guessing they both knew something that she did not about the elf.

They were settling down to sleep in the early evening, when a bird's song broke the stillness of the air. Up till that moment, Harty hadn't realised that they'd heard no birdsong since stepping into the Fire Realm. He turned in Phrack's direction to see if the dwarf had noticed and was surprised to see tears coursing down the dwarf's cheeks. Even Upala appeared touched by the haunting melody of the wren, she turned a swirly blue/mauve shade, they'd never seen before. They all sat enjoying the birdsong for several minutes then as abruptly as it started, it stopped. Instead someone called out.

"You going to sit there stargazing all night, or are we getting a move on?" Harty was first to recover, while

Phrack mumbled, "beautiful so beautiful." He quickly wiped the tears from his eyes re-composing himself. Onk wondered whether this was the same bird he'd seen earlier in the sky, but dismissed the idea, this wren was far too tiny.

"We'd given up on you coming back this evening," Harty responded. Malachi took umbrage to this statement.

"I've come back every day, twice a day as promised. Did you find my egg?"

"We did. Now give us a few minutes to re-pack and we'll be with you." Malachi, it seemed, wasn't to be put-off so easily.

"You did! You really did? You're not pulling an old bird's leg are you because my heart couldn't stand the strain? Where is it? Where is it?"

"Slow down, all in good time. We need to get out of here first. You failed to tell us how precious this egg is. There might be folk after us trying to get it back." Ignoring the last part of Harty's sentence Malachi admitted they were right.

"I did tell you. I said it was the last egg of my mate. I'll admit, I might not have said quite how precious it is. This egg is the last my soul mate laid before she died. We inter-dimensional wrens mate for life, so this is my last egg - ever."

"Your last egg ever?" repeated a stunned Harty. Even Onk and Phrack stopped packing at these words. Upala hadn't moved from her crouching position by the fire. She had nothing to pack, so hadn't bothered moving. Onk liked her style.

"Yes, my soul-mate's final egg. The most precious thing I have." Phrack, not having met the wren before, was intrigued.

"How come ye lost it in the first place, it being so precious an' all?" he asked.

"It was stolen, by a gang of ruthless ruffians," whined Malachi.

"And these 'ruthless ruffians,' who were they exactly?" he pressed. At this point Malachi became evasive, trying to change the subject.

"Who are you anyway?" he demanded, as he hopped in a circle around the stone dwarf. Turning to Harty the wren continued. "I didn't agree to transport any old Tim, Rick or Sally you know. There might be an extra charge for extra persons," he suggested.

"Really?" retaliated Harty, his wingtips curling in annoyance. He was starting to feel irritated all over again with the tiny bird and his big mouth, and he'd only just returned. Harty would never threaten anyone by using their unborn child as a threat, he'd been there, done that, but the bird needed taking down a clothes-peg or two. "And we might call in on some goblins that appear to be looking for you." Malachi emitted a high-pitched squeak at the mention of goblins.

"You wouldn't?" defied Malachi.

"I might," Harty confirmed. By now Onk was standing in his angry pose with his strong arms crossed over his chest, and Upala rising, stood likewise. They made an intimidating pair. "Besides, without Phrack here, we never would have found your egg, let alone managed to steal it."

"You didn't steal it," Malachi shouted, becoming incensed. "You were rescuing it, my baby. Please let me see my baby." Harty could never stay mad for long and his heart went out when the wren asked to see his child. He made a useless bad man. "It's with Onk." Then seeing the fear in the wren's eyes, he added. "He kept my unborn daughter safe for three weeks." Malachi looked up in awe at the huge troll. Onk winked.

14

Gussies

PURITY and Gussie had been travelling forever, or so it seemed. The furry little creature with the undulating gait didn't seem to tire, leading the young fairy towards the foothills of the mountains Purity had spied in the distance. Once they traversed the lower hills he stopped, as if to get his bearings, then turned at a right angle to them.

"So, we're not going over the top?" guessed Purity, Gussie chirped and took her through a winding track which ran along between the initial slopes. "Wherever it is I hope we reach it soon. I'm starving, and I don't think my feet can go much further." And then they stopped.

Purity gazed at the spot Gussie had brought her to. There was nothing and no one there. It was a barren, empty dead-end gorge. In despair, she sank to her knees in the dirt.

"Oh Goddess, how stupid am I to think an animal knows where to go for safety?" she scolded herself. She didn't blame Gussie, she blamed herself. "At least it'll take Gristle an age to find me," she muttered. "If she can," she mumbled, through her building tears.

Purity didn't know the Demi-Golems were even now sniffing out her trail. Feeling her whole world disintegrate and any last hope of survival crumble, Purity lowered her head and sobbed. She cried herself into a small ball and fell asleep with dirt on her face, tears running down her cheeks and Gussie laying across her feet.

How long she slept Purity didn't know, but when she woke she was lying in a bed, a soft, sweet-smelling giant bed and she could feel the ghastly rings were missing from her ankles.

She was very content to stay put and hope her dream never ended, but soon she'd have to rise from her place by the fire with Lou and begin culling animals like the day before.

Gussie moved at her feet, then it appeared he'd travelled somehow up to her arm and then, snuggled up by her neck. Realising she could feel Gussie in three places at once, Purity opened her eyes. On the huge bed with her were three Gussies, or rather three creatures looking like Gussie. All were black, and all were identical, and she didn't have a clue, which one was her Gussie. Or, more importantly whether they were friendly like her Gussie. The Gussie at her feet moved, travelling up the bed, until he pushed his head under her hand for a tickling session.

"Ah, there you are. Who are your friends Gussie?" she enquired. Outside the room a noise started up. The remaining two gussies leapt off the bed like squirrels, disappearing under the bed while her Gussie stayed at her side. *Who does this home belong to? Whoever it is they put me in this wonderful bed, so they must have a kind heart.*

A glance around the room showed no curtains or windows. She guessed she was underground, judging by the lack of windows and solid earthen walls. A ceramic cup and jug of water stood on a small table next to the bed. A tall cupboard opposite, with a rug by the bed, completed the room's décor. It was basic and functional, no female touches. A knock sounded at her door. Purity swallowed, it appeared she was about to find out whose home this belonged to.

She watched as a tall man ducked under the door lintel and entered the room. After her first glance, she wasn't sure 'man' was the correct term. He wasn't any species she'd ever seen. Not that her experience was huge, but she attended the local dimension school and learnt everything she could about the six major dimensions and their inhabitants. She knew about the dark and light realms and the In-between. This individual was completely outside her knowledge base. *He must be alright, look at the bed he's laid me in. Gussie trusts him too, which is enough for me.*

"Hello," said the man, his skin seeming to change colour as he spoke. "I made food." Without any further words, he turned and left. Purity took that as her cue to follow him, which she did.

The passage was long and winding, Purity followed the giant, and the three Gussies, as she'd christened them for now, followed her. A junction appeared, and her guide took the left fork into a brighter corridor. Where the other passage was hewn through the rock, this one was lined with stone blocks showing great skill in its formation. At intervals along its length lanterns burned. Purity had the feeling that they were lit for her benefit and decided she didn't care, the light they cast made her feel better, safer. Again, the corridor forked and again the giant man turned down the left fork. *We must be deep inside the foothills,* she thought, trying hard to remember the turns in the tunnels the man had made.

Presently, three large wooden doors appeared in front of them. The man chose the middle one and grabbing the iron handle, strode through. The room inside was homely and warm, if a little spartan. The warmth came from a large

156

fire at the far end of the tall room. Purity felt the heat seeping into her like a soothing balm. She naturally migrated towards the fire and her furry retinue followed. The man headed off through another door and proceeded to make a large amount of banging and thumping noises. Purity climbed up into one of the large arm chairs facing the fire and the Gussies joined her.

A few minutes later, the man re-emerged carrying two dishes. At his reappearance, the gussies vanished, slinking over the sides of the chair like puddles of oil. Her host placed a dish, relative in size to Purity, gently on her lap then made himself comfortable in the opposite chair, which fit him as if it was made for him – which it probably was. Purity stared at her plate, there was food she never expected to see again. Cheese and fruit, bread and jam, she sighed with delight.

"Thank you," she said simply, looking up at the man who was stuffing his mouth with something she couldn't begin to describe. He nodded his head towards her in acknowledgment of her thanks. She wasn't interested in his diet, her own plate more than captured her interest. Her fingers catapulted into action grabbing fragrant morsels of food and, like him, stuffing them into her mouth. She knew she was making those small moaning noises she made when she enjoyed a particular food. She didn't care about that either. It probably wasn't the height of manners to grunt and groan in delight, but Purity was long past caring about what other people thought. For all its horror, the Neath had taught Purity one very valuable lesson - *live your life to the full, because the life you know might be taken away from you at any moment.*

When her hands finally stopped moving, her plate was empty, and she was licking the last of the jam off her fingers, well trying to. The gussies had re-joined her on the huge chair and were trying to get their portion of licks in too. She'd never seen a plate receive so much attention and was beginning to feel a little bit guilty that she hadn't saved them any, when the man stood up.

"Come zooms, food," he murmured. As one the Gussies, or rather zooms as they were apparently called, flew off Purity's chair and bounded out to what she presumed was the kitchen. More crashing and banging, then the sound of a tin plate being set on the floor and more contented chewing filled the air. The man re-entered alone. This time he brought drinks, a flagon for himself and a small thimble of honey ale for Purity. She surmised he'd had fairy guests before judging by the fare he offered. As if catching her thoughts, he spoke.

"Fairies like it here," he stated, his words slow and measured as if recently learnt.

"I'm not surprised, you treat your guests like royalty." He smiled at her compliment and nodded again.

They both sat enjoying their drinks in silence and soon three black shadows came back to Purity and settled to sleep.

"Zooms like you." It was Purity's turn to smile and nod.

"Zooms like you too," she answered. The man laughed and nodded back.

"Zooms like my food," he replied. They both laughed.

The man didn't ask Purity any questions about her situation and she didn't ask him about his life. They were both content to enjoy the moment, each in their own thoughts. As if reading her thoughts, he rose a short while later.

"Bed," he advised, despite her just getting up. Feeling she owed this generous man some explanation Purity began to speak, but he shook his head. "Talk tomorrow." He stood, walked to the door and waited for her to join him. His tone brooked no choice, so she slid off the chair and came to his side. "Zooms, bed too," he added. A flurry of black ink scampered across the floor and the five of them repeated their earlier journey back to Purity's room. At the door, Purity was about to argue that she wasn't tired, when a huge yawn threatened to take her breath away. The man smiled.

"I guess you're right," she admitted, sheepishly. Her host nodded once more, turned and disappeared down the corridor. *He reminds me of Uncle Onk.*

Purity sat on her bed after the giant had left and considered her situation. It had improved, she realised, as she idly tickled the zooms heads. She still worried that Gristle would come after her. Her father had told her something of Gristle's determination when she hunted him and Onk. One zoom settled across her feet.

"Is that you Gussie?" she queried. The zoom addressed lifted his head in affirmation. "I need to name both of you too," she said, turning to the remaining two. They were watching her with round, black and gold eyes. "Or, I'm going to get completely muddled up," she continued. Thinking hard for a several moments she considered their monikers. "I don't know what gender you are, so I'll avoid those." She watched the two animals settling down by her waist and neck.

"Slinky and Inky," she announced, pointing to Inky lying on the covers at her waist and Slinky, who by now had curled up on her pillow. That done, she settled back onto the bed, falling asleep with all three creatures chirping happily away. They'd never been given individual names before and were delighted.

Purity rested on her comfortable bed and before sleep claimed her, felt the now familiar sensation of the other person or creature. She still couldn't explain what she felt, it didn't contain words, or visions of places, it was like a piece of her had been replaced. Something she hadn't realised she had lost till now. Thinking about this other

159

person, for Purity was sure it was another person, she drifted off to sleep to the quiet whistling snores of the zooms.

****

The rescue party traipsed close behind Malachi Maximus Mallory the sixteenth as he moved back into what he called the Shadowline. Harty didn't understand why there would be a thin piece of land separating the Fire Realm and the In-between from the Neath. *Isn't that what the In-between is for?* he pondered. He took Malachi's word for it because they'd been there and what else could it be?

As before they were all joined together. Onk had lost his piece of rope somewhere in Incandesonia, but Phrack produced another one from his Gander bag and they tied themselves at intervals along it. Nobody wanted to get lost.

The wren led the way with Harty second, followed by Onk, Upala and finally Phrack. Harty and Onk had done this before, but the other two were somewhat apprehensive. Though Phrack had been born elsewhere he'd spent many decades in the Fire Realm and this bit of the journey unnerved him the most.

Malachi disappeared without a fanfare, followed by Harty, the rope between him and Onk hanging suspended to nothing. Upala didn't move to begin with, almost jerking Onk off his feet. He turned back, taking her cold stone fingers in his and gently tugged her forward. *Onk is going to have to do something about Upala before very long,* thought Phrack echoing Harty's thoughts; even he could see she was becoming attached to him, by more than just rope.

Then, there was just Phrack left in the Fire Realm. Taking a deep breath and grasping his Gander bag firmly to his chest he lifted his right leg, stepped into nothing – and he couldn't move. His progress forward was hindered by a filthy, grey hand suddenly gripping his left arm tightly

160

and a second hand grabbing his right shoulder and yanking him backwards before letting go.

Glancing over his left shoulder, Phrack jumped as he recognised one of the goblins from Harty's description. Fortunately, his gander bag strap was secure around his neck in front of him or he would have dropped his precious bag.

"Where do'you think you're going?" asked the greasy overweight goblin leering at him. Phrack swallowed hard. His friends seemed to have vanished, the rope hanging low between him and the invisible Upala. He wasn't sure whether the goblin had seen it yet, so he side-stepped around clutching it behind him in his free right hand. The goblin's hand remained firmly attached to Phrack's left wrist.

"Don't you go trying to get away from us. We want words with you," the goblin snarled, as he motioned towards his fatter partner breathlessly struggling near - together with a squad of nasty looking Hells Pixies mercenaries.

"Yes, very important words. Seems like you know a couple of villains we're looking for."

"That's right, thieves they are," complained the second goblin, drawing level with them and resting his hands on his bent knees to catch his breath.

Phrack almost argued the point, but he didn't want them to realise he knew who they were. He did the only thing he could think of since they didn't seem to know where he was standing. He yanked hard on the rope behind him.

Yanking on a rope attached to a stone queen is probably not the safest thing to do, but what else did Phrack have? If he was nervous about stepping into nothing, then being wrenched forward by an annoyed member of royalty gave a whole new meaning to the words 'express delivery'. Gripping the rope, Phrack catapulted into Upala some-where in the dark.

"I'm sorry, so sorry," he capitulated, "but the goblins are behind me."

"Did you say disgusting goblins?" warbled Harty anxiously, somewhere ahead of them.

"Yes, two fat, horrible goblins."

"Well, they can't get us in here," trilled the smug wren.

"Look 'ere! Who you calling fat and 'orrible?" came a disgruntled reply. *Oh, Goddess save us!* thought Harty *he's dragged an awful goblin in with us.*

15

Noises

ONK wasn't having any of it. Regardless of them being tied together and everything being pitch black, he stomped past Upala and Phrack in the dark. Grabbing hold of the goblin, who was still gripping Phrack's left wrist, he removed the goblin's hand from Phrack's person, and physically ejected him from the Shadowline. Pleased with his actions, Onk sauntered back to his place in line.

"Go!" he commanded, and the chain of friends moved forward.

They came out from the Shadowline into the Neath. There was a distinct difference between the sky and ground, though not a lot. Things were mostly grey here. Malachi announced his deed was done and wanted his egg as payment.

"How will we get home without you?" whined Harty.

"There's lots of ways out of the Neath," the wren assured them. "The deal struck was to get you in, not out." Harty hung his head in defeat, the bird was correct. He'd never thought about getting out again when he made the deal.

Sighing, he gestured to Onk to hand over the box containing the egg. Malachi lifted the lid to check on his egg. Onk wasn't impressed about the wren's departure, but he had nothing to bargain with and before he could think, the wren vanished.

"That's it then?" questioned the dwarf. "You don't have a return home plan?" Harty and Onk both shook their heads. "Well, you could have told me that nugget of information before the trip. It might have made me reconsider my decision to join you."

"I didn't expect the wren to abandon us," wailed Harty.

"It's partly my fault," offered Phrack. "I think the appearance of the goblin scared him off. Maybe he'll come back?"

"I don't think so," moaned Harty. "He wasn't exactly helpful to begin with."

"Oh!" was all Phrack could think of to say.

"Oh!" agreed Onk

"Oh!" said Upala. They all stopped thinking about their predicament and turned to stare at the stone queen.

"She spoke!" exclaimed Harty, not comfortable like Onk, with long empty silences.

"Well, I never!" added Phrack. Onk and Upala just smiled. It seemed that was all Upala was going to say for now, for no amount of urging by Harty made her say more.

Making proverbial good work of a bad job they travelled a short distance in the gloom. The gloom became deeper and soon they couldn't see their hands, which cemented the unanimous decision to stop and set up camp.

Although Malachi had assured Harty that getting out of the Neath should be relatively easy, Harty wasn't convinced. *Why else did Malachi flee so quickly?* he pondered.

Wanting to take his mind off something he couldn't change, Harty gazed about him at his surroundings. There were no objects on the landscape, no trees, rocks, hills, nothing to make any one piece stand out from another.

"It's so totally tedious here," muttered Harty, as they unpacked and Phrack set about starting a fire.

"It's not all like this," answered Phrack.

"Isn't it?"

"No, there are towns and cities. I think the stupid bird put us down somewhere he felt safe rather than somewhere useful." Harty thought about it, it made sense. If so, they were probably miles from anywhere. It wasn't like Earth, there were no street signs, no one to ask. In fact, they hadn't seen anyone since they entered. He wondered whether they were in the Neath at all.

"Where are all the people, the animals and everything?" he asked Phrack.

"Oh those, they only come out at night. Why do you think I'm trying to light the fire?"

"I thought it was so we could cook food and keep warm," a naive Harty replied.

"It is…" Phrack paused in mid-sentence, "…mainly," he finished lamely.

Their first night in the Neath was everything Harty thought it might be – horrific. He was terrified out of his tiny socks several times. Without his friends new and old, beside him, he would have fled for his life and been a psychotic shell of an elf by morning, probably without his wings too. He'd forgotten about the dreaded IBS, Iced Blood Syndrome which occurred when fairies were terrified. Luckily, Onk offered to let him sit on his shoulder when he realised Harty wasn't going to be able to sleep unless he felt safe.

The night terrors began a short while after supper. Harty thought he was imagining the moans, maybe they were the result of the dry mulberries he'd eaten. Then Phrack, sitting up next to him grumbled, making him jump.

"I do wish they'd shut up!"

"You mean you can hear them too?" Harty asked, a little bit amazed that he wasn't slipping into looneyland.

"Of course, we can all hear them." Onk and Upala nodded in agreement. "They're golems." Harty nearly passed out at the mention of their names, they were so horrible.

"G, g, g, gonlims," he stuttered.

"No, golems," replied Phrack. "Or at least something like them. Usually they're not so vocal."

"Really? What are they doing?" Harty didn't really want to know, but it stopped his knees banging together if he spoke.

"They're hunting." Harty squeaked. It was a very unbecoming noise for an elf.

"Hunting?" he said, his voice two octaves higher than usual. Upala was staring at Harty with interest. She'd never seen anyone react emotionally. Unknowingly, the little tree elf was aiding her studies of magical peoples no end. Harty didn't notice the queen's stare this time for he was engrossed with Phrack's explanation.

"Yes, hunting." Realising from the elf's high tones he must be afraid, Phrack tried to reassure him. "It's okay, they're not hunting us, you'd know it if they were."

"How?" asked Harty, before he could stop himself. Despite the possibility of IBS, Harty was transfixed and hanging on the dwarf's every word. Phrack recognised the elf was terrified so he adapted his next sentence accordingly.

"When they find their prey, usually some tiny animal, they howl." He smiled inwardly, reassured in the knowledge that golems never howled, they couldn't open their mouths, they only moaned.

The howl that sounded was long and drawn out. It seemed to come from everywhere and nowhere and Harty almost wet himself on Onk's tunic.

"Now, that's different," continued an amazed Phrack, standing up. "Never heard a golem howl before." The howl sounded again followed by a second and a third. "I guess they found what they were searching for." Unbe-

166

lievably, he chuckled. "Well, I guess that's us off the menu tonight."

Harty was finding the search for his daughter exhausting, and if truth be told, he was hanging on to his sanity by a snail's trail. *It isn't bad enough that my beloved Purity's been kidnapped, but we had to accept the help of a mad tiny bird, that thinks he's king, travelled through the Fire Realm to be chased by stone serpents and hunted by goblins. We nearly die in a lava river and field of demon stones.* Harty was forgetting he was in no danger during three of the events for he could fly. *Now Phrack tells me, there are all manner of things waiting to eat me in the dark and we're no closer to finding my daughter.*

Harty could feel his heart pounding in his chest like a runaway anvil. He drew his knees up and clasped his arms around them burying his face, so the others couldn't hear him sob. He was so weary of it all, so tired and scared wingless. Though he desperately wanted Purity home safe, he wasn't sure he was up to the task before him. It seemed that just as they solved one problem, another reared its head. *I can feel in my wing-tips that something else is going to go wrong, and when it does our mission is likely to be doomed. I don't know if my heart and wings, can cope with any more surprises and delays.*

If Harty had realised how right his assumption was, he might have turned directly around and flown home after Malachi.

****

The following morning Purity awoke to the sound of dogs baying, *no howling*, she corrected. They seemed to come from somewhere nearby. She sat up in bed wondering whether she should do something about it. Gussie, Slinky and Inky were absent. Gone, she surmised, to have breakfast. It felt like she'd slept for days, she felt so relaxed and refreshed.

Rising from the bed, she washed at the small wash basin which had replaced the ceramic cup and jug of cold water, while she slept. The jug of hot water with it was still warm and bizarrely she didn't feel concerned at what this implied. She washed and dressed, then poked her nose out of the door. Two of the zooms were present and amazingly, they growled at her, causing her to step back and close her door.

"Whatever is that about?" she wondered. Shortly after, there was a scratching at the door and though she was reluctant to open it, she did. One zoom lay outside her door.

"Gussie?" she enquired. The zoom sat up and wiggled in delight, but when she stepped over the threshold of the door, he too growled.

This time she didn't shut the door. She realised they weren't going to attack her, but they weren't going to let her out either, it was a classic stalemate.

"Okay, what am I supposed to do?" she asked scrutinising the zooms. The other two had returned and all three of them sat in a line in front of her. "Wait, I guess," she concluded. When the three zooms began weaving in and out of each other, then straightening up again in a row like soldiers, Purity's growing annoyance evaporated. "How can I be cross when you all look so adorable?" she dropped to her knees and gave each a hearty scratch behind the ears.

The next noise made her start. The howling was replaced by a sound which she had never heard, and hoped she'd never hear again. It was a cacophony of different noises and screams which made her skin itch, her teeth ache and her spine judder. The zooms lay flat on the floor and put their paws up over their heads and Purity did the same. After a while, when it seemed the dreadful sounds would never stop, she retreated to her bed with the zooms following. All four huddled together under the sheets as the noise continued on and on.

★★★★

"It isn't ever going to stop, is it?" questioned Harty, covering his sensitive ears. The noise which followed the howling was like a hundred cats being skinned alive on a stone cheese grater. It vibrated down through his bones. Although they were all discomforted by the din, Upala seemed the most affected. She stared in the direction of the noise, then pieces of stone began dropping off her. Small demon stones went skittling away into the dark.

"Are they going to be safe out there?" asked Harty, concerned for Upala's safety. "Upala turned her head to face him and he noticed her eyes were gleaming like diamonds. He swallowed; she looked wonderful and scary at the same time. She smiled, her first smile to him and it scared him further, but he said nothing. Stepping away from the fire, Upala stood up. She stretched tall, and they watched mesmerised, as her body sank into the ground until nothing remained.

"Mmmm, that ability is impressive," mumbled Phrack, and he meant it. He'd never seen a demon stone before, queen or otherwise.

"Do you think she'll come back?"

"Who knows, she seems a free spirit to me." Onk looked a bit forlorn at that statement.

After Upala's abrupt exit the three remaining travellers settled down closer to the fire. Harty stayed on Onk's shoulder despite his hair waving in his face like seaweed. He was far too worried about what Phrack had said.

Several denizens of the Neath approached the fire during the hours of darkness, but they didn't interfere with the travellers directly. They were merely curious as to why anyone would stop for the night in the middle of the witch's domain. Neath residents avoided the area for fear of being transformed. They hated the witch; many had lost loved ones, pets, or both. They resented her presence all these years. She wasn't Neath and she wasn't welcome, but she stayed anyway.

Harty watched as a strange undulating black thing wove its' way around them beyond the light spreading from their fire. He couldn't identify the creature. He supposed there were a great many species he didn't know. Harty was a creature of the light, just being here was sapping his strength. *I don't know how long I can survive in this darkness, but for Purity's sake I must.* He hoped she was somewhere alive and well. He needed to find her and soon. If only they could locate the witch's lair. *Tomorrow,* he decided, *we'll seek out a resident and ask them what they know, however dangerous it is.*

16

Mothball

LONG before the darkness in the sky had lifted, the last of the gruesome visitors had departed. They didn't approach any of the party huddled around the waning campfire, seemingly more interested in their actual presence than harming them. *At least nothing tried to eat us in the night*, reflected Phrack, *which is good, but I didn't sleep a wink and I know Harty was restless too*. As a result, in the morning Harty and Phrack were in no fit state to continue.

"Is this going to happen every night?" mumbled Harty, half asleep on Onk's shoulder. "If so, I'm going to be dead soon from fright. A tree elf isn't built for this type of punishment."

Onk frowned. He didn't like his friend speaking this way. When Phrack agreed with Harty, Onk decided something had to be done.

"Town." They looked at Onk and realised he was right.

"Yes, a town, they'll have answers," beamed Harty.

"And a bed to sleep in," added Phrack wistfully. Harty smiled, his thoughts echoing Phrack. "A town it is then. Hold on, how do we wake Upala? Is she still here?"

"I don't know. Maybe she's gone," suggested Phrack. When Harty didn't catch on, he added, "You know, dissolved back into tiny demon stones." Onk wasn't amused.

"If she isn't, she'll be livid to wake up and find out we've left her behind. I know I would be," stated Harty, looking over to where Upala sank into the ground.

"To be fair Harty, I think Upala can look after herself. What with her being a seven-foot stone giantess an' all."

"Well, I don't fancy an angry stone queen coming after me," Harty advised his friends.

"You've got a point there," admitted Phrack, picturing Upala, stoning him with her own subjects.

Stalling any further discussion on the subject, Onk knelt and placed his ear to the ground. Turning his head, he spoke quietly.

"Upala up."

Upala emerged inch by inch from the grey dusty ground. As before, she dusted herself off like she'd stepped out to use the bathroom – and maybe she had.

"Phrack, you've been in the Neath before, you must recognise something." Phrack stared at the flat grey surroundings. There were no trees, boulders or houses, nothing to signify a way forward.

"I think there is a town in that direction," he finally stated.

"How do you know?" asked Harty. "It all looks the same to me."

"I believe this is the Tedium Zone," Phrack answered.

"Why am I not surprised," laughed Harty. "It certainly fits the name."

"You haven't seen anything till you've seen Reaper Falls or the Pit of Endless Suffering," replied Phrack. "They fit their titles too."

"No, I think I'll give those a miss," said Harty, sobering up.

"Maybe next time," suggested Phrack, with a malicious grin.

"There better not be a next time," huffed Harty. "Let's get going then," he continued, changing the subject. "This place gives me the collywobbles."

Phrack was still worried that the goblins might be on their trail. He kept glancing over his shoulder as they struggled onwards through the greyness.

The Tedium Zone was a flat bowl of nothingness. It was barren and grey and dismal. When it wasn't covered in a layer of gaseous mud a foot deep during the rainy season, it was covered in a layer of dust two feet deep when it dried out. The result was either struggle through the mud looking like a mud-man from a horror film, or become a grey ghost, as the dry dust floated up and stuck to everything, including the inside of your lungs. Fortunately, the stuff didn't carry germs in it, but wheezing out grey spit for a fortnight after wasn't everyone's idea of fun.

Consequently, most travellers opted to go around the outside of the grey bowl rather than through it. The Tedium Zone was home to several species who hunted folk foolhardy enough to march straight through the middle. Small creatures, like imps and elves were easily snared. Newcomers, settling down on what they thought was a simple flat plain, usually found themselves sinking into the gelatinous mud. Many had perished long before the predators and scavengers arrived, providing easy pickings.

Most of the zone was currently grey dust which ballooned up into the lifeless air with each step they took. Onk and Upala had the most trouble their heavy tread causing billowing clouds of dust. Soon all of them were covered in the stuff, except Harty, who decided to fly for this part of the journey rather than suffer inhaling "the disgusting, soul-sucking filth," as he called it.

Every now and then, without warning, an area of dust changed to grey mud. They'd have to slog their way through deep drifts, of what Harty decided to call, "sticky-ickiness." His comment was amazing seeing as how he didn't even go near the mud.

"Where does it all come from?" Harty called down, labelling Phrack as the expert on all things Neath.

"Blowed if I know," he called up. "Last time, I went around the edge not straight through the middle."

"Why didn't we do that?" muttered Harty from above.

"Because I assumed you didn't want to spend another night out here." The dwarf was correct in his assumption, even the thought of another night al fresco made Harty's wings curl.

Onk and Upala said nothing during these exchanges. They were content to travel listening to their companions rather than participating. Onk caught sight of the metallic bird again, high above them. He smiled.

They almost missed the town in the greyness. If it wasn't for Harty they would have walked past it barely twenty feet away.

The town of Mothball, such as it was, was grey. It was a typical Neath town, wood and mud construction, much of it looking as if one good blow would send it flying. Towns in the Neath didn't have parks, or churches, or leisure centres. They did have shops and taverns in abundance. Mothball was a poor excuse of a town, nothing like Incandesonia in the Fire Realm, which was almost a city in size. By comparison, Mothball was a hamlet. There was a main street, where the richer residents had homes, a market place, several side streets where nefarious activities took place, and that was all.

Nothing moved in front of them. No people wandered between buildings, no sounds came from those buildings either.

174

"Where is everyone?" asked Harty, voicing what the others were thinking.

"Mostly asleep, I'm guessing," replied Phrack. "Residents tend to wake up at night in the Neath. We're the odd ones."

"Can we get a room?" continued Harty, looking over at Upala. He wasn't sure if she needed one. Phrack ignored Harty's question and led them into a grey and black building on the left. The inside was better than Harty imagined it would be. He'd conjured up a greasy black space, full of cobwebs and earwigs, right up Onk's street. This place was clean, if a little grey, and here and there small birds sang in cages. Harty thought how cute they were, until he looked closer and discovered they were real-live fairies. He emitted a frightened squeak.

"Perhaps you better sit on Onk's shoulder and look like his pet," advised Phrack.

"Pet! Pet!" screeched Harty. "I'm nobody's pet!" He was disgusted.

"Carry on like that and you might end up somebody's dinner instead." It was then Harty realised the large room wasn't empty, there were folk sitting around the room and they were staring at him like he was supper.

He spotted two orcs, a bit like their ugly Earth cousins, the Tarmac orc, but bigger and hairier. There were several Neath demons playing a game of some sort on a large oblong table. The game appeared to involve throwing a small live animal through hoops. The demons looked up when the party entered, but quickly turned back to their game when they spied Onk and Upala amongst them.

In one corner, a warlock sat nursing a flagon of ale, while in another, an old gnarled hag crouched low over a cauldron. She smiled crookedly at the stone dwarf and gave a respectful nod to Upala, seemingly aware of her status. Harty shivered and turned away hoping the hag wasn't their cook. A young Neath demon approached

them, he was all spindly arms and legs, clearly an adolescent.

"What can I do's for's you"? he grovelled, bending so
low at the waist his wiry fingers swept the floor.

"We require a room," answered Phrack, putting on a
slight air of importance.

"Be that for's potions or spells, Sir?" the teen added,
before Phrack could chastise him for lacking manners.

"Neither, we require rest." If the teenage demon was
surprised at the bizarre request, the adult demons were
agog. They stopped their game, chucking their 'puck' into
the cold fireplace, and sidled over. The tallest among them,
made a good job of not displaying any fear or intimidation
from Onk or Upala's presence. This was the Neath and they
were kings here. The hag in the corner giggled at their
ignorance.

"Sleep is it?" the leader questioned.

"Yes sleep," Phrack squirmed. "We can pay."

"Pay? Of course you can pay." Swiping his arm through
the air he grabbed Harty capturing him in one taloned
hand. "Your pet will do as payment," he announced, and
business completed without another word he turned and
went back to his game.

Onk saw red. Nobody grabbed his friend. If any grabbing
was to be done, he'd do it. He lifted the skinny adult demon
high up into the air like he was a bag of kittens.

"Harty my friend, not pet," he roared, emphasising the
last word by shaking the demon very hard until his fangs
rattled. The demon, unable to disagree, opened his talons
and released the elf.

Harty, relieved to be liberated from the smelly hand
which threatened to damage his fragile wings, dashed back
across the room to hide behind Upala. The demon, recognising his mistake, especially with his feet dangling three
feet off the floor, capitulated.

"No, no of course not, begging my pardon. Please accept my apologies, have a room on the house." When Onk didn't release him he added, "Free." That, Onk understood. He let the demon go and he slithered down onto the floor like a red puddle of treacle. Harty had a moment of deja vu and a memory of a cat slipping through its collar in a graveyard, centuries ago. The young Neath demon re-appeared.

"I shows you's to your roomies," he spluttered, grovelling lower than before. He'd never seen anyone best his boss and he was secretly pleased, though he'd never be able to admit it. A wink in their direction was all Harty saw as they climbed the staircase in the middle of the room towards the first floor.

The room was basic, but it did boast two beds. Ever the gentleman, Onk offered one to Upala. She declined, shaking her head vigorously and pointing outside. He nodded his understanding, then sat down on the edge of the first bed. It groaned under Onk's weight, but it was made of sturdy stuff and spelled, so it was used to taking far bigger individuals than trolls.

Phrack took the second bed. Harty fluttered about, wondering where to go. He noticed a cage, like those downstairs holding fairies. Whilst he was disgusted by the practice of caging fairies, he noticed this one had a large bed in the centre of it. With a cut-out wing shape on one side, it was obviously designed with fairy anatomy in mind. He scooted over to examine it closer. It did look appealing. He could see himself settled very nicely in there, providing the door stayed open. Tying the cage door open with a piece of twine, Harty allowed himself the luxury of lying on the bed. It was wonderful. Already dwarf snores were filling the room, and these were closely followed by troll ones. Harty sighed and looked at Upala, he so wanted to sleep. He wasn't surprised when Upala addressed a snoring noise at him. He understood, she was telling him to sleep, she would keep them safe. His head hit the pillow…

****

When Purity woke for the third time, all was silent except for tiny whistles which passed for snoring amongst the zooms littered across her bed. She found the scene endearing and, reluctant to disturb the sleeping creatures, sat listening to each zoom who seemed to whistle a different note. It was almost musical.

In the stillness, she realised she could feel the undefined sensation again. A sense of belonging filled her, and for some reason it was stronger than before, like it was closer. She didn't know what, or who it belonged to.

As she lay considering this phenomenon, the bang of a door somewhere in the distance broke her revelry and the zooms sleep. All of them sat up watching the door. The handle turned, and the man entered.

"Whatever happened?" demanded Purity, leaping off the bed and crossing the room without a thought for her own safety. The zooms were beside themselves, weaving in and out of the man's legs threatening to trip him up.

"Zooms go," he ordered. They didn't need telling twice, they vanished. Purity spent a moment wondering how they'd disappeared, but she had more pressing matters in front of her. The man was injured. He staggered, and she ordered him to sit on the bed. Once there, she made him sit still while, hovering in front of him, she surveyed his ruined face.

"What happened?" she asked again. "Your face…" She didn't finish her sentence.

"Demi-Golems," he replied, answering her question, but refusing to say more. Purity didn't have a clue what a Demi-Golem was, but she did know the man needed her help.

"We need to get you cleaned up."

She went to the wash-stand and, wetting a small towel with some of the remaining water from the jug, proceeded to clean what looked like blood and greenish goo off him. The man sat and tolerated her ministrations without a word. She wasn't sure if he was too tired to take offense or alternatively, appreciated her input. She noticed that his skin wasn't like any skin she knew. It was cold and flat like stone, and the water clung to it like a puddle.

Purity took this opportunity to assess the man in more detail. He was well over eight-feet tall, his chest was broad and his arms strong. He was bigger than her uncle Onk and she guessed he was stronger too. In another place, she'd be terrified of this giant. He had kind eyes though and his act of kindness had probably saved her life. He didn't speak much, but he had a sense of humour and she liked that.

When she finished cleaning up, what had looked like obvious injuries, Purity was surprised to find there wasn't one open wound on the man's face, only colours which stained his cheeks and forehead, and didn't come off no matter how hard she rubbed.

"You need to rest," she advised, not knowing what else to say. Her mother always said, 'you need to rest,' whenever she'd been in the wars. The man nodded and stood slowly like he was in pain. He made as if to leave and then turned back to her.

"You stay?" he asked. Purity nodded, and reassured, the man left.

She waited a short while in her room. Then, deciding she didn't want to wait alone anymore, she opened the door, expecting to see the three zooms guarding her. The corridor was empty, the zooms nowhere to be seen. She hoped that was a good sign and set off in search of the room she'd been in earlier. She remembered the tunnels and the correct turnings and shortly found herself in the passage with three doors at the end. She opened the middle door.

The man was nowhere to be seen. She busied herself tidying away the remains of their previous meal, which was still on the counter in the kitchen where the man had left it. This surprised Purity, for the home looked loved and cared for and the man didn't seem the type to leave dirty dishes lying about. The spell she'd learnt from Lou for managing the animals at Gristle's home, came in useful for lifting and moving some of the items. After washing up, she set about straightening the room.

Later, settling by the fire in the large comfy chair, Purity considered her situation. *I could be in a worse place. This man is kind, his zooms are beautiful and faithful to him. I don't think they would stay with an evil person.*

Remembering the way the man ordered the zooms to go, Purity tested out a theory she'd been considering since caring for the man's injuries. She thought she had figured out what the zooms disappearing act meant and was dying to test it out. She was a fairy and her education included trans-dimensional shifting. After a few more minutes she decided to act.

"Zooms come," she called, and all three zooms appeared from out of the ether.

"So, you travel between dimensions do you, my little ones?" she crooned, stroking their slinky heads. "That explains a lot. I wonder whether you can help me?" The zooms chirped and whistled enjoying her tickling hands while she put her request to them.

By the time the man returned, Purity had organised and cooked a meal. Her mother had taught her well. She'd found food in a walk-in larder off the kitchen, food which she recognised, so it was no problem to create a simple one-pot meal for both. She hadn't been able to lift all the items she needed off the shelves, even with the spell, but found the zooms remarkably bright and strong for such little creatures. They were able to push objects with their noses and lift things with their teeth.

The man seemed surprised by Purity's actions. However, he didn't say a word, calmly seating himself at the table as she requested.

"I had to cook everything in the pot I found on the stove. I'm sorry, but I'm too small to lift it myself. Could you assist?" she asked. The man nodded and rose to gather the casserole pot and plates from the kitchen.

"Good," the man mumbled, wiping his mouth with the back of his hand then pushing his plate away after two helpings from the pot. Purity was pleased by his praise.

"Thank you," she answered humbly. "It's nice to cook. It's the first normal food I've eaten since arriving in this Goddess forsaken place." The man frowned at her comment and realising she might have insulted the man's homeland she began to apologise. He raised his left hand.

"No, no, you right. Goddess forsaken," he agreed, smiling. Then he pointed towards the kitchen. She turned her head and saw two zooms fighting over the remains of their meal in the pot, while the third had their head stuck inside an empty bottle and was running around trying to dislodge it.

They both laughed at the scene, their laughter increasing when the trapped zoom vanished, the freed bottle flipping end over end startling the second zoom who vanished in surprise. The remaining zoom stared out of the kitchen at Purity, then vanished to join his friends.

"Where do they go?" Purity asked intrigued.

"Don't know," shrugged the man. "Always come back, so never worry."

"Your zooms are lovely," she continued. This statement earned her a strange stare from the man. The 'man,' she couldn't keep calling him that.

"Not my zooms, Not your zooms. Zooms free. No-one's zooms."

"I'm sorry, I didn't mean anything by it," Purity replied,

feeling awkward. She paused to consider her next statement not wanting to upset the man who'd been so kind to
her. "I don't even know your name," she said, hoping he
might volunteer the information and change the subject.

"Jasper," he replied, then he stood and went to stoke the
dying embers of the fire. As he worked the flames, she
watched him. He was a man and he wasn't. He ate food
with her and apparently enjoyed it. He spoke and dressed
and laughed, but he wasn't a man – not really. He reminded
her a lot of Onk.

Tears welled up of their own accord at the thought of
her uncle Onk. By association it brought back thoughts of
her mother and father. Jasper turned from drawing the fire
and regarded the tiny girl sitting in his armchair with tears
in her eyes. *She's young, too young to be out in the wilds of the
Neath. Too young to have a squad of Demi-Golems after her.
What did she do to incur their wrath, or more importantly the
attention of their mistress, that diabolical Heath Witch, Gristle?
Those golems were difficult to fight and even harder to kill! Thank
goodness there were only ten of them. That's the trouble with
re-animated life, it won't die when it's supposed to.*

As fast as Jasper had knocked one golem down, the
previous one got up. When he realised he was going to lose
the battle, fighting hand-to-hand, he had reverted to utilising his elementary structure. They were still outside and
still alive, their level of life anyway, but not one of them
could move. They would never move again. He'd
entombed the lot in solid rock. Now, they would stay that
way for all time.

17

Chocolate

GRISTLE had tried her hand at shadow-watching, or far-sight as some called it, when she first arrived in the Neath. The idea of capturing the minds of birds and animals to spy on others appealed to her. So what, if they died because of the contact? She could always eat them afterwards. She'd been successful at it too. However, it seemed that creatures were a lot less common in the Neath than in the light dimensions.

On Earth, there were all manner of animals, birds, insects and fish, not to mention people. Here, the only creatures easily caught were spiders, snakes and lizards. The flying creatures were much more intelligent than the crows and seagulls of Earth, and after a few incidents of their friends dying whenever they drew near Gristle's house they quickly learnt to avoid it. Unlike Earth, there were no police cones around Gristle's estate to ward people off, but the large ring of bleached bones - from her failed spells - served the same purpose.

Never one to give in easily, Gristle had practiced with

her spiders. They were the fastest and easiest for transporting. Before she'd sent her squad of ten Demi-Golems off to re-capture the girl, she'd attached a spider to one of them, to be her eyes and ears. Retreating to her room, she placed a Do Not Disturb sign upon it and sat down to concentrate.

Through her shadow-sight, she'd witnessed the destruction of her ten golems and their incarceration inside the mountain. She was horrified, angry and excited.

"If I could harness that power, I'd be unstoppable. How do I apprehend a demon stone man? I'm sure I still have those spells lying about somewhere. I need to keep the one I've been waiting to use on that stupid oaf of a troll, but I have plenty of others to spare. I'll spend a few of those on the stone man and make him my slave." Gristle cackled in anticipation. Rubbing her hands together, she spin-danced out of her study, flipped the Do Not Disturb sign over, and headed towards her spell larder.

Lou crept out from behind the large flowerpot in the study. She'd been listening to the old crone, who never kept silent when she shadow-watched. Lou had learnt that the concentration required drained Gristle's perceptive abilities. As a result, she couldn't tell if someone was close by, wishing her ill. It was the major flaw of shadow-watching that Gristle had yet to appreciate. Twelve years earlier, she had turned the witch she learnt the skill from, Grue the Gruesome, into a toad before she could explain that Shadow-watching would sap her powers making her vulnerable.

Fortunately for Gristle, Lou wasn't thinking of revenge. She felt awful for what she'd done to Purity and was lonelier now than before she met her. Realising too late, that once you have experienced something as precious as true friendship, it's harder to survive without it. Gussie hadn't returned either, since that fateful night. Lou knew in her heart he'd left because of her treachery. She missed him terribly too.

Lou listened to Gristle grumbling about, "that dratted fairy," and a stone man too. She wondered whether they were connected in any way. The stone man had apparently defeated Gristle's squad of golems, which was awesome and unbelievable.

Lou hadn't considered that Gristle would send golems after Purity, now she knew, she felt full of remorse at her earlier jealousy fuelled actions. Sneaking into Gristle's study before the witch arrived had been a stroke of genius, but what she was going to do with that information now, she didn't know. She watched Gristle leave, flip the sign and stride off down the passageway towards her larder. Thinking the coast was clear, Lou stepped out of the room, straight into the arms of Crogg.

"Where's you going slug?" he demanded, deliberately insulting Lou, "and more importantly, where's has you been?" He looked over Lou's shoulder into the study and gasped, holding his chest in mock disbelief. "The mistress isn't in there, what's you doing in there alone?" Guessing the answer, he took a step back. "You's is spying on the mistress. Ooo! She won'ts like that when I tell's her." Lou was mortified.

"Please don't tell's her, please," begged Lou, falling to her knees. "I didn't do's anything honest." Thinking quickly, she added, "I's been so lonely since Purity ran away." Crogg knew this explanation wasn't the truth, but Gristle had believed Lou's story so, without proof he couldn't say anything. Now he'd caught Lou doing something wrong. She'd be turned into a spider for certain. He had leverage, and he used it. "Purity never did run's away, did she? Tell's me the truth or I's go to the mistress now. She's won't be happy. Turns you's into a spider I reckon." Lou wasn't very bright. She didn't realise her answer would put her deeper under Crogg's control. She began to cry.

"I didn't mean's to do it," she sobbed, her heart bursting

with unhappiness. "I got's jealous." Crogg smiled wickedly.
I thought so. She's done something with the fairy.

"Did you's kill her?" he asked, leering over her tiny kneeling figure. Lou looked up and caught the malicious glint in Crogg's eye. She knew then he was going to tell Gristle everything, regardless of what he said. She leapt up and fled down the passage, away to the kitchen.

Once there, she secreted herself high up the flue and waited, terrified and alone, in the dark. And that's where Gussie found her. She almost died of fright when something moved below. Thinking it was Crogg, or that monster called a Demi-Golem, Lou forced herself to climb higher up the narrowing chimney. Then the chirping started up and she knew at once Gussie had returned. Wrapping her arms tight around him, she sobbed her unhappiness into his slinky pelt.

****

After they'd eaten, Purity joined Jasper by the fire while the zooms, who had re-appeared earlier, snuggled down in front of the heat, burrowing their noses in each other's pelts until they looked like a black puddle of oil on the rug.

Purity recounted the tale of her kidnapping at Jasper's request. Her story caused him to growl in places, not unlike her uncle. She told him of her birth too, though an abridged version, not the one her father told about spiders, and cats called Tenamunday.

She told him of the bizarre feeling she'd had ever since arriving of someone, or something, being aware of her presence here.

"I don't feel any malice or ill-intention," she confided to Jasper, "but I don't feel any care or goodness either, just curiosity." The feeling of being watched continued to puzzle her and Purity hated puzzles.

Lastly, Purity spoke with sadness of Lou, still trapped, a prisoner in Gristle's home and how she now understood Lou's feelings. She didn't hold Lou's actions against her despite her jealousy and deceit. Without Lou's intervention, Purity would never have met Gussie or had his help, or Jasper's.

At that point in Purity's story, one of the zooms lifted its sleepy head and vanished. The puddle became smaller and the remaining two zooms wriggled about to reposition themselves. Purity hadn't noticed the change in numbers, but Jasper had. He smiled. Purity smiled wider when Gussie returned with Lou's arms wrapped around his neck.

When she lifted her head from his fur, she wasn't in the flue in Gristle's kitchen anymore. She was in a comfy room with a roaring fire and the smell of real food coming from somewhere nearby, and there were three Gussies, Purity and a giant man. Lou fainted.

They put Lou to bed in Purity's room and Gussie stayed with her. The other two hadn't budged from their place at the fire.

"Chocolate?" asked Purity, once they settled. Jasper tilted his head in confusion.

"Chocolate?" he repeated. Purity had found a tin of cocoa powder in the kitchen larder and thought to make them a cup before bed. Her uncle Onk loved it.

"Yes, would you like some before bed?"

"Don't know," came the reply. "Never had it before."

"But you have some here in your larder."

"Do I?"

"Yes." Realising the conversation was going nowhere, Purity jumped up. "Look you wait here and the zooms can help me make it." Without waiting for any more comments from Jasper, Purity set about making hot chocolate.

A stone man with a chocolate moustache said goodnight to Purity at her door. Purity giggled, Jasper couldn't get enough of the stuff, forcing Purity to make him three mugs full before she raised her hands.

"Enough! My father says, too much of a good thing isn't good for you."

"It isn't?" Jasper questioned, his new moustache making Purity smile. He was of the opinion, if you liked something you should have it all the time.

"No. Besides, its traditional to have a cup of hot chocolate before bed, so it's time for bed." Jasper's smile dropped. Apparently, he'd never tried the brown powder in the tin wondering what it was in his larder. Now he asserted he was going to buy chocolate every week. That meant he went somewhere to shop and he agreed to take Purity the following day.

Lou's dark wet eyes shone, as Purity entered the room and neared the bed.

"Please say you's forgive me," Lou begged, her voice trembling with anxiety. After a moment's thought, Purity replied.

"Yes, I do forgive you Lou," she answered, "but if you ever do anything like that again I will never, ever, be your friend again. Is that clear?"

Lou jumped off the bed and hugged her new found-again friend. Purity would never entirely trust Lou, though she'd never tell the little imp that. They settled down for a good rest after Lou finished her own hot chocolate, and Gussie had licked the inside of the cup clean.

****

It was a strange group of folks searching the town for information the following morning. Many residents had never seen a city troll let alone a mulberry tree elf. More than a few looked like they might have eaten Harty, if he hadn't been glued to Onk's shoulder like some pet parrot.

"It's horrible here," moaned Harty. "I feel like dinner. I wish they would stop licking their lips and rubbing their hands when they look at me."

"Onk keep Harty safe."

"I know Onk, but it's unsettling to a fragile being like me. One twist, or splat, and I'd be eaten." Onk growled his displeasure at such a thought and Upala closed ranks at the suggestion.

They made their way towards the market place, as no one they spoke to on route admitted to knowing any witches locally. Phrack reasoned the market traders might have more knowledge of other regions than the locals. It seemed like a good idea and he was right. The first trader they spoke to stared at them and went a lighter shade of green than he already was.

The second and third turned their backs once they heard who Phrack was enquiring about. The fourth trader didn't answer their question verbally, but tilted his head left and shrugged his shoulder like some cockney wheeler-dealer. His deliberate twitch caused Harty to glance left and there, down a small side street, was another shabbier market-stall selling goods.

The trader, a slime troll, appeared to be selling ingredients for spells and potions.

"What do you want to know?" he asked, looking at them furtively and shifting his eyes sideways. *A shifty manoeuvre, if ever there was one*, reflected Harty, and he'd seen a few since arriving in this town.

"We're looking for witch," requested Onk, using his best words in his politest tone. He'd witnessed lots of folk getting what they wanted that way. It didn't seem to take nearly as much energy as attitude and bad behaviour. *Teenagers could learn a lot from Onk*, thought Harty.

"Ah, but which witch?" replied the cryptic trader, grinning to himself at his witty joke. Onk observed the slime troll, he seemed familiar, but he couldn't figure out why. He had the same features as Earth trolls, but was shorter, much shorter and his complexion was dark green. Then Onk noticed Harty and Phrack looking back and forth between the two trolls.

"He could be your brother Onk," announced Harty, unhelpfully.

"Your younger brother," put in Phrack, then after a moment's thought added, "much younger." Onk frowned. He didn't like them comparing him to this ugly green stranger. He turned to Upala for support. She was also eyeing them both up and down. It unnerved him.

"Onk has no brothers," he stated loudly. The trader nodded.

"And I have no brothers either."

"Maybe you're cousins. You could be cousins," suggested Harty. It was the trader's turn to stare at Onk.

"No more staring," bellowed Onk, causing everyone to jump. It seemed Harty had hit a proverbial nerve. "Witches?" he said, rounding on the trader.

"It depends on two things," the trader replied, raising his hands in surrender. "First." He counted on his three fingers. "Which witch? And second, how much you got?"

"Nope, he's not your cousin Onk. He's only got three fingers," stated Harty.

Onk smiled. The trader wondered whether the elf was always that dim, or should he inform him that he lost his other finger and thumb in a fight. He decided no, maybe not. Ignoring the elf, the trader turned to Onk.

"There's stone witches, hedgerow witches, fire witches, heath witches…"

"Heath Witch, it's a heath witch," Harty squawked, unable to contain himself any longer.

"Heath witches then, they'll be more expensive."

"Funny, I thought they might," sneered Phrack, the sarcastic edge missed by those present.

"Why, how many have you got?"

"Well, heath witches don't normally live in the Neath, and there's only one living here now, so naturally, it'll cost more."

"How does that work?" queried Harty. "Surely if you have only one heath witch, everyone will know where she is and that makes her details cheaper."

"You'd think so wouldn't you," replied the trader, busily thinking on his feet "However, there's only one because she is so powerful, she scared all the other witches away."

"Let me get this straight. You don't actually have any witches here, except this one heath witch?" The trader was starting to realise he might have fallen into his own trap. "So," continued Phrack. "We don't actually need you at all, we just need to ask where 'the witch' lives?"

"Ah, ah, ah," the slime troll stuttered, trying to recover control of the situation. "As you've found out, no one else will tell you where she lives." *That's it,* he congratulated himself.

"Oh!" sighed Harty. *It feels like we've been had.*

"Did we really need to pay him so much?" asked Harty, noticing from his elevated position on Onk's shoulder, that they seemed to be travelling back the way they'd come the day before.

"Yes," Phrack answered. "Because it was him or no one. Did you still want to be in that excuse for a town, or would you rather be finding your daughter, so we can all go home?"

"Do we have to go through the Tedium Zone again though?" Asked a fretful Harty, biting his nails. "Can't we go around it this time? Please?" he beseeched his friends.

It seemed Onk wasn't the only one who realised manners got more out of people than rudeness.

"We could go around, but it will take longer than one night," answered Phrack. "The other option is to place a guard and take it in turns to watch through the night." Harty wasn't sure he liked the sound of that. How could he, a four-and-a-half-inch high elf, protect the camp?

Realising what Harty was thinking Phrack added, "Of course for safety we'd watch in pairs."

"Onk watch all night," Onk declared. Harty knew his friend's sleeping habits and while he was impressed by Onk's offer, he knew Onk would soon struggle without sleep. Onk was rare for a troll in many ways and most managed quite well with just a few hours. Since Onk's episode caring for Harty's unborn sleeping daughter, he seemed to require many more hours than the average troll. Phrack didn't know about Onk's need for sleep, regardless, he was against the same person watching all night.

"You might not need sleep, but your watch partner will. May I suggest Onk and Harty take the first watch till midnight? Upala and I will take the second watch till what passes for dawn here. That way we can cross the zone quickly and safely." And that's exactly what they did.

"That was easy," breathed Harty, when they reached the far side of the zone the following afternoon. "Isn't this where we heard that awful noise before?" he asked, looking about. Onk nodded, scanning the sky for his pretty bird.

"The trader's directions are to bear left when we see the foothills on the far side of the zone," continued Harty.

They stared at the horizon. Far off in the distance they could just make out a low range of hills, possibly the foothills the trader mentioned, which led to a higher range of mountains. In between the ground was flat and grey and endless.

"Where's this witch's house then? I can't see it," muttered Phrack.

"The trader said, we'd need to travel further," replied Harty, who understood how Phrack felt. It was annoying having to cover the same ground. "If only we'd known that Gristle's home was near the beginning of our journey, think of the time we'd have saved."

"Can't be helped I suppose," grumbled the dwarf.

"I know, I'll fly up and see if I can spot it," suggested Harty, thinking to help his friends.

"You think it's safe up there?" asked Phrack, "Only you haven't flown at all in the Neath."

"I've been watching and haven't seen anything in the sky, things mainly seem to be grounded."

"That's because a lot of flying critters sleep at night, on account of not wanting to fly into things," replied Phrack. Feeling brave Harty stressed, "I've got to try."

Taking a deep breath, the mulberry elf launched himself high into the sky. It was a weird sensation flying without much light, clouds, or wind. There weren't many thermals to use, or currents to glide on, it was all wing power.

When he got to a reasonable level he hovered, checking for other sky traffic first, and then focusing his efforts on searching for the witch's house. He found it in minutes; they weren't that far away. He pointed to the direction where the house was located, and they stood below waving their arms and shouting to indicate they understood his directions.

One minute, Harty was hanging in the air pointing the way. The next he'd been elf-napped, it was the only word for it. Pulled around the waist and yanked away by another flying creature. Fortunately, it wasn't a creature set on eating him, but a larger version of elf.

"What are you doing?" Harty yelled at his attacker. "Put me down this instant," he demanded. The fairy ignored him. It was much younger than Harty, fitter and stronger too. It was a he, and he resembled someone, but Harty couldn't place who that might be.

"Put me down," Harty repeated. The big elf continued to ignore Harty's demands. Harty knew he should be afraid, very afraid, but right now his indignation won out over fear – that would come later.

Onk and the others had watched in disbelief as Harty, pointing the way to the witch's house, had been accosted in mid-air by a second elf. An elf, who'd grappled him and flown off with Harty tucked under his arm like a daily newspaper. They'd tried to warn him, by waving and shouting up, but the other creature was too fast and Harty seemed to think they were only waving.

"Did that just happen?" asked a stunned Phrack. "Or, did I imagine another elf kidnapped Harty?"

"Harty gone," confirmed Onk, his emotions rolling between anger and sadness as he searched the skies for his friend. He caught sight of the metallic bird following in the elf-nappers wake.

"It isn't too difficult to figure out where the elf must have taken Harty," muttered Phrack. "Initially anyway, because the town of Mothball is where we've just come from. I wish I'd known someone had their eye on our tree elf."

Onk looked at the dwarf sceptically. "There's nothing for it, but to backtrack to town." Phrack sighed in resignation. He and Onk packed their belongings – Upala didn't appear to need any - and the remaining companions re-traced their steps with heavy hearts.

Arriving later in Mothball, the silent elf, with Harty grasped under one arm, zeroed in on one of the houses. *So, someone has been watching me. I hope I'm not about to become fairy fricassee,* Harty mused, remaining curiously calm considering his frightening predicament. The kidnapping elf re-adjusted his heavy load and flew like a supersonic jet in through one of the house's lower windows. In seconds, he had Harty locked inside a filthy bird cage. *Great! Another kidnapping! What is it about my family and people stealing us? I wish I was big and strong like Onk. Nobody thinks about kidnapping him,* bemoaned Harty as he flopped down onto the gritty cage floor.

****

Although Jasper loved having Purity as company, - she was far more delightful than the zooms, - he knew she couldn't stay, she needed to find a way back to Earth. He wasn't aware of the location of any portals through the dimensions but felt sure someone in the nearby town would. He suggested they travel to Mothball and ask there.

The journey was perhaps two days, no more. Purity could ride on his shoulder. Purity blinked away the tears which threatened to fall. Jasper's kind offer of transport reminded her of her Uncle Onk and her home, so very far away.

"What about Lou?" Purity asked, taking her emotions in hand. They hadn't considered what Lou would do with them gone for days. Turning towards Lou, who had cuddled up by Jasper's fire with Slinky and Inky, she leant down. "What do you want to do, Lou?"

Lou had become the happiest hedgerow imp alive, since arriving at Jasper's home. Not only had she found Purity, who had forgiven her, but had been reunited with Gussie too. There was almost no work to do, and definitely no critters to kill. Plus, there was not one, but three Gussies, or zooms, as the stone giant Jasper called them. And, they were asking her, what she wanted to do, rather than ordering her about. *Could my life get any better?* she wondered.

"I'm so sorry Lou," apologised Purity, thinking Lou's silence was due to her unhappiness. "I should have asked what you wanted to do earlier."

"Me's?" Lou replied amazed. "No one's ever asked

what's I's wanted before. I's so happy. To be away's from's that awful witch and that's disgusting smelly demons." Lou shivered at the thought of them. "You's could take's me anywhere's, even down's a worm-hole and I's be happy." She grinned manically, to support her statement of happiness.

Purity surmised Lou didn't mean an actual space-time worm-hole, since it was unlikely Lou had ever attended school, let alone left the Neath Realm. She was speaking literally about a worm-hole, *and she'd be small enough to fit too,* thought Purity, smiling at the picture it created in her head before putting her mind back to work.

"No, I meant do you have a place to go home to?" Lou thought about it. Like Purity, she was born in the manner of all fairies, from the ether, before her parents claimed her. Unlike Purity, she didn't remember much of her early years before Gristle.

"I remember's orphanages. Then there was cages. Then there was Crogg. He bought's me. He give's me to Gristle. I don't remember's when. It was a long's time ago." Lou paused a moment. "Parents never came's for me," she added, in a wistful tone.

"How long have you lived with Gristle?" asked Purity, shocked at Lou's sad tale of childhood compared to her own loving one. "Since I was tiny." Jasper smiled. Lou was still tiny. Hedgerow imps only grew to the size of large beetles.

"That's awful!" sighed a depressed Purity, sinking into one of the armchairs by Jasper's eternally lit fire. "I can't imagine growing up so alone and unloved."

"It wasn't so bad's. There was warm space's by the fires to sleeps and food to eats. I's hated the works most. Killing those beautiful critters. Then Gussie comes. He made's it better." Purity shuddered. She had a problem thinking of snakes, spiders and lizards as 'beautiful,' but she didn't think they should have been slaughtered either. "You know, I's lets a few get away," admitted Lou, lowering her voice to give her confession. "She never knew. It gave me strengths to do the works, knowing I's rescues a few here and there. One of the spiders lives with me, for a while's, after I's releases him. He sleeps in the chimney flue. It's where I's got the idea to hides from Crogg, before Gussie found me." She glanced at the zooms nestled in their favourite spot in front of the fire; a living black puddle.

"So where do you want to stay now?" asked Purity. Lou looked about the room and sighed. Making eye contact with Jasper she spoke.

"Could I's stay here? It's so nice and warms and zooms are beautiful. I's not be any bothers. I's clean and mends and keeps place nice. Please?" Lou stared at Jasper with pleading eyes.

"I can vouch for that, Lou is a hard worker," added Purity, seeing a way to support Lou and find a home for her.

"Zooms, not my zooms," Jasper answered, ignoring her soulful gaze. "Zooms free." Realising she might have said something to jeopardise her chances at staying, Lou tried to re-correct her previous statement.

"Yes, zooms free. Not your zooms, Not my zooms. No-one's zooms." Purity and Jasper looked at each other, then burst out laughing. Lou couldn't see the funny side of it though, her whole future depended on Jasper's response. When he finished laughing and sobered up he noticed Lou seemed a bit puzzled.

"Don't worry Lou," he said, addressing her by her name for the first time. "You're welcome to stay."

"Really? You mean's it? You's not just saying that, because Purity's here?" Jasper frowned and shook his head in the negative. "I's be the best house guest you's ever had. You see if I's not." Lou threw her tiny body onto Jasper's chest and clung to him like a beached limpet at high tide.

Purity was glad to see Lou happy, but it made her miss her parents more. Luckily, neither of them saw the tear she hastily wiped away, before it could ruin the happy moment.

****

Gristle and Crogg were not happy in the slightest. Gristle more so, because she had lost not one, but two servants. She would need to head over to that pathetic excuse for a town and purchase another one, maybe two. She almost turned Crogg into a toad for his lack of discipline in her anger. Obviously, her spelled bangles weren't sufficient. *Crogg should have kept those girls chained up in the kitchen, rather than let them go fiddle-faddling about all over the place. I should have thought of chains. Next time, that's exactly what I'll do. They won't be able to get away so easily then.* Gristle grinned wickedly at her new plan, rubbing her hands together in anticipation.

Crogg wasn't happy either. The work of culling and skinning the animals had fallen to him following the girls' disappearance. He hated that there was no one around to do the dirty work. The sooner Gristle bought new servants the better, in his opinion.

He grabbed another snake with the grabber and carried it at arms-length to the culling tank. He liked snakes, kept one in his pocket as a pet. He wasn't sure how his pet would feel with him killing off hordes of its cousins. It was a bit like keeping a pet chicken and eating take-away chicken, difficult to reconcile.

Yanking her cloak down from the petrified coat stand, one of her earlier failed experiments with golems, Gristle regarded it, then called to Crogg.

"We're leaving. Get your skinny red bottom down here unless you want to become coat-stand number two." Crogg was at her side quicker than a greased whippet down a butter slide.

"Yes, mistress," he whimpered. Listening to Crogg's fawning, Gristle decided she was becoming bored with her 'mistress' title. It didn't carry enough weight. It didn't exude enough power.

"You may call me 'My Queen' from now on," she said, stroking her grey hair as she uttered the word queen.

"Yes… my queen."

Gristle purred in response. *Yes, I like the sound of that.*

"Come, serf." Crogg wasn't sure he liked being referred to as a serf. It was only one step above slave, squire would have been nicer, but there wasn't much he could do about it. Muttering under his breath he followed his queen to town.

Despite living in the Neath umpteen years Gristle had never learnt to fly. There weren't many witches in the Neath to begin with, and now none lived in the immediate area anymore, thanks to Gristle scaring them off. With the local coven abandoned, no one in the region remained to ridicule her inability to command a broomstick.

Gristle marched to town, using her fast witches pace. Crogg, with his mis-jointed spindly red legs and flat feet, struggled to keep up with her. As they travelled, every now and then, Gristle would bellow.

"Crogg!" in her high, screechy voice.

"Coming my queen," Crogg would answer, his voice wheezy and weak, not that Gristle cared about Crogg's well-being. She was a self-centred old woman, who only considered one person's needs – her own.

Poor Crogg was exhausted when Gristle decided to stop for the night. He was expected to set up camp, start a fire and supply Gristle with a meal before he could rest.

Gristle always took the long way around the Tedium Zone. She couldn't abide the noisy residents of the area.

"All that moaning and groaning," she moaned, watching Crogg work his magic. "Can't get a wink of sleep there," she groaned, as Crogg hurriedly laid out her night things and bed-roll. He made do with a tatty blanket, and using his arm as a pillow, fell into slumber listening to Gristle moaning and groaning about the moaning and groaning some more.

When they arrived in Mothball late the following afternoon, Gristle headed straight to the blacksmiths. She ordered several lengths of strong rolo chain and adjustable manacles suitable for fairies. She sent Crogg to secure rooms for the night at the only habitable establishment.

Gristle hated the town and didn't want to be there any longer than necessary, but she needed to sleep before making the long march home. *Tomorrow is the spell trader's last day here till next month. I'll purchase the fairies in the morning, collect a few spell ingredients from that criminal disguised as a trader in the marketplace, have my new servants chained, and be off.*

Sometimes, Gristle sent Crogg in the company of a Demi-Golem to collect the goods she'd ordered, but today she wanted to pick these servants personally, and get a good deal. Besides, the next batch of Demi-Golems wouldn't be ready to hatch for another couple of days. Without them, she didn't fancy tackling that impossible troll. Especially, after her previous disastrous encounter with the oafish brute.

****

Gristle laughed and sniggered at her two new servants. One in particular, had her evil face grinning like a shark who'd cornered a seal. Folk came out of their shops and homes to witness the rare spectacle of the witch Gristle, cavorting like a teenager, down the main high street of their sleepy grey town. She nodded and smiled at the surprised faces oblivious to the reason for their interest. Nothing could mar her happiness today. She was a queen. She had her revenge, and it was sweet.

In her right hand, extended high in the air, Gristle held a cage, and inside the cage, Harty Springfield the Mulberry elf, was holding onto the bars trying not to be sick. Crogg ran beside his queen carrying a second cage, with another male fairy inside. This fairy was young, with black hair and dark eyes. He showed no fear and no concern in his face. He held the bars as if he'd been born behind them.

"Oh happy, happy days," crowed Gristle. "If I can't have the daughter, I'll have the father," she cackled. "Either or both, will bring that dratted troll to me," she sang. "Come Crogg, lets make haste to get home and hatch my darlings."

"Yes, my queen," grovelled Crogg, astounded at Gristle's behaviour. Happiness was so out of character for her. The last time he remembered Gristle this happy, was when she terrified a goblin trader so much, he stepped backwards off a cliff and was eaten by a serpent.

The residents shuddered, shutting their doors and hiding inside after she passed by. They knew nasty things were afoot and they were Gristle-shaped.

18

Gander

As Gristle danced and pranced in sheer delight back to her home, Jasper led Purity through the winding foothill track, that skirted round the edge of the Tedium Zone, towards Mothball. At the same time Onk, Phrack and Upala went in a straight line through the centre of the zone. They didn't bother going around the edge or setting guards when Phrack begged to stop for the night. They didn't light a fire. None of them were as fragile as the little tree elf, and Onk and Upala were sufficient intimidation for any curious night-folk wishing them harm. Despite his concerns, Phrack was snoring like a badger with two pegs up its nose within ten minutes of lying down.

Onk regarded Upala. He noticed that she hadn't sunk into the soil yet, as she did most nights when they stopped. Instead she moved over, coming to stand as close as possible next to him. Regardless what the others thought, he wasn't completely unaware of her feelings towards him. He knew he needed to speak to her about their budding relationship, but he liked Upala's company, preferred it, if truth be told to Harty and Phrack's noisy business. She didn't speak, and her stillness and manner reminded him of his beautiful wife Gem, back on Earth. He missed Gem and the children a great deal. It was the first time they'd been separated in all their years of wedlock. He hadn't acknowledged how much that affected him and realised his homesickness might have given Upala the wrong impression.

"Onk has children," he said, thinking this sentence by itself might be enough to let Upala know he was committed, without him having to say any more. Upala nodded. That didn't seem to do the trick.

"Five children, many years," he confirmed, hoping this would give Upala a stronger hint that he'd been in a relationship for a long time and was off the boyfriend menu. Nothing. She nodded a second time. He had to be explicit, he realised. Show her he was off-limits completely. He was saddened that he'd have to be so blunt, but there was no helping it.

"I miss my wife," he stated, turning to face her. *There! That should do it,* he thought. Upala either didn't understand what Onk was trying to say, or she didn't care. *She'll care when I get home if Gem finds out she's been making up to me and standing this close.* Onk sighed, then he had a brainwave. *Maybe she doesn't know the title 'wife'.*

"My woman misses me," he added, as an afterthought. Upala moved closer upon hearing these words. Onk was baffled by her behaviour and surrendered, acknowledging his defeat at not being able to deter this inflexible stone maiden's advances.

Phrack turned over, apparently rousing briefly from his sleep, or so Onk thought. However, Phrack had not been asleep as Onk imagined. He'd listened to Onk's clumsy attempt to resolve his tricky predicament with Upala, before falling asleep with a knowing grin on his face.

Late afternoon found them back in Mothball, for the second time. They'd observed fairies hanging in cages at the tavern where they had spent the night, so that's where they headed first for information. They spoke to a crusty individual behind the counter, asking him about the fairies suspended overhead.

"Many townsfolk purchase fairies, as pets or servants, from traders in the town," he informed them. "The main trader in Mothball is just along the high street."

The trader seemed to be a gaggle gnome with a penchant for humorous slogans. His shop was four doors down from the tavern, full of fairies and imps in cages, and wooden slogans hanging from chains saying things like 'Gnomeless and 'In need of love,'. 'A gnome is no good without one,' and the ever popular 'Gnome Sweet Gnome'. Phrack cringed at the cheesy humour, but they needed more information, and according to the tavern worker, this was the best place to start.

Onk wasn't happy seeing sentient species in cages. He started growling as soon as they entered the store. The gaggle gnome was a species known for their propensity to talk endlessly, hence gaggle. They made good traders, wearing many customers down by their expansive verbosity until the customer mumbled, "Just take my money. Please!"

The three would-be heroes browsed the cages hanging for sale in the store. None contained their mulberry elf, so Phrack decided to question the owner.

"We're looking for our friend," he murmured softly, not wanting to cause a scene. The gaggle gnome stared at the three individuals, then glanced around his shop, and then over his shoulder, like some crook checking the coast was clear. He ignored the life forms residing in their cage cells looking down.

"There's no one here but us," the gnome assured Phrack, after satisfying himself the place was empty of other customers. It was obvious to the gnome that this buyer was sensitive about talking business in front of the merchandise. "If its privacy you're after…"

Onk was trembling with pent-up rage by this point, disgusted by the gaggle gnome's wicked livelihood in the slave trade. His pacing had begun, causing the cages nearby to rock alarmingly. The inmates were holding on to their bars in fear, and Upala was looking very impressed with his sudden bout of marching. She remembered what happened last time Onk began marching, next to the lava river.

Unfortunately, the hapless slave trader was concentrating on Phrack, where he assumed the sale, and hence his next amount of money was coming from. He saw the two giants as mere employees of Phrack. That was, right until Onk marched past Phrack, plucked the gnome off the ground by his shirt and roared into his face, spraying troll spittle in a large area around the offending gnome.

"Where is Harty Springfield?" Onk bellowed. Surprisingly, the Gnome wasn't deterred as expected. Phrack guessed this type of thing must happen a lot based on the gaggle gnome's calm reaction in the face of Onk's purple-faced fury.

"Springfield, Springfield?" He mumbled, hanging like a piece of damp washing from Onk's outstretched arm. "I don't recall the name."

"What my friend is trying to say," interjected Phrack, "is that someone stole our friend, a tree elf, and we'd like him back please."

"Oh yes, yes, I can see how you would want that. Losing a friend is terrible, terrible. I lost a friend once…" Onk shook the gnome till his teeth rattled.

"No flannel! Where is Harty?" Onk snarled, his voice dropping a decibel.

"My friend Onk here doesn't take well to flannel," smiled Phrack. "We just want the friend you stole back."

"Steal, steal!" squeaked the gnome, who it appeared was in the habit of repeating himself when under stress. "I don't steal anything, anything. What type of trader do you take me for?" He appeared genuinely horrified at such a suggestion. "I'll have you know every fairy and elf here has volunteered, volunteered." The three companions looked stunned.

Onk opened his hand and the gnome sort of slid out. Straightening up his clothes into a semblance of order, the gnome addressed the would-be heroes who were obviously in dire need of educating.

"Yes, volunteered. Roxley Routan the third doesn't 'steal' anything. As if I would." He gazed round at his collection of cages. Inside, every inhabitant was shaking their head at the unjust treatment of their boss.

"Let me get this straight. Folk come to you to be sold as slaves?"

"No, no, no. Never slaves. Fairies and elves come to me to earn money. We complete a contract, work out the percentages and they sell their time. Some agree to complete difficult fiddly tasks for species with large hands, or no hands at all, who can't manage. Others undertake speciality work like jewellery making or sewing. Some offer to be pets for a specified time. It's all up to them." Onk was amazed, so was Upala judging by her face. The gnome went on, "These…" He spread his arms wide to indicate the cages suspended above him, "…are my clients. They need somewhere to sit and highlight their abilities otherwise they might get missed, or worse still, trodden on." They regarded the hanging cages more closely and saw several fairy species doing intricate activities, like sewing or working with precious gems. It made perfect sense when they thought about it.

"You aren't a slave trader?" probed Phrack, suddenly unsure that their indignant position was the right one.

"No, no no, far from it," answered Roxley truthfully, relieved that the penny had finally dropped.

"So, where is Harty?"

"Not here my friend, not here. I don't need to steal anyone, they all come to my door freely. Though I can't say the same for other unscrupulous criminals," he whispered, lowering his voice. They trooped out of Roxley's shop heads low and out of ideas.

With no clue what to do next they headed towards the edge of town, where Upala, gave Onk and Phrack their second surprise of the afternoon. Holding up her hand she spoke her first clear word.

"Wait," she mumbled. Her voice, not accustomed to talking sounded like a large bag of marbles on a conveyor belt. She sank to her knees and literally dissolved into the dirt. There was nothing more they could do, so Onk and Phrack got a fire going and sat down by it.

"Where do you suppose she's gone?" asked Phrack. Onk shrugged. The sky moved to the darker grey they'd become accustomed to which heralded the advance of night. Phrack was settling down to sleep since nothing else seemed imminent, when the soil to his left erupted in a cacophony of stones. After much rattling and sliding, they morphed into Upala.

She looked disturbed, more disturbed than the stones trying to form a cohesive body around her. That had taken several minutes and usually she stood fully formed in seconds. Something had unsettled her usual calm demeanour. She looked at Onk the need for reassurance clear in her eyes.

Despite his earlier one-sided conversation with her, he went to her and held her. He couldn't believe it, she was trembling. What could intimidate a stone queen he wondered – and then he found out. The ground began shaking like an earthquake was starting up. Their campfire snuffed out and darkness drew in. The dwarf felt the stirrings of panic in his chest.

"Maybe we should head back into town for the night? he suggested. Onk and Upala rapidly agreed. Phrack turned to pick up his Gander bag when a stone hand shot out of the soil and grabbed Phrack's precious heirloom. He squealed in alarm, grasping the bag in turn, but the hand wouldn't release it and the dwarf was no match for it. It drew its treasure down into the ground and vanished. The soil settled, the groaning stopped, and all was silent, except for Phrack wailing about his priceless bag being stolen.

"Everything I own is in that Gander bag!" he lamented, sobbing loudly. "All me possessions. All me memories!" He sat on the ground holding his head in his hands, shaking it to and fro in disbelief. Onk felt a bit embarrassed by a grown man crying over a bag. He didn't understand the meaning of a Gander bag to a dwarf.

The Gander bag was given to each male stone dwarf as a child. It was magicked to hold more on the inside than could be seen on the outside, a bit like a Tardis. However, unlike a Tardis the more items put inside the heavier the bag became until, when a dwarf was full grown, it was almost impossible to lift. At that point, the dwarf placed it on the ground and custom dictated, that was where he married and settled down.

Phrack had settled down in the Fire Realm, marrying his love and living with her till her death during the birth of their last child, five years ago. He'd lost his wife and newborn son and understandably had never really got over it. Everything he had belonging to his wife and family was in that bag. Losing it tore what was left of his heart apart and he fell to pieces.

Upala was touched by the short man's anguish. She knelt beside him and whispered in her gravelly voice, not unlike Onk's.

"We find."

Phrack lifted his head, his face a mess of tears and tried to look convinced. He failed miserably and dropping his head back down, rested his chin on his chest.

Onk wasn't happy. First, they'd lost Harty and now, despite him not understanding its importance, they'd lost Phrack's bag. He thumped down onto the ground beside the dwarf.

"We find Harty and Gander," he bellowed, daring Phrack to disagree. This time Phrack lifted his head and smiled in earnest.

"I guess with you's two helping we ken but try," Phrack sniffed, drying his tears. He stood. "And I think I know exactly whom we can ask, come morning."

19

Reunion

MORNING found the reduced party of three stomping into the east end of Mothball, as Jasper and Purity arrived from the west, after spending the night on the outskirts of town.

Purity had been more than a little stunned when they camped for the evening. As she unrolled her blanket Jasper sank into the ground before her and seemed to disintegrate into a pile of small stones. It was almost more unnerving when he returned, clutching a bag full to the brim with supplies, but sadly for Jasper no tin of chocolate.

Jasper travelled to the town to trade on numerous occasions, so Purity assumed this was his way of procuring supplies, she had no idea he had stolen the bag. After Purity and Jasper had eaten a quick breakfast, she packed up her bedroll, then they headed straight towards Mothball and Jasper's goal, the slime troll selling potions and spells.

"I think we can find out everything we need from the potion trader," postulated Phrack, as they trod their way towards the market at the west end of town. "I bet that troll will know where Harty is and what, or who, took my gander bag."

In addition to those two concerns, Onk was also worried about Upala. Her behaviour had changed since the disappearance of Phrack's Gander bag. She was quieter, if that was possible for a person who had hardly spoken since she materialised. For Onk, that meant her body language was less animated. In fact, she hadn't displayed any facial expressions since the previous night, but a vast array of colours strobed across her skin which Onk knew was her basic form of communication.

He correctly surmised that she knew something about the bag's disappearance, maybe even Harty's location. He said nothing. He was confident that when she was ready Upala would speak either verbally or non-verbally.

****

Jasper, with Purity on his shoulder, entered the market from the west side. While Onk, Phrack and Upala arrived on the east. Phrack noticed the market seemed to be buzzing with more than its usual frenzy of buying and selling. *Something's not quite right here,* he concluded.

Phrack thought he saw someone he knew heading through the milling crowd – an old comrade. He watched as the towering demon left the market on the far side and entered one of the local taverns. The dwarf briefly considered going over to say hello, for it had been ages since they had met, but he had other priorities and now wasn't the time for a drinking reunion.

Distracted by catching sight of his old friend, Phrack failed to notice the second, tall man, striding with purpose through the market place. This one was made of stone, like Upala, and had a pet fairy resting on his shoulder. Upala froze in place at the sight of the man, and Onk, seeing Upala's posture freeze turned to face her, missing the stone giant who passed behind him intent on reaching a trader's stall.

It was Purity who recognised her uncle Onk's back and squealed such a high-pitched scream that the whole marketplace - along with Upala - froze. Without thinking, Purity launched herself from the safety of Jasper's shoulder towards her favourite Uncle. She struggled to stay level and fly true, due to her infantile wings, but her mind was too preoccupied with seeing her uncle again to curse their incompetence.

"Uncle Onk! Uncle Onk!" she sobbed, tears of happiness falling from her cheeks. "I knew it. I knew you'd come looking for me." Despite the difficulty, she landed like thistledown on his shoulder and hugged her uncle's wide neck, not caring for once, who watched her obvious display of affection.

Using his little finger, Onk patted Purity's back and uttered sweet reassurances in her ear, like he'd been taught to do by his wife for their own children. It brought a lump to his throat, reminding him of all the hours he spent with his offspring, and Purity too on occasion. When they were unwell, when they had nightmares, when they were scared of doing, or asking for something, when they were playing, usually at Onk's expense. His eyes filled with tears, though he held them tight within his eyes, using his hand to quickly wipe away any which threatened to fall.

The market folk stood around in various degrees of embarrassment and discomfort at such an open outpouring of emotion. A few shed a tear at the unusual sight. Residents of the dark dimensions didn't do tears often. One by one, the traders and their customers slowly returned to their wares.

Purity stayed where she was for several minutes, happy

to be with her uncle, happy to be found. She forgot the others momentarily as her mind hung on to the realisation that she might be going home. When she'd hugged her uncle for what she felt was a good amount of time, she leaned back and stared into his eyes.

"Thank you for coming to get me Uncle Onk." Onk smiled down at his favourite niece perched on his shoulder.

"Uncle Onk," he declared, pointing to his chest as if those two words said it all.

"Yes," smiled Purity, then glancing round she asked the question he was dreading. "Where's dad?"

Leaning out from Onk's shoulder, as she'd done many times as a small child, she gazed around the market, which was getting back to normal. "I can't see him anywhere," she continued, lifting up onto her tippy-toes, like two millimetres would make any difference to her view.

"Gone," said Onk simply. There was nothing else to say. Purity swivelled from looking out at the market to staring up at her uncle.

"What do you mean, gone?" she demanded, a puzzled look on her face.

"Stolen."

"Stolen?" she repeated, her mouth dropping open in surprise. Phrack felt the time for happy-families was over and besides, he'd noticed something Onk hadn't.

"Yes, stolen," Phrack announced angrily, interrupting the reunion. "Just like my Gander bag was stolen by this big galoot with you." As Phrack spoke, he stomped across to where Jasper stood riveted to the spot, and without a thank-you-very-much, grabbed the bag hanging from Jasper's limp hand. It was Phrack's precious missing gander bag. He hugged it close, then ducked his head in the bag to check all the contents were in order. That done, in moments he was back by Onk's side.

While Onk and Purity had been re-uniting, another

union, of a sort was occurring without them knowing. If Phrack noticed, he said nothing.

Upala and Jasper stood immobile, staring at each other across the ten-foot space. Upala appeared to sigh every now and then, but otherwise they were both as still as stone. Then, the ground started rumbling, stopping Purity's next question about her father. She turned to Jasper with a different question on her lips, then noticed he seemed to be shaking or vibrating like a washing machine. To Onk's left, stood a strange stone female who appeared similar to Jasper in build and colour. She was twitching uncontrollably too.

Upala had understood the meaning of the rumbling ground the night before. When the strong, definitely male hand protruded from the ground, she knew its significance, but how to tell the others was beyond her vocal ability. She hadn't been formed into 'The One' for long and wasn't able to talk well enough, let alone express her emotions ver-bally. She felt like a baby learning to walk and talk, she couldn't do all the things the others in her party took for granted. They had mistakenly assumed because she was queen, she'd been around for years. She had, in demon stone form, but not in 'The One' shape, her first ever 'One' shape.

The arrival of the other 'One' had stunned Upala. She didn't know what to make of him, or what to do next. She'd followed Phrack and Onk because like a child, she didn't know any better. She hadn't expected to sense him again, let alone see him. Now they were joining. It was supposed to be instinctual, but she was terrified. She wanted to run and hide behind Onk. Uncle Onk, the tiny fairy had called him. Upala would like Onk to be her uncle too, she decided, Onk was strong and safe.

Again, the marketplace stopped to observe the bizarre goings-on of the strangers in their midst. Those with any sense and knowledge of demon stones moved to a safe distance. Noticing folk around them getting out of the way, Phrack suggested they give Upala and the man some room, he had a sneaky suspicion it was about to get busy. They had just reached the other side of a stall when an explosion lifted them, and most of the market people, off their feet.

When Onk, Purity and Phrack had recovered from being thrown to the ground, they rose and peered cautiously over the edge of the up-turned stalls. There was no sign of Upala or Jasper. What had become of their fellow travellers? The ground appeared undamaged, despite the massive explosion which should have ripped a crater the size of a dragon in the soil. The same couldn't be said of the market, many of the stalls were on their sides. Stock from dozens of traders had been strewn across the area like confetti. Most of the food produce was spoilt, even the hardware gnome suffered, groaning at seeing his pots missing lids and his pans dented. Several street urchins took advantage of the free food, ignoring the stall-holders shouts to bring it back. In the epicentre, a few solitary demon stones were seen burrowing into the ground.

"What happened?" asked Purity, amazed and concerned too. "Thank goodness Lou decided to stay home," she murmured. "She might have been on Jasper's shoulder when that happened." The others didn't have a clue who Purity was talking about. Onk was saddened that Upala was gone. Then Purity gasped. "Oh goodness, where's Gussie? He came along with us, while the other two stayed at home with Lou."

Phrack and Onk still didn't have a clue who, or what, Purity was rambling on about. *What's a Gussie?* wondered Onk.

"Let's go and catch-up somewhere," suggested a helpful Phrack. Without thinking, they walked back to the same tavern Harty, Phrack and Onk had stayed in overnight, sitting down at a table near the fire.

It was the first time Purity had seen fairies sitting in cages suspended from the ceiling. She was appalled. Phrack explained the idea of bartering contracts and then went on to tell her what he knew of her father's search. Onk nodded in the relevant places when she looked to him for confirmation of Phrack's account.

Purity, in turn, told them of her flight from Gristle's home. Of Lou, the hedgerow imp's deception and the fact they'd made up since, Purity forgiving the imp, as was her nature. She told them of Jasper's kindness and of Gussie and the other zooms. Then she realised Lou was home alone and Purity had no idea how to get there.

"Oh, my goddess, what shall I do?" Her concern for Lou was clear, though from what Onk heard Lou wasn't the best example of a friend, unlike his niece.

"Don't you worry about Lou," smiled Phrack. "Somehow I don't think our stone friends are gone forever." Onk was relieved to hear that and said so.

"Onk misses Upala."

"Yes uncle. I miss Jasper too."

"Well, I think both of them will be back shortly," stated Phrack, with his adult-wise head on. Onk and Purity turned to Phrack expecting an explanation, but he refused to say any more on the subject. Failing to get a response, Purity moved the conversation to her father.

"Where is he?" she asked. "I can't believe he came all this way to find me and got captured himself. How are we ever going to find him now? He could be anywhere."

"I have an idea about that too," said Phrack. "We were going there when we came across you." Purity decided she might like this new companion. Phrack reminded her of her father, full of ideas, and solutions, a glass-half-full type of person.

The day was half gone by the time they had finished swapping stories and eating. The newly formed trio decided to have an early night and tackle the slime troll trader in the morning. There was also the outside chance that Upala and Jasper might return. Phrack slept soundly with his gander bag wrapped tightly in his arms. Purity slept peacefully lying across her uncle Onk's chest. Onk however, struggled to sleep. He was worried about his friends, Harty and Upala.

The following morning the three of them headed off to the market, they found most of the traders packing up. They stopped one trader to ask what was happening.

"We's only do's a seven day in each's towns," the gnome lisped. "Then we's moves on." The trio were horrified. They ran to where the slime troll stall was situated. It was gone, and so was any chance of getting information to locate Purity's father.

"That's it," groaned Phrack, sinking to the ground. He was beginning to think he should have stayed in the Fire Realm. *All this running around is tiring and I'm not getting any younger.* He remembered his grandfather used to say that phrase a lot. *Am I turning into him?* he wondered.

The slime troll in question, Tory Tello, had packed up his stall early. He was fed up with the lack of trade. *I could have made more money giving out information, based on the last few days enquiries,* he grumbled. As he pushed his cart along, Tory considered this phenomenon. *I wonder whether there's profit to be made running a business which buys and sells knowledge. Knowledge about folks' whereabouts, about the weather, about where to find someone who could do specific things, I could direct folk to their goal.* Then Tory recognised a potential flaw in his business idea. *I couldn't possibly hold all that information in my head though, I'd need to write it down, maybe more than once.*

If I did that I might as well sell copies. I'd call it a… 'Direct-Tory', he decided, *… and it would need updating every year. Businesses might pay me to place their information in the Direct-Tory, then I could give out free copies each year to* townsfolk. *I might call it the 'Tello-Pages' after me, because it would tell people what they needed to know. Or, perhaps I'll use my date of birth 11, 8, 118*, based on the new Neath calendar. Calendars were changed every time another demon took over the realm.

As the creative slime troll thought about his latest flash in the pan idea, he shook his head and frowned. *It will never catch on*, he decided, as he pushed his wares out through the town and into the grey countryside. *Who would be gullible enough to want one?*

★★★★

Gristle meanwhile was still skipping around at home.

"My new Demi-Golems will be ripe enough to pick in three hours," she giggled, in that uncharacteristic school-girl voice she used when she was happy. "That infernal tree elf is locked up nice and tight too," she continued, rubbing her palms together in glee. "There be no letting him sleep in the kitchen. I was just too kind to that other lazy wretch. Fancy her running away after all my years of care, the ungrateful imp. The other male I purchased can do the culling with Crogg," she concluded, cavorting around her dining room chairs as she moved towards her study.

Crogg wasn't happy at having to restart the awful work of killing every day. He wasn't a very wicked demon, and though he didn't have a very kind heart, he didn't like cruelty. He had hoped both the new boys would be put to work on the farm.

"Why should I's have to get me's hands dirty?" he groused. "Should be those new 'uns." Plus, he'd been ordered to feed the older, locked up one. Well, that wasn't going to happen. He'd let the new servant do the serving of food to the prisoner or he could starve.

The new 'boy' didn't speak. Crogg reckoned he was

about the same age as Purity who'd run away. "That's the problem with young uns," he continued. "No stamina. I's going to make sure this one's doesn't scarper." Crogg manacled the young boy's ankles tight so he could walk, but not run.

Harty observed the young elf closely when he hobbled into the room with a plate of food for him. There wasn't much on the plate, only scraps from Gristle's table. Harty wasn't impressed with the food, but there was something familiar about the elf. He appeared roughly the same age as his daughter, but where Purity was blonde with blue eyes, this elf was dark-haired with even darker almost-black eyes. Yet, the way he moved, the shape of his face, reminded Harty a lot of Purity. On his back, were adult wings in bud just like his daughter's too. He wouldn't be able to fly free yet, his infantile wings were far too small and weak to lift his growing body any great distance from the ground. He could probably just about manage to hover, but not fly free. *It's likely how he got caught,* Harty accurately guessed. Harty bet, like Purity too, his buds were itching terribly. He would have offered to scratch his back if he didn't think the youth would find it a bit odd. *His parents must be missing him terribly.*

For some reason, that single thought caused a pain deep inside Harty's chest which he couldn't explain. The boy didn't speak, his whole demeanour was solemn and withdrawn. He didn't look up, just laid the plate in reach as he'd been instructed and left. Harty missed his opportunity to start a conversation with the boy.

****

Back in Mothball, the others had to decide on their next step.

"We need to find and rescue my father," stated Purity, taking no argument from the frowning burly stone dwarf.

On second thoughts, she wasn't sure if she liked Phrack, let alone trusted him, after observing his obsessive behaviour over his stupid supply bag. However, her Uncle Onk did, and that was recommendation enough, she supposed. "What happened exactly?"

Phrack explained how her father had been up in the air trying to locate Gristle's house from above, when another fairy, possibly an elf, snatched him from the sky. As Mothball was the only populated place for miles, they naturally retraced their steps to the town in the hope of finding him there. However, their quest had proved fruitless when they discovered the slime troll trader, their only source of information, had vanished. What's more, they learnt the majority of fairies in the Neath, actually sold themselves into servitude legally, rather than be stolen and sold into slavery.

"But that's what happened to Lou," Purity insisted. "Lou told me she was stolen and sold, so not all traders of fairies are honest. There must be someone else in this town, apart from that slime troll, who knows where such unscrupulous deals are made.

Roxley Routan the third wasn't happy to see the strangers back in his shop again. At least the stone female was missing. He took an immediate professional interest in the young female fairy accompanying them this time, thinking she'd fetch a high price in certain areas.

"Remember us?" started Phrack. "We came to see you yesterday."

"'Yes. Yes, I remember," commented Roxley wryly. He almost added how happy he be to see them go again too. "I've already told you I don't have your friend."

Phrack wasn't sure how to phrase his next question without upsetting the gaggle gnome.

"We know, and we understand you are a reputable dealer in fairy skills." A few tiny eyebrows went up around the room. "We know now that our friend has been stolen and we need to know who might have done such a thing."

"And you think I would know of such an occurrence," countered Roxley, clutching his chest in mock indignation.

"You are the only bonafide dealer in town…" agreed Phrack, his voice trailing off as he ran out of more to say which wouldn't sound contrived. More eyebrows rose in the room and several cage occupants stopped what they were doing to listen in on the conversation.

Roxley was well aware his employees were listening. He couldn't afford to look deceitful, or else these fairy clients might not utilise his services. Lowering his voice to whisper he beckoned the three into a huddle so as not to be overheard.

"I don't agree with the selling of slaves you understand." They all nodded conspiratorially. "However, I'll admit I have heard of this happening." Roxley lifted his head to check on the room. Every fairy was leaning forward to catch any words they could. "I have been aware for some time of an establishment in Mothball, on Slavers Row, where this type of disgusting deed is practiced."

"Slavers Row!" huffed Phrack. "It's unbelievable! We didn't need to speak to that greasy gaggle gnome. We could have walked around town and found it ourselves in five minutes. It cost me two pairs of good fire lizard boots for that information." Onk and Purity felt embarrassed. When Roxley Routan had requested payment for the information on the illicit slaver trade, they had nothing on them to sell, but Phrack had his precious Gander bag and in it…

"Day-night gnome robbery! That's what it is," he groused. "Some people have no idea about morals."

"Luckily for us," suggested Purity. Onk nodded. "We weren't to know," she continued, trying to appease the stressed stone dwarf. "We might have spent hours looking for somewhere and missed Slavers Row altogether."

Phrack gave her a disbelieving glance. It turned out to be the exact place where the slime troll trader ran his stall. He couldn't believe they hadn't noticed it before, but then they were searching for the trader not the address of slavers.

They found the shop Roxley had described and he was right, there was no comparison between it, and Roxley Routan's establishment. This was a shabby little back-street premises where one expected bad things to happen – regularly.

Onk had to duck to get through the doorway, then lean his head to the left once inside, unless he sat down. He sat down. Phrack approached the orc behind the counter. There were hanging cages here too, but these were all covered in thick black sacking.

"I'm looking for a tree elf," Phrack began.

"I's give you's two for the fairy," spat the toothless orc, leering at Purity. Purity shuddered in revulsion, his ogling stare made her feel unclean.

"I'm not here to sell, or buy, I'm here to…"

"Then get's lost, before I set's the security ghouls on you's," interrupted the orc, before Phrack could finish his sentence. The dwarf glanced over his shoulder checking the room for ghouls, before he began again. "No. We believe you obtained a tree elf illegally, and probably sold him recently too."

"Ghouls, ghouls," shouted the orc, expecting Phrack and his friends to run. Onk had had enough. He wasn't stressed out like his friends, but there was a limit to his patience. He rose with his head on one side - due to the low ceiling - and lunged at the orc. The good thing about lunging was it lowered his head away from the ceiling, so he could hold it upright and roar more effectively into the orc's face.

"Elf. Who?" he bellowed, enjoying the moment, as the orc closed his watering eyes to escape Onk's fetid breath. The orc managed to squeak one word.

"Gristle."

That was enough for Onk. *Will that horrid witch ever leave my friends and family alone?* he fumed. After that, the orc dealer was very amenable and happy to assist with their enquiries, he even provided explicit directions to Gristle's home. Anything to get the fearsome troll out of his shop. The orc's eardrums had burst under Onk's verbal assault, and all his hair, what he had of it, had turned white and fallen out in shock. Phrack and Purity felt a little guilty about that. They left the grubby orc standing in the middle of his dirty room with hair all around him on the floor, like fallen snow.

Onk marched out of Slavers Row, across the town of Mothball and straight into the Tedium Zone like it didn't exist. Purity rode on his shoulder and Phrack stomped on behind. They stopped overnight in the middle of the zone, because Phrack still needed to rest. Nothing came to bother them. Phrack was beginning to wonder if the stories he'd heard of ferocious nocturnal beasts, who ate dwarves, was just a rumour to scare folk. He'd never seen anything nasty and they'd crossed it three times now, not counting their current trek across the grey wasteland. In reality, the creatures that dwelt in the zone, sensing that the troll and his companions were in no mood for their tomfoolery, no matter how hungry they were, stayed away from the three travellers.

Onk remained distressed over Upala's disappearance. She hadn't returned to them as she usually did, despite Phrack's reassurance that she would. Onk worried about her safety. The last time they had been close, she had been trembling badly. He didn't think that was a good sign.

Next morning, they rose early and followed their previous footprints which remained visible in the grey dust and mud. Onk led them, turning left to face the foothills as the orc advised once they reached the edge of the zone.

They saw the house long before they reached it and

halted. It wasn't the house that stopped them in their tracks, but the row upon row of Demi-Golems standing to attention in front of it. Gristle knew they'd be coming. She'd been preparing for their arrival.

"Did they think they could dance up to my door and ask for that pathetic tree elf back? Did they think I'd whimper and whine and give in to their demands?" she monologued. "What fools!"

The golems didn't move, they didn't blink or smile, or breathe. They waited for their instructions from their mistress. Then the moaning began.

20

Hungry

PHRACK and Onk recognised the sound. They'd heard it before when they first travelled over the Tedium Zone on their way to Mothball. Now they were experiencing it up close and personal. To Purity, it sounded and looked like all her worst night-terrors rolled into one massive throat-stopping, gut-wrenching nightmare. What's more, she thought she had heard that sound before. The tiny hairs on her arms and the back of her neck rose as her fear escalated ten-fold.

Gristle sat at an upstairs window, watching the scene below with anticipation. She clapped her gnarled hands together in glee at the havoc she was about to wreak. Harty had been given a birds-eye view too from his cage. He wasn't going anywhere. He had no chance of gaining his freedom on his own. He was imprisoned inside an iron cage, a silver manacle welded around his left ankle. Both his palms bore blisters where he had grabbed hold of the iron, fearing for his life, when Gristle swung his cage back and forth as she pranced out of Mothball on her journey home. The manacle was welded to a length of silver chain, which was in turn welded to one of the bars. The manacle had been personally welded on by Crogg, and Harty had the burns to prove it. If he was rescued, it would have to be like a bird in a cage. He didn't have much hope for his own survival, but he was terrified for his friends.

"Why are you doing this?" he asked the mad witch. "What have we ever done to you?" he implored, calling down to Gristle from his prison cage as it swung wildly from a hook hammered into the ceiling, also courtesy of Crogg.

Admittedly, Onk had accidentally banished Gristle into the Neath Realm, but she started it with her persecution of Purity even before she was born. "Can't you just leave us alone?"

"No," she crowed, turning to look up at Harty. It was the first time she'd addressed the elf since his incarceration. *If only I can keep the witch talking, keep her distracted. Maybe the others might have a chance to get away.* "You ruined my spell. You ruined my life and now I'm going to ruin yours and make you watch." Gristle sprayed Harty with a face-full of spittle, as she eyeballed him through the bars whilst balancing on her tippy-toes on her chair. To Gristle's way of thinking, after the blasted troll, this elf was directly responsible for all her troubles. "You're a no-good interfering busy-body," she harped on. "If you hadn't helped that stupid lump of a troll, rescue that cocoon, that unborn fairy would have been my property, to use in any way I wanted."

This was Harty's daughter Purity, who the witch was prattling on about. Harty swallowed hard and fought for control of his emotions. He realised how close he'd come to never having a family at all, not a wife, not a child – nothing. He couldn't imagine life without either. There was no way this disgusting old hag was going to jeopardise their future happiness.

Onk was always up for a fight, but he had to admit the odds

here weren't good. There was him, an ageing stone dwarf and a fairy three inches tall.

The three companies of Demi-Golems, twenty to each company, spread out in three horizontal rows facing the would-be rescuers. The golems stood, voicing their classic pre-attack moaners drone, a tactic guaranteed to make grown demons shudder and lesser mortals run away - very fast. The golems didn't move, because they hadn't been commanded to move. Until they were given that command, they would stay put as per their current orders – whatever they were!

"What shall we do?" asked Purity. "Why aren't they attacking us?"

"I don't know, but why don't we turn around and go away very quietly?" suggested Phrack. He didn't like their odds and frankly, running away and hiding in the dark somewhere seemed an excellent idea. Purity glared at him.

"That's my father in there," she growled, the sound a miniature version of her uncle.

"I know, my dear, I really do," replied Phrack, realising his comment might have been the wrong thing to say. Trying to placate her he added, "I'm not sure what we can accomplish on our own, that's all. I think we might need reinforcements."

"And you happen to know of some in the middle of nowhere, do you?" she retorted tartly, shades of a sullen teenager emerging.

"I just might do," answered the cryptic dwarf, staring at the immovable company.

"Darrr!" grumbled Gristle. "They're backing off. They're not supposed to do that!"

"I'd do that," offered Harty. Gristle immediately took her frustration out on the tree elf.

"Why are they backing off, elf?" she cursed, scowling up

at him. "Answer me," she insisted. "Or I'll pull your wings off."

"Why are you asking me?" replied Harty, his face up close between the bars despite his fears. "I'd back away too if faced with sixty Demi-Golems." Suddenly, something clicked into place inside Harty's head. He realised he'd had enough of being afraid all the time There was only so much fear one person could carry in their head. *So what if my wings fall off with the dreaded IBS? A lot of folk seem to manage without the use of wings and it doesn't look like I'm going to get out of here anytime soon.* This change in thinking made the mulberry elf fearless. "Maybe they've gone to get something to eat first?" he offered, surprising himself at his flippant tone. "They must be starving after trooping all the way here," he suggested, struggling to keep the sarcasm out of his voice. *What's wrong with me? Have I got a death wish to be killed by this horrible witch?* Harty wondered.

The truth was that whenever Harty Springfield was faced with the prospect of imminent death, he became flippant and couldn't help seeing humour in every precious moment. Gristle, on the other hand, was seriously contemplating the possibility that the daft elf might be right.

"I suppose it is possible," she conceded. "Trolls eat a great deal and are led by their stomachs." Harty nodded his head vigorously encouraging Gristle's thoughts in that direction. Gristle continued her one-sided conversation oblivious to Harty's intended misdirection. "There isn't a lot to eat in the Neath unless, like me, you can turn things and people into food. I know trolls don't have that ability. Ok elf, they've gone to get food," she agreed, and stomped away to her kitchen because all this talk about food had made Gristle hungry.

The travel weary trio meanwhile, were traipsing back to Mothball for the fifth time.

"Tell me again why we're running away," queried Purity petulantly. She was revising her assessment of the stone dwarf's personality yet again, and now, with his plan to run away, she wasn't sure whether she liked him or not. He wasn't displaying positive qualities she admired in any great amount. "I saw my father in a cage next to the witch, in that upstairs window," she told them, pointing to the first floor. Though she couldn't fly freely, Purity had managed, with effort, to hover high enough to get a better view of the stand-off.

At least he isn't dead yet. I mustn't think like that, she admonished herself. *Gristle's more likely to keep him secure and fed, like she did me, than injure a potential worker.*

"We're not 'running away' as you so aptly put it child," said Phrack, interrupting Purity's deliberations. He used the term 'child' to highlight the fact that she wasn't in charge. "We are retreating to gather reinforcements, as I said earlier."

"Reinforcements! What reinforcements? We don't know anyone in the Neath." Purity wanted to scream, and she didn't miss his put-down of her either. Outwardly, she tried to remain calm for her father's sake.

"You might not know anyone in the Neath, but I do," smiled Phrack, tapping the side of his nose to suggest he had a secret. *He is so infuriating*, Purity decided.

The hidden inhabitants of the Tedium Zone left the group of commuters alone on their trek back again. Onk, like Phrack, was also starting to think the stories about scary creatures were made-up. Either that, or they weren't interested in catching and eating a troll or a stone dwarf.

Their arrival back in town, caused a greater stir than them leaving, since word had got around that they were going to challenge Gristle. Nobody did that and kept their original shape.

The locals peered, crawled or slithered around their

doors to stare at the troll, the dwarf and their new pet. High above, a speck no more than a metallic glint soared in the sky. Onk lifted his eyes skyward, checking that his follower was still there.

Phrack led them down the main street towards a less affluent part of town. They looked down Slavers Row as they passed – it was empty. They passed Gallows Retreat and Deadman's passage and still Phrack walked. He called a stop outside a building, *presumably some kind of tavern*, Purity thought, *judging by the stench of stale beer wafting through the doorway.*

It was seedy and rundown, not the type of establishment someone like Purity, or her mother Shine, would ever think of putting a delicate foot inside. The name plate, hanging at a jaunty angle by one chain announced the place to be called, 'The Executioner'. *Folk in Mothball sure have a funny sense of humour*, she thought.

Inside, The Executioner was no different to ten other taverns in Mothball, folk were drinking or drunk, gambling or broke, awake or asleep. It was the outside of the tavern which made it stand out from the crowd. Lined up on either side of the western-style saloon doors were two rows of motorcycles. These weren't shiny café racer bikes, with full fairings and comfy seats, these were what mortals would have called rat bikes, if they could have seen them.

Each motorbike was held together by an odd assortment of different materials, from the expected rivets, bolts and screws to string, glue and elastic. Not one bike had any paint left on it unless rust had become a shade. The overall assembly of each vehicle resembled an art installation in a metal recycling plant, rather than any form of transportation.

Onk was impressed by the amazing array of heavy metal. He walked along the row admiring each rat bike in turn. He liked the raised handlebars, the cross-shaped mirrors and the high sissy bars. He stopped beside the second bike, after his quick review of the others, to admire it more closely.

"Pretty," he announced loudly almost crooning. "Very pretty." Phrack smiled.

"Yes, one of my better designs I think."

Purity, sitting on Onk's shoulder was astonished.

"You made this?" she asked gobsmacked, daring the dwarf to confirm his statement and say yes.

"Actually, I made five of these bikes. The black one Onk has taken a shine to, that grey one next to it. The camouflage rat bike with drop handlebars, and those two at the end." Phrack pointed to a matching pair of hybrid trail bikes.

"I thought you said you made shoes?" accused Purity.

"Mmm yes, I make shoes now, but when I lived elsewhere I made motorbikes." Purity couldn't believe it. "I've made a bunch of other items in my time, but these are my favourite." Onk wasn't just impressed, he was mesmerised. Before either could ask more, Phrack added his most vital piece of information, "I also made friends."

As he uttered the word friends, a stream of huge, menacing individuals poured from the tavern and crowded around the three of them. The bikers wanted to know who was eyeing up their machines.

Purity saw folk of different species, sizes and genders, most were demons, but all of them without exception, were wearing the same shabby clothes, mainly greasy jeans and worn leather jackets. They smelt of grease, beer and body odour. The crowd of demon bikers recognised Phrack immediately. Some patted him on the back, then several picked him up and squeezed him to their chest. *Not a very manly act,* thought Purity, though secretly she was a bit jealous. After this Phrack was hoisted up onto their shoulders and hauled inside the tavern. He remembered to duck his head under the wooden lintel at the last moment.

Onk, with Purity riding shoulder saddle, followed in their wake, their thoughts of rescuing Purity's father, temporarily side-tracked.

"Well met Blaster," greeted the tallest one, a Rokurokubi demon. Onk watched while they all shook hands using some bizarre kind of hand thumping ritual. He liked that too. The Rokurokubi demon appeared very much like a tall wide human to Onk, except for the bright red, two-inch high tattoo around his neck. Purity counted several other demons including; a full-grown Neath demon, a Nybbas demon, a howler demon, an orc, two trolls and a Yan-gant-y-tan. They had all moved aside to let in the person who was obviously their leader.

"Well met Xaphan," acknowledged Phrack, *or should that be Blaster,* smirked Purity as she watched Phrack and the large demon thump fists.

"Well met Blaster," repeated Xaphan. "I hope you haven't appeared wanting your old position back?" he enquired. The leader was a little squirrelly that the dwarf had appeared at their current base of operations unannounced.

"No, no, nothing like that," reassured Phrack. "Having a bit of trouble with a witch and wondered whether any of you might like to help?"

Xaphan turned to his posse for their views. They nodded in unison at their boss. "It's possible," he agreed, shrugging his shoulders, hoping he didn't appear too over-eager. "The only witch hereabouts is that mad heath witch, Gristle," he volunteered.

"That's the one," confirmed Phrack, who saw no point wasting his friend's time with stalling tactics.

"You need a bike?" Xaphan queried.

"Be nice," grinned Phrack like a small child. "Like old times."

"Two," interjected Onk. Phrack looked over at Onk.

"You sure Onk?" Onk nodded enthusiastically. It seemed Phrack had found another kindred spirit in Onk.

The roar of ten motorbikes, complete with misfires and broken baffles starting up, brought folk out of their homes to stare in wonderment and admiration. Some, hating their noisy neighbours, were hoping the bikers would move to a new tavern permanently, preferably in a new town. Unfortunately for them, seven of the bikers had permanent commitments in Mothball, but over half of them joined the leader Xaphan on their latest quest.

It didn't take half as much time covering the distance as before. Purity didn't know what her father would make of it, her riding pillion on a motorbike, while Onk rode at speed, his hair rippling out behind them. Technically, she was riding shoulder saddle, but somehow, she was sure her father would disapprove even if she was with her uncle Onk.

For some reason the sensation thrilled her, which was good because it created a distraction from her itching wing buds. They hadn't bothered her in days, choosing this moment to begin itching violently between her shoulder blades. *I wish they would emerge and get it over with!* she grumbled to herself. *I want to yank them out of their coverings right now, then shout to the world that I'm all grown up,* but she didn't. Her mother had warned her of the dangers of forcing her wings to release early, how they could become deformed and damaged with tears in them. She might never fly again. She couldn't risk that, sooner IBS than deformity.

They had to take the long way around the Tedium Zone; the bikes didn't fare well with the grey mud and dust. Something to do with clogging up their carbs. *Whatever that is?* reflected Purity. *I thought carbs were what mortals didn't eat when dieting. I still haven't found Carbs in the supermarket. It must be purchased from a speciality shop,* she surmised.

Despite this lengthy detour, they managed to produce a good rolling cloud of dust, announcing to everyone for miles that Demon MCC was on the move.

Onk was loving his new ride. He'd taken to it like a proverbial duck. He wasn't looking forward to handing the wondrous machine back to its owner when this escapade was over. He made himself a promise that he'd buy his very own motorbike when they returned to Earth, even if Gem said no. He knew she wouldn't though, she'd probably want one herself. Onk grinned at the idea, conjuring up the image of the two of them riding out across the sands like mortals did on horse-back. Why they didn't use the beaches for bikes was beyond Onk, he thought it the ideal place to ride, very flat with few stones. He planned to try it out the first chance he got. He was loving the smell of the leather jacket some-one had lent him too. *Have to get one of these,* he decided.

The Demi-Golems remained motionless and moaning outside Gristle's place, when they returned with Phrack's promised reinforcements. During the rescuers absence, Gristle had hot-stepped it outside to re-programme her three companies of golems with new orders. Her initial thwarted command had been for the golems to "attack when attacked". Since Onk's group hadn't attacked, the golems had remained stationary and foiled her plan.

Demi-Golems were notoriously difficult to command. They would only follow very short, direct orders and that was their main weakness. So, no matter how powerful, or how indestructible golems were, i.e. not sleeping, eating etc. they were only able to cope with a few correctly selected words. They couldn't think for themselves, let alone outside-the-box.

This time, if the group approached to within a certain distance, the Demi-Golems would act. Having re-set their parameters, Gristle returned inside to await the fools' return. She didn't have too long to wait either. Gristle guessed they'd gone to Mothball, it was the only inhabited place for miles. What they had eaten there, she didn't care, but she heard them long before they arrived.

The row of demons on motorbikes faced up to the Golem army. If the bikers crossed over the invisible line set by Gristle, her golems would activate. They would not cease fighting until their objective was met - obliteration of her enemies. Gristle resumed her position at her command headquarters in the upstairs bedroom as before. She'd dragged Harty in his cage back up there to watch his friends' annihilation. Harty was initially impressed by the row of demons on bikes.

"They look quite cool," he murmured, the typical boys-toys influence that motorised engines have on males, working its charm on him. That was until…*Oh my Goddess, is that my daughter on Onk's shoulder?*

"They're horrible, and stinky, and noisy," rattled Gristle, turning around to glare at the pesky elf, "… and I'm going to destroy them all, all that is except your daughter. Her, I shall keep as my personal slave to replace that unreliable wretch of a hedgerow imp." Gristle remained vexed over the disappearance of Lou, who'd been with her for years. She knew nothing of Crogg's skulduggery.

Gristle hit Harty's weak spot perfectly. His beautiful daughter, slave to that mad heath witch? "Never," he yelled, as he realised that Purity was outside with his rescurers.

"You'll never have her. You horrible hag. You never caught her before and you won't now." Gristle grinned, her taunting had worked a treat on Harty Springfield. Moving closer to his cage she crooned.

"Yes, but I have you now. What loving child wouldn't give up their freedom for the sake of their adored father?" Harty caught her off-guard when he replied.

"Would you?" This question stymied Gristle, she thought back to her youth. She hadn't cared about her parents. They were always going on at her to wash and clean her room. Annoying individuals that's what they were. Much better behaved once she'd turned them both into Canadian Geese.

Gristle had never been a parent either. She only had a spoilt lazy child's opinion, of caring and love. All children were self-centred and uncaring in her view of the dimensions. Lou had run away after the lovely home Gristle had given her, the ungrateful imp. For once in her evil life Gristle spoke the truth when she answered.

"Well, no."

"And, my daughter won't either," Harty challenged, muscling up to the bars and hoping desperately that she would believe his lie to save his beloved child.

Fortunately for Harty, a movement outside the window distracted Gristle as she fleetingly considered turning the meddlesome tree elf into a goldfish - without water.

"What in blazes are they doing?" she grumbled, watching the scene below. "Why aren't my golems ripping your lot to pieces?

From their elevated position, it wasn't easy to see the sudden change in the landscape in front of the golems. Without warning, the ground had fallen away in front of the first row of golems revealing a deep chasm, the depth of which was unknown. The golems bent their necks and stared down into the darkness, unsure how it fitted with their new command orders. They didn't perceive this as a threat, or an attack, to them it was simply an act of nature, but they were wrong, nature had nothing to do with it.

Five golems at the ends of each row edged round the chasm and reformed in front of it. This meant the numbers facing Phrack and Onk was halved to thirty instead of sixty.

The original thirty stayed where they were behind the newly-made ravine, gazing downwards.

"Much better," decided Onk, rubbing his hands together in anticipation of a good brawl. It had been months since his last one with Gank, his friend. Gank had been invited to Onk and Gem's mating ceremony and stayed on in Thanet ever since. He loved the seaside and fish and chips as much as Onk. He'd joined Onk's karate club too and they loved nothing better than having a jolly good scrap together.

"Gank love this," he told Stinkley, the Nybbas demon on the bike next to him. Stinkley not having a clue who Gank was, nodded and grinned. Nybbas demons were often the buffoons of any group and Stinkley was no exception. He was an inferior demon as demons go, only able to influence folk through dreams and visions. Joining the motor cycle club had given him status and prestige and his smile, once seen as idiotic, was heralded as menacing and scary when dressed in leather and demin.

No one knew how or why the ravine had appeared, but it made the odds better and they weren't going to question fate. At Xaphan's command, the bikers divided into two groups. The Yan-gant-y-tan, a huge demon wearing long black gloves and flourishing a rat-like tail led one group, while Xaphan himself led the other, each sub-group planning to tackle their chosen targets, east and west. They started towards the reduced row of golems, at each end of the ravine, who in turn, began marching towards them, when the ground at their feet shifted again. The combatants halted as two more sections of land fell away. This time the ravines that appeared were at forty-five-degree angles to the initial cut. Because these were at an angle to the first trench Gristle and Harty could see the gaping holes in the ground.

"What's that?" Gristle screamed, shaking her pointing finger and shoving Harty's cage violently.

"I've no idea," he answered honestly, through clenched teeth. Despite the searing pain, he gripped the bars tightly, as his body hung at right angles to his tethered ankle. It felt like his joints were being pulled apart. He wanted to add, "you dim-witted witch," to that sentence, but reckoned Gristle might hurl the cage through the window. And, though he could fly, he couldn't levitate cages.

The odds against the bikers reduced again, as the new angled ravines bisected the original one. These effectively cut off the advance of several more segments of the golems, in one move. What was left facing Onk and the rescue squad, was a further reduced row of Demi-Golems inside the angled gaps.

Xaphan ordered his brothers to park-up and dismount. Moving their beloved bikes out of harm's way, the bikers proceeded on foot towards the remaining golems, who now numbered twelve. Xaphan decided the odds were much more in their favour until the other golems found a way around the ravines. He had eight bikers including himself, then there was Onk and Phrack to join in the fun.

The Demi-Golems were predictable in their fighting style. Whatever skill they had in life was gone, replaced by Gristle's command to "bash 'em till they're good and dead." As a result, each one moved forwards with their arms outstretched ready to bash their opponent senseless like some horror film zombie. They didn't understand the element of surprise, or stealth or misdirection. Onk had a great time bopping a few golems and knocking them flat. Without any initiative most ended up inside one of the chasms.

"This is easy," shouted Purity, sitting high on Onk's shoulders. She hadn't bothered to move after watching Xaphan and Stinkley with their first four opponents. She felt she could probably knock a few down herself but decided not to risk it.

To one side, she watched the other troll and the Howler demon named Beatroot, lay into two Demi-Golems. Beatroot was the most bizarre demon she had seen. A strange dog-like individual with long floppy ears, warm brown eyes and a brown and white pelt. He even sported a dog collar adding to his canine appearance. But what unnerved her most, was the howl he gave with each blow, making everyone of Purity's bones vibrate.

Phrack had given her the low-down on all the demons before they left Mothball, so Purity wouldn't be afraid of their new-found friends. He'd said that Howlers were loyal to a fault to those they cared about, in this case his biker club pack. They were big softies too, but Phrack advised her not to say that to Beatroot's face. She'd taken that as a warning, but Phrack knew the Howler was more likely to lick her than bite her, if she said anything.

It was like lining up targets to shoot at a fairground. Bop, bop dong, another one went in the hole. The thirty golems behind the first chasm, stood stoically by watching their comrades fall ungracefully into the darkness. Nothing had activated their orders, so they waited moaning in a low monotone drone.

The remaining inactive golems finally seemed to catch on and began shuffling through the gaps on either side. If the thirty Demi-Golems reached the band of heroes they'd be outnumbered and Gristle would win.

21

Spider

THE remaining Demi-Golems never stood a chance. Coming in low behind them, was the equivalent of a huge aeroplane-sized, metallic bowling ball on wings. The creature, a dragon, hit the three shortened rows of golems who had been about to move forward, with a blast of roaring flames from the rear. They went down like skittles. Strike!

Most of them tumbled into the pit, black and charred. Just in case they didn't, the 'ball' banked around and went in for another shot. It was dragon two, Demi-Golems zero, as the last one toppled over the edge.

The large male dragon hovered in the sky beyond Gristle's house, while Onk and his band of merry men cleared up the odd stragglers. If the chasms hadn't mysteriously opened they wouldn't have won the battle, because golems never stop once their command has been activated. Inside, the chasms were filling up with golem bodies. *None of them dead, and all of them dead. It's eerie*, reflected Purity.

With the last one gone over the edge Purity peered

down. In the darkness below, the Demi-Golems seemed to have sorted themselves back into rows. They were unmoving because, although they were closer horizontally to the bikers and their pals, they were further away vertically. Thus the command Gristle had given was negated. As everyone watched, the gap at the top of each chasm closed, until the light entering through the hole blinked out. Sixty golems were left entombed, standing alone in the dark.

"Hoorah!" cried Purity. "Only dad to rescue."

Within seconds, as if in response to her words, the ground began to grumble again. Concerned for their safety, the biker group ran to protect their machines. They needn't have bothered. Behind the now closed ravines, the ground began to vibrate. First Jasper, then Upala, rose out of the loose surface stones, or so it appeared.

Onk breathed a huge sigh of relief, Upala was safe. Phrack understood the deeper meaning of their arrival together. These were the mysterious ravine makers, and Upala had found her partner in Jasper. Neither stone person made a move towards the group. They simply stood on the far side of the secured golems and smiled at the assembled heroes.

Upala waved at Onk, her eyes alight with mischief and love. Onk, realising she had found her life partner and was happy, waved back. The couple sank back down into the ground until no evidence remained that they had ever existed. Onk wiped a tear of sadness away which threatened to fall, knowing his new friend was gone for good this time. He wished Upala well, but it made him think of how much he missed Gem and his children.

"Cheer up Onk, Upala's okay now," Phrack insisted. Onk nodded. To cover his emotion, he stomped towards the place he'd last seen Upala and Jasper, on the pretence of inspecting the ravines.

He looked up from the closed chasms and stared across

to where a large male dragon sat watching him. It tilted its head to one side, its golden eye fixing him with a pointed glare.

"Dog?"

Dog nodded his huge scaly head, and with a mouthful of grinning teeth, send a roasting breath over to Onk, almost singeing his eyebrows off – but not quite. Onk's grin was wider than Dog's. He launched himself at the dragon, who purred with delight as Onk threw his massive arms around his neck regardless of the danger. Onk was over-joyed to see Dog, all grown-up and heroic.

"Big," said Onk, stepping back and admiring the beast in front of him. "And strong." Dog purred with pleasure at Onk's assessment till his chest plates vibrated. The rest of the crew stayed well back from the dragon. Dragons had a nasty reputation for accidentally roasting folk, and no one wanted to be demon flambé.

****

Gristle was mortified when she saw her Demi-Golems rousted and roasted so easily. Granted they weren't very smart, they weren't smart at all. More like robots following orders than sentient beings, but that was the third batch and her fourth were a long way from maturing. She had no ammunition left, except her spells and that irritating tree elf. When she spied his would-be-rescuers staring up at her sitting in the window, she decided a full retreat was in order.

Grabbing Crogg by the earlobe, she pulled him down-stairs ignoring his yelps of pain. In her other hand, she grasped Harty's cage by the hoop at the top. Her grip caused it to swing alarmingly as she re-negotiated the steep stairs. It was a perilous journey for one, for all three, it was almost suicidal. Twice, she almost stumbled missing her step, taking them tumbling down with her.

Miraculously surviving, at the bottom Gristle turned right, then right again, until she faced her locked potions cupboard under the stairs. Crogg had never been allowed inside the cupboard under the stairs. Releasing Crogg's ear and placing Harty's cage on the floor, Gristle produced a small key from her skirt pocket and unlocked the low door.

Crogg was intrigued. He always wondered what items she stored in the cupboard. He knew about the other door, the one beyond the house. That's where she had him store bones for the fires. She'd told him of the extensive tunnel system beyond the bone pile too, but cautioned him about straying too far inside, telling him he would get lost forever. With his gullibility spell firmly in place, Crogg believed every word Gristle uttered.

When a flight of stairs leading downwards presented itself, and below he spied a room leading into darkness, he was agog. *I bets the outer door ends up here. I remembers thinking it was strange having a house without a cellar.* What Crogg also didn't know, was that Gristle had conveniently cast a forgetting spell upon him, so he couldn't remember any details of the house he'd actually built for her.

Crogg didn't have long to dwell on his surprise. At the top of the cellar stairs, Gristle pulled him forward and kicked him off the top step. He bounced and tumbled down the short flight, landing in a bruised heap at the bottom. Stepping across the threshold, Gristle lobbed Harty's cage at him. He caught it moments before it smashed onto the stone floor – luckily for Harty. Gristle turned and locked the door behind them before she descended.

"Good luck finding us now," she muttered.

Harty considered shouting for help before the door closed, but Gristle seemed to know what he was thinking because the look she gave him almost made his heart freeze over. It said, 'try it and you'll be a vole quicker than you can speak.' Harty wisely decided to stay quiet and see what developed instead. After his near-death plunge down the stairs he was in no condition to do anything but breathe, let alone escape.

Striding over to the centre of the room, Gristle bent down and began chanting as she chalked out a shape on the dusty floor. Crogg had seen her perform the chant before, up in her study, and he knew it opened small tears in the dimensions to Earth, because she had learnt the chant from him. What he didn't understand was the meaning of the chalk markings on the floor.

Why does she wants to check on Earth now? he wondered. Then the truth struck him as the tear widened briefly, to the size of a witch. This tear was much more advanced than Crogg's own ability, more impressive and more stable too. *She isn't planning to spys on them. She's planning to enter the tear.* Crogg was stunned anew. *The chalk markings must be another spell to enhance the chant. Opening a tear that big, big enough for a witch to pass through is mind-bogglingly difficult's, but if anyone can do it's, Gristle is the witch who can,* he concluded.

However, two things were against Gristle's plan. Firstly, every time she stopped chanting the tear failed, collapsing in on itself like melted cheese. To create a tear big enough for her to use successfully, might take hours or even days of chanting. Secondly, Crogg knew that Gristle didn't have the patience or perseverance to complete such a task alone.

As Gristle chanted she too recognised her limits, but she also thought she knew a way around her problem. Taking the stairs two at a time, she launched herself back up the cellar steps, unlocked the door, and vanished up into the house. Crogg was tempted to follow, but he was aching all over from being thrown down the stairs the first time. He didn't feel much like being kicked down for a second time. He glared over at Harty, daring him to say something which would give him a reason to shake his cage. Harty didn't, much to Crogg's annoyance, so he went over and kicked his cage anyway, out of spite. The cage rolled away from the spot near the chalk marking to a place nearer the foot of the stairs.

Outside Gristle's home everyone was in celebratory mood, despite not yet gaining access to the evil witch's dwelling, or rescuing Harty. Destruction, or rather incarceration, of the Demi-Golems and the arrival of a wondrous dragon, who Onk greeted by name as Dog, and who was evidently on their side, had created a festive feel to the whole proceedings.

Stinkley, the club's cook, had got a decent fire going courtesy of Dog, and the beginnings of a meal was stirring. Onk, always a keen follower of his gastronomic needs sat and waited for 'foooood'. Hunkered next to him was his old, new friend, Dog. Onk hugged Dog over and over and Dog, revelling in the affection despite his grown-up status, wrapped his tail around Onk in much the same way. It reminded them both of their times together in the tunnels under Ramsgate long ago, before Onk met his wife Gem, and Dog was reunited with his long-lost mother.

Gristle peeped over the sill of her bedroom window and glared out at the scene below. Her invincible army was vanquished to below ground level where they stood to attention ready to fight.

"What the blazes are they up to now?" she grumbled, referring to the biker gang. "I'm fed up with the lot of them. First, they come over here uninvited. Then they return and destroy my army. Now they're having a party with a blasted infernal dragon! I hate dragons. Why aren't they storming my house?"

Purity was pondering much the same question. She had found a comfortable spot resting on top of one of the bike's saddlebags.

"One moment they're fighting and the next they're

partying." Purity was perplexed. She didn't understand the bikers code, to work hard and play harder. They'd done their work, as they saw it, fighting the Demi-Golems, even if the majority were incapacitated by Jasper and Dog. Now it was time to play, which generally meant eating, drinking, then sleeping, though not always in that order.

Glancing over at Phrack and Onk, she saw they had entered into the spirit of the biker merriments. Dog, after an initial welcoming session, had flown up to Gristle's roof where he roosted like a chicken with his head under his wing. Purity lay back and looked up at the sky. It was getting darker and though she hadn't seen Gristle again, she was aware that the witch was still in the house and her father remained a captive there.

Purity realised the sensations she'd been experiencing since entering the Neath were stronger here. She believed the answer to these feelings were linked to the horrible Gristle's house. She briefly considered continuing on her own, but she could almost hear her father berating her, "You're too small, too young, too weak and only one fairy." Agreeing with her absent father's assessment Purity decided to rest till morning, if she could, but the sensation in her head was loud, which sounded a bit silly since no one but her could hear it. *It calls to me like a friend, or a relative*, she decided, closing her eyes in an attempt to sleep.

When Gristle realised her pursuers weren't coming after her immediately, she calmed down.

"If that stupid lot are resting, I might as well take a rest too." she concluded. "No need for me to panic and leave. My home is impregnable." With her decision made she headed to the kitchen to make some supper, then off to bed, not caring about her minions remaining in the basement.

Crogg and Harty spent the night in the cellar. Crogg had been too afraid to leave the dark and damp room. Morning saw the male fairy appear and descend the stairs to bring them food. *He's a bizarre fairy,* Harty decided. *Like Purity in so many ways, but so different. Where she is sunshine, this fairy is rainfall. Where she smiles and giggles, he scowls and grimaces. Where she is chatty and sociable, he is silent and withdrawn.* The male fairy fed them and left without saying a word.

Harty and Crogg looked at each other, the same thought passing through their heads. *Who is he?* Before they could think much more on the subject, Gristle's silhouette appeared briefly in the doorway above. She glared down at them then continued past without saying a word, going to check on the ripening process of her next batch of Demi-Golems. She was loath to leave her budding golems behind.

"Those buffoons outside might damage them, if they find a way in and chance upon my new army maturing." So, Gristle invoked a spell, hiding her army behind a false wall to wait until her return - if she were forced to flee. That done she returned to her study to rehearse her spells.

Purity was amazed when she woke the following morning. The biker party seemed to have fizzled out some time during the night. Phrack was nowhere to be seen. Onk was snoring as he leaned up against his friend Dog, who must have come down from the roof in the early hours. Purity admired the dragon as he slept. He was beautiful. His shimmering, metallic scales iridescent in the insipid morning light.

I wonder what he'd look like on a bright summer's day on Earth, she reflected, smiling at the image she could see in her mind. As if hearing her thoughts, Dog turned his head in her direction, opened his eyes and fixed her with a long gaze. *When did he wake up?* she gulped and found it hard to look away. It felt like he was examining her soul, which was unusual because fairies don't have souls, they return to the ether from which they were created when they die.

The dragon's mouth opened, and Purity held her breath. She was near enough to be singed like toast. She'd make a tasty, if small snack, but instead the dragon's lips lifted at the edges and Purity could swear he was smiling. Feeling more at ease, she smiled back, and leaving the saddlebag where she had spent the night, rose into the air and went to sort her personal needs. Afterwards, she decided, she would survey the land ahead. Although Purity's wings were infantile she was able to hover some distance off the ground. What she wouldn't give though to fly like her father, to dance like a butterfly and soar like a bird. Still, it was enough height to figure out the layout surrounding the house and give her friends information to help formulate a plan to free her father.

****

Gristle had been up a while before the rescuers got themselves together. She'd completed her spell to protect her growing army, set a couple of traps to catch the would-be rescuers and had a decent breakfast. Now she sat pondering her next move. She didn't want to leave her home, if she didn't have to.

"Maybe, that rabble outside will turn around and go home, if they think they've won," she mumbled. "If those dratted Demons on their stupid machines go, I'm sure I can manage one measly troll and a pathetic dwarf." Gristle didn't include Purity in her plans. Fairies were no more dangerous, in her opinion, than caterpillars on cabbages. Gristle had a lot to learn.

Purity surveyed the landscape around Gristle's house with new eyes. Although she'd lived within the building for several weeks, she'd never been able to hover over it due to the spelled anklet. Now she was getting her bearings on its size and location.

From above, the house looked like your average witch's hovel. It was a wooden house rapidly built, with two floors, all of which had strange angles and corners; nothing was at ninety degrees. Consequently, the building leaned alarmingly to the left, giving the appearance that it was going to launch itself off in the next few minutes.

Around the jaunty-shaped house was a depressing garden with grey soil and even greyer plants. Behind it was a large wooden shed from which, even this high up, Purity could smell the stench of animals kept caged. This was where she had worked with Lou. Purity's heart ached when she recalled the vile tasks she and Lou had been forced to carry out on the defenceless animals inside. No matter how hideous and scary the creatures were, they didn't deserve to die. She shuddered at the unpleasant memory, dropping in flight to an altitude that put her level with the first-floor windows.

Gristle stared out in hatred at the despicable fairy, who she had kindly given food and shelter to, hovering so tantalizingly close outside her study window. If the witch could have grabbed the irritating flying menace by her ankles and torn off her annoying wings, she would have. It had nothing to do with the fact Gristle couldn't fly - whatsoever.

"The ungrateful wretch," she whined, watching Purity come closer. "Come any closer my dearie and I'll turn you into tadpoles," she muttered, beginning the casting of that specific spell. As her fingers left the table to focus her magic, the male fairy attending her accidentally swamped her drink-refill, momentarily deflecting Gristle's attention.

"You stupid, idiotic fool!" she ranted, forgetting about Purity as the hot snail tea soaked through her ragged skirts and ran down her skinny legs on to the floor. "If my favourite skirt is the slightest bit stained," she hollered into his face, dancing manically around the room. "It'll be the last time you ever see daylight." Not that there was much daylight in the Neath Realms to begin with.

The male fairy backed away as if honestly mortified and upset about what he had done. Glancing towards the window he watched as Purity flew out of range, then ducked as a metal tray flew through the air towards him. It skimmed the top of his wings and clanged into the wall behind him, leaving a dent as big as a troll's fist. He ran from Gristle's anger, worried for his own safety, but pleased that his diversion had been a success.

Flying back to her friends, Purity didn't have a clue that her life had just been saved by a stranger. She was buzzing with excitement to tell her friends that she might have found a way inside. Hovering over the grounds, she suddenly remembered there was a large cellar beneath the house. While she was held prisoner there, she'd considered it as a means of escape, until she realised that she didn't have a clue where in the house the cellar began. Lou had mentioned a door key which Gristle kept on her person and Purity wondered if this was the key to the cellar. She was as likely to acquire the key from Gristle as a frog was to turn into a prince.

"Gristle uses the dry bones of the animals we slaughtered to fuel her fires," Purity informed the group, once she'd landed. Phrack gave a slight shudder at the thought, while Onk and several of the others, licked their lips, especially Beatroot. "I remembered Lou telling me that the bones were stored inside the back door to the cellar." The demons gathered closer struggling to hear Purity's reed thin voice. They stared at her blankly. Noticing their vacant expressions, she explained, "That means, there is a way inside the house from outdoors, somewhere." Not much change in the faces around her. "Don't you see?" she insisted. "If there's an inner door in the house and an outer door too, they must connect somewhere underground - in the cellar." Phrack thought he understood.

"There's some kind of tunnel system into the house?"

"Exactly." The group smiled as one, tunnels they understood. "So that's our way in," she clarified to the assembled crew. "We find the entrance to the cellar and enter the house under Gristle's nose. Though not literally." The thought of being under Gristle's nose, or anybody else's nose for that matter, made Purity feel physically sick.

"Any idea where the outside entrance might be?" asked Xaphan, the Demon leader.

"I'm not sure, but I think it might be between the shed and the kitchen door. It was Crogg's job to put the bones there because once the lightening spell wore off, they were too heavy for Lou and me to lift in large amounts. He was never gone very long so it can't be far. Gussie often came in with one in his mouth too," she added with hindsight.

"In that case, it's probably a type of trapdoor, or hatch," offered Phrack in explanation. Xaphan nodded.

"Makes sense," he acknowledged, eager to get going.

His biker gang, who were easily bored, were getting restless with the inactivity. It was the reason why Xaphan had accepted this undertaking on their behalf. Beatroot, the Howler demon, had wandered off into the grey garden to sniff the plants. Hanor, the mixed-race stone troll, appeared to be cooing softly to three black rocks near the shed. Meanwhile, Brett the Yan-gant-y-tan demon, was using a sharp knife to carve a long candle into a finger. He seemed to always have a candle on his person Purity noted, and when he wasn't lighting or carving them he was bizarrely, eating them.

Onk, deciding there'd been enough standing about, began pacing back and forth. In his mind, now was the time for action, especially seeing as how Dog was back with him again.

"Onk find," he stated loudly, and with his decision made, he headed off towards their enemy's home. Without another word everyone else followed Onk. He had a way about him, a leader's authority; if he said something it became so. Onk was a man's man, or in this case a biker's man or troll. Dog watched the progress of the rescuers from his temporary perch on top of Gristle's roof.

Gristle watched the band of Demons traipse along behind the troll. They wandered through her beautifully maintained garden around to the back of her house. She saw them trample her beloved plants into the dust, plants she had spent years growing. Several excreted rare exotic poisons, these plants were her living. Gristle raised her hands and pulled her hair in frustration.

"Look what they're doing! Look what they are doing!" she wailed, repeating herself. "My plants! My lovely plants trampled to pieces." In reality, the party of rescuers, worried about stepping on something deadly, had all walked following Onk's footsteps, so very few of Gristle's precious plants had been destroyed, but she didn't care. "I'll teach them a lesson they won't forget."

Leaning forward, she began casting a spell and directed it through her partially open window. It fell on the last two members of the biker group, a couple of unsuspecting orcs. They didn't stand a chance. Gristle's spell activated so rapidly they didn't have time to even call for help let alone open their mouths. First, it froze them in place, then it turned their legs into roots and those roots tunnelled underground in search of water, dragging their poor unfortunate victims under the soil. Gristle was delighted. She rubbed her palms together in glee, skipping across the room like a seven-year-old girl who'd discovered her birthday present under her parents' bed.

"Tee hee hee," she tittered, just like a schoolgirl. "This is fun. Maybe I don't need to go anywhere." She watched the group turn the corner of the house, oblivious to the fact that two of their party had vanished. Their minds were totally focused on locating the cellar entrance and Onk was busy stamping, hoping he would discover the way in through sheer brute force. Gristle scurried to the room on the other side of the corridor, so she could continue her spellcasting on the next unsuspecting person.

Reaching the back of the property, they all heard the frantic chittering and angry hisses coming from the shed. This was where Purity and Lou used to labour. The residents inside were getting upset. Purity wondered whether Crogg had bothered feeding them or changing their bedding recently. Considering their level of distress, she doubted it.

Onk heard their pitiful calls as cries for help, and without a sound he turned towards the shed. Onk's wife, Gem, told everyone that he was 'a big softie' and no one believed her. Onk proved her correct by ripping the lock off the shed door and flinging it high in the air, it vanished into the distance.

Inside, the creatures became more agitated, many figuring they were about to be fed at last – they weren't. Onk was torn for a moment between eating them or releasing them. He blinked twice, then started opening cages at random. Hordes of captives scuttled this way and that seeking freedom. Purity hovered up behind Onk. She'd had enough of animals in cages and though they terrified her and gave her the screaming ab-dabs, she helped him releasing them. Both watched, smiling, as the freed creatures slithered, crawled or scuttled away into the greyness of the Neath.

Several shy snakes stayed put where they were, even with the cage doors wide open. They were so indoctrinated to living in their cramped space, they didn't understand that Onk was offering them their freedom.

In exasperation, Onk grabbed the back of the two wire cages, one in each hand and shook them vigorously, forcing the inhabitants out onto the floor. Disgruntled at being dislodged from their homes so inelegantly, they spat and hissed at Onk before slithering out the door, following the speedy fire lizards who had hot-footed it, the instant their prisons were sprung.

The spiders, the most intelligent of the three types of creature in Gristle's captivity, took to the rafters aware they might otherwise become dinner for the other two species. All except one, who, taking his life in his legs, ran up Onk's right arm and stopped on Onk's shoulder staring at the city troll through eight shiny bead-black eyes. Onk had two thoughts in his mind, should he splat the arachnid with the palm of his left hand, or see what happened next.

Onk was never a stereotypical troll. He dumbfounded Harty and everyone who met him at each and every turn. From rescuing an unborn fairy to finding a lost baby dragon. Onk's deeds were legendary. *Why should today be any different.* He smiled down at the defiant hairy-legged creature, which wasn't small by any standard. It was the size of a small side plate and it quivered up and down apparently undecided about its next move. *Is it going to spring onto Onk's head, or bite him, or both?* wondered Phrack, astounded and intrigued at the things which seemed to happen involving this remarkable city troll.

"Sharp," commented Onk, looking with intensity at the spider's razor-sharp fangs. Deciding this spider, with its pretty iridescent body, was harmless, Onk turned his thoughts elsewhere, letting the spider be. If it didn't harm him, he wasn't about to harm it.

Onk returned to the waiting queue of folk watching this exchange. Most of them had not moved while Onk side-tracked on his new rescue mission. None of them mentioned to him that the spider now resting, like a favoured pet, on

254

the top of his shoulder was the rarest of creatures, a Neath death spider, its name the only explanation required.

Xaphan and Phrack smiled and shook their heads. The remaining bikers swallowed hard and the group continued their trek around the premises in search of the elusive basement entrance. The spider on Onk's shoulder, sighed and nestled down onto the huge troll's tunic. It sent out several threads of silk to secure its position as Onk's pace demanded. It didn't plan to be shaken off by accident.

Gristle lost track of the band of heroes once they disappeared around the back of her home. It was a flaw in her house design that she hadn't appreciated till this point. At the time it had seemed like a good idea, not bothering to put windows into the rear of the house since all her customers came via the Tedium Zone. Now, she couldn't see where the intruders had gone.

"Hogs-whittle and piffle-spit, where have those imbeciles gone? she groused, leaning out of the side window as far as she could without plummeting to the dusty grey ground below. "It won't be long before they find a way in I suppose," she grumbled, admitting the reality of her situation. "And, I can't zap anymore of those dratted snoopers either from this angle. Bah!"

Gristle was extremely fortunate in this moment, for Dog was occupied watching Onk's progress below. If he had noticed Gristle hanging out her window like a windblown curtain he might have frazzled her to a cinder and ended the whole debacle.

As the reality of her home being over-run by trolls, demons, and orcs - not to mention a dragon - hit her, Gristle began dashing around the house collecting her precious herbs and other spell ingredients which were priceless in the Neath.

Stuffing everything into three large cloth bags, including a raggedy assortment of clothes to wear, Gristle hurled herself downstairs towards the cellar calling for the male fairy on the way.

She still hadn't given the boy a name. Normally, she insisted on her servants having new names when she purchased them, though Crogg and Lou had been exceptions. She hadn't bothered to ask the fairy his original name either, it wasn't important to her. Except for times like now, when she needed to call him to her.

"You, Fairy, you," she screeched, using her old granny voice which carried further and echoed through the house like a banshee. The creatures taking refuge within the walls of Gristle's home, secreted themselves deeper into the cracks and crevices. These were fortunate escapees from earlier times and included within their number, a new bunch of snakes, lizards and spiders. None wanted to come to Gristle's attention, if they could help it.

"I'm here," came the reedy reply, as the fairy in question fluttered towards her from the corner up ahead. "You have need of me mistress?" he enquired humbly, lowering his head in acknowledgement of her greatness.

"Have need of you? Have need of you!" she repeated, her voice rising shrill in pitch. "Of course, I have need of you, you fool. Why else would I be calling you? You think I'm doing it for practice? You dolt!" She felt like batting the idiot from the air, but she actually did need him. She needed a go-fer and he fitted the bill nicely. "Go fetch my expensive spices from the kitchen and be careful not to spill one speck or else…" She left the sentence hanging in the hope the threat would inspire the fairy and make him work faster collecting her supplies.

"Yes, mistress," the fairy mumbled, bowing his head so low he almost fell out of the air on his own. Gristle couldn't detect any sarcasm in the fairy's voice and decided she liked this deferential tone and body language. "Where shall I bring them to?"

"To the cellar fool," she berated, wondering whether he might be a bit simple-minded. "Do I have to think of everything myself? Oh, and its queen now, not mistress."

"Yes, my queen," and with that the fairy left on his errand.

Gristle visibly preened at being called Queen, his reply putting her in a much better mood as she skipped towards the open cellar door, holding her makeshift luggage bundles under one arm. Gristle had almost forgotten that she'd left Crogg and Harty in the cold dark room all night. She continued down the cellar steps surprised to find they were both at the bottom of the stairs.

How powerful am I? she congratulated herself. *I love having power to make lesser beings obey me so totally. Crogg and the elf are still here just as they should be.* Deciding it was important to make sure they continued to know their place, she addressed Crogg with what she felt was the appropriate criticism.

"There you are, you lazy worthless creature. What have you been doing while I've been hard at work?" She was tempted to kick Crogg across the floor just for fun, but refrained this once, her good mood prevailing.

"Waiting for you my queen," Crogg grovelled, bending on his knees before his queen, his hairless head scraping the floor – he wasn't stupid.

"Well, get up," she replied, appeased. "I have work for you all."

****

The biker group, led by Onk, found the kitchen door easily enough. Thinking access to the property would be simplest through the kitchen, Onk grabbed the door handle with the intention of wrenching the door off its hinges. The biggest electric shock he'd ever experienced, powered through his body catapulting him across the poor excuse for a garden, into the now empty animal shed.

Several bikers landed beside him in quick succession.

"Stop, stop!" yelled Phrack, rushing in front of the door, effectively making a barrier of his body. A foolhardy action with orcs and demons bearing down on him. "It's clear, we can't get in this way," he advised the waiting entrants. "I'm guessing not everyone is going to get away with burnt fingers and frizzy hair."

Phrack glanced over at the bikers returning to the queue. He was guessing that the smaller folk in the group, namely him and Purity, might be seriously damaged, if not killed outright, if they tried the lethal doorknob. "We've already decided we're going in through the cellar. Let's carry on looking for the hatch, maybe the old witch forgot to secure that." The bikers didn't sound convinced. There were various head shakings and grunts coming from them as they considered Phrack's words. They were looking forward to having a go at the door; the electricity, whatever that was, looked like good fun.

As for the ones who'd been on the receiving end already, they felt violated. The dose of electrocution had got their 'dander up.' No one wanted to be seen with hair sticking out from their head like a wayward toilet brush, except those who didn't have hair. It was an affront to their hard biker image, and they wanted revenge.

Sensing disorder was in the offing, Xaphan called his brothers to him, especially when he saw they seemed about to launch a mass attack on the offending portal, going straight through the stone dwarf, if they had to.

"Hold brothers," he shouted, gaining their attention above the growing din. He focused on the three individuals who now sported hair like woolly lambs. "We are bikers. We are strong." The assembled bikers turned and listened to their leader's words. "We will continue on our quest to locate this secret hatch." He brooked no rebellion, staring at each member in turn hard and long to assert his dominance. Once he was sure they were his to command, he addressed Phrack. "Lead on Blaster. Let us finish this deed."

And they would have continued marching around the whole house in pursuit of the elusive basement trap-door when Onk, emerging from the dark shed, yelled.

"Hatch," and promptly fell through it.

22

Tunnels

A LARGE black hole appeared in the grey featureless ground. The bikers, Phrack and Purity peered down into it. Onk was nowhere to be seen. Three snakes who'd been hiding underneath the shed since their forced release saw this as an opportunity for a safer hidey-hole. They side-winded over the dusty ground and plopped down into the blackness, their hopes pinned on a safe landing. They found one.

"Oww, Ahh, Oooee," came various vowel sounds from below in the gravelly tones of a city troll.

"Uncle Onk?" called Purity, hovering above the hole. There was no reply to her call.

"I think Onk is okay," suggested Phrack. "Until now anyway," he suppressed a snigger.

"Uncle Onk, are you alright?" repeated Purity, becoming more worried by the second. A few more seconds passed with a large amount of shuffling noise coming from below.

"Onk okay," came the reassuring response. Everyone gave a collective sigh, not realising they'd been holding their breaths until now. Stinkley and Beatroot giggled like adolescent teenagers and Xaphan, trying to stay calm, gave his fellow bikers a disapproving frown. Then, looking around he thought they'd lost someone. Doing a quick head count he identified that two of his brother orcs were missing. He decided not to say anything, they might have gone back to take care of the bikes. He didn't like to believe any of his brothers would run away like fire lizards.

Phrack reached into his Gander bag, which was fast becoming a celebrity in its own right, in the eyes of the bikers. He withdrew two lanterns, complete with oil and tapers, and a glow stick. *How on earth did Phrack get a glow stick here?* Purity wondered, watching in amazement as Phrack broke the vial inside the stick and lobbed it into the hole.

The stick dropped down into the darkness, striking Onk on the forehead before coming to rest at the foot of the soil-covered troll. Purity fluttered down following the path of light, settling as softly as a flower unfolding on her uncle's left shoulder. Which was fortunate, because the pile of soil on top of Onk's right shoulder covered the shape of his new pet, the Neath Death spider.

Ignoring calls from above for Onk to help the others down, Onk decided introductions were the highest priority. He didn't want his spider-friend to eat his niece-daughter.

"Purity, Knife. Knife, Purity." Purity sat looking confused. She wasn't sure whether her uncle was asking her to go get a knife, or something more sinister. Until she could figure out what he meant she stayed exactly where she was, not moving an inch. She was pretty sure her uncle didn't mean any harm to her, or the scary spider clamped on his other shoulder.

What Purity couldn't, and didn't know, was that Onk had already named his new pet spider - Knife. He'd stared hard at the spider when it first sailed up his right arm, and then settled down seemingly at home on his right shoulder. He'd been acutely aware of the razor-sharp fangs too, which reminded him of the knife he used for cutting fish. Knife, seemed a good name. It wasn't clear yet whether Knife knew Onk's chosen name for him, or not at this point.

Purity watched her uncle use his little finger to wipe away the soil on his other shoulder. Slowly, a small mound resolved into a hairy lump with thick jointed legs. The eight legs lifted up and down, one after the other, allowing Onk to stroke and clean them. Purity jumped as eight bead-black eyes opened and gazed at her.

"Knife," Onk said, speaking to the hairy creature. The spider appeared to understand Onk through his gentleness and tone. Purity watched amazed, as the spider twirled and danced around Onk's fingers like they were another spider. She smiled. *My uncle is so awesome.*

While Onk cleaned himself and Knife up, the remaining members of the band descended into the cellar. Phrack retrieved his glow stick, he'd already handed the two lanterns out. Holding the glow stick above his head like an umbrella Phrack led them into the darkness.

****

Up above in the house, and a long way from the outside entrance to the cellar, Gristle's preparations to leave were almost complete. Her new servant fairy, who she referred to simply as Fool, had his own name. It was Courage, but he'd never tell the hideous witch that, for names were power.

As far as he knew, Courage was born and had grown up in the Neath. Named by his first owner as a joke, he was cared for by no one. He remembered, it was always dark and he was always hungry for food, attention and love. Only one of these needs was ever met. Despite obviously being a fairy of the light realms, he was never collected by parents and no one ever loved him. He had been sold continually throughout his twelve short years of life, purchased by Demons, orcs and now a witch who thought he was a fool - but he wasn't.

His life had been a sad lonely one so far; no family, no friends and often no food, but that situation had changed in recent weeks. He had felt something. Someone's feelings and emotions touched him, they were a new experience and made him wonder. *What sort of creature is it? How could they have survived all this time in the Neath Realm without me knowing?*

Over the last few days the feelings had grown stronger, sometimes overwhelming him in their intensity. He could identify some of them. The first, all-out terror, wasn't new to him, but it was the first of many transmitted to him. He understood guilt and fear too, but he'd also felt strange emotions which caused a warm feeling in his chest. *Is this what love feels like?* he had wondered, when assaulted by the unusual sensation days ago. Courage shook his head to clear his mind. He figured out that whatever was making him feel differently, was getting closer.

He was still upset and annoyed at being caught by the trader visiting Mothball a few days before. He'd been following the sensations which were calling to him, and not focusing on his surroundings. Before he knew what was happening, he'd had a black cloth thrown over his head, and been bundled into a metal cage – harmful to light fairies if they touched it – and sold.

Prior to his capture, Courage had spent the last few weeks as a free fairy, His previous owner, a wealthy orc, had foolishly decided to cross the middle of the Tedium Zone in an attempt to out-wit any thieves. The plan had worked before, but it didn't this time, as a result the orc had been robbed by two smelly goblins. They hit him hard on the head and he passed out like a wimp at the sight of his own blood.

Courage saw the robbery as the opportunity he needed. While the goblins were busy ransacking the orc's belongings, he scrabbled away into the darkness hiding at a safe distance. After the goblins left, Courage checked the elderly orc was still breathing, he didn't wish him dead. Then, taking the tiny key to his chains from his master's jacket pocket, he unlocked and removed the chains from his ankles, so he could hover. He went directly to Mothball and some sixth sense told him to stay there in hiding.

The individuals outside the house harassing Gristle, arrived roughly the same time the sensations he was feeling increased. *Is this a co-incidence, or does it mean something? Could one of those people out there be causing these feelings?* He felt both excited and a little afraid at the prospect of finding answers to his questions.

At present, Courage had no time to consider the interesting emotions he felt. Gristle kept him occupied fetching and carrying her supplies from upstairs in her home to downstairs in the cellar. Courage was small, but he was strong for a fairy, and this was the reason why Gristle had purchased him. However, even with his impressive strength, Courage couldn't hold everything in his arms, no matter how much Gristle goaded and threatened him. She didn't know her threats had no effect on Courage. He was used to far worse intimidation from Neath demons and the like. Over the years, he'd been kicked, punched, scratched, locked up, manacled, held underwater and almost strangled - on more than one occasion. Gristle was like a school-girl by comparison, except she was a witch, and, she had spelled him to remain nearby, as she had with Crogg, otherwise she knew they'd disappear.

Finally, pleased with the assortment of bundles and boxes accumulated inside the chalk markings on the cellar floor, Gristle called Crogg and Courage to her. She considered using Harty too, but the tree elf was untrustworthy and liable to sabotage any request made of him. Fortunately, Crogg knew what to do; she only had to teach Fool, to do the same.

"Crogg. Stand there and start chanting."

"Yes mis... my Queen," he corrected himself, bowing low as he felt her icy stare fall upon him. She was furious at Crogg's mistake addressing her incorrectly but didn't have time to punish him. Courage caught on fast; he had to in the Neath.

"My Queen, what is your wish?" he asked, bowing low like a courtier to distract her from inflicting pain on Crogg. The young Neath demon inclined his head one inch in Courage's direction by way of thanks. Pleased with his manners, Gristle instructed Courage in the chant, setting him up opposite Crogg.

"Now, see neither of you stop. I want that escape route fully open when we leave." After several minutes, the thinnest tear began forming from their combined chanting. She leaned forward to determine its exit location. The vague outline of a large unkempt garden appeared, and beyond that a derelict Victorian house.

"Good, good," she murmured, rubbing her palms together, then proceeded to throw her smaller items through the narrow opening.

Harty watched Gristle's activity with interest from inside his prison. The cage was where Crogg had kicked it at the bottom of the stairs and fortunately nowhere near the tear. *She's leaving*, he realised, his expression of worry relaxing slightly on his face. That was until he noticed Gristle treating him to a cunning stare. His heart sank. *She's leaving and she's going to take me with her!* As if guessing Harty's thoughts, Gristle giggled and sidled over to him.

"Yes, my slave, you're coming with us," she crooned,

re-igniting Harty's fear. "You'll like that won't you?" Harty's fear escalated ten-fold. He thought she'd forgotten all about him. He swallowed hard, the tears threatening to fall, but he needed to stay strong for Purity's sake.

****

Xaphan had decided - following the disappearance of his two orc members - that he wasn't going to tolerate losing any more. He made Hanor remain behind, stationing him above the entrance to the tunnel with instructions, to raise the alarm should anything hostile appear. He would have positioned another member there, but Dog had alighted from the roof curious about the black hole. He was settled with both feet, or more accurately paws, on the edge, his heavy head resting on them as he peered down into the darkness with undisguised curiosity.

The young troll called Hanor, was an unusual mixed-race hybrid troll, he had a stone troll mother and Neath troll father. Both had recently died in the last Neath uprising, leaving him without any close family. The Neath was permanently full of unrest. Individuals living there always felt they could do better than this or that reigning person. Neath Demons did not follow orders well. They were much better at ordering people about, so uprisings happened fairly frequently. The result was that the surrounding population was usually injured, maimed or killed during the violent Demonic battles which ensued. The warring factions called it Realm politics, but honest folk knew better.

Hanon hunkered down on the opposite side to Dog. He'd noticed the two orcs were missing. They were both new to the club and he'd felt they were a bit dodgy. He reckoned they were running away from something, or someone, and he didn't trust them as much as hedgerow imps, who were notoriously unreliable. If they hadn't left of their own accord, he didn't want to be the next one to vanish. On the other hand, the Dragon staring at him with golden eyes, looked as if he was assessing his next meal. That didn't make him feel any safer either. He accepted his leader's command, but part of him wished he was down in the tunnels with the others instead of babysitting a humongous hungry beast.

They guessed that the passage that led to the cellar might be long and convoluted, but none of them expected it to wind back and forth like some deranged snake.

"If this carries on much further I think I'm going to be sick," announced Purity, holding her stomach in both hands.

"I know what you mean," replied Phrack, wiping his sweaty forehead and swallowing back bile which threatened to erupt.

"You don't suppose the tunnel is spelled, do you?" asked Xaphan. Without thinking, Phrack smacked himself on his aching forehead.

"Why didn't I think of that?" he grumbled rubbing his head, realising this was precisely what had occurred. "That blasted witch has spelled us. She's got us deliberately walking around in circles until we're sick. We could have been down here for hours if you hadn't suggested it Xaphan. Well done brother."

"Or days," suggested Purity under her breath, dropping gently to the ground as her stomach pains increased. "What do we do? How do we get out of it?" she queried, trying hard not to throw up.

"We need to leave this tunnel, somehow."

Onk didn't need any more explanations. He was feeling sick to his stomach and it had nothing to do with any food he'd eaten.

"Door," he stated. Lifting both arms high above his head, he hammered his fists repeatedly into the earthen wall on the right side like it didn't exist, and very soon it didn't.

There was only so long anything could stand up against

a frustrated city troll. The area Onk was punching wasn't really a structured wall. It was a build-up of soil cast aside from earlier activity and it didn't have much strength. Within a few minutes, it surrendered completely like a sandcastle meeting the sea. The soil cascaded down from a point roughly three feet above Onk's arms, creating a river of earth which flowed into their current tunnel like a chocolate fountain.

Leading the way again, Phrack stepped through the newly made 'door' which Onk had thoughtfully created and continued down the uncovered passage. Immediately, everyone felt much better. The increasing sickness and belly aches subsided, the pounding headaches ceased. It was with a lighter step they continued in their search for the cellar down a straight tunnel.

As they walked, Phrack couldn't help but wonder. *What would've happened if Onk's door had opened onto the troop of incarcerated Demi-Golems?* He shuddered at the thought and, hugging his Gander bag closer, strode on.

Gristle heard the thudding beneath her house and guessed it was her intruders trying to break in. She sniggered to herself.

"They have only found the first of my traps by the sound of it," she snorted. "The next won't be so easy to bypass."

Harty's rescuers continued along the new tunnel. It wound back and forth occasionally, but they didn't feel so sick anymore. In fact, they were starting to feel relaxed and happy, if a little tired. When Onk suggested they stop for a short break, nobody disagreed. Each person found an area to settle down. Some decided to eat, others took a drink, but what was surprising was that Onk took a nap immediately.

A nap by itself was not uncommon for Onk, however Purity knew her uncle well and he generally took his naps after he had eaten a very big meal. *He hasn't eaten anything recently, why is he falling asleep now?* she asked herself, stifling a huge yawn. *I'll think about it in a minute,* she decided, her heavy eyelids closing. Her wings, small as they were, folded flat onto her shoulder blades. As her eyelids fell, she noticed out of the corner of her eye that the rest of the party were also going to sleep. *Spell,* was the last thought that flitted across her mind before she too was slumbering.

****

Above in the house, Gristle was becoming frustrated. Having two servants chanting instead of her, didn't seem to be sufficient to open a tear big enough for her body to get through. She'd managed to get one arm into the tear a short while ago, but it was too small for her head, shoulders, or the rest of her.

"Digidy Spit," she swore, turning on her two subjects. "Can't you chant any louder, or faster?" she harangued them. "At this rate it's going to be tomorrow before we can leave."

Crogg and Courage couldn't answer their queen without stopping. Already both were beginning to struggle, their voices growing hoarse. In a few hours, they would have to stop completely, and Gristle knew it. It didn't make her mood any better. She glanced over at Harty in his cage and wondered whether she should use him. It would solve her immediate problem and enlarge the tear quicker.

Harty would have been very happy to chant providing Gristle agreed to leave him behind in the Neath. Somehow, he didn't think she'd agree to his condition.

****

Purity could feel the heavy weight on her legs.

"Oh Gussie, move over," she grumbled, receiving a nip on her ankle for her comment. "Owww Gussie, that hurt!

Whatever did you do that for?" she asked, opening her eyes. There was the zoom, wide-eyed and stretched across both her legs and there was uncle Onk on the ground opposite snoring. "Hold on a minute!" she exclaimed for a second time, rising groggily to her feet. "Uncle Onk, Uncle Onk, wake up." She shouted in his ear, knowing her tiny voice wouldn't wake up the slumbering troll unless she yelled. He didn't budge, and though she didn't know Phrack that well, she needed to wake everyone up and he was her next choice.

"Phrack, wake up, wake up," she hollered, right into his earhole. Phrack's hand came up to wipe the pesky insect away. Purity backed off before she was swatted like a fly, but she was determined and this time Gussie decided to lend a helping hand, or in this case mouth.

"Owww, Ow, Ow," roared the irritated dwarf, smacking his ankles in his sleep. Gussie, it seemed, had bitten Phrack a good deal harder than he had Purity.

"Phrack, please wake up," Purity pleaded, sticking two fingers into his ear for good measure.

"What? What is it?" he groused, opening his bleary eyes and seeing Purity hovering at eye level in front of him.

"Wake up Phrack. We've been spelled. I can't wake up Uncle Onk."

"Spelled?" he queried, scratching his head as his mind attempted to come around. *What's that dratted girl going on about? Spelled?* He glanced around the room and quickly realised it wasn't a room. He was lying in the dirt on the tunnel floor and littered around him were Onk and his biker pals, sound asleep. He glared down at the furry abomination skipping around his feet. "Is that the devil that bit me?" he asked Purity. She nodded.

"I'm sorry, it was the only way he could wake you and me up," she apologised. Phrack robbed his sore ankles.

"Well, keep that furry fuzzball away from me." Gussie backed away at Phrack's harsh words.

"You've hurt his feelings," Purity insisted, rushing over to Gussie. "He was trying to help. We could have been here days or longer without his help." Purity hugged Gussie to reassure him. "As it is I don't know how long we've been asleep," she advised the irritated dwarf. *Obviously, not a morning person*, she decided.

"I suppose I better wake the others up," Phrack grumbled, tramping over to Onk first. "Keep that thing away because Onk is likely to eat it if he's hungry." The tiny zoom started trembling under Purity's hands.

"Stop that," she admonished Phrack. "You're scaring him. We might need his help again, so be nice,"

Phrack huffed and Gussie settled his head back into Purity's arms. He didn't seem to have any plans to leave.

Once Onk and the others had been woken, Purity explained who Gussie was, and that Jasper must have sent him.

"Upala and Jasper," Onk mumbled, saying much about his feelings in those two words. He'd started to see Upala as a younger sister he'd never had, regardless of her initial feelings towards him. Purity patted her uncle's hand.

"Come on, let's go," she suggested, they'd been in the tunnels far too long for her liking.

Once everyone was sufficiently alert, they set off once more with Onk taking the lead. After a while one of the biker Demons decided to voice his concerns.

"Is it me, or is it getting hotter in here?" asked Stinkley, the Nybbas demon. The others nodded in confirmation.

"Hot," announced Onk from the front, turning his head back towards his troop of followers. "Like Fire Realm," he suggested.

"It is like the Fire Realm, you're right Onk," agreed Phrack, the most knowledgeable of their group on the subject of the Fire Realm. "It even smells like it." Onk sniffed the air and nodded.

"That isn't good, is it?" queried Purity, riding on her uncle's left shoulder as before. The Neath spider, Knife, appeared to be sound asleep on Onk's right shoulder. Nobody had thought to wake the little creature, they were all too scared to approach him. Purity sighed, *Knife is lucky to be missing whatever dangers lie ahead of us*, she thought. "You don't suppose Gristle teleported us to the Fire Realm while we slept, do you?" she asked, imagining all the places they could have been transported to.

Onk shook his head, his hair flowing out in all directions despite the lack of wind. It brushed over the sleeping spider who moved one leg capturing the strand of hair. From here Knife catapulted himself onto the top of Onk's head. It appeared he hadn't been sleeping after all.

Onk swallowed and tried to look up at the spider who was out of sight on the very top of his skull. For some reason, not being able to see the spider unsettled Onk. When he could see it, it was fine; now he couldn't, it wasn't so good. He came to the decision that though he'd like to entice it back down onto his shoulder, he currently had other problems to deal with so, against his better judgement, Onk left Knife where he was.

"Too much Star Trek," Onk mumbled, getting back into the conversation. Purity blushed. She knew what her uncle was referring to. Her father was always telling her that she watched too much mortal television, but she was addicted to the old Sci-Fi series and had found a human trekkie who lived in Nethercourt, who felt the same way. Of course, he never knew that Purity sat outside his window watching the old programmes with him.

"No teleport," Onk growled, bringing Purity's thoughts boldly back down to Earth.

"What's a teleport?" asked Xaphan, interested in the strange new word.

Purity was about to launch into a long explanation regarding the crew of the USS Enterprise, when another disapproving glare from her uncle squelched her enthusiasm for the subject.

"It's just something from a show I watch," she replied, sighing like a teenager and editing her words to reduce any complications on the subject. Xaphan realised he wasn't going to get any further information, but he remained intrigued. Maybe later, when they weren't fighting the wicked witch and her hordes of Demi-Golems, he'd ask again.

Gussie the zoom, was skipping along ahead of the band of heroes, when suddenly without warning, he pulled up short. Onk, a couple of feet behind him, almost stood on the furry fuzzball and had to sidestep like he was getting off a small horse to avoid trampling the zoom into the ground. Purity floated down from Onk's shoulder concerned for Gussie's safety.

"Oh, my poor Gussie, what's wrong?" she murmured, wrapping her arms around him. One second the group were watching Purity make a fuss of the little zoom, the next both Purity and the zoom were gone.

23

Zoom

"WHAT just happened?" asked Phrack amazed. "I didn't know he could do that, did you?" Phrack turned to Xaphan for confirmation.

"Yes, Purity did tell us, but I didn't know he could take passengers. It would have made our progress so much quicker if we had known that," Xaphan replied somewhat tersely. Onk wasn't happy, while he understood the zoom would do nothing to harm Purity, he didn't like the creature zooming off with her.

No sooner had he considered this issue, than the zoom in question, with Purity attached, returned to Onk's side.

"Where did you go?" Phrack asked Purity.

"Gussie took me further down the tunnel, to the source of the heat," she replied, aware of her uncle staring at her oddly. Onk marched over to Purity.

"Never, Go, Without Saying Where, Again," the troll boomed at his niece and the zoom. Though she was used to her uncle shouting, this was the longest sentence Purity had ever heard Onk bellow. His whole body was physically bristling with unexpended energy, a clear sign he was very upset with her. Gussie trembled, tucking himself behind her ankles. Her uncle was right of course, she always told her parents where she was going and when she'd be home. Her uncle had taken on the role of guardian and he must have been worried for her safety.

"You're right Uncle Onk, we should have told you where we were going, but in truth Gussie didn't give me any time to explain." Onk glared at the zoom hiding behind Purity who shivered even more. "Gussie was just trying to help by showing me what our next hurdle is." Onk was slightly appeased by Purity's explanation, but like any parent he didn't want Purity to know. He stomped about, settling his mind down.

"So, what did you find out?" asked Phrack, forestalling any further delay, but dreading her reply. It was bound to involve more danger and life-threatening activities. The dwarf could only cope with so much excitement. Since he'd partnered with the troll and the mulberry elf, he felt he'd experienced enough thrills for several decades.

"The source of the heat," she replied smugly. "It's a massive lava river."

"Well, that's that," moaned the defeated dwarf. "There's no way we can cross that. We might as well turn around and try electrocution via the kitchen door." Several of the Demons liked that idea and nodded in support of it. Xaphan scowled, it was hard work keeping his biker club alive.

"What about the zoom?" he queried, watching the furball shivering behind Purity. "Can he tele..." Xaphan couldn't remember the rest of the word.

"...port, teleport us?" Purity finished for him. Onk frowned and Purity turned to looked down at Gussie.

"Gussie, can you do that? Can you teleport others?" The zoom seemed to understand Purity's question and her new word, but he did nothing. He remained where he was for several seconds, unmoving, then he vanished.

"Great! Thanks, Xaphan," growled Phrack, in a good imitation of Onk. "You've scared him away." Xaphan raised an eyebrow at Blaster but said nothing. Within a minute, Gussie returned with an egg. He vanished and was back again with a comb. A narrow shoe arrived after that and finally a packet of herbs. The group formed a circle around the objects to try and determine what the zoom was trying to say.

"A comb, a shoe, an egg and a packet of herbs," listed Phrack. "What do they all have in common? I'm guessing they all came from the witch's house. That's definitely a shoe a witch would wear," he concluded, pointing at the bright red sparkly shoe. Onk nodded, he'd seen a shoe like that before, on the legs of that hateful witch Gristle before he threw her into another dimension. "Okay, they all belong to the witch. Is that all?"

Beatroot sidled forward with his cute, doglike ears looking decidedly out of place on his demonic head. He looked at the objects and then at Purity. "They're all small," he gestured, pointing first to the objects on the ground and then Purity including her in his assessment. Gussie leapt out from behind Purity's legs where he'd retreated after depositing his finds. He cantered over to Beatroot and nuzzled at his feet.

"Be careful he doesn't bite you," warned Phrack. "He's got a vicious bite on him." Gussie whined and Beatroot reached down to scratch Gussie's head, wherever that was.

"Seems ok to me," replied Beatroot.

"I told you," commented Purity turning on Phrack. "He only did that to wake you up."

"So you say," answered Phrack. "Maybe he's partial to the taste of stone dwarf." Purity raised her eyebrows in annoyance. It was clear the dwarf wasn't going to let the biting incident go. She knew dwarves were renowned for bearing grudges, for as long as it takes a volcano to run dry.

"They are all small," contemplated Stinkley, repeating the Howler demon's words. "He took Purity and she's small too." He stood considering the clues. The Yan-gant-y-tan demon named Brett, hadn't taken part in any discussions regarding their quest until this point.

"I believe it is trying to say, 'e cannot take anything with 'im larger than these objects." Purity pondered on the Yan-gant-y-tan's statement marvelling at the demon's clear French accent, amazed to hear it in the Neath Realm. She didn't know the origins of the Yan-gant-y-tan, a night creature who evolved on Earth.

"That's it!" she announced. "The only other thing I've seen him teleport apart from himself is Lou." Onk frowned, he didn't know who Lou was. "She's a hedgerow imp tinier than me," volunteered Purity, catching her uncle's expression.

"So, we're right back where we started after all that conjecture. Come on then, let's see another lava river," Phrack sighed, resigned to visiting the thing he hated most in all the dimensions, but he wasn't going to tell anyone that.

The heat soon became unbearable. Clothing came off, initially folk carried it in their arms, but soon the novelty of that lost its appeal and pieces were scattered about the tunnel like some forgotten jumble sale.

"If it gets any hotter," complained Purity crossly. "I'm turning around and flying out of here."

"What about saving your father," Phrack reminded her. "Have you forgotten him?"

Purity swallowed the hard lump in her throat. She had forgotten her father in all the drama and excitement of the spells and freeing the creatures outside. Phrack's remark made her feel a little guilty, but that didn't last long as they turned the corner and stared at the incredulous sight which greeted them.

The river was hot. The heat seared their skin and they were yards away from the actual lava. It was unbelievable. It wasn't as wide as the river Onk and Phrack had traversed leaving the Fire Realm, but it was impressive.

"How in the Goddess's name, has something this big not been noticed?" Phrack asked, turning to Xaphan for an explanation. Xaphan shrugged his shoulders, his arms held out in the unspoken universal gesture meaning, 'I haven't got a clue.' The river flowed downhill to the left of them. On the far side, they could just discern a door, and was that cackling? The cackling sound a witch might make when she thinks she has outsmarted someone?

Facing right, Onk discovered how this monstrous flow had come about. Half-way up the side of what used to be the tunnel wall, was a tear - a tear into the Fire Realm.

"Gristle has re-directed the Fire Realm river here to be her private defence perimeter," stated Phrack, verbalising what Onk was thinking. "She must have paid a wizard to seal it in place, that's not cheap. I wonder what will happen to life within the Fire Realm with its river undermined?"

All rivers brought life and prosperity to the cities they served and Incandesonia was no exception. The river could not remain like this for long. Somehow, the tear had to be unsealed then closed, but that was a job for another day. First, they needed to get over to the other side and rescue Harty before who-knows-what happened to him.

Onk briefly considered making another boat, but they were too many in number and he didn't think he had enough time, or energy to make so many boats. They sat back from the edge of the lava considering their next move. No one had any ideas.

****

Gristle, realising her foes were nearing her home, checked on their whereabouts using a location spell. Discovering they'd reached the lava river she let out a girlish giggle of pleasure.

"Ah ha! There they are, stuck on the other side of my beautiful lava river. How delightful!" she cooed. "I might install one of these around my next home," she warbled, pleased her enemies were trapped. In fact, she felt so powerful she decided to pay them a visit to lord it over them. Stepping through the doorway on the far side, she grinned with glee.

Purity noticed her first and pointed her out to the others.

"Look!" she said raising the alarm. "The witch has come down to gloat." The others, following Purity's gaze, stared over at Gristle skipping up and down on the far bank. Onk growled, treating Gristle to his fiercest unhappy face, but Gristle had seen far worse in her life, an angry troll at a safe distance didn't faze her. Even if this one was the cause of all her problems, past and present.

"Think you're going to rescue your pathetic tree elf, do you? You feeble excuse for a troll?" she crowed, shouting across the river the worse insult she could think of. Onk growled. "Think again, you smelly breathing toad." Onk's growl grew louder. "You and your disgusting rabble are never going to get over that lava. And if you do, I'll be long gone with my new slaves by then."

Phrack didn't know the witch and already he wanted to throttle her. Purity had narrated the story surrounding her birth to them earlier. He couldn't see any reason why someone as evil as Gristle should be allowed to carry on making people's lives a misery.

After Gristle had shouted her abuse at the folk opposite there really wasn't any reason for her to remain. Besides, she wanted to see how the chanting was going. *These fools aren't going anywhere,* she concluded.

With Gristle gone, the group settled on the ground to decide what to do. The way forward seemed unreachable. Their spirits were low, and it seemed the only way left to them, was back the way they'd come.

"I don't fancy going back the way we came," Phrack stated, remembering Gussie biting him awake. The bite marks on his ankles were painful, no matter how cute and harmless Purity thought the animal was. "We might end up falling asleep again if we pass through those tunnels or get sick. No, we need to think of something else," he continued, not giving anyone the opportunity to disagree.

"We could look further into the tunnels," suggested Xaphan.

"Or, try to close the tear," added Purity.

"Maybe the river goes somewhere, we could follow the flow," voiced Stinkley, getting the knack of this conversation lark. Xaphan glanced at Stinkley, he wasn't used to the Nybbas demon being so talkative and adding constructive ideas.

"Okay, that's three ideas," clarified the dwarf. "Which one do we do?"

"Why don't we do all three?" continued Stinkley, on a roll.

"Good idea. Let's break into three groups and meet back here… emm, sometime later," Phrack proposed.

"Phrack, we need some way of telling the time, else some of us could get lost in here," suggested Purity slyly.

Time pieces weren't common in the Neath. Folk tended to set their day by the sky getting lighter or growing darker. They would arrange appointments and meetings, 'when the sky is at its lightest', or 'when the sky is just about to grow dark.' In the tunnel, the 'sky' was the reflection on the roof from the lava. It didn't change.

Phrack knew what Purity was getting at, but he didn't have to like what she was suggesting.

"Alright," he grumbled, realising Purity must have seen inside his treasured bag when it was stolen from him. "But, I want them back."

"Yes of course," Purity agreed.

The bikers where interested and then in awe when Phrack delved into his precious gander bag and produced not one, but three wrist watches. Lots of oooo's and ahhhs echoed around the chamber where they stood. The remaining orc, Thistle, had never seen a watch before, neither had Beatroot. The Yan-gant-y-tan called Brett, knew all about them, they were part of his heritage.

"What is it?" asked Beatroot, looking down mesmerised as Phrack strapped a watch onto his hairy wrist. A second timepiece was attached to Xaphan's arm, he stood silently, acting like this sort of thing happened to him every day. In reality, he was terrified, but couldn't afford to show his fellow bikers his fear – he was their leader and had to set an example. Sadly, Onk's arm was far too large to fit any strap. He actually pouted when Phrack told him so. Purity was far too small, the watch could have circumnavigated her waist – twice - she didn't mind, she couldn't wear one anyway because they had metal parts. She didn't mention this to Phrack because he had parted – all be it briefly – with some of his belongings.

"Beatroot, you and Onk go and investigate the river flow. Be back in two hours." Beatroot stared blankly at Phrack. Phrack stumped over to show the excited demon how to read the dial. He emphasised that they had to return to the cavern when the little hand was on the shape called number two. Beatroot nodded vigorously, hardly able to contain his excitement. Together with Onk, Purity and Knife, Beatroot left on their mission holding his watch arm high in the air like it was capable of leading the way. Phrack explained telling the time to Xaphan and he left with Thistle backtracking to explore the tunnels. Finally, Phrack, Brett and Stinkley's group sat down to consider how to close the tear.

It was a very dispirited group of people who trudged back two hours later. No one had discovered anything to help their situation. The river appeared to flow on for miles, though it could be another spell they concluded. The tear was too high up the wall and they had no magic to seal it, let alone reach it. And the other tunnel, the one they'd originally come through, had been re-spelled winding around in a complete circle before ending back at this cavern. It appeared, as well as no way across presenting itself, there was no way back either. Gristle had either applied a spell or removed the tunnel. Beatroot watched sadly as his wristwatch was handed back and disappeared into Phrack's gander bag. He felt like howling at its loss, but he knew it made Purity frightened, so he refrained.

They'd all become Gristle's prisoners without knowing it.

24

Trapped

THEY sat on the ground and shared out their remaining food and beverages. They'd plenty of provisions, so they weren't going to starve immediately. It was then that Purity noticed Gussie had vanished again.

"Where's he gone this time?" she asked, her gaze searching around the cavern floor.

Maybe he's gone for help?" Xaphan offered, looking up from his food.

"Yes, that's it. I bet he's gone to find Jasper."

"Well, don't get your hopes up Purity. I've a feeling Jasper has other things on his mind," added Phrack.

Onk grunted, the rescuers had become the ones who needed rescuing. He considered punching his way to the entrance, but something Phrack said earlier made him re-think that plan. What if he uncovered the Demi-Golems? Even Onk, strong as he was, couldn't fight them all.

When Gristle returned to the main cellar room she wasn't happy with what she discovered. The tear was a thin slither like a rip in silk and Crogg was curled up on the ground asleep. She kicked him awake as she stormed over to Courage whose voice, at barely a whisper, was struggling to keep the connection open.

"Want anything done, do it yourself, that's what my mother always used to say," she complained. Gristle's mother would never had said anything of the sort. Her parents, a witch and a wizard, were kind considerate people, who did nothing but their best for Gristle.

Gristle was rapidly reaching the conclusion that neither Crogg, nor the elf, had the ability to create a tear large enough for her to fit through. She'd have to be involved in the spell-casting for it to work. The idea of working alongside her minions increased her displeasure, but it couldn't be helped. Plonking her bottom down on a nearby packing crate she addressed her 'team'.

"You two have to keep that tear open now, we're going to be overrun by vicious demons soon," she whined, appealing to their instincts for survival. "I've sent most of our things through the tear." That meant her stuff. "So, we can't stay here," she urged, hoping to get them on her side. Crogg was aware that if the current tear closed now, it wouldn't naturally re-open at the same place. Gristle would lose everything.

While she was focused on Courage, looking at him in what she thought was a kindly expression, Crogg sniggered under his breath. Quicker than a rattlesnake on a rapid rat, her head snapped round to face him. He froze in mid-breath, terrified she'd heard his chuckle. This time Courage watched on as Gristle issued out instructions.

"Crogg, you take over from Fool now you've had a nap." She uttered the words softly and nicely, but Crogg knew when he was being ordered no matter how sweetly she tried to wrap the words up. Aware Courage was about to lose his voice she added another 'nice' request.

"Fool. Go get something to help your throat."

Courage stared at Gristle wide-eyed. It was the first kind

thing she'd ever said to him. Crogg blinked twice in disbelief, she'd never said anything that nice to him, for as long as he could remember. He took over from Courage continuing the chanting, so the boy could stop. Courage trotted away, glancing sideways at Harty, silent in his cage, and continued up the stairs. He half-expected Gristle to call him back, saying she was joking and he should get back to work – but she didn't. He left and headed to the kitchen to see if there were any herbs and spices that hadn't been thrown through the hole.

In the cellar, Gristle, who hadn't missed Crogg's disrespectful snigger, decided she could afford to be lenient. *Those stupid biking creatures aren't going anywhere*. When she giggled for no apparent reason, Crogg reassessed his earlier assumption. She was happy because something horrible was happening to someone else. It made sense.

Gristle surmised she had plenty of time now her foes were effectively trapped. Later, she would join her slaves in widening the tear and leave the Neath behind. This home had out-lived its usefulness, she decided.

Back in the lava river cavern, the temperature had increased dramatically. Since Gristle had locked off their only exit, everyone was starting to sweat. They'd removed as much clothing as was decent in Purity's company. The beverages were running low too. Onk was almost at the end of his patience, he was going to pound the walls into submission and Demi-Golems be dammed.

Purity was wondering about Gussie. She hadn't expected him to leave her again, at least not until they'd freed her father. She felt like crying because this cavern wasn't where she expected to finish her short life. She rested on a small rock the size of a grapefruit, trying to hold back her sobs, when she saw something move on the ground at the edge of her vision.

Turning her head, she watched a pebble, or more accurately a stone, roll across to the edge of the river. It was joined by a second, then a third. By now, the ever watchful Onk had noticed it too. He jumped up and shoved an elbow in Phrack's side. Phrack, who was facing away from the river to reduce the heat on his face, was about to 'have a go' at Onk when he saw what Onk saw. Both understood what a rolling stone meant, and it wasn't about gathering any moss.

"Upala!" they announced simultaneously. They ran to the bank with grins so wide Purity thought their smiles might fall off the ends of their faces.

"What's going on?" she laughed, their grins and happiness infectious, though she didn't know why. Xaphan, Stinkley and the others joined them watching the spectacle as more and more small stones rolled in.

The stones built a small mound, then appeared to stop.

"That's a great deal of help," responded Beatroot, sarcastically. The stones changed colour and turned yellow. "Well, I suppose that's interesting if nothing else," he added.

"No, no no!" panicked Phrack, waving his arms about. "Don't make them angry, can't you see they're here to help." The stones changed to green.

"What by changing colour?" Beatroot asked. "How's that supposed to help? We don't need a traffic light." The stones turned yellow and a few started to roll down off the pile they'd created. Phrack grabbed his head in both his hands.

"Stop speaking stupid demon. We need their help."

"Look ere, who you calling stupid?" Beatroot challenged, a definite growl edging his voice.

"Xaphan, help me, make him understand. These are sentient stones." Xaphan was interested in what Phrack had to say. *These folks seem to know more about these realms than I do*, he realised.

"Why don't you enlighten us Phrack," he suggested calmly. Onk had had enough.

"Stones belong to Upala," he stated, butting in before

286

Phrack could utter another syllable. "They build us way out." The stones turned green.

"Why didn't the silly dwarf say that," muttered Beatroot, moving off to sit down and watch the spectacle. Phrack knelt down by the stones.

"We are truly sorry. We know you are trying to help us." Beatroot spun one finger in a circle next to his head to indicate he thought the dwarf was looney.

The few stones who had left, rolled back to the pile. Nothing seemed to happen for a short while, then the ground groaned, the surface moved, and several small boulders began pushing up through the rocky soil.

"That's more like it!" exclaimed Beatroot, standing up. "Now we're getting somewhere."

The group watched as bit by bit the coloured stones and later boulders, built a tower, then they stopped. It was a very tall tower almost reaching the cavern roof and it stood at the very edge of the river bank, careful not to let the lava touch it.

"What now?" asked Stinkley, curious about the bizarre stones.

"We wait," replied Phrack mysteriously. "I don't know exactly what we're waiting for, but I trust Upala."

They didn't have long to wait. Stinkley noticed it first. Stones were moving on the far side of the river where Gristle had been haranguing them.

"Look, look," he bellowed, waving and pointing across the lava. "The stones, they're moving over there."

"Shhh! You'll have that blasted witch back down here," cautioned Xaphan to his insubordinate. Stinkley hung his head in apology.

"Sorry boss, I forgot."

They watched, struggling to contain their excitement as stones on the far side, replicated an identical tower to the one on their own side.

"Okay, what happens next?" said Thistle, feeling it was his turn to say something intelligent. "Do we sling a rope between the towers and climb over?" They all looked to Phrack's gander bag, it was bound to have the answers.

"I don't think so," Phrack answered. "If we did anything like that I think the towers would fall apart."

It happened slowly at the beginning. Both towers began leaning towards each other very, very slightly.

"Oh Gosh! All that work and they're going to collapse!" Purity wailed in horror. But they didn't collapse. They fell towards each other, and because they were so precisely made, in exactly the correct place and position, they met in one complete union, butting up against each other and holding themselves secure. A bridge built only of stones, without cement or glue, held itself in place before them.

"It's impossible," murmured Phrack. Walking closer he repeated his words. "It's impossible." The dwarf, being a stone dwarf, knew everything there was to know about construction, despite his current profession as a cobbler. "Where's the keystone and the springer?" he demanded, moving closer to inspect the edifice before him. The others didn't have a clue what Phrack was muttering on about. They worried the dwarf might have gone more than a bit looney, talking to himself as he peered at the pristine bridge.

"Be careful Phrack, or you'll fall in." The dwarf looked down, his toes were mere inches from the lava. He shuffled back. "I don't understand how this is possible," he said turning to face the group. "It shouldn't be here. No one can build an Etrusco arch like this."

"Well, whatever an Etrunko bridge iz, zey did it, and I for one am extremely grateful," answered Brett. The Yan-gant-y-tan always had a difficulty pronouncing his 's'. "Are we going to crozz?" he questioned. "Iz it zafe?"

The stone bridge turned the colour green.

"I guess that answers your question," smirked Purity,

taking first dibbs across the bridge though she could have hovered over it.

The passage over was smooth enough, the stones making up the surface formed a type of cobbled pavement roughly three feet wide. It didn't do to look down and check on the river, unless you wanted your eyebrows burnt off and any other pieces of hair. All of them made it safely over without mishap.

"What happens now?" queried Beatroot. Purity glanced back at the bridge.

"I think it will stay here, until we need it again," she answered. The bridge glowed differing shades of green.

Leaving the lava cavern behind, they used the door Gristle had vanished through earlier, and entered a new tunnel system, made of brick not earth. Purity thought she could hear mumbling. She wondered if they were finally drawing closer to Gristle's lair.

None of them were expecting to find anything on the other side of Gristle's artificially diverted lava flow, so finding several rooms at regular intervals along their route caused them some concern. Onk wondered who had been held prisoner in the small pokey rooms, which were locked on the outside with hatches to check on in-mates. Looking through the door hatches as they went, all the cells were empty save one.

Inside the furthest, two very dirty biker orcs huddled tight in a corner. They were cold and hungry and didn't look like they'd slept very much. Xaphan decided, the pitiful creatures were in no condition to assist with the current rescue. However, their appearance answered Xaphan's earlier question about their whereabouts.

Without a word, the two orcs rose, heads down, hearts heavy. They weren't bad orcs who'd run away as everyone had thought. They were creatures who had fallen foul of one of Gristle's nasty spells. The pair described how some type of spell paralyzed them, then their legs turned to roots and dragged them below the ground before they could cry for help. The next moment, they were dropped inside the locked cell from above, and left without food water or a toilet. *Well that explains the smell,* thought Purity, holding her tiny nose. *Thank goodness I had sense to go before entering the tunnels.* She had noticed several individuals disappearing briefly on their journey. *For toilet breaks,* she guessed. That made her realise she was glad they couldn't go back that way.

It was fortunate their brother bikers found and rescued them, from what could have been a very nasty ending. After supplying the two orcs with the last of their supplies of food and drink, Xaphan ordered them to follow on behind at a safe distance. He recognised that they weren't up to any fighting, should it happen.

The party slowed as all of them, and not just Purity, began to hear voices, or rather one voice. It belonged to Gristle. It seemed she was berating her servants for not working hard enough. Recognising that they had almost reached their destination, the party stopped their forward progress. They needed some kind of plan.

"We need to know what we're walking into," suggested Phrack. Everyone nodded. "One of us needs to creep forward and check it out." He gazed around at the assembled crew, assessing their potential for the task. None of them were really built for stealth and creeping. They were all loud stomping individuals, guaranteed to make the most noise and violence possible, Onk especially. Phrack shook his head in defeat. He was their only option.

"I'll do it," came Purity's tiny voice. Stopping their objections before they started, she added. "It makes sense, I'm the smallest and quietest." What she said was true. They all nodded a second time.

Purity was terrified. Onk remembered, it was only a

short while ago that his friend Harty, had offered to do much the same thing in Incandesonia. Her offering to check out whatever lay ahead made sense, but Onk didn't have to like it. None of them except her had the ability to be quiet and mostly invisible. She edged slowly forward. Behind her, Phrack made little shooing motions with his hand like she was some child going off to school on the first day.

That was the problem with being small, people often thought small meant young, and the reverse was also true. She had friends her own age, who complained that people expected more of them because they were taller, they assumed they were older. They often grumbled to Purity about how annoying it was. She seemed to be a person lots of people came to with their problems. She quite liked that. *Maybe, that's what I'll do when I'm older, counsel people about their problems.* Purity smiled, she liked that idea a lot.

Glancing over her shoulder, Phrack was still shooing her on. Taking a deep breath, she advanced around the next corner. She made sure to float high up against the ceiling where folk hardly ever looked – that's what her father had told her anyway.

Gristle had her back to Purity as she edged into the room. Purity saw a large space with stairs on the far side leading back up into the house. Gristle was speaking to something or someone, held captive inside one of those horrid hiring cages. Purity slammed her hand over her mouth to smother her huge intake of breath, as she realised the captive was her father. He was caged, and Gristle appeared to be addressing him politely, for a witch.

Her instincts told her to rush over and free her father from his prison, but she knew she didn't stand a ghost of a chance against the evil witch. Settling her raging emotions, she concentrated on assessing the situation, just as Phrack had instructed her to do.

In the middle of the room, was a witch's chalk circle. Crogg knelt outside it, eyes closed, muttering words. In the air above the circle, a thin wavy fluorescent line floated. Purity didn't know what she was seeing, but if Gristle was involved it had to be bad. She couldn't hear what Gristle and her father were discussing, and where she was hovering she was vulnerable, so she scoured the room for someplace to hide.

There weren't many suitable places. She briefly considered returning to Phrack with the knowledge of the room layout and the fact her father was here, but it didn't feel useful enough. They needed to know what the witch was doing.

Noticing a box, apparently ignored, on a high shelf several feet to her left, Purity floated over to it. It was small, just four inches high, but with her winglets folded flat she could hide behind it. She almost fell off the shelf in surprise when the box in front of her jumped.

Gristle had spent much of her life being nasty. Over the decades, after turning her parents into birds, she'd turned many people into animals. The most common thing for her to do was turn them into rabbits for her supper. On occasion, she turned folk into other things too. One such transformation was Maddrigrew the Gruesome, who she'd turned into a toad, twelve years earlier during her search to locate Onk.

Maddrigrew, or Grue for short, had tried to teach Gristle how to far-see. In return, the ungrateful witch had turned her colleague into an amphibian. Gristle knew Grue would seek out a white witch, so she had placed an extra spell, a time delay, so her spell couldn't be reversed for several years.

One of the first things Gristle did, once she learnt how to manipulate tears, was to seek out Maddrigrew and capture her before she found a white witch. A toad was the largest thing she had been able to transport through a tear, and it had taken all of her energy to do it. Chucking things through from the Neath side it seemed, was effortless, but dragging things from Earth was equivalent to moving a mountain. Purity was the largest thing Crogg had ever lugged into the Neath.

Grue had lived a captive in her box at Gristle's beck and call for years. She was a broken forgotten witch, who held on to a thin strand of revenge. This kept her alive, gave her purpose, plus she had retained her ability to far-see and cast a few basic spells, otherwise she would have passed away years ago. All those years had given her time to think, think about the life she had before and the life she could have had, with a family and children and a home.

Bad witches didn't want those things. When Grue was young she didn't want those things either. She had moved naturally and smoothly into darkness and evil. Nowadays, Grue wasn't so sure that she wanted to be evil. The idea of a home and family appealed more, not that it was ever going to happen with her living as a toad, in a box, in the Neath.

Grue felt Purity's presence as she entered the room. Her far-seeing skills were hugely superior to Gristle's own. She'd been observing the situation both outside and inside the cellar. She knew Harty's rescuers were close too, and she needed help to get away from Gristle's clutches. *If I help them,* Grue reasoned, *they might help me in turn.* But she couldn't speak as a toad, and far-seeing tended to kill creatures if she used them too much. She'd managed to improve her technique of possession with much practice over the years, so the creatures she used didn't die, providing she only stayed inside their minds a few minutes at any one time. In the Neath Realm, Gristle had practiced on plenty of creatures over the years mainly fire lizards, stone snakes and Neath Death spiders.

The spider on Onk's shoulder, shook itself and rose up on its legs. It turned and scrutinized its host. Onk was busy trying to 'speak' to two stones. He wasn't doing very well, neither of them were Demon stones, just ones he had found on the ground, but it gave Grue an idea and she retreated from the spider's brain.

The demon stone bridge was still in place. The stones, sent by Upala, had come to the conclusion that some of them would have to be sacrificed to save the majority, so stone by stone they scrambled down the structure, each stone sinking immediately into the ground rather than stay to see their friends and family fall into the lava and dissolve.

Utilising a stone snake, Grue slid closer to the bridge of stones which existed now as a single strand. It was an amazing and unbelievable feat, one guaranteed to make Phrack swoon if he had the opportunity to observe it.

Grue had never captured the mind of a demon stone before. None had ever come close till this moment. It was tricky, like wading through toffee with an orc on your shoulders and a harmonica in your mouth, but if anything, Grue was used to hardship being a toad. She continued trying to establish contact with one of the stones and succeeded – in an odd way.

It was the most bizarre experience she ever felt. She could far-see through the stone, but also feel that she wasn't in command of it. Two unknown beings were with her and they remained in control of the stone's movements no matter how hard she tried, to first persuade and later force, the issue. She wasn't doing anything or going anywhere without their agreement and help. *So be it,* she decided. Getting home to Earth was her highest priority and she needed their assistance to get there.

Grue watched using her far-sight, as the stones continued moving and rolling. Thousands had died as the final section of the bridge sides collapsed into the fiery lava, but it appeared their work wasn't finished. She got the impression they had one more task to complete, before any stone would be allowed to assist her.

The stones rolled towards the tear set half way up the earthen wall. It was from this tear the lava poured out to make Gristle's river. Stone by stone, they placed themselves at the very edge of the opening, forming a thin crust with their bodies as the lava's heat melted their cores. Round and around in circles the stones continued to pile into the tear and eventually, Grue noticed, the tear began reducing in size. The stones were succeeding in stopping the flow of lava. They slowed the flow until the river became a stream, then a trickle, then was no more. It was an amazing feat of what was possible, if enough individuals were willing to sacrifice themselves for the greater good. It made Grue feel humble to witness it.

When it was over, one solitary stone rolled away and headed through the door, into the cellar complex beyond. It by-passed Onk and the others without them noticing, whilst Maddrigrew the Gruesome, accompanied the stone, from within the snake.

****

The box jumped towards Purity a second time and she moved back against the wall. It was a stand-off, until Purity heard a thin gravelly sound getting louder. Thinking it came from Gristle, she peered out from behind the box. Gristle had stopped speaking to her father and was sitting eating food provided by another elf.

It was a servant Purity hadn't seen before when she lived in Gristle's home. *He must be new,* she concluded. She didn't know why, but she couldn't take her eyes off the stranger. She risked discovery if she continued standing out in the open staring at him. She noticed he was the opposite to her in appearance, dark where she was light. Then it hit her. *He's the one I've been sensing. The one who's been giving me these feelings of belonging.*

The elf lifted his head and looked over in Purity's direction as if searching for something. Then his gaze landed on her. He stared straight into her eyes as Purity stood at the side of the box on the high shelf. She froze. He didn't say a word, didn't raise the alarm. If he had, she'd be joining her father in the cage.

Courage pulled his gaze away from Purity's location. His heart was pounding in his chest. This was the source of the sensations he'd been feeling. He didn't want Gristle to know he'd seen the female fairy next to the box. He daren't signal to her. Nothing to give her away, so he turned and walked back up the steps. Gristle continued eating and the tiny gravelly noise drew closer.

When a small stone tumbled out from the wall onto the shelf, Purity, her stress levels at maximum, released a small shriek of alarm. Gristle heard it, she rose from her place on the bottom step and shouted out.

"Who's there?"

Grue, inside her box, thought fast. She grabbed a stone snake resting in a dark corner of the cellar with her mind, momentarily dropping the stone's essence. The snake woke with a surprised start, Grue's mental touch making it hiss twice. Gristle pounced on it.

"You are disturbing my meal," she groused, stressing each word. She held the reptile by its jaws, so it couldn't turn her hand to stone. "Stop it at once, or I'll turn you into a rabbit." The snake, living all its years in the Neath, hadn't a clue what a rabbit was, but it didn't like the sound of it. It sounded far too cute and cuddly. It hung loosely in Gristle's hand like a wet tie, broadcasting its submission. She cast it to the floor like a forgotten toy. Relieved, the snake side-winded away into the darkness hiding underneath the stairs as fast as its scales could slither.

Grue gave a silent sigh and re-captured the stone, which surprisingly was still alive. She didn't realise this was because of Upala's control of her subjects. The stone rolled towards Purity and changed colour. Purity knelt down.

"Thank the Goddess you're a demon stone," she whispered, breathing on its surface gently, so Gristle couldn't detect their conversation. The stone turned green. "What are we going to do?" she asked. No change in colour, she tried a different tact. "Do you know what is in the box?" The stone flashed pink briefly, then returned to green. "Ohhh, is it good or bad?" The stone turned mauve, highlighting mixed emotions and leaving Purity none the wiser.

Deciding that the thing in the box was a friend, not a foe, because otherwise the stone wouldn't want to help, Purity continued. "Do we need to get whatever it is, out of the box?" The stone turned green for 'yes.' "Next question, how do we do that without Gristle noticing? It doesn't look like she's leaving any time soon." The stone stubbornly remained the same colour, either that was its answer, or it didn't know.

The stone rolled closer to Purity. It nudged at her side tapping the pointy needle she wore. She'd found it inside Phrack's gander bag after Jasper had pilfered it. The weapon wasn't much good for fighting anything except ants, but she felt comforted by its presence and besides Phrack hadn't asked for it back.

Taking the hint, she removed the weapon and brandished it in the air. The stone rolled towards the box and tapped it. "There?" The stone turned emerald green. Trusting the stone, whose brethren had seen them safely over the bridge and destroyed the golems, she gently pushed the needle point into the cardboard, careful to ensure it didn't make a sound. No one screamed or shouted, so she did it again slightly to the left. Continuing in this way she made an impressive dot-to-dot circle approximately three inches in diameter.

With Gristle and Crogg in the cellar, Purity dare not try tearing open the outlined shape she had made.

"We must wait," she informed the stone. The stone turned green in agreement.

Gristle chose this point to leave the cellar, much to everyone's relief, and her own. She hadn't planned on it taking so long to create the tear. Now, Mother Nature had decided to raise her voice and shout at her. Well, she'd shouted at one particular part of her, and Gristle needed to answer her call – soon. The lack of a toilet in her cellar was an annoying oversight. Stamping up the steps, she headed to the toilet irritated by her body's earthly needs. If she could have spelled herself not to need the toilet forever, then she would have.

"Blasted nuisance," she muttered, stamping out through the door above and disappearing into the house. Without any one to watch him, Crogg decided he too needed relief, this time for sustenance. He hadn't eaten for hours. He called for Courage to return to the cellar and take over his job of keeping the tear open, for every time Crogg stopped mumbling the spell it began to close.

It took several attempts, but eventually Courage's head re-appeared at the top of the cellar steps. Crogg couldn't chase up after him unless he wanted to incur Gristle's displeasure. He knew from experience it didn't do to anger the evil unbalanced Heath witch.

Courage, wanting to see the fairy on the shelf again, appeared to take pity on Crogg. He descended the steps and nodded to Crogg, who took off up the stairs like a cannonball. Courage stared at the tear as it began to close, edging in from the sides till it was a thin sliver. He couldn't face Gristle's anger either, so he settled himself on the floor and took up the spell-casting.

With the witch and the Neath demon gone, the stone leapt up and threw itself at the shape on the box. Taking its cue, Purity took turns joining it in its labours. It was tiring work, but soon the cardboard in one spot gave in and tore, followed in slow repetition by the rest of the holes.

Purity peeked in through the jagged hole, there was a creature inside and it was staring out at her with very intelligent eyes. She stepped back as the rotund shape of a toad crawled into view. With much exertion on the toad's part and yanking from Purity, the animal plopped on to the shelf beside her. Its gratitude at being out of the box was apparent by the way it rubbed itself up her arm. That, and there were tears in its eyes.

"Are you ok?" Purity asked, wiping away the toad's tears with her fingers as they began to fall, toads didn't cry. The toad nodded. "You're human, right?" The toad shrugged its shoulders. "Almost human, then." Purity amended her statement, understanding the toad's unspoken words. "Like me." Again, the toad nodded.

Grue was so relieved to be out the box that she had been hibernating in for months, that she had snuggled up to the girl's arm without thinking. This slip of a girl was being kind to her, even wiped away her tears in an effort to comfort her. *If I can get off this shelf, I might help her*, she decided, taking a shine to her.

"We need to get down from here," Purity advised the toad, patting her gently on the back. "Wait here a moment," she requested, "while I check whether it's safe to go." Purity peered around the box, while Grue and the stone waited in the shadow of the box. Leaning back towards the toad, Purity asked the question that had been bothering her since she landed on the shelf.

"Do you know what she's doing?" she asked the toad who she was sure, wasn't a toad, but one of Gristle's hideous transmutations. The stone turned green answering for Maddrigrew. "Oh, you're controlling the stone." Maddrigrew shrugged once more. "You're sort of controlling it?" The stone flashed green.

Purity felt Courage when he re-entered the cellar and she knew, he must know she was there too, but he hadn't done anything about it. He hadn't called Gristle or informed Crogg, before the demon galloped up the stairs. She saw the elf sitting outside the chalk circle chanting, he didn't stop or come over. He sat with his eyes closed concentrating on his task.

Purity decided now was the time to descend the shelving unit. She wasn't strong, and she wasn't big, but she figured she and the toad could descend using her baby wings. It would be a kind of controlled fall rather than flight, but they needed to get moving before the others returned, and she needed to free her father.

They dropped off the shelf in a half-falling, half-gliding manner, plummeting more rapidly then she would have liked. Courage opened his eyes at the sound of their heavy landing. He didn't stop chanting, but his eyes were wide like he'd seen a spirit. As soon as they sorted themselves out, the toad scuttled across the floor towards the dark tunnel beyond. Grue didn't have the skills physically to be an asset. Her strengths lay in stealth, cunning and spell-casting, along with her ability to far-see. It was a talent Gristle had managed to learn during her time in the Neath, despite her insistence to Grue, that it was impossible and beneath her.

Purity rushed over to her father, who was lying with his eyes closed and his body almost up against the bars of the cage, which lay on its side by the bottom step.

"Father, father," she called softly, reaching through the bars to shake his shoulder. Harty Springfield jumped to life like a man electrocuted. He'd been dozing and imagining a giant spider coming to devour him. He had taken Purity's hand to be one of its fangs touching him.

Harty had never recovered from his terrifying ordeal with a spider, twelve years ago. Then, a nasty wingless elf and a villainous Tarmac orc had trapped him in a tree, food for a hungry spider. He screamed like he was being eaten alive.

"AHhhhhhhhhhhhh!"

Though Harty's voice wasn't loud in volume, it was enough to bring everyone running. Crogg scampered back down the stairs with Gristle on his heels, the back of her skirt tucked in her knickers in her haste to reach the cellar.

From the other direction, several large biker demons hove into view from the tunnel beyond. Included in their number, was a very angry city troll who roared his displeasure so loudly the building itself shook in terror. Creatures for miles around shivered and hid. The bikers standing closest to Onk were deaf for weeks afterwards.

Gristle grabbed Crogg by the ears.

"Spell," she screeched, throwing Crogg across the room towards the chalk circle. More scared of Gristle than demons or trolls, Crogg joined Courage chanting. The tear widened.

"Come one foot closer and I'll turn you all into frog-spawn," Gristle bellowed. That stopped everyone. The demons had no idea what frog-spawn was, but they weren't taking any chances just in case it proved fatal. When Onk didn't move a muscle either, they knew they were correct in their assumption that the witch's threat was genuine and deadly.

It should have been easy to cross over to Gristle and grab her, but the first biker who did, Thistle the orc, turned into a large puddle of jelly containing a plethora of things resembling little black peas.

Harty couldn't help feeling this was all familiar. The same witch, same troll, same tear. Only this time he was at the witch's mercy.

Onk, Phrack and the bikers lined up on one side of the witch's chalk circle containing the now expanding tear, while Gristle, Crogg and Courage stood on the other. Purity and her father remained at the foot of the stairs.

The Demon bikers froze. It was a stalemate.

25

Malachi

BACK in Earth's dimension, the wren Malachi Maximus
Mallory the Sixteenth, was feeling ever so slightly
guilty. His egg was home, and he'd spent a vast amount of
time seeing to its needs, settling it into its new nest,
ensuring there were no draughts and that it was warm and
safe.

Unknown to mortals, wrens were a different species to
Earth-bound birds. Ornithologists speculated how the tiny
birds managed to disappear from one place, only to re-
appear somewhere entirely different moments later. They
theorized it was because they were so small. They never
guessed these avians, like mermaids and unicorns and the
occasional grey cat, were in reality trans-dimensional
creatures.

In the same way, their eggs were special too. Not
restricted to Earthly conventions of time and location, these
oval orbs could be incubated and hatched wherever and
whenever the parent deemed the place, or more importantly the time, was right. Malachi snuggled down on his

egg. It looked a lot like the eggs children purchased loose in bags at Easter, speckled and roughly a centimetre in diameter. Malachi shivered at the thought, *No one is going to eat my young – ever.*

In his mind's eye, he saw Harty Springfield, the tiny Mulberry elf not much bigger than him, vowing to rescue his daughter and return her home safely. The wren's guilt grew. He'd left them all adrift in the Neath, after they'd entered the Fire Realm and rescued his unborn child for him. He wondered how they were faring, how they were going to get home. *It won't hurt to check on their progress,* he concluded.

Leaving his beloved one safe and snuggled inside a large bundle of sheep wool, Malachi ventured out. He hadn't told Harty and Onk all his secrets. He had more than one way into the other dimensions, he just tended to use the one at the Viking ship for convenience. It was the closest and the largest.

Over the last few decades, activity in and around the tiny village of Manston, north of Ramsgate, had dwindled. At one time, between the nineteen-forties and seventies, the place had been a thriving community, busy twenty-four seven. First packed with airmen and fighter craft, and later with huge sweeping cargo planes and their allocated transport lorries. Malachi had been put off travelling to his portal at the end of the runaway for this very reason.

Now the runway and airport stood closed and empty. Nothing and nobody moved as the wren surveyed the barren landscape that had once teemed with life. On the boundary wire fencing, yards of yellow ribbon festooned the highway, signalling a silent protest to passers-by on the cruelty and short-sightedness of individuals' in high places. Malachi shook his head. None of Thanet's creatures or its fairy folk, could understand why they had closed down such a treasured, much-loved icon of Thanet's history and commerce.

Although Malachi didn't like the hustle and bustle of the past, he hated the current state of affairs. It didn't seem fair that the place had been left, abandoned to the elements, while humans wrangled over whether it deserved to live again, or be demoted to the nothingness of an insipid housing estate. Surely, he thought, there were other places to build houses that didn't upset the local spirits who resided within the airport boundaries.

There were pilots and serving officers who'd given their lives to protect the airfield, and the little island realm during the wars. Some of the spirits he knew by name, like Bernard Stevens who'd given him tit-bits at the RAF kitchen window. Many of the spirits were upset at the planned changes. *Why build houses at all, if there isn't much local employment? How are island people going to afford new homes? Probably for more off-islanders to commute like the last time.* It was clear Malachi would never understand the plans of mortals.

Grabbing a few berries to eat on the way, Malachi slipped into a gap in the link fence and waited. He'd learnt to his peril to be watchful. This was not a safe portal, wildlife was in abundance here, from the graceful butterflies and placid hares, to the evil-eyed kestrel, ever on the hover for tasty morsels. Malachi didn't intend becoming one of those any time soon.

Satisfied the maundering bird was occupied elsewhere, probably on the verges of the dual-carriageway beyond the roundabout, where the bank voles thrived, Malachi flew inside the boundary perimeter. The portal wasn't visible to everyone, but to him it stood proud and elegant, a large standing stone several feet beyond the runway's end. Naturally, it had been spelled by wizards and couldn't be seen by mortals. They were known to dig up anything they couldn't understand and move it indoors, supposedly to help them understand it better.

Malachi shook his feathery head, landing lightly on the stone's apex. Every portal to the realms was unique and this was no different. The doorway to the In-between here, lay in the shadow of the stone, wherever the shadow happened to be at any given time, on any given day. Trying to enter the portal when the sun was directly overhead was pointless as the standing stone cast no shadow. As the daylight hours ended, like now, the shadow was long and stretched out behind the stone.

Malachi hopped down into the grass. Unlike the wide opening at the Viking ship, where a city troll could meander through like an elephant playing twister, passing through at this place was trickier, as the shadow was the portal not the stone. The wren needed to ensure no part of his body, including his wing tips, caught the light. He concentrated and focusing on his task shuffled forward inch by inch.

Glancing up for one brief nano-second, Malachi caught sight of the kestrel's move moments before it dropped.

306

Instinctively, he shimmied forward and vanished. Leaving the disgruntled hawk to rise, an empty clump of grass clenched in its outstretched talons and not the plump wren he'd been scrutinising. The kestrel voiced his irritation and, banking into the wind, spiralled away to find easier pickings on the dual carriageway over by Minster.

If Malachi had been human, he would have wiped the sweat from his brow at his narrow escape. Instead, he shook his plumage violently to eradicate the moment of terror he'd experienced sensing the kestrel plummet, almost unnoticed from the sky.

My poor baby! Malachi exclaimed, remembering his precious egg was now unguarded, and alone. *Imagine if anything had happened to me then,* he gasped, leaning against a nearby boulder for strength. *It doesn't bear thinking about. The sooner I find these folk, the quicker I'll be home.*

Travelling through the In-between settled the petite wren's frazzled nerves. He waved to the merfolk and the friendly dolphins who, like him, visited the place often. Drawing closer to the Neath Realm, he leaned forward to listen in case someone or something was close to the portal, like the kestrel earlier. He was feeling fragile after his near-death experience and didn't think his heart could stand another shock. He knew this portal came out underground in a disused basement. It wasn't ideal, but it had never been occupied so he felt safer than arriving out in the open, where predators might be lying in wait.

****

In the cellar below Gristle's home, Maddrigrew the Gruesome watched from her hiding place under the stairs. *The tear isn't big enough and isn't growing quick enough either. It won't take long before those biker Demons realise Gristle doesn't have enough energy to vaporise a second one.* Grue wanted to help Purity, but she also desperately wanted to go home, back to Earth. Her desire overrode her feelings towards the young fairy. She knew Gristle and her servants didn't have sufficient power to make a large enough tear by themselves, so she started chanting. In her mind, she spoke the words she had learnt listening from her box, mouthing the words as much as her toad mouth would allow.

"The tear!" yelled Phrack, to his assembled group of friends. "It's growing! Quick, the witch is going to escape."

Gristle couldn't believe her eyes. There were her two servants chanting as they had done for hours on end, without making one wit of difference in the tear's size. Suddenly it was expanding like an inflated balloon. She smelt a rat, or rather a toad, but she didn't have time to contemplate her good fortune. She needed to leave right now, for she sensed the bikers were building up to tackle her as a group, head on. Reaching over to her far left she grasped Harty's cage.

"No!" screamed Purity, instinctively knowing what the witch was about to do. An image of her father gripping the poisonous bars of the cage as it hurtled through the air, etched onto her brain. He'd come all this way to rescue her, only to be made a prisoner instead. She couldn't imagine life without her father. She couldn't consider facing life without him supporting and loving her. He was her father, rescuing her as an unborn baby, even before he knew she would become his daughter. That's how much love he had. Her body began to quiver uncontrollably as her desperation tore through her.

Without warning, Purity's body rose off the ground until, within a few short seconds, she became a blurred vibrating outline hovering in the air. As her body shook, it gave off waves of power and heat. Beams of light like lasers strobed the entire basement until everyone, including Gristle, had to stop what they were doing and cover their eyes, or risk being blinded. The light reached a point where, to Onk, it was like staring directly at the sun, even with his eyelids closed and his arm across his eyes. Then it vanished.

In the dim black light which replaced it, he watched amazed as a pair of magnificent pink gossamer wings unfurled from between Purity's shoulders. The wingspan was equal to her height. They shone iridescent in the pale lamp-light, the edges glistening like polished pink diamonds as they continued to expand.

Peeping through their fingers, the demons were in awe of this miracle occurring in their midst. Everyone turned to watch the amazing spectacle, they'd never witnessed a fairy's adult wings emerging before. It was an unbelievable sight for creatures of the Neath.

Purity on the other hand, was frozen in place with pain. Her father had warned her it would be painful, but she hadn't realised just how bad. She couldn't move, think or speak, as the wings she'd complained so bitterly about, burst from her skin. The pain was like someone had thrust two red-hot knives into her back. She felt her blood pulsing out into her wings to fill and strengthen them. Slowly and gently she concentrated on moving them. They had sprouted from the same muscles she had used as a child for her baby winglets. Now she needed to learn how to control and manage these impressive extensions. The demons in the cellar remained enraptured at this wonderous rare sight. They uttered various sounds of disbelief at Purity's transformation before their eyes and someone definitely squeaked, though no one admitted it later.

Gristle saw this incredible event as the diversion she needed. She took the opportunity, when everyone was concentrating on Purity's wings, to throw Harty's cage at the tear.

No one had time to think. It all happened so fast.

Onk roared again, making everyone duck because it sounded like the building was coming down. Seeing the witch's intention, he rushed over to the tear as Harty's cage sailed towards it, but he was too late. The tips of his fingers brushed the metal bars fleetingly, but he couldn't grab it.

Onk's violent actions caused Knife the spider to lose his grip on the troll's shoulder. His little body went flying towards the tear spinning end-over-end like some eight-legged Catherine-wheel frisbee. Knife headed across the tear and into the realm beyond, a long thread of silk trailing behind him. Faster than Purity thought possible, the toad she'd helped escape rushed past her, grasped the trailing edge of thread and vanished too.

Gristle grabbed Crogg and Courage by their wrists the second she let go of Harty's cage. She dove recklessly through the tear, with both servants clutched to her, heading for freedom. Courage took one last backwards glance over his shoulder to Purity as Gristle dragged him through. Purity's eyes widened as he mouthed one word.

"Sister."

Then he vanished along with Gristle and Crogg. Without any chanting to sustain it, the tear began to collapse in on itself.

A huge rubbery arm shot out of nowhere. It stretched through the diminishing tear, disappearing into the void beyond. Crossing the space between the two realms, it snagged Harty's cage and abruptly halted its progress into the unknown realm.

Brett, the Yan-gant-y-tan, grinned widely as his amazingly long arm and fingers retracted back to their normal size, pulling Harty in his cage to safety. He smiled down at his surrounding friends surprised faces.

"Zou like?" he asked, enjoying their expressions because

he hadn't mentioned, or demonstrated, this unusual ability until now.

The tear made an undignified 'pop' as it vanished from the Neath Realm, sounding more like someone passing gas, than a dimension sealing shut.

In place of the tear, inside the chalk circle, fluttered a tiny bird - a wren. Who, noticing a horde of biker demons within wing's reach, promptly fainted onto the ground in a heap of ruffled brown feathers.

It was somewhat anticlimactic after that. The biker Demons were thanked profusely by Phrack and left temporarily, via the front door, to check on their bikes.

Sadly, nothing could be done to save poor Thistle. There were no white witches in the Neath. Purity offered to take him home with her, once they found a way back. They collected every black polly-wog and placed the whole mess in a large glass jar for safe-keeping.

Onk scooped up the tiny passed-out wren and put him in the web nest created by Knife on his shoulder. He didn't reckon Knife the spider would be returning to the Neath any time soon.

The first priority after that, was freeing Harty from his cage. Onk had thought to pull it apart, but Phrack suggested a better solution. And besides, he pointed out to Onk, his way though effective, was likely to sever Harty's foot. Onk acknowledged this was a time for finesse rather than brute strength.

Fortunately, they had a dwarf in their midst, a dwarf used to working with metals. Using a fine jewellery file and a soft piece of leather - courtesy of his gander bag - Phrack made short work of the silver chain, gently filing one link open to release Harty's trapped ankle.

"I thought I'd never walk on two legs again," Harty complained, rubbing his ankle and grinning up at his best friend Onk. Onk wasn't sure what to make of that statement, but he knew his friend joked a lot, so he smiled back.

Harty hugged his daughter close. He'd been through a lot to find her and they both had tales to tell, but that could wait. She had superb adult wings and he was dying to take her flying with him.

"You up for a quick aerial?"

"You think I'm ready?"

"As ready as ever."

"What about being kidnapped?" Harty laughed.

"What with a dragon beside us?" Purity smiled.

"I forgot about that. Last one out is a worm." She yelled over her shoulder running for the door.

Onk stood in the hallway of Gristle's home slightly envious of his niece. He didn't have anything as wonderful as wings to enjoy. *Maybe I'll ask Dog for a trip one day.*

At that moment, Xaphan's head appeared around the doorframe.

"Coming out for a ride before you go Onk?"

"You bet!" he answered, all thoughts of flying forgotten.

****

Later, in the quiet of the house before they considered how to get back home, Purity spoke to her father.

"He called me sister," she told him, speaking about the elf in Gristle's service.

"Maybe he meant it like a term of endearment."

"No, he meant it as sister," she insisted. "You know, I think I've known ever since I stepped into the Neath. That elf was, is, my brother." It took Harty a moment to consider Purity's statement and then he realised what that meant for him.

"My son," he stated, astonished at the feelings which rose up in those two short words. They squeezed his heart. "It feels right," he confirmed.

"My nephew," mumbled Onk, stamping across the room to join them.

Purity ran over and hugged her Uncle. "Oh, Uncle Onk," she whimpered. Onk ran his finger over his niece's beautiful shiny halo of golden hair, careful of her new wings. He made this promise to her.

"If on Earth, we find him."

"And if he's not?" she asked, staring up into his broad craggy face, her trusting blue eyes wet with unshed tears.

"Then we search other realms," Onk added, glancing over to Harty for confirmation. Harty nodded to his friend, wondering what new dangers they would be facing by making his daughter this promise.

Purity returned to his side. He closed his eyes and hugged his daughter close again. It didn't matter, whatever the cost, she was worth it. For the present, Harty was content that Purity was safe and unharmed.

Malachi came around a few minutes after his faint in the cellar, before Onk had left on his final bike ride. He assured the four travel-weary wanderers that he could get them back to Earth, provided they went via the portal in Pegwell Bay. He recounted his narrow escape from the kestrel at the Manston portal, and refused point blank to go home via that route, even though it was quite literally on their doorstep. The trio agreed to the wren's demands. They couldn't really refuse because they had no way of getting home otherwise.

No one was keen to leave, once what passed for night in the Neath had fallen. As there were plenty of rooms in Gristle's home they all stayed the night. The bikers left for Mothball the following morning. They said their farewells to Harty, Onk and Purity before departing. Xaphan tried to persuade Phrack once more to re-join them and come back to their clubhouse in Mothball. He offered the dwarf the second-in-command position, but Phrack wouldn't be budged. He wanted to find his daughter and make it up to her. This adventure with Harty and Onk had taught him much. *My family is the most important thing in my life. All other things are nothing compared to it. I should have gone with my daughter when she asked me.*

The last any of them saw of Phrack was as he rode away, on a bike donated to him by Xaphan. He rode along the right boundary edge of the Tedium zone heading towards the last known place his daughter lived.

The trip back through the centre of the Tedium Zone was pretty uneventful, except for Upala and Jasper, emerging from the ground during the evening. It scared Malachi half to death for a second time in as many days. Though he didn't faint, Harty thought his feathers might fall out in shock. The couple had returned to say their final farewells. Slipping in and out amongst them, were the three Gussies and a very timid Lou. Purity hugged them all, vowing to see them again one day, if she could.

"You will always be welcome at our home, won't they father?" she said, glancing over at her father. Harty wasn't so sure given their size, but he gave his fatherly nod as was expected of him. Onk hugged Upala close while Jasper frowned at their contact.

"Stay safe," he grumbled.

"I will," she rumbled back. Jasper took his partner physically back from Onk, a possessive gleam in his eye. He wasn't sure he liked his wife having such an attractive male friend.

The In-between came as a welcome diversion to Harty's thoughts. It delighted Purity, who'd never witnessed it before. She 'Ohhed' and 'Ahhed' at the beautiful creatures living where no mortal had ever been.

"Can't we stay a while?"

Harty explained about the time difference in the In-between, how someone could lose themselves inside it.

"Imagine," he said to her, "staying here a while, then going home and finding out years have passed." Purity shivered, she'd done enough travelling.

Epilogue

"Let's go home." she said. Harty and Onk nodded wisely. "Besides, I have a brother and one day I intend to find him."

"LET them find me now," cackled Gristle, leaving the Neath Realm and taking her second step, which closed the portal behind her. Crogg and Courage stood at the end of a long path which led to the front of a Victorian house. She remembered the building from her last time on Earth. Crogg hissed and cowered, hating the sunlight, while Courage stood tall, drinking in the sunshine he'd never seen.

The West Wood was smaller than Gristle remembered. The gates were nearer too and outside the traffic layout had altered. The busy road remained, but now a large disgusting roundabout filled the space. The lane to the left was wider, with hideous iron railings.

Above in the trees, the rooks had managed to hang on to some of their ancestral rookery. It was from there one of them spied the witch scuttling down into the West

Wood. Normally, they ignored witches and their shenanigans, but this one was dragging an elf and a young Neath demon along with her. The trees of the West Wood took a collective gasp. They remembered this witch.

Gristle wasn't concerned with the grumbles of rooks and trees, she was concentrating on booting Crogg up the path towards her new home.

Acknowledgements

My thanks go to:

Charlie Mayhew - for her loud, but lovely pet Beatroot who provided me with such inspiration, and for giving permission to use his name. Thanks to her I can also do a passable Moon-Walk and Wave.

David, my son - for listening to the draft excerpts and offering useful insights and suggestions.

Geoff Fisher - for agreeing to format this, my third full-length novel.

Jim Scott - for the idea of incorporating a Motor Cycle Club into the mix.

Karen Ince - for agreeing, yet again to assist in the line and proof editing.

Michael, my husband - for not telling me to be quiet at the thousands, no millions, of times I've mentioned my writing to him.

Lucie at Pegu Designs - for her wonderful jacket design.

Tara Moore - International author, for her continued support and encouragement plus agreeing to let me use one of her beautiful photos for the cover.

Lastly, my fellow authors and writers, both in and out of Inspirations Writers Group, for support, reassurance and keeping me grounded.

Photograph & Illustration Accreditations

1. **https://travelsoutsidelondon.wordpress.com/about/**
   Chapter 5 - The Hugin, Viking Ship, Pegwell Bay
   by Adrian Prockter.

2. **http://pixabay.com/**
   Chapter 7 – Fire, Chapter 13 – Egg, Chapter 20 –
   Motorbike, Chapter 21 – Spider, Chapter 24 –
   Toad, Chapter 25 – Kestrel.

3. **Pencil Drawings & Front Cover Image of Onk &
   Tenamunday by Dom Channing**
   Chapter 8 – Hedgerow Imp, Chapter 14 – Foothills,
   Chapter 15 – Phrack Apprehended, Chapter 19 –
   The Marketplace, Chapter 22 – Tunnels.

4. **Pencil drawings by Louise Morse**
   Chapter 4 – Tenamunday, Chapter 12 – Fruiting
   Trees, Chapter 17 – Hot Chocolate

5. **Remaining photos and illustrations by author
   Carol Salter**

About the Author

Carol Salter is pleased to offer this her third full-length, independently published novel.

Gristle's Revenge chronicles the further adventures of Onk, the city troll and his life-long friend Harty Springfield. The story follows on from her first novel, *Witch on The Warpath*.

Carol continues to work full-time since retiring from the NHS four years ago. She still practises kyokushin karate. In 2017, Carol decided to add hip-hop dance lessons to her fitness regime in a vain attempt to stall the escalating progress of time.

She continues to chair and run Inspiration Writers Group (IWG), the group she founded in 2010. IWG has grown from strength to strength, publishing not one, but two anthologies, *Red* and *Orange,* in 2017. The IWG achieved acclaim as finalists in the 2017 Kent Creative Awards. Their third anthology, *Yellow,* will be launched in November 2018.

Above all these things she reads, and when she isn't reading - she writes...

You can find more about Carol's writing and follow her blog on carolmsalter.com

In addition to all reputable book retailers, you can purchase her books and related merchandise on https://carolmstore.phy.sx/

Authors survive by reviews. Please leave one on either; Amazon, Goodreads or Carol's EStore. Thank you.